Love *and* *Other* SURPRISES

EMILY LARKIN

www.emilylarkin.com

Love and Other Surprises / Emily Larkin. – 1st ed.

ISBN 978-0-9951428-7-9

Cover Design: JD Smith Design

Dear Reader

This duo consists of a novel, *Lady Isabella's Ogre,* and its companion novella, *Lieutenant Mayhew's Catastrophes.*

This is first time these two books have been published together, allowing readers to follow the fortunes of a certain litter of kittens.

I hope you enjoy the kittens' story, as well as the stories of the people who rescue and care for them. Love is a wonderful thing, but kittens make it even better!

Happy reading.

Emily

Contents

Lady Isabella's OGRE

A NOVEL

A note to readers

Lady Isabella's Ogre was originally published as *Beauty and the Scarred Hero*, under the penname Emily May. When I set about revising it, all I intended to do was get rid of a few exclamation marks and give it a fresh copyedit, but towards the end of the book I encountered a scene that I didn't like.

In fact, I didn't like the last few chapters at all, which was a disconcerting discovery. But being a writer, I had a solution: I rewrote those chapters!

This version of the story works much better for me. I hope it works better for you, too.

Emily

CHAPTER 1

"This is a respectable establishment. It's not for the likes of you."

Lady Isabella Knox, sister of the Duke of Middlebury, paused in the act of removing her gloves. She looked down at her dog. Rufus cocked his head and gazed back at her with mismatched eyes. His tail wagged, brushing the muddy hem of her walking dress.

"I beg of you, don't turn me away." The speaker was tearful, young, and well-bred.

"The Hogshead will take you." The landlady's voice came clearly from the taproom, cold and dismissive.

"Oh, but, please—" The girl's entreaty ended on a sob.

Isabella pulled one kidskin glove off, finger by finger. She glanced at the half-open door to the taproom and then at the staircase, at the top of which a comfortable and very private parlor awaited her. *Curiosity is a sin,* she told herself.

She heard brisk footsteps behind her: her maid, Partridge.

"Fresh air," Partridge muttered, shutting the parasol with a snap. "Dirt and puddles and yokels gaping—"

Isabella raised a finger. "Hush a moment, Partridge."

"I beg you, please . . ." The girl sounded so like her niece Felicity that Isabella made up her mind. She stepped towards the taproom door. Rufus followed, his claws clicking briskly on the flagstones.

"A fine thing it would be if I let you put up here, with her Ladyship in the house—"

Isabella laid her hand on the door. It swung open at her touch. She took in the taproom with a glance: the low, beamed ceiling, the wide fireplace, the landlady in her white apron and widow's cap, and the girl, pretty and tear-stained, with a portmanteau at her feet.

The landlady drew herself up, stout and starched, and then sank into an obsequious curtsy. "Your Ladyship."

"Mrs. Botham." Isabella looked at the girl. Yes, very like Felicity. Dark-haired and slender and scarcely out of the schoolroom. "I couldn't help but overhear. Pray, don't turn this child out into the street on my account."

The landlady straightened. Her face was round-cheeked, her complexion florid, her expression righteous. "The Hogshead will do very well for her."

Isabella looked at the girl's clothing—the green sarcenet pelisse, the straw bonnet trimmed with ribbon, the jaconet muslin gown, all neat and well-made. "Do you think so?"

She spoke gently, but the color in Mrs. Botham's cheeks heightened.

The girl curtsied. "Ma'am, if you please, I don't wish to put up at the Hogshead."

"I should think not." There was nothing common about the girl's vowels, or her curtsy. "Where is your maid?"

The girl flushed. "I don't have one, ma'am."

"I run a respectable establishment—" Mrs. Botham began.

"Precisely." Isabella pulled off her other glove. "Which is why this child must stay here."

The girl cast her a grateful glance.

"Unfortunately I don't have suitable accommodation, your Ladyship." The landlady's smile was polite and insincere.

"I find that hard to believe," Isabella said, beginning to lose her temper.

"Nothing suiting the young person's requirements."

The girl flushed again. "I can't afford a room," she whispered. "I thought . . . I thought I could sleep in the servants' quarters, but—"

"No money and no maid?" Isabella looked at her. "You are in a predicament, aren't you, my dear?"

Tears welled in the girl's eyes.

"You may share my maid's bedchamber," Isabella said. She heard Partridge sniff behind her, and ignored it.

The landlady inhaled, swelling in her starched apron. "I won't have a fallen woman in this house!"

"I'm not, ma'am! Indeed, I'm not!"

Do I care whether she is or not? Not when the girl was so young and so clearly in need of aid. "A truckle bed in my maid's room," Isabella said briskly. "And refreshments in my parlor." She folded her gloves and waited for the landlady to protest.

Mrs. Botham inhaled again, her apron swelling, but uttered no sound.

"Come along, my dear." Isabella smiled and held out her hand to the girl.

"My portmanteau?"

"One of the servants will bring it up, won't they, Mrs. Botham?"

The landlady smiled tightly and nodded.

The girl clutched her hand. "Come upstairs and have a cup of tea," Isabella said as they exited the taproom, Rufus following closely at their heels. She ignored Partridge's silent disapproval. "And do tell me your name, my dear."

The girl's hand was small and warm. "My name is Harriet," she confided as they climbed the staircase. "Harriet Durham."

"Tell me, my dear . . . how is it you're in such a fix?"

Harriet's cheeks colored. She looked down at her cup. "I'm running away."

"Running away?" Isabella sipped her tea and studied the girl's face. She could discern no boldness. Harriet had soft brown hair and soft brown eyes and an air of timidity. Her expression when she glanced at Rufus was wary. *Surely not the type of girl to run away?* "From your parents?"

"My parents are dead." Harriet looked up from her study of the teacup. "I live with my grandfather."

"You're running away from him?"

"Yes." Harriet shivered. "And from Major Reynolds."

"Major Reynolds?" Isabella lowered her cup. "Who is he?"

Tears filled Harriet's eyes. "I'm to marry him."

"And you don't wish to?"

Harriet shivered again. She shook her head. "No."

Isabella placed her teacup on the little cherrywood table beside her. The tabletop gleamed and the parlor had a pleasing smell of beeswax polish. Mrs. Botham kept a very clean—and extremely respectable—establishment.

"Did you tell your grandfather that you don't want to marry Major Reynolds?"

Harriet nodded. "He said I was being foolish. And he shouted at me and—" She groped for her handkerchief. The tiny lace-trimmed square of fabric was sodden.

Isabella picked up her teacup and sipped, while Harriet wiped her eyes. "How old are you, my dear?" she asked once the girl had composed herself.

"Seventeen."

Felicity's age. Too young to be in the world alone. "Where are you going?"

"My Aunt Lavinia." Harriet's smile was tremulous. "Only I hadn't realized that the stage would be so slow, or that it would cost so much to take a room at an inn."

Isabella placed her teacup on its saucer. She reached down

to pat Rufus. His eyes opened, one blue, one brown, and his tail gave a thump on the floor. "Where does your aunt live?"

"Penrith. In the Lake District."

Isabella frowned. "My dear child, do you realize how far that is?"

"Is it very distant from here?" Harriet twisted the handkerchief.

Isabella looked at the tears shining in the girl's eyes and decided not to answer that question. Instead she asked, "Is your aunt expecting you?"

Harriet shook her head.

"But you're certain she'll give you refuge?"

"Oh, yes." Harriet nodded. "She said that I was always welcome to stay with her, only . . . only my grandfather wouldn't let me speak her name, or write to her, or . . . or—"

"How gothic!" Isabella said lightly, to forestall more tears. "What did she do to incur such wrath?"

"She married Mr. Mortlock. Grandfather said he wasn't good enough—and Aunt Lavinia told him he was a tyrant and married Mr. Mortlock anyway!" Admiration was patent in Harriet's voice. "Only Mr. Mortlock died, which Grandfather said served her right, and so now she lives alone."

"How long ago was this?" Isabella asked.

"When I was a child."

The girl was still a child. Too young to be forced into marriage—and too young to travel halfway across England on her own. Isabella glanced out the window at the roofs of Stony Stratford and the deepening dusk and made up her mind. *It's not really meddling. I'm merely helping her on a path she has already chosen.* "I shall take you home with me," she said. "To London. And then—"

"London? Oh, no!" Harriet dropped the handkerchief in her agitation.

Rufus opened his eyes again. His ears pricked. He lifted his head and looked at Harriet.

"Why ever not, child?" Isabella said, resting her hand on

Rufus's head, feeling the warmth and smoothness of his coat.

"Because Major Reynolds is there!" Harriet's face twisted. "If he should find me—"

"Major Reynolds won't find you," Isabella said firmly, "because you shall be at my house, quite snug and safe. And once we've received an assurance from your aunt that she's expecting you—for she may be away, you know!—then you shall travel to stay with her."

"But Major Reynolds—"

Isabella looked at her with some amusement. "Is he such an ogre, child?"

"An ogre?" Harriet shuddered. "Oh, yes. Yes, he is!"

"Then I promise to keep you safe from him."

"He'll be very angry." Harriet blinked back tears. "My grandfather has announced our engagement."

Isabella experienced a moment's misgiving. If the engagement had been announced in the newspapers, then the scandal . . .

I should restore her to her grandfather.

The girl was as young as Felicity, with no parents to dote on her. *Even so, I should . . .*

She looked down at Rufus. He glanced up at her with his mismatched eyes and thumped his tail on the rug again, content, trusting.

"Tell me about Major Reynolds," Isabella said, giving her own handkerchief to Harriet.

"He's a soldier."

Isabella suppressed a smile. "Yes, my dear, I had gathered that. Is he a friend of your grandfather's?"

"Oh, no. Grandfather had never met him until we came to London." Harriet unfolded the handkerchief. "It's my first Season, you see. Grandfather was so pleased when Major Reynolds asked permission to pay his addresses." More tears welled in her eyes. She dabbed at them with the handkerchief.

"Is the major very old?" Isabella asked. "What's his disposition?"

"Old? Oh, yes, ma'am. He's quite as old as you." Harriet's cheeks colored. "I mean, he's *much* older than you. He's as old as my father . . . that is to say, as old as my father would be if he were alive." She bit her lip, and looked down at the handkerchief she clutched.

That settled it, Isabella decided. She wasn't about to allow this child to be married to a man old enough to be her father.

"And as to his disposition, he looks so . . . so *stern,* and . . . and—"

"I collect he's quite an ogre," Isabella said lightly, to avert more tears. "Is he ugly, too? I'm persuaded he must be!"

Harriet shivered. "His face is quite scarred, ma'am. And he shouts and—"

Isabella's eyebrows rose. "Major Reynolds has shouted at you?"

"No, ma'am," the girl said, earnest and wide-eyed. "But he's a military man, so I know he will."

Isabella suppressed another smile. "You have experience of military men?"

Harriet nodded. "They stomp and they have loud voices and they're always angry and—"

Isabella had a moment of enlightenment. "Your grandfather is a military man?"

"A colonel, ma'am."

A maid tapped on the door and entered, bobbing a curtsy. Rufus sat up, alert. "Just seeing to the shutters, ma'am."

They sat in silence while the maid placed more wood on the fire, lit the candles with a taper, and then busied herself closing the shutters against the dusk.

"Then it's settled," Isabella said briskly, once the woman was gone. "You shall travel with me to London tomorrow and stay until we know that your aunt is ready to receive you."

Harriet gripped the handkerchief tightly. "And your husband, ma'am? Are you certain he'll allow it?"

"I have no husband. A widowed cousin keeps house with

me in London. She doesn't often venture out, and will be pleased to have your company."

The girl's eyes widened. "No husband?"

"Yes," Isabella said, smiling. "I know it's odd, but I find it very comfortable to live without one!"

"How is the child?" Isabella asked later that evening, as she sat in front of the mirror brushing her hair. The bedchamber was more shadows than candlelight.

"Asleep."

Isabella laughed. "Partridge, such disapprobation in one word!"

Partridge sniffed, and said nothing.

Isabella laid down the hairbrush. The silver back glinted in the candlelight. "You may tell me that I'm meddling, Partridge, and you would be quite right."

Partridge silently folded the day's clothes.

She *was* meddling, quite dreadfully, but Mrs. Botham had annoyed her, with her bristling, pious indignation. "She reminds me of Felicity." Isabella ran a fingertip over the silver crest on the hairbrush. *I will stand in her mother's stead for a while.* "We shall keep her reputation intact, until her aunt can claim her."

Partridge sniffed again.

Isabella turned to look at her. "You think I should return her to her grandfather? You are perfectly correct, my dear Partridge. Only I fear he has already disowned her."

Partridge said nothing.

Isabella turned back to the mirror. She picked up the hairbrush again. A strand of hair was caught in the soft bristles. She pulled it out and wound it meditatively around her fingertip, where it gleamed like gold thread in the candlelight.

Yes, she would take the place of Harriet's mother for a few days—although no one would think the girl her daughter. Harriet was dark and dainty; she was tall and fair. The goddess of the harvest, an admirer had once likened her to. He'd even penned a poem. *To the harvest goddess with her corn-ripe hair . . .*

Isabella snorted under her breath. She leaned closer to the mirror, but the light was too dim to discern the faint lines she knew were at her eyes. *And I am merely twenty-nine.* Too young to be Harriet's mother.

"She won't be with us long," she said aloud to Partridge. "She shall write to her aunt tomorrow—and to her grandfather, to inform him that she is safe in a respectable household."

And Harriet must write to Major Reynolds, too, to beg his pardon for jilting him. One must be polite, even to an ogre.

Partridge finally broke her silence: "She's not one of your strays, Miss Isabella. I hope you don't live to regret this."

Isabella met her own eyes in the mirror. *So do I.* "Nonsense," she said, with a light laugh. "What can possibly go wrong? No one will ever know!"

CHAPTER 2

*M*ajor Nicholas Reynolds, late of the Ninety-Fifth Rifles, looked across the expanse of his desk, with its tidy piles of paper and the sturdy inkpot and the sharp-nibbed quills and the letter knife he'd picked up in Spain, and said, "No."

"But, sir—"

Nicholas sighed. He laid down his quill and pushed aside the letter he'd been writing. "What did I say last time?"

"That you wouldn't pay off any more of my debts," his nephew said sulkily, not meeting his eyes.

"Precisely. And I always keep my word, Harry."

He spoke quietly, but his nephew flushed, his cheeks reddening above the high points of his collar.

Nicholas sighed again. He rubbed his forehead. "Did your father refuse to advance your allowance?"

"I haven't asked him," Harry said gruffly. "You know how he is, sir. He'll scold me like a fishwife, and go on and *on*."

Nicholas did know. He looked across the desk at his nephew. Harry's hair was styled in the latest cut, his blue coat had padded shoulders, a nipped-in waist, and extremely large gold buttons, and the intricacies of his neckcloth must have taken a good hour to achieve.

A bandbox creature. And Nicholas had no time for

bandbox creatures. There were more important things in life than one's clothing.

But beneath the extravagant attire was a young man who was in trouble.

Nicholas ran his fingertips lightly over the scar that ridged his cheek. *What to do?* He came to a decision: "I'll buy that black horse of yours. How much do you want for him?"

"What?" Startled, Harry looked up and met his eyes for the first time during the interview.

"How much for your black horse?"

"But . . . but I like that horse!"

"Then learn not to outrun the carpenter," Nicholas said mildly.

Harry flushed. His eyes lowered. "Yes, sir," he said, sulky again.

He found his manners when Nicholas handed him a roll of guineas, stammering his thanks and bowing. Nicholas watched as he walked towards the door. Somewhere beneath that expensive, frivolous exterior was the rough-and-tumble boy who'd cared more for his horses than for his clothes. "Harry. Would you like a commission in the army?"

His nephew paused with his hand on the door knob. "Sir?"

"A commission, Harry. Would you like one?"

Harry blinked. He looked slightly appalled. "Thank you, sir, but . . . that is to say, I prefer . . ."

You prefer to be a man-milliner instead of a man.

"Let me know if you should ever change your mind." Nicholas picked up his quill again, dismissing his nephew. He didn't look up as the door closed.

An hour later he finished his business correspondence and sealed the letters. At home he'd go for a ride, but in London there was little pleasure to be had in riding, with its busy streets and crowded parks and the *properness* of everything. There was no place for a man to gallop.

Unless he rode out to Richmond.

Nicholas glanced at the window. Fresh air. That's what he

needed. Away from the fug of London. He pushed back his chair.

A footman knocked and opened the door. "Your mail, sir."

Nicholas looked at the pile of invitations on the silver tray. This was another thing he disliked about London: all the balls and assemblies where the object wasn't to dance but to determine the eligibility of possible spouses. Looks, breeding, fortune—all were assessed in meticulous detail. *As if we were cattle at an auction.* "Throw them in the fire." He'd chosen a bride. The Marriage Mart—and all those appraising sideways glances—was behind him.

The footman halted. "Sir?"

"Give them here," Nicholas said resignedly, holding out his hand. "And send round to the stables. I'd like Douro ready in twenty minutes."

He went through the pile of mail swiftly, rejecting the invitations without reading them. A letter from Colonel Durham he put to one side. And there was another, written in a feminine hand that he didn't recognize. He reached for the letter knife, slit it open and unfolded it, pausing as the butler knocked.

"Sir? Lord Reynolds desires a word with you."

Nicholas closed his eyes for a moment. He toyed—briefly—with the thought of not being home to his brother, then he opened his eyes and put down the letter. "Send him in, Frye."

He pushed out of the chair and walked across to the decanters. He needed brandy if he was to talk with Gerald this early in the day.

"Nicholas! I must speak with you."

"Brandy?" Nicholas asked, pouring himself a glass. He turned to face his brother.

It was like seeing himself in a mirror—only paler and soft with fat. No one would ever mistake him for Gerald, though, and not merely because of the scar. Gerald's clothes were as elaborate as his own were plain—the neckcloth extravagantly high, the waistcoat exotically embroidered. Fobs and seals and diamond pins adorned his person and tassels dangled from his boots. His hair was pomaded and he brought the scent of Steele's lavender water with him into the room. *Decked out like a prize pig at a fair,* Nicholas thought, barely managing to prevent his lip from curling.

Gerald shook his head. His eyebrows drew together in a frown. "You gave my son money!"

Nicholas swallowed a mouthful of brandy. It was smoky on his tongue and warm in his throat. "I bought that black horse of his."

"To pay off his debts!"

Nicholas shrugged. "I bought his horse. What he does with the money is up to him."

His brother swung away. "I give him a generous allowance," he said, a bitter note in his voice. "And yet he can never—" He swung back to face Nicholas. "And you! Why does he come to you and not me?"

Because you scold like a fishwife. Nicholas shrugged again. "He runs with a fast set," he said. "He would do better to find new friends."

"And you encourage him by paying his debts!"

Nicholas sighed. "Gerald—"

"I must request that you not give my son money," Gerald said, with stiff pomposity.

"I didn't *give* him money," Nicholas said, nettled. "I bought his damned horse!"

"And I must ask that you don't put ideas into his head."

"What ideas?"

"The army."

"I don't think he's interested," Nicholas said dryly. Although it would do the boy good to learn there was more to life than clothes and gambling.

"I should forbid it!"

"He's of age," Nicholas pointed out. "If he wishes to join the army, he may."

"Not if I have any say in the matter!"

Nicholas discovered that his fingers were clenched around the glass. He relaxed them and drained the last of the brandy. "Very well," he said. "I shan't mention it to him again."

"Make certain you don't," Gerald snapped. "He pays far too much attention to what you say."

"Does he?" Nicholas shrugged. "I hadn't noticed."

"He looks up to you as a hero." The bitter note was back in Gerald's voice.

Nicholas was suddenly uncomfortable. He turned away and placed his empty glass on the sideboard. "You have my word that I won't speak of it to him again," he said, not looking at his brother.

But Gerald, with the tenacity that had earned him the nickname *Terrier* at Eton, persisted. "I can think of nothing worse than for him to enter the army!"

"Really?" Nicholas turned back to face him. "I can think of many worse things."

Gerald flushed, hearing the sarcasm in his voice. "The army—"

"A little discipline would do him good."

Gerald stiffened. "Are you implying that my son lacks—"

"I'm not implying anything," Nicholas said, impatient with the conversation. "I'm merely saying that I think the army would do him good. And—" he held up his hand to forestall Gerald's interruption, "—that you have my word I shan't mention the matter to him again."

"Good!" Gerald snapped. "Heaven forbid that my son should become like you!"

"Or you!" Nicholas retorted, stung into losing his temper.

Gerald drew himself up. "What do you mean?"

Soft and useless is what I mean. "Nothing," he said. "Forget it."

"Damn it, Nicholas—"

Nicholas sighed and closed his eyes. Why did he always end up arguing with Gerald? "Is that all?" he asked, opening his eyes. "Because I have other business to attend to." He walked back to his desk and sat down, reaching for the opened letter.

Gerald hesitated, and then turned on his heel and stalked across the study. "I shall see you at Augusta's tonight," he said, and shut the door with a snap.

Nicholas put down the letter. Damn. Gussie's ball was this evening. He'd have to go.

He rubbed his face, feeling the scar beneath his fingers, the smoothness and roughness of his ruined cheek. *Why must Gerald and I always argue?*

He knew the answer. Even when they were children it had been like this; no matter that Gerald was the eldest, the viscount, it was Nicholas people turned to for help. That Gerald's own son did it merely made it worse.

Nicholas sighed and opened his eyes. He looked down at the letter lying open on his desk. It was very short.

Dear Sir,

I regret that I find myself unable to marry you. Please accept my apologies.

Harriet Durham

Nicholas pinched the bridge of his nose. He swore under his breath, quietly, then got up and poured himself another brandy. He drank it slowly and deliberately, then went back to the desk and reached for Colonel Durham's letter. He slit it open with a swift, sharp movement.

The butler knocked on the door.

"What?" Nicholas said, frowning at him.

"Colonel Durham to see you, sir."

Nicholas clenched his jaw. He exhaled sharply through his nose. "Send him in."

"Your horse, sir?"

Nicholas closed his eyes briefly. An ache was building in his temples. "Another twenty minutes, Frye."

"The weather, sir—"

He turned to look out the window. A light, gray drizzle

was falling. *Damn.* "Twenty minutes," he repeated. Because if he didn't gallop he was going to smash something.

He inhaled a deep breath, kept the thought of Richmond and Douro and a thundering gallop firmly in his mind, and turned to face Colonel Durham as Frye ushered him into the study.

The colonel was a heavy man. He had the bearing of a soldier despite his graying hair, and wore his clothes as if they were a uniform. Age hadn't been kind to him: his face had lost its flesh, falling into deep, ill-humored wrinkles. Uncompromising furrows bracketed his mouth and pinched between his eyebrows.

Nicholas bowed. "I was just about to read your letter, sir."

"Don't bother," the colonel said brusquely. "I had hoped to avert—" His mouth tightened. "But it's too late."

"Brandy, sir? Or shall I have Frye bring up a bottle of claret?"

"Brandy," the colonel said, glaring at him.

He's embarrassed, Nicholas realized. *Embarrassed—and angry.*

Frye withdrew, closing the door. Nicholas walked across to the sideboard. He poured the colonel a large glass of brandy and himself a small one. "Please be seated, sir."

Colonel Durham sat.

"I've received a letter from your granddaughter," Nicholas said, handing him the brandy. "I understand she wishes to terminate our engagement."

Rage flushed the colonel's face. He swallowed his brandy, grimacing. "I must apologize for my granddaughter's behavior."

Nicholas sat behind his desk. "May I speak with her, sir?"

"Speak with her?" Colonel Durham uttered a harsh laugh. "By all means. If you can find her!"

Nicholas frowned. "I beg your pardon?"

"The stupid chit has run away!"

Nicholas placed his brandy glass carefully on the desk. "Run away? Why?"

"Because she doesn't wish to marry you."

Nicholas looked down his brandy. There was a bitter taste in his mouth. "If she had told me," he said quietly, "I would have withdrawn my suit—"

"Ridiculous nonsense!" Colonel Durham said. "And so I told her."

Nicholas raised his head. "She spoke to you about it, sir?"

The colonel nodded.

"And you said . . . ?"

"That it was her duty to marry you."

Nicholas positioned his glass precisely in the middle of his blotter. He could feel anger rising in him. "And then she ran away?"

Colonel Durham's face reddened. "She makes a fool out of me!"

No, Nicholas thought sourly. *She makes a fool out of me.* He drank a mouthful of brandy, not tasting it. "Where is she?"

"I don't know, and I don't care! I've wiped my hands of her."

Nicholas put down his glass. Colonel Durham was a rigid, narrow-minded bully—he'd known that before he'd offered for Harriet's hand—but to disown the girl when she was so young, was . . . *Criminal, that's what it is.* "She's only seventeen. You can hardly—"

"What business is it of yours?" the colonel snapped.

Nicholas looked at him coldly. "It is entirely my business. If you recall, sir, it is *me* she is betrothed to." *And me she ran away from.*

The colonel's mouth twisted. "Some interfering busybody has her." He dug inside his coat and tossed a wad of paper on Nicholas's desk. "Here."

Nicholas separated the sheets of paper and smoothed them. Two letters. He recognized the writing.

Dear Grandfather,

I have gone to live with my aunt. I know it is my duty to marry Major Reynolds, but I find myself unable to.

Your granddaughter, Harriet

He glanced at the colonel. "This is dated four days ago."

Colonel Durham shifted in his chair, as if he heard the unspoken accusation. "I thought it would be an easy matter to find her and bring her back."

And then what? Nicholas didn't ask the question. The answer was obvious: the colonel had intended to browbeat Harriet into marriage.

And I was never to know.

Anger surged inside him. He gritted his teeth together and read the second letter. It was dated yesterday.

Dear Grandfather,

Please do not be concerned for my safety. A kind benefactress has given me shelter until I can be united with my aunt.

Your granddaughter, Harriet.

Nicholas put down the letter. "Who is the benefactress?"

"I don't know. And I don't care!"

"You should care." His voice held a note of reprimand. "Your granddaughter's safety is entirely in her hands."

Colonel Durham's face grew redder. "Without her inter-ference, I would have had Harriet back by now. The matter could have been kept quiet! Now—"

"It can still be kept quiet," Nicholas said calmly. His hands wanted to clench. He spread his fingers on the desk. "No one need know why the engagement has been terminated."

The colonel's eyes slid away from him. "I stopped at my club on the way here—" He cleared his throat. "I may have uttered a few imprudent words."

Nicholas exhaled through his teeth, silently. He didn't need to be told what Colonel Durham meant: the colonel was a man of loud rages. By tonight half of London would know of Harriet's flight. *And because you can't control your temper, we will both feature in Society's latest scandal.*

"Stupid girl!" Colonel Durham said savagely. "If I could lay my hands on her, I'd horsewhip her!"

Nicholas looked at him with dislike. *It's you I'd like to*

horsewhip. "I'll send a notice to the newspapers," he said, speaking with careful politeness. "Stating that my engagement to your granddaughter is terminated." He stood and bowed. "Good day, sir."

The furrows in the colonel's face deepened, showing his displeasure. For a moment it looked as if he'd say more, then he pushed to his feet and nodded curtly. "Good day."

Nicholas watched him depart. Anger thumped inside his skull. He picked up the letters again. *I know it is my duty to marry Major Reynolds,* Harriet had written, *but I find myself unable to.*

He clenched his hands, crumpling the paper. Now he'd have to start again—attending balls and assemblies, dancing, making polite conversation, selecting a girl who was quiet and biddable and easily molded into the wife he wanted. While the *ton* watched with sideways glances and amused whispers.

He threw the letters aside and went in search of his riding gloves.

CHAPTER 3

Isabella looked around the ballroom. She gave a sigh of pleasure. London. The gaiety, the busyness. "I do love the Season."

"Yes." But her companion was frowning.

"Have you a headache, Gussie?"

"Headache?" Augusta Washburne's brow cleared. "No, I'm cross."

"Cross?" Isabella glanced around the ballroom again, her gaze catching on the shimmer of expensive fabric and the glitter of jewels, the bright flare of the candles in the chandeliers. The room was crowded to its farthest extent; beneath the music the babble of voices was loud. She could see no reason for Gussie to be cross. The ball was undeniably a success.

"It's this business with Nicholas," Gussie said. "Everyone's talking about it."

"Nicholas?"

"What a dreadful squeeze, darling!" Lady Faraday swooped on Gussie. "One can scarcely move!" She turned to Isabella, the three tall feathers in her turban swaying and nodding. Her gown was pink and trimmed with an astonishing number of flounces. "Isabella, darling! You're finally back in town!"

"Sarah, how do you do?" Isabella said politely, but Lady

Faraday had already turned back to Gussie, her eyes bright and expectant.

"What's this I hear about your cousin? Is it true? His bride ran away?"

Gussie's face tightened. She glanced at Isabella. "Yes."

Isabella's pleasure in the ball became tinged with unease. "Your cousin?"

"Major Nicholas Reynolds."

Isabella stared at Gussie. "The ogre? He's your cousin?"

"Ogre?" Lady Faraday uttered a tittering laugh.

"Ogre?" said Gussie, in quite a different tone of voice. Her eyebrows pinched together again. "Who called him that?"

Isabella bit the tip of her tongue. *Fool.* "Major Reynolds is your cousin?"

Gussie nodded.

"And his bride has run away!" Lady Faraday exclaimed. "Now tell me, Augusta—"

Her gleeful curiosity was too much for Isabella. "Sarah, I believe Mrs. Drummond-Burrell is trying to catch your attention."

"She is? Oh, pray excuse me—"

Isabella watched her go—feathers bobbing above the pink ball gown—and frowned. How had Lady Faraday known about Harriet? The child had written her letters barely a day ago.

"An ogre!" Gussie said. "Where did you hear that?"

"Oh . . . I've received a number of callers," Isabella said, skirting around the truth. "You know how it is when one first arrives in town."

Gussie's frown was fierce. "But who *said* it?"

The temptation to lie was strong. Isabella moistened her lips. She looked down at her fan and spread the pierced ivory sticks. *Don't lie,* she told herself. *Don't compound your first mistake with a second.* "I believe it was the person who's sheltering Miss Durham."

Breath hissed between Gussie's teeth. "She had no right!"

I know.

"Who is she?" Gussie demanded.

Isabella closed her fan. "No one I've spoken to knows." *Not a lie. Not quite.* She smoothed the long gloves up her arms, deeply uncomfortable. "I didn't realize Major Reynolds was your cousin."

"Second cousin. He's Lord Reynolds' brother."

Isabella experienced a sinking sensation in her stomach. The major was a nobleman? "I don't believe I've met him."

"He'll be here tonight," Gussie said, turning to scan the ballroom. "I'll introduce you."

"Oh." Isabella followed her glance, suddenly nervous. "Perhaps he won't come if everyone is talking—"

"Nicholas is not a coward," Gussie said staunchly.

"Oh," Isabella said again. She swallowed. "I look forward to meeting him."

Nicholas halted. He looked across the street. Flambeaux burned and a red carpet had been laid up the steps. He braced himself for what was to come—the stares and the whispers—and silently cursed Colonel Durham. Damn the man for having no control over his temper, no control over his tongue, for venting his spleen in his *club* of all places.

Harriet's flight would be common knowledge by now.

I don't have to attend. I can just turn and walk away.

On the heels of that thought came anger. He was used to stares—his face made certain of that—and he was damned if he was going to hide from tattlemongers.

Nicholas strode across the street and up the steps. He handed his hat to a footman and walked up the curving staircase towards the sound of music.

He was late. The ball was well underway. The large room

was stuffy, the air warm and overscented, the flowers in the vases wilting.

A *contredanse* was playing. Nicholas stood inside the doorway, watching the dancers go through their sets. His gaze slid over débutantes in pale gowns, officers in uniform, matrons with curling feathers in their headdresses. The officers and the matrons were of no interest; the débutantes were.

The dark-haired, laughing girl was pretty, but . . . *Too bold,* he decided. He didn't want a *coquette* for a wife. Beside her in the set was a redhead who looked possible. Shy, not flirting.

"Nicholas! I'd quite given up on you."

Nicholas turned. "Gussie." He bowed. "You must forgive me for being late."

"You're forgiven," his cousin said with a laugh, and stood on tiptoe to kiss him.

"You look well," Nicholas said, smiling. With her shining brown hair and shining brown eyes and the scattering of freckles on her nose, Gussie looked more like a schoolgirl than the mother of two children.

His cousin ignored the compliment. She clasped his hand tightly. "Now Nicholas, you mustn't run away."

Nicholas lost his smile. "As bad as that, is it?"

"You know how London gossips." She pulled a face. "But you must dance before you hide in the card room."

"An order, Gussie?" He raised his eyebrows.

"Yes," she said frankly. "Because you know what people will say if you don't!"

He did. It was another reason to dislike London: everyone watching and passing judgment.

"I have saved the next dance for you," Gussie said. "It's to be a waltz."

"My timing is fortunate, then," he said, smiling.

Gussie showed him a dimple. She placed her hand on his sleeve as the sets broke up and the dancers left the floor. There was barely room for anyone to move.

"Congratulations," Nicholas said. "A squeeze."

"Yes," Gussie said, with no attempt at modesty. "It's most gratifying."

Nicholas laughed at her candor. It took his attention from the glances that were directed his way. No one was ill-bred enough to point, but he was aware of heads turning, a stir of conversation. *Ignore them,* he told himself.

He had learned to hold his head up, to not hide his ruined cheek; he would learn to ignore this. It couldn't last forever; the London gossips would be talking of someone else soon enough.

He scanned the ballroom. Gerald stood in the far corner, his face flushed with heat and alcohol. And there was Gussie's husband, Lucas, in the company of a striking blonde in a blue gown. Nicholas kept his gaze on the blonde in a long moment of appreciation, liking her height, her generous figure, her full mouth.

Gussie maintained a stream of light chatter as they took their places on the dance floor, but once the music started, her tone changed. "I'm very sorry about what's happened, Nicholas."

Nicholas looked past her. *So am I.* He caught someone's eye: a lady dressed in pink with three feathers in her hair, who colored at being caught staring and hastily averted her gaze.

Nicholas's jaw tightened. He returned his attention to Gussie.

"I should warn you . . ." She grimaced, a brief screwing-up of her face.

"Warn me?" He tried to laugh. "About what?"

"Nicholas . . . you're being called an ogre."

"What?" Nicholas almost halted in the middle of the ballroom.

Habit—and the tug of Gussie's hand—kept him dancing. "It's merely someone's foolishness," she said. "You mustn't pay any attention to it."

They danced in silence. Beneath the music was the murmur of voices. He saw quick glances directed his way, saw lips shaping words. He didn't need to hear them to know what was being said.

If the name didn't suit him so well he would laugh it off, but it fitted perfectly—the scarred face, the runaway bride. *An ogre.*

Anger built inside him, growing with each step that he took. He tasted it on his tongue, bitter—

"You mustn't think about it," Gussie said, as the music came to an end.

Nicholas forced a smile. "I assure you, I shan't."

Gussie chose to believe him. "Good," she said, with a quick smile that showed her dimples. "And now, Nicholas, I must introduce you to a particular friend of mine."

He wanted to balk. His mood was too unpleasant—

"Her name is Isabella," Gussie said, tucking her hand into his arm. "Lady Isabella Knox. She was dancing with Lucas." She stood on tiptoe and glanced around the ballroom. "Do you see them?"

The blonde? He saw her. She stood out among the débutantes and the matrons, tall and elegant and deliciously curved. Her hair was an extraordinary color, like ripe wheat in sunlight.

Nicholas's mood improved slightly. *One more dance,* he decided. And then he would take his rage to the card room.

CHAPTER 4

There was no mistaking Major Reynolds. The scar was livid across the left side of his face, stretching from temple to jaw. He was a soldier; that was clear as he escorted Gussie across the dance floor. It wasn't just the military cut of his clothes, it was the way he held himself, the unconscious air of authority, the alertness with which he scanned the room, the hardness of his mouth and eyes. *A dangerous man.*

Isabella looked away. She tried to concentrate on Lucas Washburne's conversation.

"The ogre comes," a lady murmured behind her, and smothered a laugh.

Irritation surged in Isabella's chest. That word—ogre—was her fault, but the spreading of it was purely Sarah Faraday's doing. Wretched, wretched woman.

"Isabella, I'd like you to meet my cousin, Major Nicholas Reynolds."

Isabella swallowed her crossness. She fixed a smile on her lips and turned her head.

Major Reynolds stood before her, tall, with cold eyes and a scarred face, precisely as Harriet had described.

No, not precisely. Major Reynolds wasn't old. Early thirties, at a guess.

". . . ogre," she heard whispered behind her.

"How do you do, Major Reynolds?" Isabella said hastily, giving him her hand, hoping that guilt wasn't stamped across her face. *If he discovers that I'm the source of that appellation . . .* She suppressed a nervous shiver.

The major made no sign that he'd heard the whisper. "It's a pleasure to meet you, Lady Isabella." He bowed over her gloved fingers.

"Be warned, Nicholas," Gussie said with a bubbling laugh. "She'll try to thrust a stray animal upon you."

The major released her hand. "No lapdogs, I beg of you, ma'am." His smile didn't reach his eyes.

Unease prickled over Isabella's skin. *He's angry.*

"It will more likely be a kitten with half a tail," Gussie said. "Or a flea-ridden puppy."

"Both of which we have," her husband said dryly.

For a fleeting second the major looked amused. He smiled faintly. The corner of his right eye creased slightly. The left side of his face, scarred, showed no sign of amusement.

The musicians began to tune their instruments again. "The quadrille," Lucas Washburne said, holding out his hand to his wife. "This is our dance. If you'll excuse us?"

Isabella watched them go. She transferred her gaze to Major Reynolds and smiled at him politely. "How long have you been in town, Major?" She knew the answer. Harriet had told her in the carriage: Major Reynolds had come to London three weeks ago, in search of a bride.

A man who acts swiftly.

"Three weeks." The major's eyes were on her face. Their color was disconcerting, a clear, chilly green. "Are you claimed for this dance?"

Isabella hesitated. *I wish I were.* "No," she said. "I'm not."

The major's face hardened. He'd seen the hesitation.

Shame made her flush. "It would be my pleasure to dance with you," she said, opening her fan.

Major Reynolds offered her his arm. "Then let us join a

set." The words were politely spoken, but she heard an edge of irony in his voice.

Isabella bit her lip. She fanned herself, hoping to take the heat from her cheeks, and laid her hand lightly on the major's sleeve. The cut of his coat was plain, almost austere, and the fabric was a green so dark it was nearly black.

They walked onto the dance floor amid the murmur of conversation and rustle of fabric. "How long have you been in town?" Major Reynolds asked.

Isabella heard the word *ogre* whispered to her right. "I arrived two days ago," she said hastily, loudly. "On Saturday. I've been in Derbyshire visiting my brother and making the acquaintance of my newest nephew."

The major had heard the whisper. Anger glinted in his eyes. He halted. "Perhaps you'd prefer not to dance, Lady Isabella?"

I would prefer not to. But guilt made it impossible to take the proffered escape. "Nonsense!" Isabella said, shutting the fan.

"You can hardly wish to dance with an ogre, ma'am." The major's voice was light, his expression sardonic, his eyes glittering with anger.

"You are mistaken," Isabella said, lifting her chin and silently condemned Sarah Faraday to perdition.

Major Reynolds made no answer. He led her to a set that was forming. His manner was quite composed. He paid no attention to the sideways glances, the whispers.

Isabella took her place opposite him. She met his eyes—bright and hard and so clear they seemed to look right through her—and curtsied as the musicians played the opening chords. She understood why Harriet was afraid of him. *Not the scar, but his eyes.*

She observed Major Reynolds obliquely as they danced. His resemblance to his brother was strong. The bones of his face were well-shaped, his features regular. Without the scar he would have been an attractive man. With it . . .

An ogre.

The major had a soldier's physique; in that he didn't resemble Lord Reynolds. His body was lean, not fleshy, hard-muscled, not soft. Like his brother, his hair was the color of honey—a shade between brown and gold—but his skin was bronzed from the sun. The scar covered the left side of his face, a thickly ridged burn, purplish-pink, barbaric, making him look half savage.

Was it a legacy of Waterloo, the battle that had claimed so many of England's finest last year? Or did it date back to the conflict in Spain?

They weren't questions she could ask.

Major Reynolds moved through the quadrille with calm confidence, seemingly oblivious to the sideways glances, whispers, and muffled giggles that his progress afforded. Only his eyes, bright with anger, showed that he was aware of the stir he was creating.

With each step that he took, Isabella's guilt grew. It had been unforgivable, uttering the word *ogre* in front of Sarah Faraday. The major was no husband for Harriet, but he didn't deserve this. And however much she might blame Lady Faraday, she knew who was truly at fault: *Me. My wretched tongue did this.*

And with the guilt was a reluctant admiration. The major had courage to hold his head up in the face of so much attention, that scar blazoned across his cheek.

There was no pleasure in the quadrille tonight, in the steps of *l'été* and *la pastourelle*. Each half-heard whisper, each muffled giggle, served to enhance Isabella's guilt. *Shut up!* she wanted to hiss to the dark-haired débutante in the neighboring set. Her hand itched to box the girl's ears.

The word she had uttered only a few hours ago was on everyone's lips. *I've turned him into an object of ridicule.* The worst of it was, she couldn't undo it.

The quadrille had never been so interminably long before, so filled with discomfort. Her relief, when the musicians played the last chord, was intense.

Major Reynolds escorted her from the dance floor, calm and smiling, with anger in his eyes. "Thank you," he said politely, bowing.

"It was a pleasure, Major."

He acknowledged her words with a slight lifting of his eyebrows, a tiny, wry movement.

The wryness gave her courage. Isabella took a deep breath and laid her hand on his arm. "Major Reynolds, you must dance every dance tonight."

The wryness vanished. He seemed to stiffen. "Must I?"

"Yes." The bright, cold anger in his eyes was daunting, but she held tightly to her courage. "Major, you must pay no attention to what is being said—and you must *not* leave early."

His jaw seemed to harden. *He thinks me impertinent.*

Isabella took another deep breath. Guilt was lodged in her chest, a hard lump. "Come," she said, smiling, coaxing, aware of nervous perspiration prickling across her skin. *I owe him this.* "I will dance the next waltz with you."

"Charity, ma'am?" His eyes were bright and hard.

No, guilt. "Not at all," Isabella said, lifting her chin. "I save my charity for animals."

The major smiled abruptly, a genuine smile that took the anger from his eyes. "Lapdogs."

He looked quite different, smiling. Isabella relaxed fractionally. "They are usually much larger," she said. "And often quite ugly. It can be difficult to find them homes."

Major Reynolds gave a grunt of amusement. "Very well. The waltz." He bowed. "It's been a pleasure to meet you, Lady Isabella."

Isabella watched as he walked around the perimeter of the ballroom. Heads turned as he passed. Someone laughed, and turned it hastily into a cough. *I did that.*

She couldn't take the word back, but she could try to undo the harm of it.

Nicholas endured a cotillion, two country dances, and a *boulanger*—the latter with a partner who met his eyes once, blushed vividly, and stared steadfastly at the floor for the rest of the dance—before the second waltz was played. He didn't need to search for Lady Isabella Knox; he knew exactly where she was.

He returned his partner to her mother and walked around the ballroom.

"There he is. The ogre."

It was a whisper, but loud enough to reach his ears. Nicholas gritted his teeth. He kept a determined smile on his face as he took the final steps that brought him to Lady Isabella's side. His mood lifted as he led her onto the dance floor. It lifted still further when the musicians began to play. They made their bows to each other; Lady Isabella gave him her hand. Nicholas drew her close. For the next few minutes he'd forget about runaway brides and simply enjoy the pleasure of waltzing with a beautiful woman.

"How has your evening been, Major Reynolds?"

He met Lady Isabella's eyes. They were a shade between gray and blue, and quite serious.

"I've had more comfortable evenings," he admitted.

"Yes," she said. "So have I." A small frown marred her brow. "In fact, Major, I've given the matter some thought, and I think I know how to come about. You must become my beau."

Surprise made him laugh. Heads turned as people looked at them. Nicholas ignored the stares. "Your beau?" He shook his head and almost laughed again. "I think your husband would have something to say about that!"

"I have no husband."

No husband? He was suddenly aware of the curve of her waist beneath his hand in a way he hadn't been before, of her gloved fingers clasping his, of the soft fullness of her lips.

"Knox was my father's name, Major Reynolds, not my husband's."

Nicholas cleared his throat. "Oh," he said, inadequately.

"I'm the daughter of a duke. London does not laugh at me." There was no arrogance in Lady Isabella's tone, merely a matter-of-factness. "And if you're my beau . . ."

"London won't laugh at me, either." He was abruptly angry. "Thank you for the offer, Lady Isabella, but I don't need your—"

"It's not charity," she said calmly, meeting his eyes.

His mouth tightened. "No?"

"No. I don't like what has happened, Major Reynolds. It makes me quite cross!"

It seemed she told the truth: her lips pressed together and her eyebrows pinched into another frown. The frown faded as he watched. "I don't like being cross," she said, with that same matter-of-factness. "So I should like to fix this." Her lips turned up in a smile. "What do you say?"

His own anger wasn't so easy to relinquish. He frowned at her. "Are you in the habit of taking beaux?"

"No," she said, apparently unruffled by his disapproval. "But given the circumstances, I'm prepared to make an exception. It will only be for a week, two at the most."

"No one would believe it," Nicholas said flatly.

Her eyebrows rose. "Why not?"

"In case you hadn't noticed, madam, I'm somewhat disfigured." There was a bitter edge to his words he hadn't intended.

Her gaze shifted to his cheek. Her brow furrowed again, faintly.

Nicholas gritted his teeth. He knew what she saw; he'd seen it often enough in the mirror: the thick ridges of scar tissue, the melted skin.

"It's not important," Lady Isabella said.

She meant it. He heard the truth in her voice.

Nicholas almost missed a step. He cleared his throat again. "Madam—"

"I'm an eccentric," Lady Isabella said. "If I choose you as my beau, London will believe it." She smiled at him, golden and beautiful. "Now, how shall we go about it? Two dances tonight, and then . . . tomorrow I shall meet you in Hyde Park and take you up in my phaeton. Are you free in the afternoon, Major?"

He eyed her circumspectly.

"Well, Major Reynolds?"

He turned her offer over in his mind. As a charade it had its appeals. Playing beau to a woman as lovely as Lady Isabella, driving in Hyde Park with her, dancing . . . "Yes," he said, feeling almost cheerful.

"Five o'clock in the park," Lady Isabella said as the waltz ended. "By the Stanhope Gate."

Nicholas's ill-humor returned as he escorted her from the dance floor. His ears heard the word *ogre*, half-whispered, to his right.

Lady Isabella heard it, too. He saw her bite her lower lip. She glanced at him.

Nicholas smiled tightly. *If I knew to whom I owe that name, I'd make them sorry.*

The candles in the chandeliers seemed to burn brighter for a moment. The crystal drops glittered, as sharp-edged as shards of glass. Nicholas inhaled, smelling the mingled scents of perfume and perspiration, and beneath them something darker: his own anger. Determination solidified inside him. He'd find out. It couldn't be impossible. Someone must know. Ladies always talked among themselves. Perhaps Gussie knew, or even Lady Isabella . . .

Nicholas looked at his companion with renewed interest. "Lady Isabella?"

"Yes?"

"Do you know to whom I owe my *sobriquet*?" He tried to speak as lightly as he could, to hide the anger in his voice, but she must have heard it. Her cheeks flushed faintly. She opened her fan.

"Why do you wish to know, Major Reynolds?"

He shrugged. "It's useful to know one's enemies."

"Enemies?" She glanced at him quickly. "I'm certain there was no malice intended, Major. Indeed, you must not think it!"

Nicholas's interest sharpened. "You know who it was?"

Lady Isabella fingered the delicate ivory sticks of her fan. She didn't meet his eyes. "I believe . . . it came from the lady who is sheltering Miss Durham."

Harriet's kind benefactress. Anger flared in his belly.

Lady Isabella glanced up at him. "I'm certain it wasn't ill-meant, Major Reynolds. It was foolishness, nothing more. Pray, don't think about it!"

He smiled, tightly. "I assure you, madam, I shan't." He wouldn't think; he'd *do*. He'd find Harriet's benefactress, and when he did . . .

He'd teach her a lesson.

*C*HAPTER 5

*I*sabella took a deep breath as the phaeton entered Hyde Park beneath the arch of the Stanhope Gate. *Be calm. Be confident.* But it was hard to be either calm or confident when she was this nervous.

She glanced down at Rufus. He, at least, was enjoying himself. He sat up, alert, his tongue hanging out and his ears pricked. His tail wagged, stirring the vandyked hem of her carriage dress.

Isabella took another deep breath. She squared her shoulders and scanned the thoroughfare. Curricles and a barouche, gentlemen on horseback, ladies walking—fashionable London had turned out to see and be seen. *Where are you, Major Reynolds?*

Despite the nerves, her conscience was easier. This was something she had to do. Her penance, if it could be called that. Not for sheltering Harriet—she had no qualms about her rôle as protector—but for her disastrous slip of the tongue last night.

Her fingers tightened on the reins. *There he is.*

The major stood to one side of the drive, looking towards the Serpentine and the trees of Kensington Gardens. Isabella observed him as she slowed the horses. He wore a gentleman's clothes—tailcoat and breeches and top boots—but even so he looked like a soldier. His attitude was alert as he waited, watchful and unsmiling.

Her opinion was the same as it had been last night: *A dangerous man*. He stood quietly and yet there was something hard-edged about his figure, his face. She had no difficulty believing that he had killed.

In profile the scar wasn't visible. The lines of his face— brow and cheekbone, nose and jaw—were strong. He was attractive—and then he turned his head, showing her his left cheek. The scar was vivid on his face, almost shocking. Something tightened inside her, a tiny recoil at the pain that scar represented.

Isabella lifted her chin and fixed a smile on her face. "Major Reynolds." She brought the horses to a halt. "Fancy meeting you here."

His lips twitched. "Yes," he said. "Fancy that."

Some of Isabella's tension eased. Her smile felt more natural. "Shall we take a turn around the park together?"

The major bowed, with none of a dandy's flourishes. *Very much a soldier,* she thought. "I would be delighted," he said.

Her groom jumped down and Major Reynolds climbed up into the phaeton. Rufus, true to his mongrel origins, wasn't fastidious when it came to new acquaintances. He welcomed the major eagerly and tried to lick his face.

"Not quite a lapdog," the major said.

Isabella looked at Rufus's long legs and unruly tail. "Not quite." She brought the horses to a walk again. "Tell me, Major, did you receive an invitation to the Harringtons' ball tonight?"

"Yes," he said, rubbing one of Rufus's ears. "But I hadn't thought to go." He glanced at her. His expression became wry. "I take it I'm attending?"

"Yes," said Isabella. "We shall dance the first waltz and the closing dance."

The major stopped rubbing Rufus's ear. He sat back and observed her. "The closing dance?"

"Yes." Isabella said. *So that you can't leave early.*

His eyes narrowed slightly.

Isabella smiled. "And you may take me to supper, Major."

Major Reynolds observed her a few seconds longer, and then said with the utmost politeness, "It will be my pleasure, Lady Isabella."

That cold, green gaze was oddly intimidating. Isabella cleared her throat. "And tomorrow is Wednesday, which means Almack's."

An expression of dismay briefly crossed the major's face. "Must I—"

"Yes."

Major Reynolds observed her for a moment. The set of his jaw was almost grim. "Very well."

Isabella transferred her attention to the horses. "Which dances would you like? A waltz and—"

"Two waltzes," the major said firmly.

She glanced at him, startled. "Two?"

"If I'm to endure Almack's, then it must be two waltzes."

"Oh." She was suddenly—disconcertingly—aware of him as a man. The broad, strong hands, the muscled length of his thigh, the sheer size of him as he sat alongside her. She swallowed and looked away. "Now, we must meet as many people as possible," she said briskly. "Do you see anyone you know? Oh, Lady Cowper! Are you ready, Major?"

An hour later, her jaw ached from smiling. Rufus lay across the major's boots, asleep. "I think that's enough for one day," Isabella said.

"More than enough," the major said dryly.

It was draining to be the object of so much attention. But the first step was now behind them, and in a few hours they'd

41

take the second. By midnight London would be talking about Major Reynolds, and not merely to call him an ogre.

"We'll do this again tomorrow," Isabella said, trying to sound cheerful. *My penance*.

"If you think it necessary, Lady Isabella." There was no inflection in the major's voice.

She glanced at him. He had to have enjoyed the polite, meaningless conversations and the bright-eyed curiosity even less than she had.

"Yes," she said firmly. It was necessary. *I won't have you laughed at because of me*. She bit her lip, wishing she could apologize, but his face made it impossible: the hardness at his mouth, the hardness in his eyes. "I wish to be of assistance, Major." It was the closest she could come to an apology. "If there's any way that I can help you in this matter, please inform me."

Major Reynolds looked at her for a few seconds, and then seemed to come to an abrupt decision. "There is one thing, Lady Isabella."

"Oh?"

"If you should discover the whereabouts of Miss Durham's benefactress, I would be pleased to know it." His voice was light, but his eyes . . .

Cold. Angry.

Isabella swallowed.

"You may put me down here," the major said.

Isabella obeyed automatically, reining in the horses. Her mouth was dry. *Don't panic*. She moistened her lips. "Why do you wish to know?"

"I'd like to make her acquaintance."

"Why, Major?"

Major Reynolds touched the scar on his cheek. "She coined my new name, did she not?"

Isabella bit her lip. She nodded.

"Then I should like to meet her." He lowered his hand. Anger glittered in his eyes. "Do you know who she is?"

Isabella's heart gave a panicked thump in her chest. She stared at Major Reynolds, at the hard-edged face and bright, angry eyes, and found herself unable to tell the truth. She moistened her lips, found her voice, and said, "No."

Major Reynolds accepted this with a nod.

Isabella felt a rush of shame, but there was no way she could tell him the truth. Not now. Not when he was looking so angry, so dangerous.

Major Reynolds leapt lightly down from the phaeton. He looked up at her, his eyes narrowed against the sun. "Thank you for your company, Lady Isabella."

She attempted a smile. "It's been a pleasure, Major."

The major bowed. "Good day, ma'am."

Isabella watched him go. *I lied to him.* But the shame she felt was eclipsed by another emotion: panic. She had the sensation that she couldn't breathe. Fear prickled over her skin.

Major Reynolds was hunting her.

The first thing Isabella did when she set foot in her house on Clarges Street was to send for her man of business; the second was to speak with her cousin.

Mrs. Westin was in her parlor, a comfortable room with walls of pale green and a white marble fireplace. Sèvres china adorned the mantelpiece: bowls and cachepots and a particularly fine vase gilded with chinoiserie decoration. Figurines perched on side tables and peered from the glass-fronted mahogany cabinet, looking at her with tiny, painted eyes.

Mrs. Westin was engaged in her favorite occupation: knitting for the poor. Harriet sat on a chair alongside her, reading aloud from what Isabella recognized as An Improving Work. Mrs. Westin, while never deprecating Isabella's preference for novels, refused to read such books herself.

Harriet looked up. "Lady Isabella!" She put the book aside, rose, and curtsied. Her expression was shyly adoring.

Isabella forced a smile. "Hello, my dear. Would you be so kind as to give me a moment alone with my cousin?"

She waited until the door had shut behind Harriet before turning to her cousin. "Elinor . . ."

Mrs. Westin had laid down her knitting. She sat with her hands folded in her lap and an expression of mild enquiry in her faded blue eyes. "Yes, my dear?"

"Elinor, I have come to ask you . . ." Isabella felt heat rise in her cheeks. She turned away and walked to stand at the window, kneading her hands together.

"Is everything quite all right, my dear?"

"Oh, yes! That is to say . . ." She turned resolutely back to face her cousin. "Major Reynolds has it in his head to find me."

Mrs. Westin's brow creased. "Find you? But I thought you were meeting him in Hyde Park today? Although I can't see why it's *your* responsibility to stop London laughing at him. It has nothing to do with you!"

Isabella found herself unable to meet her cousin's eyes—or make a full confession. "You misunderstand me, Elinor," she said, looking down at her clasped hands, shame burning in her cheeks. "Major Reynolds means to discover where Harriet is staying. And . . . and he's very angry!"

"Oh," said Mrs. Westin. "Oh, dear."

"He will be much in my company the next week or so, and . . . and it's possible you'll meet him, and . . ." She glanced up, twisting her hands together. "I have come to beg you to . . . to not tell him that Harriet is here, even if he should ask you."

Mrs. Westin's expression became one of gentle reproach. "Thou shalt not lie, my dear Isabella," she said in her soft voice. "The good Lord commands it of us."

Isabella's cheeks grew hotter. "I know," she said "But . . . but could you please not tell him that it is I who—"

"If Major Reynolds should ask me," Mrs. Westin said,

picking up her knitting again, "I shall tell him that I pay no attention to gossip. *That* is the truth."

Isabella released the breath she'd been holding. "Thank you, dearest Elinor."

"You did quite right to rescue that poor child," her cousin said, setting neat stitches of gray wool. "But I should have thought you would have returned her to her grandfather. Surely he wouldn't have been so hard-hearted as to turn her away? However, I'm sure you did what you thought was right."

Isabella bit her lip.

"I own, I can't like the subterfuge. There's something distasteful about it."

Isabella agreed. *Extremely distasteful.* She'd not thought it would be when she'd so blithely offered Harriet sanctuary. But the skirting around the truth last night, the lie she had uttered today, the begging of her cousin's complicity . . .

Abhorrent, that's what it is.

"And it must be said that Harriet should *not* have run away." Mrs. Westin glanced up from her knitting. "One must always do one's duty to one's family, however unpleasant it may be."

Isabella opened her mouth to disagree—*Surely not an unhappy marriage!*—and then prudently closed it. Duty was the tenet Mrs. Westin lived by; she continued to wear black for a husband she had neither loved nor liked.

"However, what's done is done, and we must make the best of it."

"Yes." Isabella managed a smile. "Indeed we must."

The interview with her cousin over, she hurried downstairs, but her man of business hadn't yet arrived. After a moment's indecision Isabella climbed the stairs again and sat purposefully down at the pianoforte. She turned the sheets of music, looking for the latest piece she'd purchased. Sonata no. 14, by Beethoven. She blew out a breath and sat still for a moment, her hands poised above the keys. *Calm.* Then she began to play.

The first movement was soft, almost a lamentation, but

the music came jerkily from her fingertips, choppy and dis-jointed. After a few minutes her ears could bear it no longer. Isabella pushed back the thimble-footed piano stool and went downstairs again, where she refrained from opening the front door and peering out into the street. Instead, she paced in the library while Rufus watched from the rug before the fireplace. The walnut mantle clock ticked the minutes away on its gilded face. Half an hour passed before the butler announced Mr. Tremaine's arrival.

He bowed and advanced across the floor towards her. "Good evening, Lady Isabella. I understand you have urgent business for me?"

Mr. Tremaine was a stocky man with a square, blunt face and an air of solidity. The sight of him should have calmed her. It didn't. Mr. Tremaine was no match for Major Reynolds.

Isabella tried to smile. "I need you to go to Stony Stratford, to an inn called the Rose and Crown."

"Tonight?"

"Yes," she said. "As soon as possible."

"And my task, ma'am?"

"You must speak with the landlady. A Mrs. Botham." She turned and walked to the fireplace. The clock kept time on the mantelpiece, *tick tick tick*. "I stayed there three nights ago on my way back from Derbyshire. While I was there I made the acquaintance of a young lady. A Miss Harriet Durham." She glanced at Mr. Tremaine. "I need you to ensure that my name cannot be connected with hers. Either she was not there, or I was not there. I don't care which."

"You wish me to, er . . . pay Mrs. Botham?"

"Yes," Isabella said, aware that she was flushing. "You may draw upon my funds. I shall leave the sum up to you."

Mr. Tremaine bowed. "Very well, ma'am. I'll depart immediately."

Isabella bit her lip as she watched the door close behind him. *First I lie, and now I bribe.* She looked down at her hands. They were clenched tightly together.

She released them and blew out a breath. A glance at the clock showed that it was time to prepare for the Harringtons' ball. Two dances with Major Reynolds, and supper.

Isabella squared her shoulders. "I am not afraid of him," she told Rufus, but deep inside herself she knew it for another lie. Major Reynolds would be a formidable enemy. If he ever discovered her rôle in this . . .

Fear shivered over her skin.

"He won't find out!" she said to Rufus.

Rufus wagged his tail.

CHAPTER 6

Nicholas looked at himself dourly in the tall mahogany-framed mirror. He was dressed in the long-tailed coat, knee breeches, and silk stockings that were requisite attire in the ballroom. Another evening of being stared at, he thought sourly. Of being laughed at.

His gaze rose to the scar on his cheek. *Lucky,* he told himself, touching light fingertips to the ridges of melted skin. *I am lucky.* But he didn't feel lucky at this moment.

A footman entered, bearing a note. "Sir?"

His mood lifted as he turned to take it. It must be from Lady Isabella, crying off—

No, his name was inscribed in his brother's hand.

His mood became sourer. He broke the seal and unfolded the paper, skimming the few lines of writing quickly. *Unfortunate circumstance . . . distressing for the family . . .* The final sentence arrested his gaze: *Therefore I judge it best for you to leave town.*

Nicholas felt a quick flare of anger. "You judge, do you?" he said beneath his breath.

"Sir?" the footman said.

Nicholas glanced at him.

"The servant who brought the note wishes to know if there will be a reply."

48

"Indeed!" He strode down the stairs, his shoes making sharp, slapping sounds, and into his study. At his desk he penned a curt note to his brother. The quill rasped across the paper: *I have no intention of leaving town like a dog with its tail between its legs.* He sealed the note briskly and handed it to the footman.

Nicholas turned to the long mirror that hung over the mantelpiece, adjusting the crisp muslin folds of his neckcloth. His mood was no longer unenthusiastic. Indeed, he felt almost martial, as if the Harringtons' ball was a battle to be fought.

A battle that included two dances with Lady Isabella.

He turned away from the mirror. For all her golden-haired beauty, Lady Isabella was a better judge of how to handle this mess than his brother was. *Meet them head on.*

At the Harringtons' ball Nicholas was aware of sniggers and amused sideways glances. He was also aware of his brother's angry glare and early departure. At Almack's, the following night, there were fewer sniggers, and the glances were more speculative than amused. Neither Gerald nor his wife was present.

"It's working," Lady Isabella said, as they danced their second waltz together. Gossip and music swirled around them, and beneath those sounds were the rustle of silk gowns and the soft scuff of dancing slippers on the chalked floor.

"Yes." But he had come no closer to finding Harriet's secret benefactress—nor to finding a bride of his own. Mothers who had previously regarded him with interest now viewed him with disfavor. *As if they truly believe I'm an ogre.*

Although a few were still throwing their daughters at him, most notably Mrs. Pennington.

"Tomorrow there's a balloon ascension at Turnham

Green," Lady Isabella said, her gloved hand warm in his. "I'm going with Lucas and Gussie and the children. Would you like to accompany us?"

It was phrased as a question, but he knew what answer she expected. The balloon ascension was another opportunity to show themselves together.

"It would be my pleasure," he said politely.

The true question was: How was he to find Harriet's benefactress if he spent all his time in Lady Isabella's pocket? And, equally as important, how was he to find himself a bride?

"How are you at matchmaking?" he asked abruptly.

Lady Isabella's eyebrows went up. She studied him for a moment, with some curiosity. She wore a gown of Turkish red tonight, a warm, vivid color. Above the crossed bodice her skin glowed, milk-white. Rubies and diamonds nestled in her golden hair. "If you'll forgive my impertinence, Major Reynolds . . . what is it you're looking for in a bride?"

Not a Pennington. A quiet, soft-voiced girl.

"I want peace and quiet," Nicholas said. "I want a marriage with no arguments."

"Quiet," Lady Isabella said. She glanced around the ballroom, a thoughtful crease on her brow. "Have you considered Miss Thornton? She's—"

"Too old."

"Too old?" Her eyes flew to his, startled. "But she's barely twenty-two!"

"I want a young bride." Too late, Nicholas realized that Lady Isabella was well past the age of twenty-two.

But Lady Isabella appeared not to have noticed the unintended insult. "Why?" she asked, frankly.

Nicholas concentrated on his steps for a moment. He chose his words judiciously, careful not to give offense. "While I was in the army, I observed that the more youthful a recruit was, the more easily he could be molded into a soldier one wanted to serve with."

Lady Isabella surveyed him, the thoughtful crease still on

her brow. "You wish to mold your bride into a wife who suits you."

Stated so baldly, it sounded . . . arrogant. "Yes," Nicholas said firmly. *I have nothing to be ashamed of,* he told himself, and yet his cheeks felt faintly hot, as if he flushed.

"And would you expect your wife to mold you into the husband she would like to have?"

"Mold me?" he said, affronted. "Of course not!"

Lady Isabella's lips tucked in at the corners, as if she suppressed a smile.

"My wife would have no need to mold me," Nicholas said stiffly.

Her lips tucked more deeply in at the corners. "You have no flaws, Major?"

Nicholas eyed her with suspicion. Was she laughing at him? "None that a wife should care about," he said, even more stiffly. *I sound like Gerald. Pompous.* "Apart from the scar."

Lady Isabella's mouth lost its tucked-in look. Her gaze touched his left cheek. "The scar is unimportant," she said. "A woman who didn't see that would be a poor wife."

Nicholas found himself without any words to utter.

"Quiet and malleable," she said, glancing around the ballroom again. "And young. Are those your only criteria?"

He nodded.

Her eyes lighted on someone to his left. "How about Miss Bourne? Have you considered her?"

He didn't turn his head to follow her gaze. He knew precisely what Miss Bourne looked like: hazel eyes, light brown hair, shy smile. She had been on his list of suitable brides. "Unfortunately Miss Bourne's mother seems to believe I *am* an ogre."

Lady Isabella's gaze jerked back to his face.

"No smoke without a fire, as they say." His tone was light and wry, but it didn't elicit a smile. Instead, Lady Isabella frowned and said tartly, "Mrs. Bourne is a very foolish woman!"

"She merely conforms to public opinion. And she's not the only mother in this room to do so."

Lady Isabella's frown deepened. "But surely—"

"Would you wish your daughter to marry a man rumored to be an ogre?"

Lady Isabella bit her lip.

"No," Nicholas agreed. "Neither would I." He smiled, but beneath the smile was anger. When he found Harriet's secret benefactress . . .

He almost misstepped. With effort he brought his attention back to Almack's, the waltz, his dance partner. She stood out from the débutantes in their pale silks and satins. It wasn't merely the richly colored gown or her beauty, it was her manner, her easy confidence. In contrast to the young ladies who crowded the dance floor, Lady Isabella seemed entirely without vanity. She didn't preen or pose, she did nothing to draw attention to herself—and yet no man could be unaware of her presence in the ballroom.

She didn't fit the current fashion for slenderness. Her figure was ripe and curvaceous and . . .

Nicholas cleared his throat. *She is not the woman for me*. He knew what he wanted in a wife, and it wasn't Lady Isabella.

He glanced around the ballroom, noting the flicker of gazes hastily averted. Ladies watched from behind the cover of painted fans. He saw curiosity, amusement, incredulity. *London watches and wonders.*

The dance came to a close. "Now you may escort me to supper," Lady Isabella said cheerfully.

Dry cake and tepid lemonade? Nicholas repressed a shudder of revulsion. "It would be my pleasure."

Nicholas drove to Turnham Green in his curricle, with Lady Isabella seated beside him and the groom perched behind. The day was perfect for a balloon ascension; the sky was the color of duck eggs and the only clouds were high and to the east, a faint white swathe rippled like sand on a beach. The warm breeze was fragrant with the scents of summer, of grass and sunshine and wildflowers.

Nicholas found himself enjoying the excursion more than he'd anticipated. It was amusing to watch Viscount Washburne play the father, lifting his son up onto his shoulders for a better view of the balloon as the envelope filled with gas, swinging his four-year-old daughter in the air until she shrieked with laughter. Except, he realized, Lucas wasn't *playing* at being a father, he was *being* a father, his attention wholly on his children and his wife. *That is what I want. Life instead of death, laughter instead of war.*

Envy came, sudden and unexpected—and so strong that he had to turn away. Behind him were the sounds of the ascension: excited voices, the creak of rope, a loud shout—*Stand back, ladies and gentlemen! Stand back!*—while inside him was a dark, bitter knot of jealousy.

For an instant he didn't recognize himself, didn't like himself—and then the knot of jealousy unraveled and the familiar sense of who he was returned. The sound of the crowd swelled behind him—indrawn breaths, cries rising to shouts: *Look, look!*

Nicholas turned around. The envy was gone. In its place was calm determination. He rested his gaze on Lucas Washburne and his family. *I will have that.* It was a promise to himself, a vow.

Lady Isabella turned to him. Wheat-gold ringlets framed her face beneath a pretty straw bonnet. "How thrilling it must be to rise up into the air like that!"

"Very," he said.

She looked absurdly youthful—her eyes as bright as a child's, her lips parted in delight—and quite extraordinarily beautiful. His attention was caught by the curve of her cheek and the perfect line of her throat, the rosy lips, the smooth skin.

Desire clenched in his belly, where only moments before had been jealousy. Nicholas pushed it hastily aside. "Would you ride in a balloon if the opportunity arose, Lady Isabella?"

Her eyes brightened still further, as if he'd issued a challenge. "Yes!"

But the question he wanted to ask, the question that burned on his tongue, the question he didn't dare ask, was: *Why aren't you married?*

He asked Gussie later, while Lucas was swinging Grace in the air again and Lady Isabella was listening to young Timothy explain the intricacies of aerodynamics.

"Her fiancé died," Gussie said quietly.

"Oh." He glanced at Lady Isabella. "Was it recent?"

"Ten years ago, I think. Or maybe eleven."

"Ten years!" His attention jerked back to Gussie. "She must have loved him very much."

Gussie lifted one shoulder in a shrug. "I suppose so."

"But . . ." He glanced back at Lady Isabella. She was listening quite solemnly to Timothy's tangled explanation, her expression serious, a hint of laughter in her eyes. "But doesn't she want children?"

"She has a great many nephews and nieces." Gussie followed the direction of his gaze. "Isabella is everyone's favorite aunt."

But doesn't she want to be someone's mother?

"She should marry," Nicholas said.

"Perhaps she doesn't want to."

"But . . ."

But it was such a *waste*.

He dared not say the words aloud, either to Gussie, or to Lady Isabella as she sat beside him in the curricle on the way back to London. The barouche, with children, parents, and nurse inside, was some distance behind them. Rufus, confined to the curricle while the ascension had taken place, was happily sprawled across his mistress's feet.

"Were you terribly bored?" Lady Isabella asked.

"No," Nicholas said, truthfully. "Although I was less entranced than young Timothy."

Her face lit with amusement. "Wasn't he adorable? Such enthusiasm."

Don't you want children of your own? Nicholas wanted to ask. He bit back the words and concentrated instead on his driving, trimming the reins slightly as the curricle passed over a narrow stone bridge.

Lady Isabella clutched his sleeve. "Oh, stop! Stop!"

He reined in the horses, alarmed. "What?"

But Lady Isabella was already scrambling from the curricle and didn't answer him.

"Get down," Nicholas said to his groom. "Hold them!" And he jumped down onto the road.

Isabella was hurrying back towards the bridge, but she didn't cross it, instead she cut across the grass towards the river. Rufus loped alongside her, ears up and tail wagging, as if it were a game.

Nicholas followed at a run. "What's wrong?"

Lady Isabella knelt on the bank and reached down for something in the water. "A sack," she said. "It's moving. There's an animal in it."

Nicholas halted alongside her. "Are you certain?" He saw, now, what she was reaching for: a coarse sack, its neck bound with twine, lying partly in the river. The fabric moved slightly, stirring with weak movement.

Lady Isabella didn't answer. She reached for the sack again. It was just beyond her fingertips.

She scrambled to her feet and lifted her skirts, as if to step down into the river.

Nicholas uttered a silent sigh. "Allow me," he said.

Lady Isabella turned to him. "Oh, would you? Quickly! Whatever's in there must be drowning!"

Nicholas clambered down into the river. He bent and grabbed the sack. Water streamed from the coarse fabric.

He turned towards the bank, aware of tiny, high-pitched sounds of distress coming from the sack. Lady Isabella stood there, still holding her skirts up and allowing him a fine view of shapely, silk-clad ankles. Rufus stood alongside her, his head cocked and his ears pricked, as if he, too, heard the tiny sounds.

Lady Isabella dropped her skirts and reached out her hands for the sack.

"It's wet," he said. "Your gown—"

"As if I care!"

Nicholas handed her the sack and climbed out of the river. His boots were filled ankle-deep with water.

Lady Isabella knelt on the grass and undid the twine with hasty fingers. She opened the sack carefully. The cries of distress became louder: squeaking, peeping noises.

"Kittens," Lady Isabella said.

Nicholas stepped closer and peered inside. Kittens, wet and squirming. Rufus peered inside, too, pushing his nose into the sack. His tail was wagging.

"I hope they're old enough . . ." Lady Isabella said, her tone worried. She lifted a tiny creature from the sack and examined it. The kitten shivered in the palm of her hand. It was gray, striped with black.

The Washburnes' barouche clattered over the bridge and halted alongside his curricle. "Is everything all right?" Viscount Washburne called.

"Yes," Nicholas said, taking a step towards the road. "Just a sack of kittens."

He realized his mistake as soon as he heard young Timothy's upraised voice. "Kittens!"

Nicholas turned quickly back to Lady Isabella. "I hope they're all alive," he said in a low voice, "because the children are coming."

Lady Isabella glanced up. She looked past him and nodded.

"Kittens, Mama! Kittens!"

Lady Isabella pulled the shawl from her shoulders—a shawl that even he could see was of very expensive Norwich silk—and briskly dried the kitten she held. "Here." She handed it to him and reached into the sack for another.

Nicholas held the shivering kitten and watched Lucas and Gussie shepherd their children across the grass. Gussie's expression was concerned, Lucas's was merely resigned.

Six-year-old Timothy crouched to look in the sack. "Where's the mother?"

"Not here, darling," Isabella said as she dried another kitten, this one ginger with stripes.

"I want that one," Grace said, holding onto her mother's skirt. "It's pretty."

Isabella smiled at her. "But you already have a kitten, sweetheart."

"But I want *that* one." Grace reached out a cautious finger-tip towards the mewing creature.

Nicholas watched Gussie and Lucas exchange a glance above their daughter's head. He saw resignation and amusement and acceptance, and swallowed a laugh.

"Don't you think your kitten might be jealous if you brought another one home?" Isabella said. "Here, you may hold her for me while I dry her brothers and sisters."

"I think they'd be friends," Grace announced, clasping the ginger kitten to her chest.

The sack held five kittens. "But what about the mother?" Timothy said worriedly.

"I shall be their mother," Lady Isabella said, smiling at him. "Until they're old enough to have homes of their own."

"They're very small," Timothy said dubiously, looking down at the kitten he held cupped in his hands.

Nicholas was privately dubious, too, but he didn't express it aloud. Instead he fetched a blanket from the curricle. His boots squelched with every step he took.

"Thank you," Lady Isabella said, when they were in the

curricle again, the kittens bundled in the blanket on her lap and the barouche once more behind them. "I'm sorry. Your boots . . ." She bit her lip. "You must be quite uncomfortable."

"I was a soldier, ma'am. Wet boots are nothing."

Her gaze flicked to his cheek, and then down to the bundle on her lap. "Well . . . thank you. I'm very grateful."

He took in her appearance—the wet, grass-stained gown, the muddy shoes, the ruined shawl lying on the floor of the curricle. "Your maid won't be pleased with you."

She met his eyes again. To his surprise, she grinned. Her bottom teeth were slightly crooked. "Partridge is used to it."

"Oh?"

Her grin faded. "These aren't the first animals I've found."

He glanced down at Rufus. "Was he in a sack?"

Lady Isabella's expression became sober. No, not sober; grim. "I found Rufus on the street. He was only a few weeks old. Half-starved and beaten and—" She bit her lip. Her face softened as she looked at the dog. She reached down to rub his ears. "By rights he should hate people. But he doesn't. He has a very generous heart."

As do you. "He was lucky you found him."

"Yes." She continued stroking the dog's head. There was adoration in Rufus's mismatched eyes as he gazed up at her. "He was so tiny, so frightened, so desperate . . ." She glanced up at him. "Sometimes I don't like people at all. They do such terrible things!"

Her words triggered memory: the fall of Badajoz, the British Army gone mad, soldiers looting, raping, murdering—

Nicholas pushed the memory aside. "Human beings are capable of great cruelty," he said, hoping that she would never experience more than she had: kittens drowning in a sack, a puppy starved and beaten. "But they're also capable of great kindness."

Lady Isabella looked down at the bundled blanket in her lap. She didn't look convinced.

"Do you think they'll live?" he asked.

"I don't know. They're very young." She lifted her gaze to him again. "Do you mind, Major, if I don't attend the Fancotts' musicale tonight?"

"Not at all."

Some of his relief must have made it into his voice. Lady Isabella grinned again, giving him a glimpse of crooked white teeth. The imperfection seemed somehow to accentuate her beauty: the flawless skin, the golden hair, the soft, rosy lips. "You can still go, Major, if you wish . . ."

"Heaven forbid!"

Lady Isabella laughed. As if in echo, one of the kittens uttered a tiny, muffled squeak. She looked down instantly, her hands curving protectively around the bundle in her lap.

Her animals are like children to her, Nicholas realized suddenly. *She gives them her heart.*

Having made that observation, he very much hoped that the kittens would live.

*C*HAPTER 7

*I*sabella listened with one ear to the housekeeper. Most of her attention was on the kittens.

"I don't know what to do about young Becky Brown, ma'am. Her mother has taken ill and she's asking for leave—"

"Of course she must go! How much time would she like?"

"She asked for five days, ma'am."

"Tell her she may have it."

"Very well, ma'am," Mrs. Early said in a dubious voice, as if the absence of a housemaid would cast the household into chaos.

One of the gray-striped kittens was busily licking its sister's face.

"Is that all?"

"No, ma'am." The housekeeper's tone was ominous.

Isabella stopped watching the kittens. She shifted her attention to Mrs. Early's plump face.

"I have reason to believe that one of the servants is stealing."

"What? Surely not!"

"We're going through the beeswax candles too fast, ma'am."

Isabella was silent a moment. She didn't need to be told that wax candles were both expensive and easily sold. "If your suspicion is true, then it must be dealt with." *A thief. In this house*. It was a disturbing thought. She paid her servants generously—too generously some might say. And yet someone was stealing. "Where are they kept? The dresser between the butler's pantry and the still-room?"

Mrs. Early nodded. "But I can lock them in my parlor, ma'am, if you wish."

Isabella considered this suggestion, and then shook her head decisively. "No. I should like to catch whoever is responsible. They have no place in this house. Leave the candles where they are, Mrs. Early, but keep a close eye on that dresser."

"I shall, ma'am."

Isabella's next visitor in the morning room was Harriet.

"The mail has arrived, ma'am, and there's no letter from my aunt." There was a quiver in the girl's voice, and a corresponding quiver to her lower lip. She picked up a black kitten.

"It's been less than a week," Isabella said calmly. "It's far too soon to worry."

Tears brimmed in Harriet's eyes. "But ma'am, what shall I do if—"

Isabella welcomed a footman's entrance into the room. "Major Reynolds?" she said, glancing at the card he presented on a salver. "Tell him I'll be down shortly."

The footman bowed and retreated from the room, taking care not to step on a wandering kitten.

"Major Reynolds!" Harriet put down the kitten she was holding. The color drained from her face. "He's here?"

"Don't be afraid, child. He will have come to see about the kittens." Isabella spoke calmly, but her pulse was beating slightly faster. "May I suggest that you go to your room?"

"Of course." Harriet's eyes were wide and dilated. She looked pale enough to faint.

"Don't be afraid," Isabella said again. "He has no idea that you're here."

"But the footman—"

"The servants all understand that your presence here is not to be mentioned to anyone."

Harriet looked as if she didn't believe these words. She fled the morning room.

"Foolish girl!" Isabella said to the kitten she was holding. "He's not an ogre!" But the words were to herself, as much as to Harriet.

She placed the kitten in the basket with its kin and smoothed her gown. "Come along, Rufus," she said, holding the door open for him. He preceded her, his tail waving. "He is not an ogre," she repeated to herself, under her breath. But her heart beat even faster as she went downstairs.

The silent fear faded as Major Reynolds made his bow. There was nothing ogreish about him. The green eyes were smiling as he looked at her. "You look well, ma'am."

"As do you."

His expression changed, becoming faintly derisive. Isabella suddenly saw the scar. She hadn't noticed it—broad and livid across his left cheek—until that slight lifting of his eyebrows.

"Dare I hope that the kittens survived the night?" He reached down to pat Rufus.

"They most definitely survived," she said, smiling as Rufus licked the major's hand. "Would you like to come upstairs and see them?"

Major Reynolds walked up the stairs alongside her, and she was uneasily aware of Harriet Durham one floor above their heads. Her deception had never seemed so precarious—nor so abhorrent. The compulsion to confess all seized her.

Isabella glanced at the major. She opened her mouth, and then closed it.

Major Reynolds' eyebrows rose in enquiry. "Yes?"

Isabella bit her lip. His eyes smiled at her today, but two days ago in Hyde Park he had declared his desire to find Harriet's benefactress. His eyes hadn't smiled then; they had glittered with cold, hard anger. She had looked at him and been afraid. "Your boots," she blurted out. "Are they ruined?"

"Alas," the major said, with a rueful smile.

Isabella looked away from him. *He's smiling now,* she told

herself, *but remember your first impression. He's a dangerous man to cross*. She opened the door to the morning room.

"Luxurious quarters," Major Reynolds said. "I had thought they'd be in a box in the kitchen."

The morning room was decorated in shades of yellow. The giltwood armchairs, the pale satinwood side tables, the fanciful ormolu clock on the mantelpiece with its bower of flowers, enhanced the feeling of sunshine, of brightness and light.

"The staff wouldn't be happy with me if I gave them kittens to care for," Isabella said. "We'll be short a housemaid soon. I couldn't expect them to care for kittens on top of their other duties." She stepped aside for the major to enter. "And besides, I prefer to look after them myself."

Major Reynolds advanced into the room. "They're eating?" he asked, with a glance at the saucers on the floor. "I confess, I thought they might be too young."

"As did I. Major . . . do you mind if I close the door?"

The major glanced at her swiftly. He hesitated for a moment, and then said, "I imagine that we're both of an age where we can be in the same room without being said to have compromised one another."

Isabella closed the door. "Precisely my opinion." She bent to pick up a tiny black kitten that was exploring the room on unsteady legs. Curiosity nibbled at her. She bit her lip, and then asked, "Major . . . if you don't mind me asking, how old are you?"

"Thirty-four," Major Reynolds said. He politely refrained from returning the question.

Not old at all, Isabella thought. Only five years older than herself.

Rufus crossed to the basket. He nosed among the tangle of kittens. The kittens squirmed, squeaking for his attention. The major watched as the dog licked an upturned gray-striped face. "Extraordinary," he said.

"Rufus is very good with kittens," Isabella said. She stroked the kitten she held. Its purr vibrated in her palm. "He's had practice."

"As have you, I see." He glanced at the accoutrements—the bowls of water, milk, and meat broth, the blanket-lined basket, the box of dry dirt. A laugh came to his lips. "What does your cousin think of this?"

"My cousin kindly lends me countenance, but the house is mine. If the curtains or the carpet need replacing, I shall do it gladly."

Major Reynolds crossed to the basket and crouched alongside Rufus. "I have yet to meet your cousin," he observed. "I understand she's in mourning?"

"Mr. Westin died six years ago."

The major glanced up. She saw his surprise.

"My cousin takes her duties as a wife very seriously," Isabella said.

"Evidently." The major reached into the basket and picked up a gray-striped kitten. It mewed piteously for a moment, and then quieted in the shelter of his cupped hands.

"You must have one," Isabella said. "You're their rescuer, after all."

Major Reynolds put the kitten back in the basket. He stood. "Thank you, ma'am, but I'm not very fond of cats."

"You could call it Boots," she suggested hopefully.

His mouth quirked as if he suppressed a laugh. "No, ma'am. But I thank you for the offer."

Isabella sighed. "Well, please let me know if you hear of anyone who would like a kitten."

"Grace Washburne," the major said promptly.

"Gussie would never forgive me!"

"I think Gussie and Lucas are resigned to another kitten," he said, turning to examine the room. His gaze lighted briefly on the dainty Louis XV escritoire with its gilded ormolu mounts and floral marquetry, the pianoforte with its gleaming, polished wood and ivory keys, the low, comfortable sofas upholstered in cream and gold damask.

"Oh." Isabella looked at the basket. A gray-and-black kitten was climbing determinedly over its brothers and sisters. "Perhaps . . ."

"Won't you keep one for yourself?" he asked, turning back to face her.

"I would like to, very much." The black kitten purred in her hand. "Every house should have a cat."

A slight, awkward silence fell. Abruptly Isabella realized that she hadn't offered him refreshments, or even a seat. "Please be seated, Major." She sat, flushing slightly at her lack of manners. "Would you like something to drink?"

"Thank you," Major Reynolds said, taking a seat across from her. "But no. I merely came to see how the kittens fared."

"Very well, as you can see. My cousin tells me I have a way with strays."

She was suddenly aware of Harriet in her room upstairs. *Another of my strays.* There was another awkward pause. "I'm putting together a party for the theater tomorrow," Isabella said, rushing to fill the silence. "I hope you'll come?"

The major inclined his head politely.

"Gussie and Lucas will be there."

Major Reynolds nodded again.

Isabella bit her lip. She looked down at the kitten in her hand. "And the Worthingtons' masked ball is the evening after, out at Islington Spa." She glanced at him. "Have you given any thought to a costume?"

"Costume? Is it necessary?"

Isabella lifted one shoulder in a shrug. "A mask and domino would be acceptable, but for the Worthingtons' masquerade one generally comes in costume."

"Does one?" The major looked as if he had swallowed something distasteful. "What's your costume to be?"

"You'll have to wait and see, Major."

His eyes narrowed on her face for a moment, and then he gave a shrug, too. "Very well," he said. "I'll attend the masquerade. But only if I may have two waltzes."

Isabella was suddenly aware of his maleness and of the closed door to the morning room. "Then I shall expect you to come in costume," she countered.

Major Reynolds nodded. "I will."

Another awkward pause fell. She looked for Rufus. He was lying on the floor. Two of the kittens clambered over his outstretched paws.

"Do you intend to go to Hyde Park this afternoon?" the major asked. "The weather's not particularly clement."

Isabella glanced at the window and the gray, blustery sky visible above the rooftops. She shook her head. "No."

"And what of tonight? The Alleynes' ball, or the Warwicks'?"

"I shall be attending both," Isabella said, looking at him. "Choose which one you'd like to attend, Major, and I'll save two dances for you."

The major looked as if he'd like to attend neither. "Do you enjoy it?" he asked abruptly. "London. The Season."

"Yes, immensely."

His brow furrowed slightly. "Why?"

Isabella blinked, surprised by the question. She thought for a moment. "The busyness," she said. "The gaiety. My friends." She shrugged. "There are many reasons, Major, but mostly it's because I abhor being idle. In London I'm rarely idle. It suits me."

Major Reynolds looked at her with a faint frown on his face.

"You don't like it," she ventured.

"No." The word was an uncompromising monosyllable.

Guilt made her lower her eyes. "But if circumstances were different, Major, if . . . if—" *I hadn't called you an ogre.*

"I would still dislike it."

She glanced up. "Why?"

"The gossip," he said, a faint, biting note of contempt in his voice. "The posturing and the pretension. The insincerity."

"Those things aren't confined to London, or to the Season, Major. One may find gossip in any town or village in England."

"Perhaps." He looked unconvinced.

"And as for posturing and pretension and insincerity, I'm persuaded those aren't unique to London either. Where there's society, Major, there'll be foolishness. It is—unfortunately— part of human nature."

Major Reynolds smiled. "Well argued, ma'am." But the smile didn't reach his eyes.

Isabella looked down at the kitten she held, aware that the major's estimation of her had shrunk in the past minute. Was she so vain that she cared? It appeared so.

Major Reynolds stood. "I've trespassed on your time long enough."

"Not at all." But she rose, too. The kitten, which had been asleep in her hand, woke with an indignant squeak. Isabella bent and placed the tiny creature on the floor. It shook itself, almost falling over in the process.

Rufus rose when she opened the door. He came down the stairs with them and politely licked the major's hand goodbye.

"Which ball, Major?"

Major Reynolds accepted his hat and gloves from her butler, Hoban. "Both."

Her eyebrows rose. "Both?"

"If one is to do something, one should do it properly." The major's tone was grim, as if he spoke of battle, not dress balls.

Nicholas walked home, deep in thought. Lady Isabella wanted a costume, did she? Inspiration struck as he turned into Albemarle Street. He uttered a laugh as he ran up the steps to the house he'd hired for the Season.

"Has Mr. Shepherd arrived?"

"No, sir," the butler said, accepting his hat and gloves.

Nicholas glanced at the long clock in the hallway. It still

wanted ten minutes to the hour. "I'll be in my study. Send him in when he arrives, Frye."

"Very good, sir."

The house had come furnished, but despite the paintings on the walls and the library full of books it felt more like a hotel than a home. The study was the only room he'd made his own, clearing out all the knickknacks. The wing-backed leather armchair had, in the past few weeks, molded itself to fit him.

Mr. Shepherd was punctual to the hour. Nicholas put aside the letter he'd been writing and stood. "Mr. Shepherd. Thank you for coming."

"Not at all." Mr. Shepherd's hand was dry, his hairline receding, and his gray eyes sharp with intelligence.

"I understand you do some work for Bow Street."

"On occasion, yes."

"You've been recommended to me as being both discreet and thorough."

Mr. Shepherd made no reply. His expression was as impassive as his person was nondescript.

"I have a commission for you. Please be seated."

The details were swiftly sorted. Nicholas was conscious of a sense of satisfaction as he watched the man leave. *Soon I'll know.* And when he did . . .

He turned to look out the window, watching as Mr. Shepherd walked down the steps and along Albemarle Street. The man blended in with the other pedestrians, becoming almost invisible, so unremarkable as to be remarkable.

Nicholas lifted a hand to the scar on his cheek and let his fingertips trail over the smoothness and the ridges of hardened flesh. *Ogre.*

Soon he'd know the identity of Harriet's kind benefactress.

His next task took him into the snarl of crooked streets around Drury Lane, in search of an establishment recommended to him by one of his footman, a Londoner born and bred. He spent an hour in conference with a plump gentleman possessing a shock of wiry hair and paint-stained fingers, parted with a not inconsiderable sum of money, and exited whistling.

His next object was his club, where he dined and settled down in a winged armchair in a quiet alcove to read the newspaper and drink a glass of claret. Here, his nephew found him half an hour later.

"Sir! I've been looking everywhere for you."

Nicholas lowered the newspaper and observed his relative. Harry's face was flushed and anger was kindled in his eyes— one of which was almost buried in dark and swollen flesh.

"Been brawling, Harry?"

The color in Harry's face heightened. "Yes!" he said. "And I'll do so again! It's infamous, sir. Infamous!"

Nicholas folded the newspaper and placed it on the mahogany table beside him. "You alarm me, Harry." He gestured to an empty chair. "Please be seated. Would you like a glass of claret?"

For a moment Harry stood, fists clenched, radiating outrage with every line of his body, then he strode to the chair and pulled it closer. Some of the fire seemed to leave him as he sat.

"I haven't seen you for several days," Nicholas said mildly.

"I've been at a horse race in the country. There was this cracking mare called Winnit— But enough of that, sir!" Harry's eyes flashed. "I came back as soon as I heard. It's infamous!"

"So I gather," Nicholas said, amused. "Er . . . what's infamous?"

"What they're calling you, sir. I told Grantham it's a filthy lie!"

Nicholas glanced at his nephew's hands, curled again into fists. "Is that how you acquired your black eye?"

"Yes! And I shall do so again! I'll make them stop—"

"I thank you for your defense of me," Nicholas said. "But I don't need you to fight my battles, Harry."

"But, sir—"

Nicholas signaled to a waiter. "Two glasses of claret," he said firmly.

He eyed his nephew while they waited. Harry bore little resemblance to the young man who'd visited him only few days ago. Gone was the languor and the sullenness, and gone, too, were the pomaded hair and the absurd shirt-points. In their place were animation and anger and a plainly tied neckcloth.

"It's infamous," Harry said again, once the waiter had brought their claret. "How can you bear it, sir? It makes me so furious!"

It was odd, Nicholas thought, sipping his wine, but Harry's outrage made his own less. "Ignore it," he said.

"Ignore it!" cried Harry. "How can I? You're not an ogre, sir, and anyone who says so is—"

Nicholas put down his wineglass. "Harry, it's nonsense. Unpleasant nonsense. And best ignored."

"But, sir—"

"I beg you not to come to blows with anyone else over this."

"But—"

"To do so is to set yourself up for London's amusement." He smiled, and tried to make a joke: "One in the family is enough."

"As if I should care!"

"*I* should care." Nicholas held his nephew's eyes. "And your father would, too."

"Father?" Harry's flush deepened. "He blames you. Says you've humiliated the whole family."

The wine suddenly tasted sour in Nicholas' mouth. "Does he?"

Harry's lip curled. "He's talking of leaving town."

Nicholas put his wineglass down on the table beside the newspaper. He rubbed his forehead.

"I wish he would go!" Harry said hotly. "Of all the mean, cowardly—"

"Harry!"

Harry closed his mouth.

"You'll speak of your father with respect, or not at all. Is that understood?"

Harry's gaze dropped. "Yes, sir." The familiar, sullen note was back in his voice.

The silence between them was awkward for a moment, broken by new arrivals entering the room. "Hello, Ogre," one of the men called out cheerfully.

Nicholas returned the greeting with a nod, and glanced at Harry. His nephew's cheeks were flushed again. "How can you bear it, sir?"

"There was no malice in that."

"No, but . . ."

Nicholas laughed. He reached for his wineglass again. "So where was this horse race of yours?" he asked, turning the subject.

But Harry refused to be diverted. "I wish I knew who'd started it! I'd—"

"Don't worry," Nicholas said. "I'm handling it."

Harry's eyes lit up. The last remnants of sullenness vanished. He leaned forward. "You know?"

"I shall very soon."

Harry sat back in his chair. His expression was slightly awed. "What will you do, sir, once you know?"

Nicholas swirled the wine in his glass, considering the question. *What will I do?* It required careful thought.

He swallowed a mouthful of claret and put the glass down firmly on the table. "A salutary lesson," he said.

CHAPTER 8

Nicholas danced with Lady Isabella at the Alleynes' ball—a quadrille and a waltz—and then claimed her hand several hours later at the Warwicks', in a ballroom draped with pink silk. The champagne, when he procured two glasses after a particularly energetic country dance, was also pink.

After handing Lady Isabella to her next partner, Nicholas retired to the back of the ballroom and leaned his shoulders against the pink-swathed walls. He took an idle sip of champagne, surveying the dance floor, his eyes sliding from one débutante to the next. Clarissa Whedon would be acceptable as a wife, as would Agatha Harrow. Miss Whedon wasn't a beauty, but pulchritude was unimportant in a bride. A compliant nature, a quiet disposition, youthfulness—those were what he required, and Miss Whedon had all three. Miss Harrow was pretty, in a rather colorless way, but her air of timidity reminded him strongly of Harriet Durham.

Nicholas eyed the pink champagne distastefully and took another sip. His gaze returned to Clarissa Whedon. He tried to imagine her seated across the breakfast table from him, plain-faced and quiet. It could work. It could work very well.

He had settled on his possible choices of bride—Harriet Durham, Clarissa Whedon, Patience Bourne, and Agatha

Harrow—by careful observation over a number of days. He'd finally chosen Harriet because she was the youngest and therefore—or so he'd thought—the most easily molded into a suitable wife. *And,* he acknowledged wryly, *because she was the prettiest.*

A poor choice, as it had turned out.

Nicholas swallowed the last of the champagne. He would dance with Clarissa Whedon and perhaps take her to supper, to confirm his decision.

He straightened away from the wall, oddly reluctant to solicit Miss Whedon's hand as a dance partner.

The reason for his reluctance was easy to identify: if he had a choice, he would prefer to dance with Lady Isabella.

Nicholas shook his head, annoyed with himself. He placed his empty glass on a table cluttered with discarded glassware and strolled around the ballroom to where Clarissa Whedon sat with her mother.

Miss Whedon was of middle height, with a round face, brown hair, mild blue eyes, and a robust figure. One day she would be as stout as her mother. That was unimportant. What he liked about her was her air of calmness. She didn't blush, as Harriet had used to, when he asked her for the next dance. Her manner was unflustered as he escorted her onto the dance floor.

There was no need to ask Clarissa Whedon to join him for supper; the dance had confirmed what he already knew of her: in temperament and character she was precisely what he was looking for. Nicholas searched for a word to describe Miss Whedon as he led her from the dance floor. The only word he could come up with—stolid—he cast aside. Stolid wasn't the word he was looking for.

He returned Clarissa Whedon to her mother's care, bowed, and went in search of something to drink. The question now was: when to make his offer?

Nicholas plucked a glass of pink champagne from a tray and swallowed a mouthful. It was flat, like his mood.

He grimaced, and turned the stem of the glass between his fingers. Why not speak to Mrs. Whedon tonight? Ask if he could call on her and her husband tomorrow morning? He'd spent the past ten months preparing for this moment: selling his commission, taking over the administration of his estate, readying the house for a wife and children. He should be eager, enthusiastic—

"Nicholas."

He turned his head. His brother stood before him. Gerald's lips were tightly pursed and his nostrils ever so slightly flared, as if he smelled something unpleasant. Nicholas could only smell lavender water, which fragrance surrounded his brother.

"Gerald," he said, inclining his head in polite acknowledgment. "How do you do?"

Gerald's shirt-points and neckcloth were so high and so starched that he was unable to return the gesture. He bowed stiffly from the waist. His person was overloaded with jewelry. Diamonds glittered on his buckles, his fingers, and in the folds of his neckcloth. "I'm leaving town tomorrow."

Nicholas swallowed another mouthful of champagne and said nothing.

Gerald leaned closer. "If you had any respect for the family, you would leave town yourself!" His tone was bitter and affronted, each *s* hissed, each *t* hard. "Instead of forcing me to leave."

If you had any backbone, you would stay. Nicholas didn't utter the words; he held his temper in check.

Gerald glanced at Lady Isabella, going down the *contre-danse* with her partner. "You're wasting your time," he said contemptuously. "She won't have you. She refused two dukes."

"I have no intention of marrying Isabella Knox," Nicholas

said, stung into replying. *Fool. You let him goad you.* He tightened his grip on the champagne glass and made his voice bored, disinterested. "We're merely friends."

Gerald snorted. He turned on his heel and left, taking his outrage—and the scent of Steele's lavender water—with him.

Nicholas sipped the pink champagne, his annoyance diminishing with every mincing step that Gerald took away from him. He watched Lady Isabella dance: golden hair and creamy skin and rosy, laughing lips.

She stood out from among the other dancers, dazzling in a ball gown of forget-me-not blue stitched with seed pearls, but what drew his eyes was more than the gown and the golden hair, more than her height and her beauty. It was something else, something that was purely hers.

Nicholas narrowed his eyes, trying to identify what it was that made Lady Isabella different from every other lady in the ballroom. Not merely her poise and the easy, graceful confidence, but something more than that, something that made her seem to shine from the inside.

She had an unselfconsciousness that few people in the room had. An inner serenity.

She's happy to be herself, he realized.

How many people could say that? Could he?

Nicholas lifted his hand to the scar, caught the movement, and lowered his hand. The burn was what people saw. *But it's not who I am.*

He scanned the ballroom again, examining the débutantes. They were girls, their characters only half-formed. What would they be like as women?

He returned his gaze to Lady Isabella. Would Clarissa Whedon grow into a woman like her? Would she shine from the inside?

"Good evening, sir."

Nicholas turned his head, to discover a second member of his family standing alongside him.

"Harry?" he said, surprised. He surveyed his nephew's

clothes. Harry was no longer aping the dandy set. Gone were the extravagances of fashion. The lad was dressed neatly, but quite plainly. Almost like—

Like me.

"Isn't this rather tame for you?" he asked, wondering if Gerald had seen his son's attire.

Harry flushed faintly. "Oh, I like balls well enough," he said in an airy, careless tone.

"I had thought deep play at gaming hells was more your thing," Nicholas said sardonically.

Harry's flush deepened. "If you must know, sir, I've decided to not gamble for a while."

"Pockets to let again, Harry?"

"No, sir."

Nicholas let his gaze rest on the boy's black eye. "Fallen out with your crowd?"

Anger flared in Harry's face. "They had no right to call you an ogre. No right at all!"

"All London is doing it," Nicholas said, dryly. He swallowed the last of the pink champagne. It was lukewarm, and even less palatable than it had been before.

"Well, they shouldn't!"

Harry's loyalty was oddly touching—and if it separated the lad from the wild, expensive crowd he ran with, so much the better. "I can't recommend the champagne," Nicholas said, looking for somewhere to put the empty glass.

Harry continued, as if he hadn't heard him. "When you find out who's responsible, I hope you horsewhip him!"

"It's a woman."

"Oh," Harry said, his outrage deflating slightly.

Nicholas glanced around the ballroom, at the matrons sitting with their heads bent together in gossip, at the ladies dancing. *Perhaps even a woman in this room.*

The major danced well, his hand warm in the small of her back, but he seemed to derive little pleasure from the waltz. His face held a polite smile, but beneath that was grimness. Isabella knew the reason; she'd heard the excited exclamation as clearly as he had: *Have you seen the Ogre? I hear he's here.* The débutante who'd uttered those incautious words had flushed a vivid red when she'd turned to find Major Reynolds standing almost at her elbow. He had made no sign that he'd heard, had uttered no comment as he escorted Isabella onto the dance floor, but anger had been bright and cold in his eyes.

Isabella danced silently. Her pleasure in the evening was gone. In its place was guilt. *My fault. My tongue that did the damage.* And alongside the guilt was anger. She might disagree with Major Reynolds' decision to choose so young a bride, might feel contempt for his reasons, but in all other regards the major was a man to be admired. He was courageous. He was intelligent. He was honorable. Fine qualities; and yet London chose to laugh at him.

"Would you like something to drink?" Major Reynolds asked when the musicians had laid down their bows. "Champagne?"

Isabella looked up at his face, at the hard green eyes, at the livid scar. "Thank you. That would be nice." She laid her hand on the major's arm, aware of a foolish urge to protect him, to shield him from ridicule.

"Reynolds!"

The major turned his head swiftly. "Mayhew? By all that's marvelous!" He extended his hand. Gone were the grimness and the suppressed anger. In their place was a grin that made him look quite startlingly attractive. "Lady Isabella, may I make Lieutenant Mayhew known to you?"

Lieutenant Mayhew bowed over her hand. He was a lanky, loose-limbed man of perhaps her own age, blond-haired and brown-eyed. His face was tanned above a green Rifleman's uniform, and alive with levity. "It's a pleasure to meet you,

Lady Isabella." His gaze was openly appreciative. "May I beg the honor of a dance?"

The major made a sound beneath his breath that was almost a laugh. He turned to Isabella, still grinning. "Be warned, my lady. Mayhew is a rackety, ramshackle fellow. A regular here-and-thereian!"

The lieutenant matched Major Reynolds' grin and made no attempt to deny the charge.

Isabella laughed and allowed herself to relax. "Certainly we shall dance, Lieutenant Mayhew."

She took her place opposite him in the quadrille. "How unexpected for you to meet Major Reynolds here," she said, as they waited for the dance to start.

"Unexpected?" The lieutenant shook his head. "I should have known I'd find him at a ball."

"Really?" Isabella lifted her eyebrows. "I was under the impression that Major Reynolds didn't much care for dancing."

"Reynolds? Not like dancing?" Lieutenant Mayhew laughed and shook his head again. "I've seen him dance the night away on many an occasion."

"Oh," said Isabella.

"Why, if you'd seen the lengths he went to in Madrid to procure tickets for himself and his—er . . ." The lieutenant hesitated for a moment, and then hurried on. "It was a grand ball—in Wellington's honor, you know. The tickets were dashed hard to get hold of."

Isabella glanced across the ballroom to where Major Reynolds stood. She studied his face for a moment, trying to imagine him in Madrid with a Spanish beauty on his arm. It was a difficult image to conjure up; there was nothing of the libertine about Major Reynolds. She couldn't envisage him uttering practiced, flowery speeches and whispering sweet nothings in a lady's ear. He was too hard-faced, too disciplined, too stern.

The lieutenant was another matter. She had no doubt that he'd left a trail of broken hearts behind him, with his easy manners and the light-hearted laughter in his eyes—and the disarming thread of seriousness underlying the levity. "You served with Major Reynolds?"

"In the Peninsula, and at Waterloo. He was my brigade major. A regular Come-on."

"A Come-on?" Isabella said, baffled.

"Officers are either Come-ons or Go-ons," the lieutenant explained. "They lead from the front, or the back. Reynolds led from the front."

"Oh," she said, understanding. She turned her head again and observed Major Reynolds, now talking to a young man she recognized as his brother's oldest son. "He was a good officer?"

"The best," Lieutenant Mayhew said simply. "There's no one else I'd rather have served under."

The quadrille claimed their attention and Isabella spent an agreeable half hour, the lieutenant's tongue being light and flirtatious and never wanting for words. Their bows made and the musicians' instruments laid down, the lieutenant escorted her to where Major Reynolds stood. Young Harold Reynolds was sporting a black eye. He bowed politely to Isabella and greeted Lieutenant Mayhew most correctly, but his expression as he gazed at the lieutenant's uniform approached awe.

"Do you remember the ball at Ciudad Rodrigo?" Lieutenant Mayhew said. "These draperies remind me of it."

Major Reynolds grinned. "How could I forget?" He turned to Isabella. "Wellington claimed the best house left standing, but there was a hole in the roof where a cannon ball had come through, and one in the floor. They hung the ballroom with yellow silk, and as for the hole in the floor . . ."

"They laid a mat over it." The lieutenant took up the tale. "And posted a man to see that no one fell in!"

Reminiscent laughter lit the major's eyes. "Now *that* was a ball!"

On impulse Isabella turned to the lieutenant. "I'm hosting a party at the theater tomorrow night. *The Venetian Outlaw* is playing." She included young Harold Reynolds in her smile. "Would you care to join us?"

Both men bowed and expressed pleasure at the invitation, and Isabella was aware of a sense of relief. With the light-hearted Lieutenant Mayhew as one of her party, the major must enjoy the evening—however much London stared and laughed at him.

The theater party comprised the Washburnes, himself and Mayhew and Harry, and Lady Isabella and her cousin. Mrs. Westin was a woman of middle years with faded blue eyes and a kindly face. She was dressed in widow's black. "It's a pleasure to finally meet you, Major Reynolds," she said when they were seated. His scar appeared not to disconcert her; she looked fully at his face as she spoke. "Do you enjoy the theater?"

"I do."

Their box was private, and yet the bustle of the theater surrounded them. The ceiling echoed with the sound of hundreds of conversations, with the squawk of instruments being tuned, with laughter and catcalls as the more common members of the audience filled the pit below.

"Major Reynolds is something of a thespian," Mayhew said, leaning forward. "I've seen him tread the boards on a number of occasions."

Nicholas was aware of Lady Isabella turning her head to look at him, an expression of surprise on her face. Alongside her, Harry looked equally surprised.

"You act, sir?"

Nicholas shrugged. "It was a tradition among the Light Division."

"Is he any good, Lieutenant?" Lady Isabella asked, sounding slightly bemused.

"First rate!" Mayhew answered. "I wish you could have seen his Romeo, ma'am. It was unsurpassed."

"Romeo?" Lady Isabella said, sounding even more bemused.

Nicholas shifted uncomfortably in his chair. "A comic rôle."

"I've never laughed so much in my life," Mayhew said. "And as for Wellington, I thought he'd die choking!"

"Wellington?" said Mrs. Westin, a note of reverence in her voice.

"We were in winter quarters," Mayhew explained. "Fuentes de Oñoro, wasn't it?"

Nicholas nodded.

"We found a disused chapel in Gallegos and put on performances. Wellington rode over sometimes to watch."

"A chapel," Mrs. Westin said, with a slight frown.

"The Bishop of Ciudad Rodrigo felt just as you do, madam," Mayhew said. "He laid a solemn curse upon the enterprise."

His smile, at once apologetic and charming, won an answering smile from Mrs. Westin. "Well, if Wellington didn't disapprove . . ."

"On the contrary. I've rarely seen him so willing to be pleased. And if you could have seen Reynolds, ma'am, you would understand. His Romeo is the funniest thing I've ever witnessed."

Fortunately the curtain rose at that moment. The various pairs of eyes that had been fixed on him—Gussie amused, Harry awed, Lady Isabella astonished—turned towards the stage, where a picturesque and gothic grotto was revealed.

A man stepped onstage, a letter in his hand. He paused a moment as the hubbub of the audience subsided, and then read aloud, his voice carrying over the subdued murmur coming from the pit.

"'A man once honored with your friendship has important secrets to communicate. Repair alone this night, at the hour of eight, to the grotto in the palace gardens.'"

The actor lifted his head and gazed out over the audience, his expression perplexed. "From whom is this appointment? Its mystery bespeaks an enemy rather than a friend."

A clock offstage struck eight times, and Nicholas released the breath he'd been holding and settled himself into enjoyment of the play.

After the first act, when the actors had retired from the stage, a box attendant brought refreshments. Lady Isabella had spared no expense; the selection of cakes and beverages was excellent.

Nicholas leaned back in his chair, enjoying the noise rising from the crowd below, the indefinable scent and atmosphere of the theater. He sipped his burgundy. The wine was velvety on his tongue, slightly spicy.

"I hear that London is calling you an ogre," Mayhew said in a low, laughing voice.

Nicholas grunted. "What else have you heard?"

"That you're laying siege to an acknowledged beauty." Mayhew glanced past him at Lady Isabella. "You always did have good taste."

"We're merely friends," Nicholas said, and ignored Mayhew's expression of disbelief. He had decided on a bride: Clarissa Whedon. She had no beauty, but her nature was quiet and yielding and her mother, with four daughters to dispose of, must be pleased to receive his offer, ogre or not.

He listened with half an ear as Mayhew regaled Harry with tales of army life. ". . . ate acorns for dinner. The commissariat had sent the wagons by the wrong route . . ."

"A comic actor, Major?" a voice said quietly beside him. "You have unexpected depths."

He turned his head. Lady Isabella sat where Mrs. Westin had. Her mouth quirked into a smile. "I must confess I find it hard to imagine you as Romeo."

"I mostly took the rôle of villain." Nicholas raised a finger to his cheek, tapping the hardened skin lightly.

Her gaze flicked to it. "Major, if you don't mind me asking . . . how did you acquire the scar?"

The babble of voices faded. In his ears were shouts, the crackle of flames, the sound of a man screaming. "The billet I was in caught fire."

"Ah," she said. "How unlucky for you."

Nicholas met her eyes. "No," he said. "I was lucky."

She considered the words in silence for a moment. "There were others in the billet?"

"Four of us." Crammed into a dirt-floored hovel with a tiny, creaking loft beneath the roof. "I'm the only one who got out."

"I'm sorry," Lady Isabella said simply.

Nicholas shrugged. "It was a long time ago." He raised his glass and took a mouthful, but he tasted smoke on his tongue, smelled the scent of burning flesh. For a moment he experienced nausea, twisting in his belly. Bile climbed up his throat.

Nicholas lowered the glass, his fingers tight around the stem, and forced himself to swallow the wine.

"Forgive me for asking, Major. I apologize."

He focused on Lady Isabella. Her expression was as contrite as her voice. She had seen his discomfort.

"Not at all." He forced a smile. "It was a long time ago, and as I said, I was lucky."

Her sober expression didn't alter. Was that pity in her eyes?

Nicholas straightened in the chair. The last wisps of memory faded, the whiff of smoke, the nausea. "I was lucky," he said firmly. "Twelve years of soldiering, and no injuries in battle. Few men can say that."

Her gaze went to the scar again.

"What do you see?" he asked her bluntly. "When you look at it."

"Pain."

He raised his hand to his cheek, to the ridges of melted

flesh, the roughness, the smoothness. "When I look at myself in the mirror I remember how lucky I am."

"You do?" Her tone was dubious.

"Yes," he said firmly. *I survived.*

Lady Isabella's expression relaxed into a smile. She believed him.

Nicholas relaxed, too. No more pity.

"Do you know . . ." Lady Isabella's voice was musing. Her gaze rested on the scar again. "I hardly notice it now. Only when—" She glanced at him, meeting his eyes, and colored slightly.

"Only when someone calls me an ogre." He finished the sentence for her.

Her cheeks became pinker. "Yes."

I hope my wife will learn to see past it, too. To ignore it. "What's your opinion of Clarissa Whedon?" he asked abruptly.

"Clarissa Whedon?" Interest brightened her eyes. "Do you intend to offer for her?" She bit her lip. "Forgive me, Major, that was an impertinent question."

Nicholas made a gesture of negation. "Yes, I do intend." He tilted his glass and watched the play of light on the wine. "What do you think of her?"

"She seems a nice girl."

Nicholas glanced at her. There was a slight frown on her brow, as if she searched for a word. "Placid," Lady Isabella said at last, meeting his eyes. "She seems very placid."

"Yes," Nicholas said. That was the word he'd been searching for last night. Not stolid; placid. Calm and unruffled, quiet. And young enough not to be set in her ways. Young enough for a husband to mold her. He smiled and lifted the wineglass to his mouth. Exactly what he wanted in a wife.

After the curtain had fallen, in the bustle of movement and noise, of comments, of cloaks being sought, Gussie turned to Lady Isabella. "May I bring Grace around tomorrow?"

"Certainly. Would she like to play with the kittens?"

"She would like to have one," Gussie said wryly. "The ginger one."

"Not an hour goes past without her asking after it," her husband said from behind her, his tone a mix of amusement and resignation. "She even has a name for it: Saffron."

"We give up," Gussie said with a grimace, but there was laughter in her eyes.

Lady Isabella's mouth tucked in at the corners, as if she was trying not to smile. "Oh, dear," she said. "I'm so sorry!"

"Kittens?" Mayhew asked, stepping up alongside Nicholas. "You have kittens, ma'am?"

"Yes." Lady Isabella turned to him. "Do you know someone who'd like one?"

"Me," Mayhew said. "Would you by any chance have two?"

"Yes," Lady Isabella said again, looking at the lieutenant with all the astonishment Nicholas felt.

"Why do you want kittens?" Nicholas asked, putting up his eyebrows.

"To give to my niece and nephew," Mayhew said promptly. "They're twins," he explained to Lady Isabella. "My sister's children."

Lady Isabella smiled at him, approval warm in her eyes. "Certainly you may have two kittens, Lieutenant Mayhew. I would be very pleased to give them to you."

Nicholas pulled on his gloves. For no reason that he could identify, he felt slightly disgruntled.

CHAPTER 9

Monday didn't start auspiciously. The second housemaid fell down the back stairs and broke her leg.

"Two maids short," Mrs. Early said, stout and agitated. "It can't be done, ma'am. Not a house of this size, and with Miss Durham staying."

After Isabella had soothed the housekeeper and sent her off to the registry office to hire a new housemaid, she carried the news upstairs to Mrs. Westin's parlor, where she found not just her cousin, but Harriet as well.

"Oh, let me help!" cried Harriet, putting down the handkerchief she was hemming. "I can dust and make beds and—"

"Thank you, my dear, but it's not necessary." Isabella smiled at her. A pile of handkerchiefs lay on the sofa alongside the girl. Isabella picked up the top one. It had been hemmed so neatly that the stitches were almost invisible. In each corner a violet unfurled purple petals. "You did this?"

Harriet nodded.

The next handkerchief had yellow primroses at each corner, and the one underneath pink roses, each petal delicately rendered in thread. Isabella brushed a fingertip over one of the flowers. The needlework was superior to anything she was capable of. "Beautiful," she said. "You're a fine needlewoman."

Harriet blushed shyly at the praise.

Isabella put down the handkerchiefs and turned to leave the room, holding the door open for Rufus, who followed—as always when she was at home—at her heels.

"Ma'am?"

Isabella turned back. "Yes?"

"Has . . . has the mail come this morning?"

"Yes."

"Was there anything for me?"

"No, my dear."

Tears filled Harriet's eyes. She twisted her hands in her lap. "Oh, what shall I do if my aunt doesn't—"

"There will be time enough for worry if the moment comes." Mrs. Westin didn't pause in her knitting. "Don't borrow trouble, child." There was no censure in her voice, just calmness.

Harriet bit her lower lip. She looked down at her lap, tears trembling on her lashes.

"My cousin is right." Isabella smiled at the girl. "It's too soon to worry." But privately she *was* beginning to worry. It had been a full week. Surely a reply must come soon from the Lake District?

Little Grace Washburne came in the company of her mother, to ecstatically carry off the ginger kitten, and after a light luncheon Isabella sat down in the morning room to read the letter she had received from one of her sisters, the remaining kittens curled up in their basket and Rufus warm across her feet.

She was absorbed in a description of her nephew's first venture astride a pony when the butler entered the room, carrying a visiting card on a salver. "A gentleman to see you, ma'am."

Isabella examined the card. "Mr. Fernyhough? Who is he?"

But the butler didn't know.

"Did he say why he wishes to see me?"

"A matter of business, ma'am."

Isabella tapped the card with a fingertip. "I'll see him in the drawing room, Hoban."

She poked her head into Mrs. Westin's parlor to warn Harriet that a visitor was in the house, and then went down one flight of stairs to the drawing room.

Mr. Fernyhough was dressed with great plainness and propriety. His bow was respectful, his face earnest. He looked to be not more than twenty-five. Something about the arrangement of his features, or perhaps his manner, reminded Isabella of a half-grown puppy.

"Forgive me for intruding, ma'am," he said, upon being invited to sit. "A complete stranger! But I needed to be certain . . ." He bit his lip and then blurted: "Is Miss Durham all right?"

The name shocked Isabella into stillness. "Miss Durham?" she said cautiously.

"Miss Harriet Durham. I believe she's in your care." Mr. Fernyhough leaned forward, his expression even more earnest than it had been. "Is she all right?"

"I don't perfectly understand, Mr. Fernyhough," Isabella said, taking refuge in cool hauteur. "Why would I have a Miss Durham in my care?"

Mr. Fernyhough sat back in the crimson-upholstered armchair. His manner became flustered. "I beg your pardon, ma'am. I was given to understand— The landlady at the Rose and Crown in Stony Stratford told me that . . ." He fixed beseeching eyes on her face. "Miss Durham has run away and I'm trying to find her, to be certain she's safe and well."

"What is your relationship to Miss Durham?" Isabella asked carefully.

"We are friends," Mr. Fernyhough said, but color rose in his cheeks.

Isabella lifted her eyebrows. "Friends, Mr. Fernyhough?"

Mr. Fernyhough's face became scarlet. "At one time we hoped to marry."

Isabella looked at him with interest. A very different man

from Major Reynolds. *Mild, with that puppy-dog face.* "May I ask why you didn't?"

"Her grandfather forbade it," Mr. Fernyhough said simply. "He wanted Harriet to marry a military man, not a country parson."

"You're a man of the cloth?" Isabella asked, startled.

"Colonel Durham presented me with a living two years ago. I consider myself very fortunate to be distinguished by his patronage." But Mr. Fernyhough didn't look fortunate; he looked miserable.

Isabella abandoned the hauteur. "Harriet is upstairs. Would you like to see her?"

Mr. Fernyhough's face lit up. "She's here? Oh, yes, I should very much like to see her!" The joy left his face. "No," he said, heavily. "I'd better not. If the colonel were to ask me . . . He has already accused me of harboring her, of aiding her." His expression became indignant. "As if I'd do such a thing!"

But if you truly loved her, wouldn't you? She didn't say the words aloud, but perhaps Mr. Fernyhough read them on her face, for he flushed again and lowered his eyes. "I must support my mother and my brothers and sisters, ma'am. I depend upon Colonel Durham's patronage. If he were to withdraw it . . ."

So it wasn't backbone Mr. Fernyhough lacked, but rather an independent living. Isabella sighed.

"Would you give Miss Durham a letter from me?" Mr. Fernyhough's eyes pleaded with her.

"Of course," Isabella said. "You may be assured that Harriet is quite well. She's upstairs with my cousin."

Mr. Fernyhough hung onto those few words with painful eagerness.

"We're waiting for a letter from her aunt," Isabella continued, slightly disconcerted by the intensity of his gaze. "As soon as it comes I'll send Harriet to her. By post-chaise, of course."

"I'm most grateful to you, madam—as I'm persuaded Harriet must be, too." Emotion choked Mr. Fernyhough's voice. "Without your aid I don't dare think what may have happened to her."

"I will ensure that no harm comes to her," Isabella said, uncomfortable at the gratitude shining in his brown eyes. "Of that you may be certain."

"Her reputation . . ."

"Yes," Isabella said quietly. "The damage is irrevocable. It is unfortunate."

Mr. Fernyhough lowered his gaze to his clasped hands. His fingers were gripped tightly together. "I wish . . ." He swallowed and looked up and attempted a smile. "But it's of no use." He unclasped his hands, took a letter from his coat pocket, and extended the letter to her. "You may read it if you like, ma'am. There's nothing improper." He flushed again, faintly. "I just want to say goodbye to Harriet and . . . and wish her happy in the future."

Isabella took the letter. She turned it over in her hands. "You're certain you don't want to see her?"

"I can't," Mr. Fernyhough said simply. "If Colonel Durham were to ask me . . ." He shook his head.

"A hot-tempered man?"

"Very."

She had a vision of Mr. Fernyhough, his widowed mother, and countless brothers and sisters being turned out into the street. *If only . . .*

Mr. Fernyhough stood and bowed. "Thank you, Lady Isabella. I'm more grateful than I can express."

Inspiration struck as she rose to her feet. "I shall write to my brother, Mr. Fernyhough. He holds a number of livings in his gift. Perhaps, should one become vacant . . ."

Hope flared in Mr. Fernyhough's face.

Isabella bit her lip. *I shouldn't have said that. What if there are none?* And even if her brother had a vacant living, Mr. Fernyhough would still lack the colonel's permission to marry Harriet. Although there was a solution to that problem: Gretna Green.

Isabella looked down at the letter in her hand. It was addressed to Harriet, care of Lady Isabella Knox, Clarges Street, London.

She glanced up at Mr. Fernyhough, suddenly uneasy. "The landlady gave you my name and direction?"

Mr. Fernyhough nodded.

Isabella bit her lip again. She looked down at the letter. *Miss Harriet Durham, care of Lady Isabella Knox.* "I had hoped . . . I sent a man to ensure she wouldn't disclose the connection between Harriet and myself."

"She didn't release the information readily," Mr. Fernyhough assured her. "It was only once I mentioned my vocation that she revealed she'd seen Harriet. Mrs. Botham is a very devout woman."

Isabella pinched the letter tightly between her fingers. Dread crawled up her spine. She inhaled a deep breath and looked up at Mr. Fernyhough and smiled brightly. "I'll give this to Harriet immediately."

"Thank you." Mr. Fernyhough bowed again.

Isabella opened the door. Voices came from the foyer. She recognized Major Reynolds' baritone.

For a moment she stood frozen in panic, Mr. Fernyhough at her back, the letter in her hand, evidence of her guilt surrounding her—and then Lieutenant Mayhew's familiar laugh floated along the corridor.

The kittens. They're here for the kittens. Isabella released a shaky breath.

Mr. Fernyhough bowed once more, grateful and earnest, and took his leave. Isabella retreated into the drawing room. Her fingers trembled slightly as she hid the letter inside a book.

Her heart jerked at a knock on the door. She turned her head. A footman stood on the threshold. "Major Reynolds and Lieutenant Mayhew to see you, ma'am."

"Thank you. I'll be along in a minute." She smiled and tried to speak calmly: "Can you please tell Miss Durham that we have more guests and that I desire her to stay with my cousin?"

"Certainly, ma'am."

Isabella stood for a few moments, trying to steady her breathing. Then she smoothed her gown, arranged her lips into a smile, and went to greet her guests.

CHAPTER 10

*L*ady Isabella greeted them with a smile and an out-stretched hand. She was lovely in a gown of deep rose-pink and with her golden hair dressed in ringlets. "Major Reynolds. Lieutenant Mayhew."

"I hope we're not intruding." Nicholas indicated the front door, which had just closed behind Lady Isabella's visitor. "We can return later if—"

"Not at all. Come upstairs, gentlemen. The kittens are in the morning room."

She talked lightly of the kittens as they climbed the stairs, Rufus at their heels, and perhaps it was his imagination, but she didn't seem to be quite herself.

"Are you all right?" Nicholas asked quietly.

Lady Isabella cast him a swift glance. "Perfectly!" she said, her smile bright and wide.

No, he thought, with an internal frown. *Something is wrong.*

Lady Isabella turned to Mayhew, still smiling brightly. "They all have different personalities, you know. I can tell you exactly which one will be the first to greet us."

She opened the door to the sunny morning room. The kittens, asleep in the basket, roused at their entrance. A black one clambered out and came running across the carpet, its tiny tail held high in the air.

Lady Isabella bent to pick up the black kitten. "This is Boots," she said. "And I'm afraid you may not have her, Lieutenant."

"You're keeping her?" Nicholas asked.

"Yes," she said, stroking the kitten. "How can I give her away when she comes running to greet me every time I open the door?"

"Boots?" Mayhew asked, walking towards the basket of kittens.

"Major Reynolds ruined a pair of boots rescuing them," Isabella explained as the black kitten began to purr.

Mayhew cast a laughing glance over his shoulder. "A hero, no less!"

Nicholas ignored his friend's teasing and closed the door to prevent any escapes.

Rufus trotted over to the basket, stuck his muzzle into the tangle of kittens, and began to lick the upturned faces. Mayhew uttered a startled laugh as the kittens squeaked, scrambling over each other, vying for the dog's attention.

"Extraordinary, isn't it?" Nicholas said, walking across to join Mayhew. He patted Rufus. A very nice dog, with his gangly legs and plumy tail and his startling eyes. *I should like a dog like him.*

"The black-and-gray is the boldest," Lady Isabella said, coming to stand alongside them. "She's a girl. And of the two gray tabbies, one is a boy, and one a girl. Here—" She handed the black kitten to Nicholas, their fingers touching fleetingly, and then bent to pick up a gray-striped kitten. She checked its gender with brief matter-of-factness and gave it to Mayhew. "This is the boy. He loves to have his belly rubbed, see, if you hold him like this . . ."

Mayhew laughed again as the kitten relaxed in his grip, belly-up, purring.

"What do you think, Lieutenant?"

Nicholas retired from the conversation, listening with half an ear as he examined the paintings on the walls, Boots cupped in his hand. The black-and-gray kitten set about climbing the curtains while her boldness was discussed and the gray-striped male purred blissfully under Mayhew's ministrations.

When the discussion turned to the logistics of traveling to Southampton with two kittens, Nicholas retired to one of the sofas. The cream and gold damask appeared to be untouched, but he thought he discerned some scratches on the lion's claw feet, as if a kitten had tried to climb up them.

Boots settled happily on his lap. Nicholas stroked the kitten idly, listening to her purr. The warmth and softness of her coat, the vibration of her purr beneath his hand, brought back memories of Spain, of campfires and—

"I thought you didn't like cats, Major?"

Nicholas looked up to find two pairs of eyes on him. "Er . . ."

"Nonsense!" Mayhew said. "If he said that, he was gammoning you, ma'am." His grin widened. "What was the name of that kitten you picked up after Badajoz? That scruffy, multicolored creature? Amigo, wasn't it?"

"Compañero," Nicholas said reluctantly, and then added for Lady Isabella's sake: "Companion, in Spanish."

"He carried it around with him for months," Mayhew said, speaking to Lady Isabella. "Said it was too young to fend for itself."

"Oh," said Lady Isabella. Her eyes were slightly narrowed, her expression assessing.

Nicholas cleared his throat. He stood and placed Boots on the floor. *Shut up, Mayhew, or she'll foist the last one off on me.* "Which ones are you taking?"

"Those two," Mayhew said, pointing. He turned to Lady Isabella. "But I won't take them until next week, ma'am, if that's all right with you?"

Negotiations complete, they exited the morning room, Lady Isabella closing the door in the face of the black-and-gray kitten's attempt to explore.

"What happened to your Spanish kitten?" Lady Isabella

asked as they descended the stairs, Rufus preceding them, his tail waving.

"He refused to cross the Huebra."

She glanced at him. "Did you miss him?"

"A little," he admitted.

"Are you sure you wouldn't like—?"

"Quite certain," he said firmly. Although, truth be told, he had liked the warmth of Boots on his knee, her quiet purr, her soft fur.

In the hallway Mayhew bowed over Lady Isabella's hand and—quite unnecessarily in Nicholas's opinion—kissed it. "I'm in your debt, ma'am. You've saved my reputation!"

Lady Isabella disclaimed this with a laugh.

"What reputation?" Nicholas said, slightly sourly.

"I always give the *best* presents."

"Hyde Park this afternoon?" Nicholas asked, while Mayhew accepted his hat and gloves from the butler.

"Oh," Lady Isabella said, consternation crossing her face. "Forgive me, Major, but I don't think I can. The masquerade tonight . . . my costume . . ." She bit her lip.

"No apology is necessary," he said, but as he walked down the steps with Mayhew, he wondered whether the costume had been an excuse or a reason. Something was bothering Lady Isabella. She wasn't agitated or flustered, just . . . not completely at ease.

He couldn't lay the blame at Mayhew's feet—Lady Isabella was no straw damsel to be overset by the lieutenant's lighthearted flirting.

Nicholas took his leave of Mayhew at the end of Clarges Street. "A prime article," the lieutenant said. "No wonder you're making up to her."

Nicholas looked at him with exasperation. "I told you, we're merely friends."

Mayhew shook his head. "A word of advice," he said, leaning close and dropping his voice to a whisper. "Take that last kitten."

"Damn it, Mayhew! How many times do I have to tell you? We're merely—"

But Mayhew shook his head, his eyes alight with laughter. "I must be off!" He raised a hand in a gesture that was very like a salute and swung away.

Nicholas watched him go, torn between annoyance and amusement. Amusement won. He grunted a laugh, then set his hat more firmly on his head and strode off in the direction of Drury Lane.

Isabella retrieved Mr. Fernyhough's letter from its hiding place. Now that the major was gone, some of her tension eased. She turned the letter over in her fingers. There would be tears when she gave it to Harriet, of that she was certain. Harriet was a sweet child, mild-tempered and eager to oblige, but she was also—as Isabella's brother Julian would say—a watering pot.

Although the girl did have reason to cry.

Isabella sighed and climbed the stairs to Mrs. Westin's parlor.

The room was warm with sunlight. Harriet was reading aloud in her soft, childlike voice. Isabella didn't recognize the words, but the tenor of the book was unmistakable: another Improving Work.

Harriet finished the sentence she was reading, in which duty figured largely, and looked up, marking her place with one finger. "Your visitors have gone, ma'am?"

"Yes." Isabella braced herself for tears. "One of them was an acquaintance of yours: Mr. Fernyhough. He desired me to give you this." She advanced across the room as she spoke, holding the letter out, aware of Mrs. Westin's head lifting and the knitting needles stilling, aware of Harriet's cheeks paling and the book falling unheeded from her lap.

"Mr. Fernyhough?" Harriet spoke the name in a breathless gasp. "Here?" She rose to her feet.

"He has gone, child," Isabella said gently. "He felt it was unwise to see you."

"Oh." Tears started in Harriet's eyes.

"He was concerned for your well-being. I was able to assure him that you're safe and well."

The girl nodded. Her eyes were bright with moisture.

"He left this for you."

Harriet took the letter with a trembling hand.

"Perhaps you'd like to go to your room to read it?"

The girl nodded mutely. She clutched the letter to her breast and fled the parlor.

"Mr. Fernyhough?" Mrs. Westin asked when the door had closed behind Harriet.

Isabella sighed and sat. "A clergyman." She picked up the book that had tumbled from Harriet's lap, smoothing the pages. *There is no greater glory than a life devoted to duty,* she read. She closed the book and glanced at the spine. Sermons. "An admirer of Harriet's. He withdrew his suit when Colonel Durham forbade the match."

"Quite proper." Mrs. Westin nodded her approval. She resumed her knitting.

Isabella glanced at her. *Proper, yes, but look at the unhappiness that has resulted.* She didn't utter the words. Instead she placed the book to one side and said, "Lieutenant Mayhew has agreed to take two of the kittens."

"That's good," Mrs. Westin said, not looking up from her knitting.

Isabella bit her lip, wishing she could talk freely with her cousin and knowing that she couldn't; their views on the subject of familial duty were widely divergent. She stood. "I have a letter to write, Elinor. Please excuse me."

"Of course, my dear." Mrs. Westin smiled serenely, her needles moving with a brisk *click-click-click*. A sleeve of sturdy blue wool dangled from one knitting needle.

Isabella let herself out of the parlor. She walked back to the morning room and the kittens and sat at the escritoire to compose a letter to her brother, the Duke of Middlebury. Paper, quill, ink, sealing wax . . . The words, though, weren't easy to find. She stared down at the sheet of hot-pressed paper, aware of an ache growing behind her temples. *What to reveal and what to hide?*

"How much should I tell him, Rufus?"

Rufus was no help; he merely wagged his tail.

There was something about a masked ball—a freedom, a loosening of constraints, a slight edge of the *risqué*. One could wear clothing that in other settings, in the same company, would be shocking. Isabella glanced down at her feet in their Grecian sandals. She couldn't have gilded her toenails on any other occasion—not unless she wished to shock the Polite World and draw censure down upon her head—but hers weren't the only painted toenails, tonight. A glance around the crowded ballroom showed several other ladies had the audacity to mimic the whores of Paris. One even appeared to be dressed as a whore. *Brave,* thought Isabella. *I wouldn't care to display so much flesh.*

The music fitted the mood of the assembled guests: loud, with a slightly wild edge to it. Few débutantes were present. Their mothers had prudently kept them away. The Worthingtons' masquerade did have a reputation, after all.

Isabella scanned the ballroom through the eyeholes of her golden mask, looking for the major's chosen bride, Clarissa Whedon. She was relieved not to find her; this was scarcely the place for a girl just out of the schoolroom.

Isabella found herself frowning. How could the major wish for so young a bride? And for such a reason? A placid, biddable girl without any opinions of her own. A girl whose character was still unformed.

He'll be bored within a month.

She shrugged. If that was the sort of marriage Major Reynolds wanted, he was welcome to it.

She scanned the room again, searching for him. There were a number of men with his height and breadth of shoulder—she saw a black-bearded pirate, a Roman legionnaire, a knight in armor with a red, perspiring face beneath his visor—*Poor man; not a good choice of costume*—a monk, a sailor with a tarred ponytail, an executioner, and a rather tall Napoleon—but none who had the major's carriage.

"Isn't this fun!" Gussie said. Her eyes gleamed with merriment behind the concealment of her mask. With her red hooded cloak, pinafore and pigtails and pantalettes, and the basket of strawberries on her arm, there was no doubting who she was.

Isabella laughed. "Yes!" She reached for another strawberry. Red Riding Hood's basket was almost empty.

A winged Faerie flitted past, giggling behind her mask, pursued by a horned satyr. The ballroom boasted half a dozen Faeries, in addition to a lavishly feathered peacock, a number of shepherdesses, a mermaid with an awkward tail, a butterfly, several buxom milkmaids, two Marie Antoinettes with powdered hair, a rather clever marionette, and a Cleopatra.

And a Grecian harvest goddess.

Isabella touched the tiny golden corn sheaves that dangled from her earlobes.

"There's another goddess." Gussie pointed.

Isabella followed the direction of her finger. A Diana stood by the far pillar, boyish in a short Grecian tunic, a bow and a quiver of arrows slung over her shoulder.

"Who's that with her? Good gracious!" Gussie gave a choke of laughter. "Just look at what Sarah Faraday is wearing."

Isabella had seen. She politely refrained from commenting.

"Oh, and there's Cupid. Look!"

"Yes," Isabella said. "But have you seen your cousin? He said he'd be here."

Perhaps he hadn't realized quite how far the Worthingtons' estate was from town? Seven miles, in the dark, was no slight distance. He could have lost his way or—

A disturbance near the doorway drew her attention. Voices rose. She heard gasps, laughter.

A man emerged from the crowd near the entrance, dressed in a brown frieze coat. There was no mistaking his height or his soldier's bearing.

Isabella's mouth dropped open.

She wasn't the only one transfixed. Heads turned as Major Reynolds passed. A stir of conversation rose in his wake.

"Oh," said Isabella, finding her breath as he walked towards them. "How perfect!" She held out her hand to him. "Major, I'm truly impressed."

Major Reynolds bowed over her fingers. "I'm pleased you approve."

She could only shake her head and stare at him. An ogre confronted her, gray-skinned, with flaring, red-rimmed nostrils, a jutting, knotted brow, and matted black hair hanging past his shoulders. A livid scar deformed half his face, *papier-mâché* sculpted into scarlet ridges of burned flesh.

"Where did you get it?" Gussie reached out to touch the mask with one finger.

"A costumier near Drury Lane."

"It's perfect," Isabella said again. "Absolutely perfect." She meant more than the mask. The major was thumbing his nose at the *ton* and at the same time joining them in their laughter.

Very few men would have either the wit or the courage to do that.

"It seemed . . . apt," the major said. His face was hidden behind the mask, all but his mouth and chin.

He had a very nice mouth, Isabella realized. An expressive mouth, with nicely shaped lips. A mouth that, right now, was quirked up at the corners, as if he barely held back laughter.

Bless you for having a sense of humor, Major. There could be no more ridicule after tonight, not after Major Reynolds had invited London to laugh *with* him.

His eyes, green and glittering behind the mask, examined her costume—the elaborately upswept hair bound with gold ribbon, the tiny golden corn sheaves dangling from her earlobes, the gown of cream satin falling to her ankles in long, sheer pleats, its bodice bound with golden cord, the delicate Grecian sandals. His eyes lingered a moment on her gilded toenails and then rose to inspect the staff she held, crowned with gold-painted corn sheaves and intricately bound with golden ribbon. "Demeter," he said.

"Well done, Major."

Viscount Washburne emerged from the crowded dance floor, splendid in a huntsman's costume, a wolf skin thrown over his shoulders. "The quadrille," he said to Gussie, holding out his hand to her. He glanced at Major Reynolds and his eyes widened. For a moment he stared, and then he uttered a crack of laughter. "Magnificent!"

Major Reynolds grinned. "Thank you."

Gussie put down her basket of strawberries. She took her husband's hand. "Make sure he has some punch," she said over her shoulder, as Lucas Washburne pulled her onto the dance floor.

"Punch?"

"A Worthington tradition," Isabella said. "You must try it. It's . . . Well, you shall judge for yourself."

His mouth quirked again in amusement. "That good?"

"Better!"

"Then I must certainly try it." He held out his arm to her. "If you'll lead me to it?"

They strolled slowly around the perimeter of the room to the accompaniment of the quadrille. The familiar tune had an edge to it, a slight wildness not found at more formal balls. The dancers caught the mood of the music. Isabella watched them for a moment, enjoying their gaiety, before turning her attention to the guests clustering the edges of the dance floor.

Satisfaction grew in her breast with each indrawn breath, each startled gaze, each choke of laughter, each low-voiced murmur of admiration that Major Reynolds' mask evoked. "Major," she said, in a low voice. "You are a genius."

"Taken the wind out of their sails," he murmured, inclining his head to a rather portly Robin Hood.

The table that bore the deep, silver punch bowl was crowded with revelers. It took some minutes before they were able to procure glasses.

Major Reynolds looked at his glass dubiously. Sliced strawberries and oranges floated in the punch. "It's pink," he said. "Are you certain—?"

"Try it!"

His lips twisted in amusement. She thought she saw a gleam in the eyes hidden behind his mask.

The major's first sip was tentative. His second was not. "The deuce!" he said, examining the punch more closely. "What have they put in it?"

"It's probably best if one doesn't know," Isabella said, raising her own glass to her lips.

The punch was potent, slightly sweet, slightly tart, cool in her mouth and hot in her throat. She swallowed, feeling warmth spread beneath her skin. *Dangerous to drink too much,* she told herself.

After the quadrille came a waltz. Isabella leaned her staff against a wall and allowed Major Reynolds to lead her onto the dance floor. They made their bows and then came together, his hand at her waist, hers on his shoulder. She'd worn no gloves tonight, for the veracity of her costume, and neither had he. She was aware of the heat of the major's palm, the strength of his fingers. Their handclasp felt surprisingly intimate.

The Worthingtons' waltz was no staid Almack's dance, but something far more exhilarating and fast-paced. The musicians plied their bows with ever increasing speed. Major Reynolds kept time with the music, whirling her around the dance floor until she was breathless and laughing. He retained hold of her hand when they halted, steadying her. "More punch?" he asked, as he escorted her from the dance floor.

Recklessly she nodded.

Dance followed dance until Isabella lost all track of time. She saw Major Reynolds frequently on the dance floor: the brown coat, the mane of shaggy black hair, the scowling ogre's mask. From the set of his mouth, he was enjoying himself.

The heat in the ballroom rose. The punch bowl was frequently emptied. Eyes glittered behind masks, cheeks were flushed, and mouths were wide with laughter. The knight removed his gauntlets, gorget, and breastplate. Sweat stained his undergarments.

Isabella ate a supper of lobster patties and white soup and returned to the ballroom to dance again.

"Where's your staff, Demeter?"

The voice was familiar: Major Reynolds.

Isabella turned. "I have no idea!" she said, laughing up at him. "I've lost it!"

"For shame," he said.

The mask was grotesque above his grinning mouth. For a moment the wrongness of it almost made her dizzy. Such a strong, well-formed body, such a hideous, deformed head. *Take it off,* she wanted to say, but she bit the words back. *Too much punch,* she scolded herself silently. *I must drink no more.*

"The next dance is to be a waltz," Major Reynolds said. "And then I believe fireworks will follow."

"Isabella!"

Another familiar voice, and this one far from welcome.

Isabella lost her smile. She turned. "Sarah. Have you met Major Reynolds?"

She made the introductions with cool politeness, but if Sarah Faraday noticed the coolness she made no move to leave. She was well on the way to being intoxicated, her laugh too loud, her words slurring, her face red above the green ruff encircling her neck.

Isabella glanced down at Sarah's dress. What was she? The gown was a profusion of green frills, layer upon layer of them, thickening her already stout figure.

"How charming you look together," Sarah Faraday said. "Beauty and the Beast!"

Isabella looked up from her perusal of the green gown. "Demeter and an ogre, actually," she said coldly. "What are you? A cabbage?"

She regretted the words as soon as she'd uttered them, too spiteful, too petty, but Sarah Faraday failed to notice the insult.

"A dryad." She pirouetted, almost falling over in the process, the dozens of frills flaring out, making her look even stouter. "Dressed in spring leaves."

"Very original," Major Reynolds said, politely.

Very cabbage, Isabella thought.

The musicians struck up the waltz. "Excuse us," Major Reynolds said, holding out his hand to Isabella. "This is our dance."

Isabella let him lead her onto the dance floor. "Beauty and the Beast!" she said, her voice sharp. "If she starts putting that around London—"

"It's a compliment," the major said, sounding amused. "For you, at least."

"But you're not a beast, any more than you're an ogre!" Anger made her tone hot. "And if she—"

"You sound like my nephew." Major Reynolds was smiling at her. "And I shall give you the same answer I gave him: I can fight my own battles."

"But—"

"Ignore her."

"Yes, but what if she—"

"I don't care." Major Reynolds tugged her closer. "Dance," he said in her ear.

Isabella pursed her lips. "Is that an order, Major?"

"Most definitely."

Her ill-humor slid away. "An autocrat, I perceive."

He grinned at her, his teeth glinting white beneath the scowling ogre's mask, and tightened his grip on her hand. "Of the worst kind," he said, and swept her into the waltz.

*C*HAPTER 11

*T*he music bore no resemblance to the waltzes he was used to dancing in London. It was wild and fast, almost Bacchanalian. The musicians' exuberance was infectious. Nicholas heard the music in his ears, felt it in his blood. *Dance faster,* it urged. *Faster.* Lady Isabella must have felt the music, too; she matched him step for step as he led her into one flamboyant turn after another. They were both laughing by the time the musicians laid down their bows. Their hands clung together for a moment as they steadied one another. Nicholas dragged air into his lungs and bowed. "Thank you, Lady Isabella."

"Not at all," she said, fanning herself with a hand. "You're an excellent dancer."

"As are you." He offered her his arm. "A drink, ma'am?"

"Please!"

The line to the punch bowl was long. Lady Isabella's cheeks were flushed beneath her golden mask. She fanned herself again. "You enjoy dancing," she said, in her clear, frank way. "And yet you give the impression of a man who dislikes attending balls."

"It's not balls I dislike," Nicholas said, wishing he could remove his mask. He was so damned *hot.* "It's the Marriage

Mart. I feel like a beast up for sale at an auction, being examined by prospective buyers."

Her face lit with laughter. "How uncomfortable!"

He shrugged, knowing he'd dislike it less if he didn't have the scar blazoned across his face, but not willing to make that admission aloud.

Lady Isabella's smile faded. "You're correct, Major. That's precisely what it is: an auction. I'm glad to be out of it."

I will be, too.

They had barely received their glasses when there was a stir of movement behind them, a rise in the babble of voices. Nicholas turned his head and watched as liveried footmen flung open the French windows lining the far side of the ballroom.

Glasses in hand, they joined the drifting crowd out onto the terrace. Flambeaux burned and lamps lit the gardens. The cool night air was welcome on his chin. Nicholas inhaled deeply and wished it was time to unmask. Perspiration trickled down his cheek.

The hell with it.

He put his glass down on the stone balustrade and reached up and pulled the ogre's mask off his head.

The air was cold on his face, refreshing, welcome. He closed his eyes in a moment of sheer enjoyment.

"Much better, isn't it?"

He opened his eyes to see that Lady Isabella had untied her golden mask and was using it to fan her cheeks.

"Yes." He wiped his face with one hand and ran his fingers through his hair. It was damp with sweat.

"Look!" someone cried behind him. "They're starting!"

At the sound of the first explosion, the ballroom emptied of guests. The terrace became a jostling mass of people, pressed close to one another, laughing and exclaiming as the fireworks lit the sky. Nicholas was more conscious of Lady Isabella alongside him than he was of the display of pyrotechnics. She felt soft, warm . . .

Nicholas gave himself a mental shake and drained his glass of punch. He gazed up at the bright cascade of sparks tumbling in the sky. Around him people cried out in delight, clapping their hands.

The fireworks display over, the terrace slowly emptied, the guests drawn back into the ballroom by the light and the warmth and the lilting strains of music. Lady Isabella made no move to leave the terrace. She leaned her forearms on the balustrade and gazed out over the garden. London was several miles distant; the lights and clamor didn't intrude here. The garden was dark but for a sprinkling of lamps. It was an enchanted landscape of shadows and flickering flames.

Nicholas stayed beside her, breathing in the cool air. Pleasure hummed in his veins. He felt careless, reckless, exuberant. He knew why: the punch. The stuff was lethal.

They weren't alone; a few others lingered on the terrace, to converse, to flirt lightly with one another, and in the case of a young buck dressed in striped stockings and a jester's hat, to sit groaning with his head in his hands.

"Are you enjoying your triumph, Major?"

The ogre's mask sat on the balustrade, alongside his empty glass. Nicholas tapped the *papier-mâché* cheek, sculpted in scarlet whorls, with one finger. "Yes."

Lady Isabella laughed softly.

He turned his head to look at her. She shone in the moonlight, pale and golden. "Why Demeter?" he asked. *Why not Venus?*

Lady Isabella touched one of the golden earrings in a reflective gesture. It spun, catching the light of a flambeau, gleaming. "A suitor of mine once wrote a poem. 'To the harvest goddess with her corn-ripe hair.'"

Nicholas uttered a crack of laughter. "Good Lord!"

Lady Isabella was unoffended. She grinned.

"Who was it?" Nicholas asked, before he could catch his tongue.

"Brabington."

"Brabington?" Nicholas said, startled. "The duke?"

Lady Isabella nodded.

"Why . . . ?" He hesitated a moment, aware the question was impertinent, and then plunged onwards, knowing his recklessness was due to the punch, but not caring. It was a night for stepping beyond boundaries. The music streaming from the wide-open windows urged it; Faerie music, spiraling up into the night sky, wild and lilting and as intoxicating as the punch. "Why haven't you married?"

Lady Isabella's eyebrows lifted, but she didn't appear to be offended. "Because I haven't wished to."

"But . . ." He halted, stuck for words. Didn't every woman want to marry? And then he remembered: "Your fiancé died," he said. "I'm sorry."

"Roland? Yes. He died a month before we were to be married." She looked down at the empty glass in her hand.

"That must have been hard," he said quietly.

"It was," she said, but he heard no melancholy in her voice, saw none in her downturned face. "But it was eleven years ago, so don't picture me with a broken heart, for that's not the case!" Her expression grew thoughtful. "In fact, I've often thought it was fortunate the wedding didn't take place. Not fortunate that Roland died! But fortunate I didn't marry him." She glanced at him, and uttered a laugh. "I've shocked you, Major."

"Not at all," Nicholas said, although her words had taken him aback. "Er . . . why was it fortunate?"

"Poor Roland had no sense of humor. A necessity, I believe, in a marriage." She met his eyes, her tone serious, "Don't mistake me, Major. I was in love with Roland—as much as a child of eighteen can be!—but I'm no longer wearing the willow for him."

"But you haven't married."

"No doubt I would have, if my father hadn't died so soon after Roland, and then my mother . . . She was very ill, and by the time she passed away I was twenty-four and quite used to making my own decisions, and I found that I didn't *want* to marry. Fortunately she left me a sizable fortune, so I didn't have to."

Nicholas frowned at her. "Your brothers allowed you to set up house by yourself at twenty-four?"

"With Mrs. Westin, yes."

Lady Isabella was looking at him with some amusement. *She thinks me a stick-in-the-mud.*

"And Brabington? What was wrong with him?"

She lifted her smooth shoulders in a shrug. "I didn't wish to marry him."

"But . . . a duke!"

Her expression became slightly exasperated. "Pray, what has that to do with it?"

Nicholas stared at her. He shook his head, not understanding.

"'It is a truth universally acknowledged, that a single woman in possession of a good fortune, must be in want of a husband,'" Lady Isabella said, her tone ironic.

Nicholas blinked. "I beg your pardon?"

"A paraphrase." She put her glass down on the balustrade. It made a dull *clunk* on the stone. "The world expects me to *want* to marry. Well, I don't! I like my life precisely how it is."

"Do you dislike men?" he asked, trying to understand, and failing.

"No, not at all! But I have no need for a husband of my own."

"But—"

"Why should I trade my liberty and my independence for a husband's name? What would I gain?"

He looked at her, standing pale and golden in the moonlight, the mask with its dark, empty eyes dangling from one finger. "Children?" he ventured.

"My life isn't empty of children," Lady Isabella said. "I have twelve nephews and nieces."

"Oh," he said. Her words rang in his ears. *Liberty.*

Independence. Perhaps that was what made her shine so much brighter than the other women of the *ton*. She belonged to no one but herself. Within the strict confines of Society, she danced to her own tune.

If she were crushed into a mold—wife, mother—would she cease to shine so brightly?

Nicholas turned his head and frowned down at the shadowy, lamplit garden. Had Gussie become less of herself when she'd married? Would his own bride?

A groan drew his attention. The jester staggered to his feet, his hand clapped over his mouth.

Nicholas grabbed his mask, hastily took Lady Isabella's arm, and guided her further down the terrace. The jester reached the balustrade where they'd stood and leaned over it, noisily casting up his accounts.

It was quieter here, darker. One of the flambeaux had guttered out. They had fewer companions.

Nicholas placed the ogre's head on the balustrade again. The *papier-mâché* mask scowled at him. "Is marriage wholly repugnant to you?"

"I wouldn't say repugnant, Major. Merely . . . it holds no temptations."

But what of physical desire? Nicholas held his tongue; it wasn't a comment he could make.

Lady Isabella turned the golden mask over in her fingers. He watched her frown. "I will own that there's one drawback to my situation: I must rely on my friends to provide me with an escort."

He lifted his eyebrows. "But Mrs. Westin—"

"Certainly she will accompany me if I have no other escort, but she has no great liking for balls and rout-parties."

She leaned against the balustrade again and looked out over the garden at the darkness and the shadows and the flickering lamps. "Usually one or another of my brothers and sisters are in London for the Season, but this year they are none of them here. Julian has just been presented with

112

his fifth child and poor Marianne is in no state to come to town. Simon has taken his family to the continent, and both Clara and Amabel are expecting." She turned her face towards him, laughing, moonlight gilding her cheek. "You see, Major, there's no shortage of children in my family!"

He looked at her for a long moment. "You truly have no intention of marrying, do you?"

"No."

"But—"

"I enjoy being a spinster." He heard the truth clearly in her voice: there was no defensiveness, just a quiet sincerity.

Spinster. An ugly little word. So wrong for her.

Nicholas looked at Lady Isabella in the moonlight. She was golden and silver, beautiful. *Such a waste.*

Lady Isabella looked out over the garden again. "Legally, a wife belongs to her husband. She's his property."

He'd never thought of it quite like that, but she was perfectly correct.

"I have no desire to become another person's possession, Major."

"But. . ." He groped for words, trying to articulate his thoughts. "But if a man truly loved you he wouldn't try to make you a possession."

"I have received a number of offers, Major, from men who professed to love me. But what they loved was my face, or my rank, or my fortune—or all three!" There was no bitterness in her voice, just honesty.

"Then you're wise not to have married them."

She smiled at him. "We're in agreement, then."

"But a love match," he persisted stubbornly. "If—"

"If it was *me* he was in love with," she said with irony, "and not merely my face."

"If it was a love match," he continued doggedly. "Then surely you could have no objection?"

Lady Isabella laughed. The sound had a hard edge to it,

matching the glitter in her eyes. "It's always my face men fall in love with," she said. "And I'm much more than my face."

"I am aware of that," he said with stiff dignity.

The hard glitter left her eyes. Her mouth softened into a smile. "You are a prince among men," she said, reaching out to touch the back of his hand, resting on the balustrade, with light fingertips. "Ogre." The word was said with affection.

She turned to go inside.

"But—"

Lady Isabella looked back over her shoulder. "I shall never marry, Major. Accept it!"

She was Venus, standing silhouetted in the light streaming from the French windows. Tall and queenly and inordinately beautiful.

Their companions in this corner of the terrace were gone. Some had returned to the dancing; others, judging from the muffled giggles that rose from the gardens, were indulging in more clandestine activities. He and Lady Isabella were alone, apart from music and shadows and moonlight.

She held out her hand to him. "Come inside. Let's dance some more."

Nicholas took hold of her fingers. "You don't know what you're missing."

She laughed. "I assure you that I do!"

"No," he said. "You don't."

It was music swirling from the ballroom that made him tighten his clasp on her hand, that made him pull her closer. Faerie music, wild and reckless.

Lady Isabella became very still. "Major." There was a note of warning in her voice.

"Don't dismiss something as worthless until you've tried it."

"Major Reynolds—"

"You've set your heart against marriage, without knowing anything of the pleasures that may attend it."

"Major—"

"If you were to make a love match, you would find that the . . . er . . . physical side of marriage can be extremely enjoyable."

Lady Isabella pulled her hand free. She folded her arms across her chest, defensive. "Roland did kiss me once; I didn't like it."

"He didn't do it right, then."

Her frown vanished. She laughed. "How would you know? You weren't there!"

"How do *you* know if you've only tried it once?"

The question silenced her. She bit her lip.

He looked at her, gilded in moonlight. Desire clenched in his belly. Dear God, he *wanted* to kiss her. The music was no help, whispering in his ear, urging, enticing. "I think you should try it again."

She stood quite still for a moment, her arms crossed, her face expressionless. "Just what is it you're proposing, Major?"

He shrugged and tried to keep his tone careless. "A kiss."

There was no revulsion in her voice, merely shock: "You know I dare not!"

He glanced over his shoulder, at the shadowy gardens. "We wouldn't be the only ones."

Her brow creased. "Why, Major?"

Because I want to taste your mouth. "So that your decision may be more informed." He leaned against the balustrade. "It's a very important decision, after all."

Her lips twisted, as if she tried to hide a smile. "For my own good?"

"Yes," he said, striving for a note of piety. "I feel it's my duty."

He saw laughter in her eyes; she knew he was teasing her. "Your duty?"

"Yes. I'm a very dutiful man."

She laughed aloud at this and uncrossed her arms. "You have a glib tongue, Major. Is this how you won your battles? By sweet-talking your enemies?"

You aren't my enemy. Nor was she the woman he wanted to marry. But right now, while the mad, Bacchanalian music swirled around him and the night air was cool on his face, he had a burning desire to kiss her. "What do you say?" he asked lightly.

She bit her lip, looking uncertain. "I don't know."

It wasn't a *No.* Did the music affect her as it did him? It urged him to take her hand again and stroke his fingers lightly up her arm.

Nicholas gave into the urging. He stepped away from the balustrade and reached for her hand and ran his fingertips up the inside of her arm, over cool, smooth skin.

Lady Isabella shivered slightly.

"Aren't you the slightest bit curious?" His voice was low.

"No," she said. "I told you that Roland kissed me—and I didn't like it at all."

He bent his head and whispered in her ear. "And I told you that he did it wrong."

She laughed at this. "Major, you're more conceited than I'd thought!"

"Not conceited," he said, stroking his fingers lightly up her bare arm again, from her wrist to the sensitive hollow of her elbow. "Merely honest."

Lady Isabella shivered again. She bit her lip.

Nicholas bent his head closer. "I dare you," he whispered in her ear.

"My reputation—"

"Will still be intact. I give you my word of honor."

Lady Isabella made no demur as he led her down the steps into the garden, as they followed a barely seen path into the shadows, as he pulled her into the darkness of a gazebo.

"I've drunk too much punch," she said.

"I know I have." He pulled her close to him, cupping her face in his hands. "I shouldn't dare to do this otherwise."

"Am I so terrifying?" she asked, a tart note in her voice.

Not terrifying; untouchable. He was suddenly, painfully,

aware of his ruined cheek. Beauty and the Beast. And yet he *was* touching her, her cool skin warming beneath his fingers.

"If you dislike it, you must tell me."

Lady Isabella moistened her lips. "I will." Her voice was barely audible; she was nervous.

She wasn't the only one.

Nicholas inhaled a slow, steadying breath. He slid his hands from her face to her throat, tilting up her chin with his thumbs. Her eyes stared at him, silver in the night shadows.

"Relax," he said, smiling at her.

"That's easier said than done, Major!"

He laughed, a slight puff of breath, and angled his head and touched his lips to hers.

Slowly, he told himself, closing his eyes, inhaling the scent of her skin. Orange blossom.

He started gently, laying soft kisses on her mouth until he felt her begin to relax, then he tasted her lips lightly with his tongue. She tasted of punch, of strawberries and oranges, sweet and tart, delicious.

Heat was building in his body. When her lips parted to his tongue he almost groaned.

Slowly, damn it. Slowly.

He explored her mouth in small increments, keeping it light and teasing, playful. Arousal jolted through him when her tongue shyly touched his.

Slowly.

But it was impossible when she was kissing him back, her mouth shy and inexperienced, eager.

Nicholas abandoned his caution. He kissed her more deeply, losing himself in pleasure, in heat. His awareness of their surroundings, the gazebo and the shadowy garden, faded. Her mouth was more bewitching than the Faerie music, more intoxicating than the punch. He sank into it. His world narrowed to her lips, to her body pressed against his, to her scent, her taste. This was indulgence, this was bliss, this was—

Madness.

Nicholas forced himself to release her. He opened his eyes and stepped back a pace, struggling to breathe. His heartbeat was loud in his ears.

They stared at each other. He heard her breathing, as ragged as his own, saw the glimmer of moonlight in her eyes.

"Lady Isabella?" he asked softly.

She inhaled a sharp breath. "I need to return to the ball." Her voice was low and shaken. "If my absence has been noted—"

Nicholas took hold of her hand. "It will be all right."

Her fingers clutched his. He saw her nod, heard her try to steady her breathing. "Yes," she said. "Of course it will." But her hand trembled slightly as he escorted her along the path and up the steps to the terrace. *I shouldn't have kissed her,* he thought as he halted, letting her enter the ballroom alone. She glanced back, framed by the French window, golden in the light streaming from the chandeliers, then moved swiftly from his sight.

Nicholas stayed on the terrace for a full hour, leaning his forearms on the balustrade, frowning down at the garden. What had happened in the gazebo? A kiss, merely a kiss, spurred on by the punch they'd both consumed, by the reckless music.

Merely a kiss, and yet . . .

He was uneasily aware that his world had altered. Something was different, but he wasn't sure what.

CHAPTER 12

*W*hen dawn seeped in through the chintz curtains, Isabella gave up all pretense of trying to sleep. She had lain awake for what seemed like hours, listening to the clatter of hooves on Clarges Street, to voices raised in song as revelers made their way home, to the night watchman's cry: *Four of the clock, and all's well*.

Except that all *wasn't* well.

In the space of a few minutes, everything had changed. Her life had turned upside down.

You've set your heart against marriage, Major Reynolds had said. *Without knowing anything of the pleasures that may attend it.*

And he'd been correct: she *had* set her heart against marriage. But now . . .

Isabella shifted position inside the twisted nest of bedding. Sleep was impossible; every time she closed her eyes she remembered the major's kiss, remembered the heat that had washed through her, the spiraling coil of pleasure in her belly.

She hadn't wanted him to stop. That was what appalled her the most—more than her acquiescence to his suggestion, more than her enjoyment of it. She hadn't wanted him to stop. She had wanted more.

Am I so sunk below reproach?

It seemed that she was. Every time she closed her eyes she was aware of the heat and the tension still lingering in her body. *I want more.*

Isabella changed position again. She rearranged a pillow that seemed to have grown lumpier with each hour that passed.

I feel it's my duty, the major had said, teasing her. And then he'd kissed her. And she'd let him, she'd kissed him back, and now . . .

I want more.

Isabella closed her eyes and relived Major Reynolds' kiss. Warmth flushed inside her at the memory of his mouth, the gentleness, the hunger.

It was no longer impossible to imagine the major with Spanish paramours. If he kissed like that—

Isabella opened her eyes. The curtains shone brighter with suppressed sunlight.

Harriet's grandfather had been correct: the girl was a fool to turn down a man such as Major Reynolds.

And I am a fool for kissing him.

No, not for kissing him—for letting it affect her like this. For allowing a few minutes' pleasure to disorder her mind.

Isabella uttered an exclamation of annoyance. She pushed back the covers and sat up. Across the room, her reflection glimmered ghostlike in the mirror—pale face, shadowed eyes.

Rufus, in his basket at the foot of her bed, sat up and yawned widely.

"Did you sleep, Rufus? I didn't." She touched a light fingertip to her mouth, watching the movement in the mirror.

Major Reynolds had kissed her, tasted her . . .

Isabella lowered her hand and briskly got out of bed, reaching for her dressing gown. She pulled the belt tightly about her waist and stared at herself in the mirror. A stranger met her eyes: a woman who would consider casting aside the tenet she had lived her adult life by, a woman who would consider exchanging her liberty for a man's embrace.

Rufus climbed out of his basket, stretched, yawned again, and trotted across the carpet, tail wagging, to greet her with a lick on the hand.

Isabella patted him absently. "No," she said under her breath, turning away from the mirror. She was not such a fool. A fool to kiss Major Reynolds, yes, and an even bigger fool to enjoy it—but not such a fool as to fail to realize that it wouldn't be like that with every man. It had most certainly not been like that with Roland.

Isabella drew the curtains back. Sunlight flooded in.

Why hadn't it been like that with Roland, whom she had loved? Why Major Reynolds? A man who, by his own confession, wanted a bride barely out of childhood. A bride he could mold to suit him. She couldn't admire him for that. He was either foolish, or arrogant, or perhaps both. And yet . . .

And yet she wanted him to kiss her again.

When had she come to be so aware of the major as a man? An *attractive* man?

She leaned her hip against the windowsill, frowning down at the street without seeing it. Memory of Major Reynolds' kiss tingled on her lips, but the major wasn't a man she wanted to marry. *Any more than he wants to marry me.*

Rufus pushed his nose into her hand.

Isabella laughed suddenly, looking down at him. "Your mistress is a fool!" she said loudly. A kiss, one kiss, was no reason for this turmoil of her thoughts.

Rufus pricked his ears, alert. He wagged his tail.

"Yes, you're quite correct, Rufus. It's time for breakfast." She turned away from the window and reached for the bellpull.

121

They had formed the habit of meeting in Hyde Park between the hours of five and six. Lady Isabella would take him up in her phaeton and drive around the park and let him down; a flirtation, conducted beneath the *ton*'s interested gazes.

Except that it hadn't been a flirtation; it had been businesslike and friendly.

Until I kissed her.

The question was: Would she stop for him today?

Nicholas strolled along the drive. A light breeze ruffled the dark surface of the Serpentine.

"Reynolds!"

Nicholas turned his head.

Lieutenant Mayhew came up alongside him astride a high-stepping gray. "Joining the Grand Strut, I see."

Nicholas lifted one shoulder in a shrug. He glanced at Mayhew's companion and blinked in recognition. "Harry?"

"Sir," his nephew said.

A phaeton swept briskly past with a clatter of hooves and wheels. Perched on the high seat was a dashing young lady with dark ringlets. The glance of her eyes, the slight smile as she passed them, were full of coquetry.

Mayhew turned his head to watch her. "Very nice!" he said. His attention swung back to Nicholas. "And where's your fair Venus?"

The words brought back vivid memory of the Worthingtons' terrace: Lady Isabella standing framed in the French window, golden, goddess-like. "Ah . . ." Nicholas said. He turned to Harry. "I didn't see you at the Worthingtons' last night."

"I dined with Mayhew," his nephew said. He sounded like a schoolboy trying not to brag: a little too nonchalant.

Nicholas glanced at the lieutenant. "Taken up with this young rattle?" he asked, forcing humor into his tone.

Mayhew grinned. "Someone has to tell him about your exploits."

"My exploits?" Nicholas said, slightly taken aback.

Harry edged his horse closer. "You never told me, sir, that during the battle at Badajoz—"

Nicholas stopped listening. Another phaeton was approaching. The lady's elegant posture, her deft handling of the reins, the black-and-tan mongrel at her feet, the middle-aged groom, were all too familiar.

Lady Isabella brought the phaeton to a halt alongside them. "Mr. Reynolds, Lieutenant Mayhew." She inclined her head in greeting. "Major Reynolds." Her eyes met his for a mere instant and then slid away.

Nicholas bowed to her, and wished Mayhew and Harry gone. He listened to Mayhew's cheerful greeting with impatience, to his extravagant praise of Lady Isabella's skill with the reins with something approaching irritation.

"Prime horseflesh, ma'am! You're clearly a capital whip."

The conversation turned to the kittens, and then to Mayhew's niece and nephew, before the lieutenant finally bowed in his saddle and took Harry off, with a grinning backwards glance at Nicholas.

Silence fell between them. Nicholas cleared his throat. "Lady Isabella . . ."

"Would you care to drive with me, Major?" It was a familiar question, one she'd asked each time she had halted for him, but this time her eyes didn't quite meet his.

"Yes," he said firmly.

Major Reynolds took the groom's place alongside her. Isabella set the horses in motion. She sat stiffly, aware of an awkwardness between them where there had been no awkwardness before.

"I must apologize for my behavior last night," Major Reynolds said. "It was unforgivable."

Memory of his fingers sliding up her arm made Isabella shiver. "I was at fault, too."

"It was I who offered," the major said. His tone was hard to decipher. Grim, with something underlying it that sounded almost like regret.

Does he wish he hadn't kissed me?

She glanced at him. He didn't see. He was frowning, his brow lowered, his mouth tight.

Yes, regret.

Mortification flooded her. *I passed a sleepless night wanting more, while he's been wishing it never happened.* She gripped the reins more tightly. "And it was I who accepted."

"Yes, but—"

"Shall we argue over who is most at fault, Major?" Isabella asked, her voice sharper than she'd intended. "It seems a pointless exercise to me."

Major Reynolds was silent for a moment. "You were gone," he said quietly. "When I returned to the ballroom."

"I generally leave after the fireworks." Isabella encouraged the horses past a slow barouche with a flick of her whip. "The Worthingtons' masquerade is one of the events of the Season, but it can become a little . . . a little beyond what is truly respectable." *Like kisses stolen in a garden.* The mortification had risen to heat her cheeks. She kept her gaze on the horses, on the road. Anywhere but him.

"I feared I had offended you," Major Reynolds said. "I thought, when you were gone . . ."

Isabella glanced at him again. This time he was looking at her. "You didn't offend me."

"No?"

"No."

Major Reynolds held her gaze for a moment, his hand resting on Rufus's head, and then nodded. His face relaxed into a smile. "I'm glad."

Isabella turned her attention back to the horses. She felt

rather more cheerful. *Not regret at kissing me; regret at offending me.*

Memory of his mouth, of his fingers stroking over her skin, brought another shiver and a flush of heat. The major had been right: kissing him was nothing like kissing Roland. *How ignorant I have been.* "I didn't realize it could be like that."

"Neither did I."

Isabella glanced swiftly at him. "I beg your pardon?"

"It must have been the punch," Major Reynolds said. A meditative frown creased his brow. "It must have inflamed our senses."

Isabella stared at him. "You mean . . . it shouldn't be like that?"

"Not that good. No."

She wrenched her attention back to the horses. "So last night was . . . an aberration?"

"I can think of no other explanation."

Relief flooded through her. An aberration. The feverish pleasure she had experienced, the sleepless night, the heat, the longing, the disordered thoughts, were due to the punch, not Major Reynolds' kiss. "And how it was with Roland, *that* is how it should be."

"Er . . . what?"

A familiar carriage rounded the bend. "Lady Sefton, with Princess Esterhazy."

She slowed the horses. Lady Sefton's barouche, with its matching bays, drew up alongside them. They exchanged bows with Lady Sefton and the round-faced, sharp-tongued Princess Esterhazy.

"Major Reynolds!" Lady Sefton cried, reaching across to give him her hand. "How clever you were last night. Bravo!"

"Thank you, madam."

They finished the circuit of Hyde Park, nodding and bowing to acquaintances, stopping to converse with friends. Lady Sefton wasn't the only person to congratulate the major on his ogre's costume. *Last week they laughed at him; now they laud him.* Isabella's upper lip lifted slightly in contempt as she glanced around her. Beneath the pomaded hair and the glowing ringlets, the bright silks and crisp linens, the silver buckles and frothy lace, the members of the *beaumonde* were sheep. *Where one leads, the rest follow.*

For a brief second she saw the *ton* as Major Reynolds must see them: frivolous and shallow, full of pretention and gossip. It was a dizzying, disconcerting moment.

Isabella shook her head, banishing the notion. She drew the phaeton to a halt where her groom waited beside a tree. "My cousin and I are dining with Gussie and Lucas tonight. I understand we may see you there."

"Gussie's?" Major Reynolds said. "Yes. I'll be there." He leapt lightly down.

The groom scrambled up and took his place. Major Reynolds raised his hand in farewell. A twitch of the reins and the horses moved forward.

Isabella hummed beneath her breath as the phaeton swung out of the park. The *clop* of hooves and the rattle of wheels on stone were momentarily loud as they passed through the Stanhope Gate. *An aberration, because of the punch.*

The anxiety that had ridden beneath her breastbone all day was gone. In its place was knife-sharp relief. She'd felt . . . Isabella pursed her lips, searching for a metaphor as she slowed the horses' pace. It was as if there was a room inside her head where everything was shelved, where *she* was shelved, all the parts of herself, each neatly in its own place. And Major Reynolds' kiss had turned that room upside down. Everything had tumbled off the shelves, and the shelves themselves had become crooked so that nothing fitted and things kept sliding off to fall on the floor again.

Now everything was back in its place. She was whole, she was herself, and she knew that the path she'd chosen for herself was the right one.

CHAPTER 13

"We'll be dining *en famille*," Gussie had said. "Very informal!" And very informal it was, Nicholas discovered when he arrived. Gussie met him in the doorway to the parlor and stood on tiptoe to kiss his cheek. "I'm so glad you came," she said, tucking her hand into his arm and pulling him into the room.

The parlor was familiar, a room in crimson and mahogany. The occupants were familiar, too: his nephew Harry was good-naturedly teasing a shaggy half-grown dog that clearly had mongrel origins; Mrs. Westin sat beside the fireplace, conversing with Lucas Washburne; and Lady Isabella sat on one of the sofas, Grace on her lap and Timothy leaning over the back, both children talking excitedly, and a familiar ginger-striped kitten playing with the ruffled hem of her gown.

Harry laughed and the dog uttered an answering bark. An adolescent cat with only half a tail mewed plaintively at Nicholas's feet. He scooped it up. "That's Badger," Gussie said. "His . . . ah, whiskers are slightly out of kilter due to the arrival of young Saffron."

Nicholas rubbed beneath Badger's chin. He was a fluffy creature, wiry beneath his fur, with striking golden eyes and a patchwork coat of black and white. Nicholas glanced around the room a second time, taking in the noise, the laughter, the children, the pets. *I want this.*

Badger began to purr.

"Sir!" Harry said, noticing him. He came across the room to shake Nicholas's hand. The dog trailed at his heels. It had a rough brown coat, short legs, and bright, mischievous eyes.

"Who's this?" Nicholas asked as the dog realized it had a new acquaintance to make and reared up, planting its front paws on one of Nicholas's knees.

"Tam," said Gussie. "Down!"

The dog obeyed, sitting on the carpet and beginning to scratch beneath his chin with great determination. His tail hit the floor loudly with each jerk of his paw.

"The flea-ridden puppy?"

"No longer flea-ridden," Gussie said. She scratched her elbow absently, as if remembering a forgotten itch.

Nicholas laughed. Badger paid no attention to either the dog or his laugh. He continued to purr.

"Sir," Harry said urgently. "I really must ask you about Badajoz. Mayhew said—"

Badajoz was blood, it was slaughter, it was not what he wanted tonight. "Later," Nicholas said.

Gussie clapped her hands. "Grace, Timothy, time to go upstairs!"

The children clambered eagerly off the sofa. "I want the story with Prince Adelei," Grace said, tugging at Lady Isabella's hand.

Nicholas stood aside from the doorway as Gussie and Lady Isabella and Timothy and Grace—with Saffron now clasped tightly to her chest—exited the parlor, followed by Tam. The clamor of upraised children's voices faded down the hallway. He looked across the room and met Lucas Washburne's amused gaze.

Nicholas put the cat down and walked across to make his bow to Mrs. Westin.

"Claret?" Lucas asked.

Nicholas nodded, and took a chair alongside Mrs. Westin. Badger jumped up on his lap. He turned around once, kneaded Nicholas's knee briefly, and curled up, purring.

Nicholas accepted a glass of wine from Lucas. "How are the kittens?" he asked Mrs. Westin. "Getting up to mischief?"

"Mischief? Yes." Mrs. Westin uttered a sigh. Not such an animal lover as Lady Isabella, he deduced. "One of them made it downstairs this morning. Such a pother! The house was turned upside down, looking for it."

Nicholas laughed. He glanced down at Badger, contentedly asleep on his knee. His purr rumbled faintly. "I gather they're not the first litter your cousin has raised."

Mrs. Westin shook her head. "Isabella is forever collecting strays," she said. Then, to Nicholas's surprise, her thin cheeks flushed and she broke eye contact.

A sudden, awkward silence fell. Nicholas sipped his claret and wondered what in their conversation had embarrassed Mrs. Westin. He gave a mental shrug and changed subjects. "Tell me, Mrs. Westin, what is your opinion of Kemble?"

From actors, they moved to playwrights. Mrs. Westin had much to say about Shakespeare. She preferred the Bard's tragedies; his comedies, she said with censure in her mild voice, were too vulgar and immoral for today's modern audiences. "Fornication and deception! Women dressed as men!"

Nicholas, who numbered *Twelfth Night* among his favorites, diplomatically did not disagree with her.

"And as for *A Midsummer Night's Dream*!" Outrage gave Mrs. Westin animation, bringing color to her cheeks. "Have you read it, Major?"

Nicholas nodded, bemused.

"Such a shocking play. That *wicked* elixir." She shuddered. "Liaisons with beasts! And—" as if this were more dreadful than anything else, "—a daughter's disobedience to her father is rewarded!"

Nicholas bit the inside of his lip.

Mrs. Westin folded her hands in her lap. "It is a woman's duty to obey her parents in all matters. Especially marriage."

Abruptly he remembered Harriet. The urge to laugh deserted him. He glanced down at Badger, curled up asleep on his knee, and managed—barely—not to frown.

It was with relief that he heard Gussie and Lady Isabella enter the parlor. Dinner couldn't be far away.

When it came time to move into the dining room, Nicholas found himself with Lady Isabella on his arm. He cast Gussie a suspicious, narrow-eyed glance. Was she trying to matchmake?

Gussie met his gaze blandly.

Dinner was an agreeably relaxed and informal affair. With only six at the table they talked freely around it. When the ladies had risen, Nicholas leaned back in his chair and yawned.

"Brandy?" asked Lucas. "Or port?"

"Brandy," Nicholas said. He looked across the table at Harry, also leaning back in his chair now that the ladies were gone. "What are you doing here, young whelp? I thought you were in Mayhew's pocket."

"Lieutenant Mayhew has an engagement tonight," Harry said, with dignity.

And Gussie needed another man to even the numbers.

He glanced at Lucas, pouring from a decanter, and debated asking him whether his wife was indeed matchmaking. He decided against it. However hard Gussie tried, she couldn't succeed. He had settled upon Miss Whedon as his bride, and Lady Isabella was determined in her spinsterhood.

Nicholas accepted the glass Lucas held out to him. He frowned. Spinster. Such an ugly little word, so wrong for her. It conjured up an image of a dried-up stick figure of a woman, withered and shrunken, the exact opposite of Lady Isabella, who was so lush, so—

"Not to your taste?" Lucas asked.

Nicholas looked up. "Wool-gathering!" he said and swallowed a hurried mouthful of brandy.

"Sir," Harry said, leaning forward. "I must ask you about Badajoz! Is it true that—"

"Since when have you been interested in the military?" Nicholas asked, amused.

Harry flushed slightly. "Mayhew's been telling me about it."

"Tales of glory?" Nicholas raised his glass again. This time he sipped slowly, savoring the brandy, letting the heat and the smokiness linger in his mouth. "There's more mud than glory, you know. And fleas—"

"And blisters and boils and lice. Yes, sir, I know! Mayhew told me all about it."

Nicholas raised his eyebrows. "Did he?"

"Yes, sir." Harry pushed his brandy glass aside and leaned forward. "But what I particularly wanted to ask you about was Badajoz."

"Badajoz?" Nicholas repeated, regarding his nephew with something close to surprise. He'd never seen Harry so animated. His eyes were alight with enthusiasm. "What about it?"

"All of it, sir!"

Nicholas stroked his cheek thoughtfully, his fingertips sliding over the ridges of the scar. He'd promised his brother to say nothing to encourage Harry to join the army. Was this breaking his word?

He tapped his cheek, remembering. The battle to take Badajoz had been bloody, the loss of life appalling, and the aftermath, the sacking of the town, the raping and the murder—

No, Badajoz would scarcely encourage Harry to purchase his commission.

Nicholas lowered his hand. "Very well," he said. "Badajoz."

Isabella sipped her tea. "Have you finished that book I lent you, Gussie?"

"*Pride and Prejudice?* Yes. Very droll! Would you like it back?"

"Please. I have a . . . a friend who would like to read it. I'm hoping it will raise her spirits." The tomes Harriet read to Mrs. Westin were morally uplifting, but they were scarcely of the sort to cheer up the girl.

She glanced across the drawing room. Major Reynolds stood leaning against the mantelpiece, talking to Lucas Washburne. About horses, judging from the words she caught.

A good-looking man, taller than Washburne, leaner. And Harriet thought him ugly? *Foolish girl, to be blinded by a scar.*

"Shoo!"

Isabella's attention jerked away from the men. Badger was on the tea table, sniffing the cream jug.

Mrs. Westin clapped her hands. "Shoo!" she said again. "Away with you!"

The cat jumped down. He sat for a moment on the carpet, his tail twitching in affront, then stalked across the drawing room, sat down in front of the fireplace, and proceeded to wash himself.

"Wretched creature!" Gussie said, with a laugh. She stood. "It's in the library. Is there anything you'd like to borrow?"

Isabella rose to her feet, following Gussie from the drawing room. "What did you think of Mr. Collins?"

"Mr. Collins? A beautiful combination of pomposity and stupidity!"

"I have to confess, he was my favorite character," Isabella said as Gussie opened the door to the library.

The library had dark paneling and heavy armchairs upholstered in brown leather. *A man's room,* Isabella thought as they entered. And yet it was Gussie who used it most.

"Here are the first two volumes." Gussie walked over to one of the tables. "Now where did I put the third one? Oh, hello, Nicholas. Would you like to borrow a book?"

Isabella turned her head. Major Reynolds stood in the doorway. "Perhaps," he said, stepping into the room.

"I can recommend this," Gussie said, holding out a slim calf-bound volume. "But it's Isabella's and she's lending it to someone else."

Major Reynolds took the proffered volume. "It's good?"

"Extremely!"

He opened the book, turned to the first chapter, and read the first line silently. His eyebrows lifted fractionally. He glanced up at Isabella. She saw in his eyes that he had recognized the passage.

Isabella bit her lip.

Major Reynolds looked down at the page again. "'It is a truth universally acknowledged, that a single man in possession of a good fortune, must be in want of a wife,'" he read aloud.

Memory of last night was suddenly vivid in her mind: the terrace and the darkness, their conversation. *And after that I let him kiss me.*

The major lifted his gaze to meet hers again.

Isabella felt herself blush. She looked down at the carpet, a particularly fine Axminster in red and brown.

"Where did I put the third volume?" Gussie muttered. "Oh, it's upstairs. Excuse me, I won't be a moment!" She trod briskly from the room.

Major Reynolds closed the book. "Good," he said. "I'd hoped to be able to speak with you alone."

Isabella looked up from her perusal of the carpet. "You did?"

"Yes." Major Reynolds placed the book on the table. "What I said this afternoon about kissing. I'm afraid you misunderstood me." His gaze was as direct as his voice.

"I did?"

"What I meant was that, without the punch, it should still have been good. Just not *that* good."

Isabella crossed her arms over her chest. "It would have been like it was with Roland."

"No," Major Reynolds said. "It would have been better than that."

Isabella shook her head. "Perhaps kissing is different for men than it is for women. Men enjoy it more than women."

An expression crossed the major's face. She recognized it belatedly as frustration. "No," he said. "Lady Isabella—" He took a step towards her, and halted abruptly.

It was one step only, but awareness of him shivered over her skin, making her heart beat faster. It was suddenly difficult to breathe.

Major Reynolds felt that *frisson,* too. She saw it in the widening of his eyes, in his stillness.

For long seconds neither of them moved or spoke. Then the major cleared his throat. "It should be enjoyable," he said quietly. "For both participants. A kiss should bring heat to one's senses. It should make you want *more*."

More. It was what she'd wanted ever since those moments in the gazebo. She wanted it now. The heat that had spiraled in her belly was there again, the tension and the craving that had made it impossible to sleep.

Isabella dug her fingers more deeply into her arms. *I am not kissing him again*. She was not that weak, that foolish.

But without the punch it would be like it had been with Roland. Not repugnant, but not pleasant either. Something she could live without.

Then prove to yourself that you don't need it. Let him kiss you again.

Isabella moistened her lips. She heard the sound of her heartbeat in her ears. "Major—"

"Lady Isabella—"

They spoke at the same time.

Major Reynolds opened his hand. "You first."

They had been about to ask the same question. She knew it; Major Reynolds knew it, too. She saw the knowledge in his eyes, saw it in his mouth, in the smile hovering on his lips.

Her throat was suddenly too dry to speak. Her heart began to beat even faster.

Major Reynolds waited a few polite seconds, and then spoke: "Let us try again. Let me *prove* to you . . ."

No, let me *prove to you.*

Isabella swallowed. "Very well." She uncrossed her arms. "But only once."

"Only once," the major agreed.

He stepped close and stood for a moment, looking at her; his eyes were vivid green, and yet somehow hot and dark, too. "As before," he said, his voice little more than a whisper. "Tell me if you wish me to stop."

Isabella nodded, her gaze fixed on his.

Major Reynolds inhaled a deep, slow breath. His hands reached to cup her face. Her skin tingled beneath that light touch. *Such strong hands, so warm.*

Her heart kicked in her chest as the major bent his head. She closed her eyes.

His lips touched hers. There was nothing repugnant about it, but neither was there the madness of last night, the pleasure sweeping through her, the sense that she was losing control of herself.

Isabella began to relax. *I was right and he was wrong.*

Major Reynolds licked her lower lip. She shivered, aware of a prickle of treacherous pleasure. He licked her lips again and murmured something against her mouth. Her ears couldn't make out the words, but she parted her lips instinctively, wanting more.

No, this is wrong. I don't want—

But he was inside her mouth and she couldn't pull away, she could only kiss him back, leaning into his body, hungry for his mouth. Heat rose inside her, pleasure spiraling, and she felt *alive,* filled with urgency and want.

There was no punch, no Faerie music swirling around them, and yet the intoxication of last night, the arousal clouding Nicholas's mind, were the same. He stifled a groan and drew Lady Isabella closer, sinking into desire, into bliss. The softness of her skin beneath his hands, the sweetness of her lips, the taste of her mouth . . .

Her mouth. Dear God, her *mouth* . . .

Nicholas lifted his head and stepped back, releasing her, dragging air into his lungs, striving for a semblance of control, of sanity.

They stared at each other. Lady Isabella's cheeks were flushed, her eyes dark, her lips rosy. The sight of her mouth arrested his attention. He almost stepped forward again, almost kissed her again.

"We should stop," he said. His voice was unaccountably hoarse. "Gussie will be back any moment." The words were more for himself than for her. *Stop. Stop now. While I can.*

Lady Isabella didn't answer for a moment. He thought she was trying to catch her breath. Her expression was aghast. "You said last night was an aberration. You said it wouldn't be like that again!"

He shook his head, trying to deny what had just happened. But there was no denying it. *And without the punch this time,* a worried voice in his mind pointed out. *Without the music.* "It shouldn't."

"Then why—"

He shook his head again, still staring at her, at the temptation of her mouth. What had just happened? And why her? Why now? "I don't know."

Footsteps sounded in the hallway. "I found it."

Nicholas turned hastily away from Lady Isabella. He reached for the first volume of *Pride and Prejudice* and fumbled it open. His heart was beating loudly in his ears. He heard Gussie speak again, heard Lady Isabella reply.

He swallowed and tried to slow his breathing, his heartbeat, and to concentrate on the page he was looking at. It was upside down. Hastily he turned the book the right way up.

Gussie plucked the book from his hand and ruthlessly closed it. "You may read it later," she said.

Nicholas groped for a suitable retort and failed to find one. His mind was fogged with passion, and not a little panic. What had just happened between himself and Lady Isabella?

Mutely he followed the ladies from the library. An aberration. It had to be an aberration. But not caused by the punch. *We are the aberration, the two of us.*

It wasn't love; it was a mindless, physical desire. *Her mouth and mine fit together.* Would their bodies fit together, too?

He hastily shoved the thought aside.

An aberration. An anomaly. Something between just the two of them.

Something not to be repeated, he told himself firmly.

Back in the drawing room, Lucas Washburne proposed riding out to Richmond on the morrow.

"A picnic!" Gussie said, clapping her hands in delight. She turned to Lady Isabella. "Do say you'll come."

Lady Isabella acquiesced. To his ears she still sounded shaken. Her face, flushed in the library from his kiss, was now pale. She avoided meeting his eyes.

Mrs. Westin demurred. So, too, did Harry. "I'm engaged with Lieutenant Mayhew," he said.

Lucas turned to him. "Nicholas? Will you join us?"

"Perhaps," he said, with a glance at Lady Isabella's averted profile. Her hands were clasped tightly in her lap. *Or perhaps not.*

Mrs. Westin rose to leave not long after that. He wondered if she'd sensed her cousin's agitation.

Nicholas bowed and politely bade them good night. Lady Isabella murmured something unintelligible in return.

Nicholas resumed his seat. He frowned at the polished toe of his shoe.

Gussie came to sit beside him. "Do say you'll come tomorrow," she said coaxingly.

Nicholas looked past her to the empty doorway. *I owe Lady Isabella an apology.* He made an abrupt decision. "Yes," he said. "I will."

CHAPTER 14

*T*he room inside Isabella's head, where the parts of herself had been neatly organized, was in chaos. The shelves had collapsed. Everything lay on the floor. Some things were broken beyond repair.

Who am I?

On the outside Isabella knew she looked the same, but on the inside everything had changed. She no longer recognized herself.

She dressed in her slate-blue riding habit with the row of buttons marching militarily down the front, bade Mrs. Westin and Harriet good-bye, and went downstairs.

"Your mount is here, ma'am," the butler told her, opening the door.

Isabella trod down to the street, where her groom held the mare's reins.

"Good morning, Burgess," she said, mechanically.

Hooves clattered on the cobblestones: the Washburnes arriving. Behind them was their groom, picnic hampers strapped to his saddle.

"Nicholas is joining us, too," Gussie said cheerfully as Isabella placed her foot in her groom's cupped hands and swung up into the saddle.

"I beg your pardon?" The worry that had blanketed everything like a fog evaporated abruptly.

"Nicholas," Gussie said, as another horse and rider turned into Clarges Street. "Here he is."

Major Reynolds sat easily in the saddle, utterly in control of his mount. It took no effort of imagination to imagine him commanding in battle.

Isabella let her gaze drop to his horse; it was easier to look at the beast—huge and glossily gray, with strong haunches and a proud neck—than its rider.

"Good morning!" Gussie said cheerfully as the major halted alongside them.

"Gussie," he replied. "Lucas." A brief pause, and then, "Lady Isabella."

"Good morning, Major Reynolds."

The major's eyes met hers. He gave a nod of acknowledgment, but didn't smile.

No, I don't feel like smiling either. She looked down at her hands gripping the reins. Blue gloves, to match her blue riding habit.

"Let's be off," Gussie said. "What a beautiful day for a picnic!"

Isabella was heavy with exhaustion, tense with worry, but the fresh air and the exercise helped to clear her mind. By the time the brick walls surrounding Richmond Park were in sight she'd achieved something approaching calmness. She was able to enjoy the vista of grassy slopes, woods, and avenues.

She stole a glance at Major Reynolds. Sunlight fell on his scarred cheek. She saw how distorted the skin was, ridges and plains of melted flesh shining in the sunshine.

Something tightened in her chest. She looked away.

Parkland lay before them, scattered with copses of trees. A herd of deer grazed in the distance.

"I have to gallop!" Gussie declared.

"A race?" her husband suggested, a glint in his eyes.

Gussie accepted the challenge.

Isabella declined, shaking her head. Her mood wasn't light enough for racing. Neither, it appeared, was the major's. He did, however, play marshal, holding up the white square of his handkerchief. "Ready?"

The handkerchief descended and the horses leapt forward.

When the thunder of hooves had died, Major Reynolds turned to the groom, riding a horse burdened with picnic hampers.

"Do you know King Henry's mound?"

"Yes, sir."

"Meet us there."

The man nodded, touched his heels to the horse's flanks, and trotted away.

Silence fell. The sound of the leaves rustling in the breeze, the lilt of birdsong, the humming of bees, was suddenly loud. Somewhere a squirrel chittered. A woodpecker hammered its beak against a tree trunk, *tat-tat-tat-tat*.

The major cleared his throat. "About last night."

Isabella transferred her gaze from Gussie's and Lucas's diminishing figures to his face. His expression was sober, stern even.

The only thing she could think of saying—*You promised me it was the punch!*—was too much like accusation, so she kept silent.

"I must apologize," Major Reynolds said, his eyebrows drawing together in a frown. "I hadn't quite realized how things stood between us. I thought it was the punch, when really . . ." The frown deepened, becoming a furrow. "The aberration is *us*."

Isabella blinked. "I beg your pardon?"

"It's *us*," he said, leaning slightly forward in the saddle, as if closing the distance between them could make her understand. "Not the punch or the music or anything else. It's something between the two of us."

Isabella looked at the major doubtfully. She liked him, but she didn't think she loved him. "Love?"

"Oh, no!" Major Reynolds said, lurching backwards in his saddle, his expression so horrified that she almost smiled. "Nothing like that. Just . . . just something purely physical."

He means lust.

She should have been appalled. Instead, she was deeply relieved. "So it wouldn't be like that with other men."

"No," Major Reynolds said firmly, and then a doubtful frown creased his brow again. "At least . . . I don't think so." He met her eyes. "I've never experienced anything like that and I've, er . . ." Faint color rose in his lean, unscarred cheek. "I've kissed a number of women."

I imagine you have, to be so skilled at it. Abruptly, shamefully, Isabella wanted to kiss him again. She wrenched her thoughts in another direction. "So, if I were to kiss another man . . ." She searched her mind for one. "Lieutenant Mayhew, for example. It wouldn't be like that?"

"Mayhew has had a lot of practice," the major said, his voice dry. "I'm sure he'd be good at it."

"But it wouldn't be as good as last night."

"No, I don't believe so."

Perhaps I should kiss Lieutenant Mayhew, just to see.

Major Reynolds appeared to have the same thought. His eyes narrowed slightly and he opened his mouth to say something, and then closed it, as if he'd thought better of it.

But Isabella didn't want to kiss Lieutenant Mayhew, however blond and laughing he was.

She looked at Major Reynolds, a frank scrutiny, taking note of the tanned skin and the startlingly green eyes, the strong bones of his face, the scar.

It was strange how one's perception of a person could alter so drastically within such a short period of time. Last week she'd seen the major as hard-faced; now she struggled to remember why she'd ever thought that. Stern, yes, until his face relaxed into a smile, but not hard-faced. His mouth was resolute, his eyes disconcertingly clear, piercing almost, but his face was marked by laughter. The creases at his eyes and mouth told of laughter, not anger.

No, that was incorrect. *Half* his face was marked by laughter. The other half was marked by pain. No smile lines radiated from his left eye or bracketed the left side of his mouth. The skin there was smooth, pink, burned.

Maybe that was why she'd thought him hard-faced? When she saw his face, his whole face, with the scar so prominent, all she saw was pain. It gave a false impression of who he was—pain, hardness—instead of a man ready to laugh.

Except that she hardly noticed the scar now.

I should learn to see it as he does. Major Reynolds didn't see pain when he looked in the mirror; he saw how lucky he was.

Isabella's gaze drifted to his mouth. Memory of his lips on hers, of his hands on her skin, brought a flush of heat to her body. *I want to kiss him again.*

She had a label for that sensation now: lust.

That's what it was. Lust. An aberration between the two of them.

The relief she felt was almost exhilaration. The room in her head was no longer in chaos. Almost everything was back on the shelves again. Some things still lay on the floor, too broken to fix. Her ignorance, her innocence—whatever one wished to call it—was one of them.

I am still a virgin, but my body knows how to crave physical pleasure.

Shocking, yes, but far better than the alternative: that her brain was addled, that she had somehow fallen in love with Major Reynolds.

She was herself again, only slightly altered. The sun was shining and the birds were singing and everything was in its place again in the world, in *her* world.

Elation bubbled up inside her. "Shall we race?" She narrowed her eyes against the sun, searching for Gussie and Lucas. They were tiny figures on the hillside.

"By all means." Major Reynolds brought his horse alongside her and flashed a grin. Had he caught her mood? Her exhilaration and relief?

Isabella grinned back at him. *Only lust. Nothing as terrible as love. Nothing I can't cope with.*

They were both flushed and laughing, panting, by the time they pulled up. Lady Isabella's mount, a lively blood-bay named Firefly, had proved almost as swift as Douro.

"Congratulations, Major," she said, laughing, catching her breath. "You won!"

"Not by much."

Gussie and Lucas were no longer beneath the clump of trees. Nicholas glanced around, searching for them. They were further down the avenue, their horses ambling side by side.

Nicholas nudged Douro with his knee, bringing himself and the horse around to face Lady Isabella.

"I wish I could have brought Rufus," she said. "He would love this."

"Then let us bring him," Nicholas said. They were so close that their legs almost brushed. "And Tam, too. And Timothy and Grace. A barouche filled with dogs *and* children."

"A splendid idea, Major."

"But no kittens," he added.

Lady Isabella made a *moue* of disappointment. "Don't you think kittens would add a charming element of chaos to the expedition?"

Her eyes laughed at him and the temptation was suddenly and quite simply too great. Nicholas leaned over and kissed that teasing mouth.

Her hesitation lasted a mere fraction of a second, and then Lady Isabella kissed him back.

Nicholas deepened the kiss, savoring the softness of her lips, the exciting heat of her mouth. Arousal flared in his belly. He could lose himself in this, in the heat, the exquisite pleasure, the—

We're in Richmond Park.

With a muttered oath he tore his mouth from hers. At the jerk of his hand, Douro stepped back a pace.

He stared at her, steadying his breathing. She looked as she had last night—dark eyes, flushed cheeks, well-kissed mouth—but not aghast, not dismayed.

"Lady Isabella—"

"Isabella." Her mouth quirked up at one corner in a wry smile. "If we're to do *that,* then I think we shouldn't be so formal with each other."

Her words made hope rise swiftly in his chest. *We'll do it again,* she seemed to be saying.

But not here. Not where we can be seen.

Nicholas cleared his throat. "Very well, Isabella, . . . I think we'd best find Gussie and Lucas."

"Yes." The wry smile vanished. "We had better." She gathered her reins.

Part of him was disappointed. Had he wanted her to protest? To kiss him again?

Yes, he had. But Lady Isabella—Isabella—knew as well as he did what would happen if they were seen kissing in public. They would have to marry. And as much as he enjoyed her company—and her kisses—she was not the bride he wanted.

His thoughts swerved to Clarissa Whedon, the bride he *did* wish for. She was no beauty, but it was her mildness, her youth, that recommended her to him. She would suit him in ways Lady Isabella never would.

And vice versa, whispered a sly voice in his mind.

Nicholas shook his head, banishing the voice. He pressed his knees against Douro's warm flanks and encouraged the horse into a trot. Clarissa Whedon, he would marry; Isabella Knox, he would kiss.

But he couldn't kiss Lady Isabella if he was engaged to another woman.

Douro lengthened his stride into a canter. Lady Isabella kept pace beside them.

Nicholas glanced at her. He would put off his proposal to Miss Whedon for another week. Or two.

They ate their picnic on King Henry's mound, looking across London to the dome of St. Paul's. No opportunity arose to kiss Lady Isabella again. "Almack's tonight?" Nicholas asked her as they left the green expanse of Richmond, enclosed in its brick wall, behind them.

She shook her head. "The Peverills' musicale. My cousin particularly desires to attend."

A musicale. Nicholas managed—barely—not to grimace. Almack's, with its débutantes and its dowagers, its dry cake and tepid lemonade, was almost more appealing. Almost. "Would you and your cousin like an escort?" he asked.

Isabella glanced at him from beneath her lashes. He thought she suppressed a grin. "We would be delighted," she said demurely.

Several hours later, lounging in a lattice-work Chippendale chair, Nicholas found himself regretting his offer. The musicians were superb, the supper superior to anything Almack's could offer, but neither the performance and nor the intervals had offered the opportunity for a private word—much less anything else—with Lady Isabella.

He cast a glance around the ballroom. The guests were predominantly female, and predominantly gray-haired. With a sigh he focused his attention on the musicians again: two violinists and a pianist. The pianist was extraordinarily animated. He played with his entire body. His face changed with the mood of the music: dreamy, his eyes half-lidded; exultant, his eyes wide and his mouth open; fierce, a frown furrowing his brow and his lips drawn back from his teeth; melancholy, his mouth pulling down at the corners and his shoulders sagging.

A final trembling chord filled the ballroom. The violinists laid down their bows. The pianist bowed his head.

There was a moment of silence, as if the audience held its collective breath, and then the sound of clapping swelled into the silence. The applause grew until the ceiling seemed to resonate with it. "Excellent," said Mrs. Westin, seated between him and Isabella, as the musicians stood and bowed. "Simply excellent!"

They rose, in the clamor of conversation around them.

"Magnificent—"

"—the finger-work—"

"—such expression!"

They lingered after the crush of guests had thinned, being invited, on the strength of Mrs. Westin's friendship with Mrs. Peverill, to partake of further refreshments in one of the smaller saloons.

Mrs. Westin, almost as animated as the pianist had been, discussed the performance with their hostess. The pianist, when he and his fellow musicians joined the party, was listless and somewhat morose. Or perhaps he was merely exhausted.

From music, Mrs. Peverill and Mrs. Westin moved on to a discussion of china figurines. Nicholas stifled a yawn.

"I have just purchased two more pieces," Mrs. Peverill said. "Would you like to see them?"

Mrs. Westin expressed great interest. Nicholas stifled another yawn. He swallowed the last of his wine.

"Isabella, will you join us?"

Nicholas snapped alert as Lady Isabella assented. He placed his glass on a convenient table and drifted after the ladies, out the door, along the corridor. Behind him, from the ballroom, came the scrape of wood on wood as the servants cleared the room of a hundred chairs.

The ladies turned into another saloon. Nicholas strolled slowly after them. "Exquisite!" he heard Mrs. Westin say as he paused in the doorway.

The room was undeniably a lady's parlor, decorated in pink and white. Every surface was covered with figurines. He saw milkmaids and frolicking lambs and goatherds, minstrels and huntresses and harlequins, bright-eyed squirrels and coquettish ponies.

Nicholas blenched slightly.

Mrs. Peverill caught sight of him. "Major! Are you interested in china figurines?"

Lady Isabella glanced up swiftly.

"Er . . ." He stepped into the parlor. "In a small way."

Lady Isabella bit her lip. She picked up a figurine and began to study it.

"The larger pieces are through here." Mrs. Peverill walked across to another door. She opened it. Nicholas caught a glimpse of more pink-tinted walls.

Mrs. Westin followed her hostess. Lady Isabella didn't. She was frowning at the figurine in her hand.

Nicholas stepped closer to her.

"A small interest in china figurines, Major?" Lady Isabella said, still studying the figurine she held. It was a milkmaid with golden curls. "I would never have guessed."

"Very small," he said, glancing at the door through which the older ladies had vanished. "Minuscule."

Lady Isabella returned the milkmaid to its place on the giltwood table. "Minuscule?" she said, turning towards him, a smile on her lips, a smile in her eyes.

"Smaller than minuscule." He closed the distance between them and reached for her, capturing her face between his hands, bending his head.

Lady Isabella didn't protest. She leaned towards him. "Be careful," she whispered.

148

The kiss was brief and hurried, scorching. They broke apart at the sound of voices from the adjoining room.

Nicholas turned hastily away from Isabella and picked up a figurine. From the corner of his eye he saw the ladies emerge into the parlor. "Oh, do you like that piece, Major?" Mrs. Peverill asked. "It's one of my favorites."

He looked down at the figurine. It was a young man in a puce jacket leaning against a tree, a violin held negligently in his hand. "Er. . ." His mind was still caught in the heat of Isabella's mouth.

He glanced at Lady Isabella. Her face was slightly averted; he saw only her profile, the curve of her cheek, faintly flushed, the soft fullness of her lips. Desire clenched in his belly. He wanted to reach for her, to kiss her again, to not stop.

Nicholas cleared his throat. "Very nice," he said lamely, and put the figurine down before he could drop it.

*C*HAPTER 15

*O*n Thursday morning, the housemaid Becky Brown returned from visiting her mother. She asked to speak with Isabella.

Isabella saw her in the book room. Becky entered with Mrs. Early, the housekeeper. They sat at her gesture, Mrs. Early solidly, the girl perching nervously on the edge of her seat. One look at Becky's face told Isabella that the news was bad. "How is your mother?"

Becky shook her head, her hands fisted in her apron. "Not good, ma'am. She can't even get out of bed anymore." The girl swallowed convulsively.

"Has she seen a doctor?" Isabella asked.

The girl nodded.

Had Becky's hard-earned money paid for that bill? "What did he say?"

"He said that there was something growing inside her. That she won't get better."

Isabella was silent for a moment, remembering her mother's own illness, remembering the day when she had finally acknowledged that the dowager duchess wouldn't recover. "Would you like to be released from my service?" she asked gently.

Becky nodded. "Yes, ma'am. Someone needs to look after her and the little ones. My father has to work, you see, so he can't . . ." She twisted the apron between her hands.

Isabella nodded. She did see. She glanced at Mrs. Early. "You may leave today, if you wish."

Mrs. Early nodded.

Relief flushed the girl's cheeks, but she shook her head. "Oh, no, ma'am. I thought . . . a week, if . . . if it suits you."

"Are you certain you don't wish to leave today?"

Becky shook her head again. "One of the neighbors said she could stay for a week." She smiled shyly at Isabella. "I thought . . . a week would give you time to hire someone else."

"Thank you, Becky. That's very thoughtful."

The girl's flush deepened. "You've been good to me, ma'am. I didn't want to leave sudden-like."

"Thank you, Becky."

When the girl had curtsied and withdrawn, Isabella turned to Mrs. Early. "Will you please go to the registry office again?"

The housekeeper nodded. "Yes, ma'am."

Isabella sighed. "We seem to be going through housemaids rather fast." She stared at the square of sunlight that caught the corner of her desk, turning the pale wood golden. "We will pay her for this month and the next," she said, looking up. "And give her references."

Mrs. Early nodded.

"And please ask the cook to make up a hamper of food for Becky when she leaves. Food for her family. Meat pies, fruit, bread . . ." She frowned. What else? "Oh, and some of those plum cakes." A treat for the children, in the middle of what must be a dark and frightening time for them.

"Yes, ma'am."

Isabella nodded her dismissal, but halted the housekeeper at the door. "Mrs. Early, are the wax candles still being taken?"

Mrs. Early turned to face her. "Yes, ma'am."

After the housekeeper had gone, Isabella pulled out her ledgers. She looked back through several months of neat columns, noting how many wax candles had been bought and when. Yes, three months ago. She tapped the page with a fingertip, frowning. A slight increase at first. The following month there was a noticeable jump, as if the thief had gained confidence. And this month . . .

Her lips pursed. *I should have noticed this.*

When had she added these figures to the ledger? Last week, when her mind was occupied by Harriet and Major Reynolds.

Isabella shook her head, unimpressed with herself.

It was fairly easy to determine how many candles had been stolen, using last year's figures as a comparison. She tallied the numbers on a sheet of paper. The total made her eyebrows rise. Wax candles were an expensive luxury. If the thief had sold them for only half their true price he or she had made a significant sum.

Isabella laid down her quill. *I don't like this.* It was unsettling to think that there was a thief under her roof. No, it was more than unsettling; it was disturbing.

Major Reynolds kissed her that night at the Athertons' ball, after supper, when the quadrille was announced and the room they were in momentarily emptied of dancers. The kiss was as intoxicating as wine, and far too brief.

On Friday he kissed her at Vauxhall, where they managed to part company from Gussie and Lucas as they wandered through the dimly lit gardens. Major Reynolds held her pressed to him. His mouth burned against hers, hungry. She had the sensation that she was drowning in heat. When at last he raised his head she clung to him, dazed. Her pulse beat loudly in her ears. *More,* it said. *More, more.*

They stood in silence for a long moment, breathing

raggedly. She felt the warmth of Major Reynolds' body pressed against hers, the strength, the solidity. One of his hands stroked lightly down her back.

Isabella trembled with the pleasure of it. She clutched his lapel and closed her eyes. *Is this truly me? Have I gone mad?*

"I like to kiss you," Major Reynolds whispered against her cheek.

"I like to kiss you, too." And she turned her head, her mouth seeking his, kissing him again. *Yes, I have gone mad.*

On Saturday she looked at herself in the mirror and scarcely recognized herself. Had her eyes always been this bright, her cheeks this rosy? *This is what lust looks like.*

Isabella accompanied her cousin and the Peverills to the opera that evening. She searched the boxes with her eyes. Mrs. Westin's voice, the voices of Mr. and Mrs. Peverill, were a meaningless blur of sound. Major Reynolds had said that he might . . .

There he was, on the other side of the chamber, scanning the boxes, swiftly examining each set of occupants before dismissing them.

Isabella's heart began to beat faster. She held her breath as their eyes caught across the auditorium. For long seconds they looked at each other, and then the major smiled at her, a smile that made her blush with her whole body. A smile that *promised*.

Isabella tore her gaze from him. She looked down at her hands, clasped in her lap. Anticipation hummed in her veins. She barely heard a word her companions said. The music, when it started, was nothing but noise.

During the first interval their box filled with friends and acquaintances paying their respects. Major Reynolds didn't visit. She glanced once across at him—leaning back in his chair, watching her, an ironic twist to his mouth—before firmly turning her attention away.

When the curtain lowered for the second interval, her cousin and the Peverills expressed the intention to visit the

Seftons, in a box opposite. "I shall stay here," Isabella said, as the others rose.

"Are you feeling unwell?" Mrs. Westin asked, her brow creasing with concern.

"Oh, no," Isabella said. "I just want to sit here and be quiet."

"Shall I stay with you?" her cousin asked, half-lowering into her seat.

"Oh, no! I shall just sit and watch people."

Mrs. Westin looked dubious, but allowed herself to be persuaded. She followed the Peverills, glancing back once from the doorway.

Isabella looked across at Major Reynolds' box. It was empty.

She looked down at her hands. *I was untruthful.* How had this happened? How had she become someone who told lies, who stole secret kisses from a man she had no intention of marrying?

I should stop this. Before I can no longer stand myself.

"Isabella."

The sound of her name, quietly spoken, made her heart lurch in her chest. She turned her head swiftly.

Major Reynolds stood in the shadows at the back of the box.

"Nicholas!" She rose.

The clandestine kisses were wrong. Why, then, did it feel so *right* when the major took her hands and drew her back into the shadows? When he smiled at her? When he bent his head and kissed her?

His hands were at her waist, strong, holding her closely against him. Their lips clung together. There was heat and dizzying delight, and then Major Reynolds bowed and was gone.

Isabella stood alone in the back of the box. She touched a trembling finger to her lips. *I have gone mad.*

On Sunday Isabella accompanied her cousin to the Chapel Royal, as was her habit when in London. The day stretched ahead unbearably—no ride in Hyde Park with the major, no dancing tonight. *No kiss.*

Isabella looked down at her hymn book. It wasn't just Major Reynolds' kisses she would miss today, it was his company, his conversation.

When had the major come to be such an important part of her life?

Isabella opened the hymn book and stared blindly at the text. *And when did I become so infatuated with his kisses that I became blind to the risks?* Last night had been the height of foolishness. To steal a kiss in so public a place!

And yet she had kissed him quite willingly, had in fact *lied* to facilitate it.

Isabella frowned at the hymn book. The lines of text were like centipede tracks across the pages, unreadable. The rector's voice droned unheard in her ears.

What she was doing was profoundly wrong. *I should stop it, all of it: meeting him, kissing him.*

And yet the thought of no longer seeing Major Reynolds brought something close to panic to her chest.

When had she come to like him so much?

The answer was easy: At the Worthingtons' masked ball. When he had made everyone laugh *with* him instead of *at* him. When he'd kissed her for the first time.

The rector's voice was rising, the sermon coming to its climax. Isabella heard none of the words; they were noise in her ears. *How much do I like him?*

The answer was terrifying. She looked up blankly and stared at the rector without seeing him.

There was a rustle of sound and movement as the

congregation stood. Isabella scrambled to her feet belatedly. She had no idea what hymn was to be sung.

The organ music, when it started, made no sense. The words were unfamiliar. Isabella gripped the hymn book tightly, her fingers crumpling the pages. Was it more than lust? *Am I in love with him?*

How could she be in love with a man she'd known such a short time? And, equally as important—or perhaps even more important—how could she love a man who had admitted that he wanted to mold his wife to suit him?

The organ music stopped. Pages turned with a rustle of paper.

Isabella thumbed through the hymn book at random, opening it to a new page. She stared down at it blindly. What did she know about Major Reynolds?

He'd been a good soldier, a good leader of men. *The best,* Lieutenant Mayhew had said.

He had a sense of humor.

When he looked at his scar in the mirror he saw how lucky he was.

He was proud. He was intelligent. He was courageous.

Was that enough? *Do I want to marry him?*

By his own admission Major Reynolds was an autocrat—although surely he'd been joking? But still, joking or not, he was a man used to command, a man used to giving orders and having them obeyed.

What would it be like to be such a man's wife?

The singing stopped. The congregation sat. Isabella followed, half a second later. She tried to recall her first impression of Major Reynolds: *A dangerous man.* It was difficult to think of him like that now. When she thought of him, she thought of laughter, of kisses.

Don't let the kisses fool you; he's still a dangerous man.

How many men had he killed in his twelve years as a soldier?

Isabella shivered. She stared down at the hymn book,

gripped tightly in her hands. The rector was talking again. The words blurred together in her ears. *What do I want?*

"Isabella?"

Isabella looked up blankly. Everyone else was standing, talking, moving. The service was over.

"Isabella?" Mrs. Westin said again. "Are you all right?"

"Yes," she said hurriedly, rising. "I was just, uh . . . thinking."
What do I want?

She tried to focus on her cousin, on the conversations around her, on anything but the answer. But the answer refused to go away as she gathered her hymn book and her bible, as she donned her wrap, as she stepped out into the sunlight.

If Major Reynolds is the man I think he is, then I would like to marry him.

To acknowledge the words, to say them in her head—if not aloud—was shocking. For a moment she stood frozen. People brushed past her, their voices a meaningless babble in her ears.

"Isabella?"

With effort she focused on her cousin's face.

"Are you certain you're all right?" Concern furrowed Mrs. Westin's brow. "You look very . . ."

Lost. I'm lost. In the past week I've become someone I don't know. I no longer recognize myself.

". . . very pale."

Isabella attempted a smile. She swallowed and spoke, "I'm perfectly all right, Cousin."

She might not recognize who she was, but she recognized the emotion rising in her breast. Not dismay, but hope.

I want to marry Major Reynolds.

Isabella blinked and looked around her. The world seemed somehow different, unfamiliar. A world in which she might have a husband, children, a family.

It was a dizzying thought.

Isabella walked carefully down the steps, holding onto the railing.

The route home seemed much shorter than usual. Isabella listened with half an ear as her cousin discussed the morning's sermon. In her mind she built dreams of a husband with a scarred face and green eyes, of children, of laughter and love. Reality returned when she stepped into the cool foyer of her house in Clarges Street.

Would Major Reynolds want to marry her? She bore no resemblance to the bride he had described, youthful and biddable. *Perhaps he thinks me too old, too odd.*

Would he want to mold her into someone else? He liked her, that much she knew. And he wanted her. But to want someone and to love someone—to love someone as they were, unchanged, unmolded—were two completely different things.

Isabella climbed the stairs beside her cousin, her brow creased in thought. Was it merely lust that Major Reynolds was experiencing—his hungry kisses, the way he held her pressed so close to his body—or was it something more?

The only way to know was to ask him.

Dare I?

Rufus bounded down the second flight of stairs, his tail wagging. Isabella bent to greet him, patting him, ruffling his fur. She glanced up at the sound of footsteps. Harriet.

Isabella straightened slowly.

And dare I tell him the truth about Harriet?

How would Major Reynolds react?

If he was the man she thought him to be, a man of calm good sense, then he wouldn't judge her too harshly.

If he wasn't . . .

Isabella shivered, suddenly cold.

Monday morning brought no letter from Harriet's aunt. "Don't worry," Isabella told the girl. "If we've heard nothing by

Friday I'll send my man of business to Penrith to look for her."

"I'm sorry to be such a burden, ma'am."

"You're not a burden," Isabella said. "We're very glad of your company, believe me." She smiled cheerfully at the girl, although privately she was becoming a little worried. What if Harriet's aunt was dead?

Harriet gave her a trembling smile in return. Unshed tears brimmed in her eyes. Where those tears of gratitude or misery? *Probably both.* The poor child was as innocent as one of the kittens and almost as helpless. The world was a frightening place if one had no family, no money, no protection.

Isabella was struck by a sense of how lucky she was. She had everything Harriet lacked, not through virtue or endeavor but through a quirk of birth.

No, not everything. Harriet had had one she thing hadn't had: Major Reynolds as a bridegroom.

I want the man she ran from. How was that for irony?

After luncheon, Isabella paid a call on Gussie, ostensibly to see how Saffron was. "I still have one kitten left unhomed," she said, as ginger-striped Saffron purred in her cupped hands. They sat in Gussie's morning room, with sunlight streaming in through the lace curtains. "I was wondering . . . perhaps your cousin might take her?"

"Which cousin? Nicholas?" Gussie said, looking up from her cross-stitch. "Why don't you ask him?"

"I thought I'd ask you first what kind of man he is," Isabella said, avoiding Gussie's eyes.

"What kind of man?" Gussie laid down her needle. "You ask me that, after you've been in each other's pockets the past two weeks?"

Isabella felt a blush rise in her cheeks. "I know his social face," she said, focusing on the gilded urn clock on the mantelpiece. *And I know the lover.* "But you know him so much better than I. I just wondered . . . what your opinion of him is?"

"My opinion of him?" Gussie repeated in an amused voice. "You want to know my opinion of Nicholas before you bestow a kitten on him?"

Put like that, it did sound odd. Isabella studied the ornate metal fire guard. "Yes."

There was a moment of silence. Gussie cleared her throat. Her voice, when she spoke, was uninflected and businesslike. "Nicholas was my favorite cousin when I was a girl. My opinion of him is very high."

"Why?"

"Because . . ." Gussie's voice trailed off as she thought. "Because I trust him. Because he makes me laugh. Because he's *nice*."

"Nice?" Isabella repeated doubtfully. A bland word, a word that told her nothing. "Would you say he's domineering?"

"Domineering?"

Gussie was silent a moment. Isabella risked a glance at her. Her friend's brow was creased in thought. She was chewing on her lower lip.

"No," Gussie said finally. "I wouldn't call Nicholas domineering. He is very decided, and he has a great deal of determination, but he's not domineering. At least—" she qualified this, "—he has never been so to me." She put her embroidery frame aside. "Nicholas is a very capable man. He has a reputation for getting things done."

"He does?"

Gussie nodded. "When I was a child we used to spend our summers together, and even then, when I was . . ." she shrugged, ". . . ten years old, maybe twelve, I knew that if I needed something *done,* it was Nicholas I should go to, not Gerald." Her smile was wry. "That's why Gerald dislikes him so much. Nicholas is so much more competent than he is."

"Oh."

Gussie leaned forward. She clasped her hands together on her knees. Her expression was serious. "The Nicholas I knew was a schoolboy—kind to me and patient and he *listened* when I spoke, as Gerald never did, but that was many years ago. The man . . ." She shrugged with her face, with her hands. "I'm learning to know him again. He was gone a long time."

"At war," Isabella said. Twelve years of soldiering, of fighting, of leading men into battle, of killing. Twelve years of blood and death. Her gaze dropped to Saffron, sleeping peacefully, a warm bundle in her hands. "Such an experience must change a person. Harden them."

"Yes," Gussie said. "But I *think* Nicholas is still the person he was. I think he has not become . . . too hard. Although I have to admit that he is more restrained than he was, quieter, more controlled."

Yes, Major Reynolds, was a very self-controlled man. A disciplined man. *Except when he's kissing me.*

Isabella glanced up and met Gussie's eyes.

After a long moment of silence, while tiny motes of dust spun in the sunlight, Gussie said softly, "I think he would make a fine husband."

Heat scorched Isabella's face. Her gaze skittered to the silver teapot, the dainty porcelain cups, the plate of cakes. "I wasn't . . . I didn't mean . . . I was only asking because . . ." She bit her tongue, stopping the babble of words. She met Gussie's eyes and said, with what she hoped was dignity, "I was only asking because of the kitten."

Even to her own ears it sounded ridiculous.

Gussie's lips pursed, as if she tried not to smile. "I see," she said blandly. "More tea?"

Lady Isabella halted the phaeton. Her groom leapt down. Nicholas stepped up and sat beside her, fending off Rufus's eager tongue. "Good afternoon."

"Good afternoon, Major."

He settled back on the silk-lined seat as the horses moved into a slow trot. How many times had they done this? A dozen?

Rufus nudged his knee. Reminded, Nicholas rubbed his warm flank. The dog leaned against his booted legs and closed his eyes in pleasure.

The day was mild, the temperature warm and the sun bright. Only the faintest of breezes stirred the air. Hyde Park was busier than he'd yet seen it. Curricles, phaetons, barouches, and landaulets thronged the drive.

Lady Isabella wore a carriage dress of Clarence blue trimmed with braided ribbon. The color made her eyes seem more blue than gray, her hair even more golden. He glanced at her smooth cheek, her soft lips. *I must kiss her tonight.*

He looked ahead, not seeing the busy drive, absently pulling one of Rufus's ears between his fingers. Where would they be tonight? Oh, that was it: the Middletons' ball.

The phaeton stopped.

Nicholas focused his gaze. The roadway ahead was blocked. A curricle had clipped the wheels of an elegant barouche. The curricle's driver had lost his horses' reins and sat red-faced, enduring the scathing commentary of the barouche's coachman, while his groom attempted to gather the reins.

Lady Isabella ignored the commotion. She turned to face him. "You know why I don't wish to marry, Major," she said, in her clear, frank way. "May I ask, why do you want to?"

The question drew his attention most effectively from the disturbance ahead. He studied her for a moment, the direct gray-blue gaze, the hair gleaming golden beneath the jaunty hat, the serious set of her mouth.

"Why?"

She nodded. "Yes."

Nicholas glanced down at Rufus, leaning against his legs. He could brush off the question, give an answer that was flippant or vague, one that told her nothing . . . but she had answered his questions honestly on the Worthingtons' terrace; he owed her the truth.

"Soldiering is about death," he said slowly, pulling Rufus's ear between his fingers. "I knew that. I'd always known it. But at Waterloo . . ." His surroundings faded as memory flooded over him: the sound of cannon fire, of horses and men screaming; the smell of gunpowder and blood; death all around him.

Rufus nudged his hand. Nicholas realized he'd fallen silent, become motionless. He cleared his throat. "Waterloo was a slaughter. I watched so many men fall . . ." Memory intruded again: a welter of blood, of torn flesh and shattered limbs, of death, death everywhere, the smell of death, the taste of it on his tongue, the sound of it in his ears.

He swallowed. "It seemed that no one could survive. It seemed . . . impossible." He glanced at Lady Isabella. She was staring at him, her face pale. Was he shocking her? "I remember a moment, when I stood on the battlefield. My horse had been shot from under me, and all around me were dead men. Scores of them, hundreds, thousands. The French cavalry were attacking again and . . . and to survive seemed impossible." He had touched his cheek. *I am lucky,* he'd told himself, but he hadn't believed it.

Nicholas drew Rufus's ear slowly between his fingers. "I vowed that if I lived, if I survived that day, I would sell my commission, that I'd have nothing more to do with death." He met her eyes, held them. "I want *life.* I want children. I want to see them grow. I want to watch them go out into the world and have their own children. *Life,* not death."

Lady Isabella swallowed. He saw the muscles move in her throat. "I had heard Waterloo was bad," she said in a low voice. Her face was almost—but not quite—expressionless.

I did shock her. "It was," he said simply.

She looked away and moistened her lips. "Thank you for telling me."

This was too dark a conversation for Hyde Park, for the frivolity of the Grand Strut, the ladies with curling feathers in their hats and the gentlemen with absurdly high neckcloths, the prancing horses and the silk-lined carriages, the sunshine and birdsong. "It was a long time ago," Nicholas said, his voice hearty and cheerful.

Lady Isabella cast him a narrow-eyed glance. *Don't treat me like a child,* he read in it. "Why did you decide to become a soldier?"

So she refused to be diverted, did she? Part of him respected her for it. No milk-and-water miss, Lady Isabella.

"Why?" He had to think back. It was hard to remember the young man he'd been, fresh out of Cambridge and eager to make his mark on the world. "I had intended on a diplomatic career, but . . . I decided I wanted more of a challenge."

"And was it a challenge?"

"Oh, yes." The challenges of soldiering had been many. He'd learned how to scout terrain and assess enemy positions, how to command men, how to lead them into battle even when the odds seemed stacked against them. He'd learned how to kill, how to lose one's friends, how to survive. And then there had been the purely physical challenges: the forced marches, the filth, the bitter cold and the searing heat, the scarcity of food, the boils and the lice and the fleas, the fevers. "It was everything I'd thought it would be, and more. It was extremely challenging. But I enjoyed it . . . for the most part."

Lady Isabella nodded. She glanced ahead. The offending curricle was gone. The barouche was almost alongside them, the coachman sitting erect on the driving block, his chest puffed out, proud victor of the moment.

With a deft flick of her whip, Lady Isabella encouraged the horses into motion. "Thank you for telling me," she said again.

"You're welcome," Nicholas said. He looked past her, towards Kensington Gardens. Trees, sunlight, water.

He experienced a moment of disorientation, as if the world tilted slightly on its axis. His fingers stilled, pulling Rufus's ear. How could this greenness, this sunshine, this safety, exist in the same world as the mud and blood and carnage of Waterloo? How could that battle, that slaughter, have been less than a year ago? How was it possible?

He blinked and shook his head slightly.

Lady Isabella caught the movement. She glanced at him. Her eyebrows rose inquiringly. "Major?"

Nicholas shook his head again, more firmly this time. "Are you going to the Middletons' ball tonight?"

"Yes," she said. "Will you be there?"

"Most definitely," Nicholas said. *I have to kiss you.*

*C*HAPTER 16

*C*olonel and Lady Middleton's ball was well under way when Nicholas arrived. He gave his hat to a footman and climbed the stairs to the ballroom. It reminded him of Gussie's ball, two weeks ago: the hubbub of music and laughter and conversation, the mingled scents of perfume and perspiration, the almost-suffocating warmth.

But tonight there would be no sly laughter, no sideways glances, no whispers. *I am passé. London has moved on.*

Nicholas accepted champagne from a servant. He sipped it as he strolled around the perimeter of the ballroom, nodding to acquaintances, pausing to talk with friends, all the while scanning the room for a glimpse of wheat-gold hair. The ballroom was colorful with the dress uniforms of various regiments: the blue, scarlet, and gold of the Royal Horse Guard, the green of his own Rifle Brigade, with its black facings and silver lace, the red jacket of the Lifeguards, trimmed with rich gold lace. Lieutenant Mayhew wasn't present; Lady Isabella was. He found her going down a set with Lucas Washburne. She was tall and elegant in a white satin slip under a robe of celestial blue crêpe.

Nicholas watched her, his shoulders propped against the wall, sipping his champagne. When the cotillion had finished he pushed away from the wall and strolled across the dance floor. "Lady Isabella," he said with an inclination of his head.

"Lucas."

He observed with satisfaction as Lady Isabella's cheeks flushed faintly. *I am going to kiss you tonight,* he promised her silently. Anticipation twisted in his gut, a quicksilver flicker of desire.

"Would you like something to drink?" Lucas asked Lady Isabella. "Lemonade? Champagne?"

"Champagne, please."

She watched Lucas stride away, glanced at Nicholas, colored faintly again, and turned her gaze to the dance floor, where a quadrille was preparing to start. Her attention focused on one of the dancers, a man Nicholas recognized.

"You know him?" he asked.

"Lord Riles? Yes."

Something about her tone made him study her more closely. "Another of your suitors?"

Lady Isabella nodded.

Nicholas looked at the dance floor again. Riles was moderately tall, moderately handsome, and possessed of impeccable breeding and a large fortune. "Why didn't you marry him?" From what he knew of the man, he had a sense of humor.

"I felt that his personality was . . . too compliant."

Nicholas swallowed a laugh. *You would have led him by the nose.*

"We wouldn't have suited."

"No," he said, voicing his thoughts aloud. "You'd need a strong husband."

Lady Isabella looked sharply at him. "To dominate me?"

"To match you."

"Oh." Her gaze fell. She turned her attention to the dance floor again, watching as the partners made their bows to one another.

Clarissa Whedon was in the same set as Riles. Nicholas

observed her for a moment. *My bride,* he thought, sipping his champagne. It tasted slightly sour in his mouth.

Lady Isabella glanced sideways at him. "A strong wife would suit you, too."

Nicholas looked at her. "No."

"Not willful and obstinate," she said. "But strong-minded. To match you."

Nicholas shook his head. "I want a peaceful marriage. A marriage without arguments. For that, a young bride is best."

"Don't you think you could have a peaceful marriage with a slightly older wife?" Her tone was diffident. "Someone whose character is formed?"

"No." Young soldiers lacked experience, but they were more tractable, less likely to complain, to question orders, to argue. It stood to reason that a young wife would be similarly tractable.

Lady Isabella made no reply. She bit her lip and looked at the dancers again.

Nicholas followed the direction of her gaze. He watched as Clarissa Whedon stood placidly waiting for the quadrille to begin.

That is what I want.

But the wife he'd imagined—quiet and biddable, agreeing with everything he said—no longer seemed quite as ideal as he'd once thought. "You think I'm wrong."

Lady Isabella glanced at him. "I think that you're . . . misguided."

Misguided? What did she mean by that? Was she telling him—politely—that she thought him a fool? He opened his mouth to ask her, but at that moment Lucas Washburne returned. "Colonel Durham's here," he said to Nicholas as he handed Lady Isabella a glass of champagne. "Have you seen him?"

"No." Nicholas scanned the ballroom. *I shall take care to avoid him.*

"Colonel Durham?" Isabella said. "I would like to meet him."

168

Nicholas turned his head to stare at her. "You would?"

"From what I've heard, he's an unpleasant man."

Very, Nicholas thought. He raised his glass and paused, looking past her shoulder. *Damn.* He took a long swallow and said, "You're in luck, Lady Isabella. You're about to meet him."

"I am?" She turned her head, following the direction of his gaze. "Is that him?"

He wondered what she saw: the lines of bad temper etched into Colonel Durham's face, the sour mouth, or the man's erect carriage, forceful footsteps, and bristling, aggressive energy.

Colonel Durham halted. "Major Reynolds."

Nicholas bowed. "Colonel Durham. May I present Lady Isabella Knox and Viscount Washburne?"

Colonel Durham favored Isabella with a bow and a glance, both equally brief, and then turned to Lucas Washburne. *He doesn't see her,* Nicholas realized in disbelief.

The conversation wasn't protracted—the colonel invited him to dine at his club the following evening and spoke a few words about the weather and London traffic. Harriet wasn't mentioned. Another bow and he was gone.

Nicholas glanced at Lady Isabella. Had she noticed the colonel's dismissive manner towards her? "Well? What's your opinion of Colonel Durham?"

She glanced at him. "Truthfully? I think him a man who places no value on women."

Lucas Washburne blinked. "You do?"

"He addressed himself entirely to you both. I may as well not have existed."

"Really?" Lucas said, turning to stare after Colonel Durham.

Nicholas raised his glass and drained it. "The colonel isn't the brightest of men," he said dryly.

Lucas turned back to Lady Isabella. His expression was faintly perplexed. "Are you certain that's what he did? Because I didn't notice anything."

Lady Isabella laughed. "You're a man, Lucas. Of course you wouldn't notice."

Washburne didn't venture a reply to that; he grinned, shrugged, and went in search of his wife.

"You're correct," Nicholas said, his eyes on Isabella's face. "Colonel Durham places no value on women."

She grimaced slightly. "Poor H— Miss Durham."

The words were an unwelcome reminder. Nicholas frowned down at his empty glass. "Yes. Poor Miss Durham."

"You're nothing like the colonel," Lady Isabella said.

"I should hope not."

Her brow creased. "Then how could Harriet Durham have thought—"

"Don't forget this." He tapped his left cheek with one finger.

Lady Isabella's eyes fastened on the scar for a moment, and then she shook her head. Her lips thinned. "Foolish girl!"

"Yes, I agree." He looked at the dance floor, at the lines of dancers, at Clarissa Whedon. She didn't appear to hold him in aversion. But then, he hadn't noticed that Harriet had, either. He'd mistaken her dislike of him for shyness.

Lady Isabella was silent.

Nicholas glanced at her. She was watching Miss Whedon. Her expression was unreadable. "May I have the next waltz?" he asked.

"Do you even need to ask?" Her glance, her smile, her tone, were wry.

Nicholas looked down at his empty glass again. He turned the stem between his fingers. Soon there would be no more waltzes, no more kisses. He looked across at Miss Whedon.

Boring, whispered a voice in the back of his head.

He ignored it.

170

The waltz came after the quadrille. Nicholas enjoyed the familiar pleasure of dancing with Lady Isabella—the curve of her waist beneath his palm, the warmth of her gloved hand on his shoulder, the ease with which their steps matched. Her height, too, was a pleasure. Isabella's chin was level with his shoulder; he didn't have to bend his head to speak to her. It was easy to meet her eyes. Easy to kiss her.

Later, he told himself, sternly quashing a flicker of desire.

If there was a later. The Middletons' house seemed to be depressingly without concealed corners in which to kiss.

The music finished with a flourishing final note. Nicholas escorted Lady Isabella from the dance floor, cool and elegant in the white slip and blue robe, queenly in her height. Diamonds sparkled at her ears and around her throat.

She was the perfect Society lady, polished and glittering, graceful and poised, untouchable, unkissable—until she grinned at him and he caught a glimpse of her teeth, white and charmingly crooked. "Thank you for the dance, Major."

Desire kicked in his stomach. "The library," he said. "Five minutes."

Lady Isabella's grin faded. Her eyes held his. Blue-gray eyes. Beautiful eyes.

I want her.

Nicholas clenched his hands. He was *not* going to kiss her in the Middletons' ballroom in front of everyone. "The library," he said again, his voice slightly rough, and then he bowed and turned on his heel and walked away from her.

He knew she would come. This thing that snared him, this lust, was mutual. It twisted in her gut the same as it twisted in his. *We are in the grip of madness.*

He studied the volumes on the shelves. Poetry. Wordsworth and Coleridge and Byron's *The Corsair*.

The door opened.

Nicholas swung around. He watched Lady Isabella close the door behind her.

"Dare we?" she asked in a low voice as she came towards him.

He held out his hand. "We'll be very careful," he said, drawing her with him to the farthest, shadowy corner of the room. A wing-backed leather armchair loomed, the bronze studs gleaming faintly in the light of the two lamps that were lit.

"If anyone sees us—"

He took her face between his hands. "They won't."

She stared up at him, her eyes dark and unreadable.

"Kiss me," he whispered.

Lady Isabella lifted her mouth to him.

CHAPTER 17

$\mathcal{I}$sabella lost all track of time. The warmth of Major Reynolds' body, the strength of his arms, the urgency of his mouth, the sheer magic of kissing him, of being held by him, drove all thought from her mind.

Heat rose in her until she burned with it. She ached for more. This—his mouth on hers, his arms around her—wasn't enough. She broke their kiss. "Nicholas . . ."

He rested his cheek against her temple. His breath was ragged. "What?"

A sound at the door made them break apart.

"Down!" The major whispered fiercely, pushing her behind a winged armchair.

Isabella crouched as the door opened. She pressed her forehead against the cool leather and closed her eyes. Her heart beat rapidly. *If we're discovered . . .*

Major Reynolds knelt alongside her. His arm came around her shoulders, pulling her close. She felt the pressure of his thigh against hers.

The door shut with a *snick*. There was a moment of silence, when she strained to hear past the beating of her heart, and then she heard a man's low voice and an answering feminine whisper.

The minutes passed slowly. She leaned into the major's warmth, her eyes closed, trying not to listen to the giggles and low murmurs. *Is that what we sounded like?*

No. She and Major Reynolds had kissed silently. There'd been no coquetry between them, no teasing, no muffled laughter.

Because ours isn't a flirtation. It was something much more intense, exhilarating beyond anything she had ever imagined—and quite terrifying.

I could lose myself in him.

She knelt with her head bowed and her eyes closed while the lovers kissed, while they murmured farewells, while the door opened again and then shut.

Major Reynolds' arm tightened briefly around her, and then he released her. Isabella opened her eyes and looked at him. His face was in shadow, the scar hidden. Her heart clenched in her chest. *I love you.*

"I apologize," the major said. "This was not a good idea."

Isabella shook her head mutely.

Major Reynolds was silent a moment, looking at her, his eyes a dark gleam. He uttered a shaky laugh. "My lady, don't look at me like that, or I'll have to kiss you again."

Then kiss me.

He sat very still, staring at her, and then reached for her, pulling her towards him. His mouth was hot and hungry.

Isabella closed her eyes and kissed him back fiercely. *I love you.*

The rows of books with their leather spines, the carpet beneath her knees, the armchair casting its shadow over them, ceased to exist. Her awareness narrowed to the major's mouth, to the grip of his hands. She was drowning in sensation, drowning in *him,* in his scent, his taste, his heat, in the sound of his breathing, the sound of his heartbeat.

This time it was Major Reynolds who broke their kiss. He pulled back, putting distance between them. His face was flushed, his eyes so dark they looked black. His breath was ragged, panting.

He stared at her for a long moment, and then rubbed his hands over his face. He leaned his head back against the armchair and squeezed his eyes shut. "This is madness. We're insane."

"Yes."

He turned his head to look at her. "If we're discovered . . ."

"It would be a scandal," Isabella said quietly. She clasped her hands in her lap. "A scandal of such proportions that—"

"We'd have to marry." His words were as quiet as her own had been. His eyes held hers, his stare intense, as if he looked inside her. He wasn't offering, she knew he wasn't offering, and yet, dear God, she was mad enough to *want* him to.

"I'm not the sort of woman you'd like to marry." The words blurted from her. "Am I?"

She knew she wasn't; he'd told her precisely what he wanted—youth, and a yielding nature. *And I have neither of those.*

Isabella felt a stab of jealousy for Clarissa Whedon, as sudden and intense as it was shameful. She looked down again, at her lap, at the crumpled fabric of her gown, at her hands clasped tightly together. *Tell me I'm not what you want.*

"I . . . uh—"

The door to the library opened again.

Major Reynolds ducked his head. He slid further back behind the armchair and reached for her, pulling her close, shielding her.

Footsteps entered the room. She heard the stealthy *clink* of decanters, furtive male voices, laughter. Servants stealing a little brandy.

The servants were quicker than the lovers had been. Barely two minutes passed, while she leaned into the major's warmth and listened to his heartbeat.

More laughter came, then the sound of the door opening and closing. They were alone again.

Major Reynolds released her. He stood.

Answer my question, Major. Am I someone you could marry?

The major held out his hand. "We've got to get out of here."

She let him pull her to her feet. "Nicholas—"

He tightened his grip on her hand and drew her across the library. His mouth was grim. "This was one of my more stupid ideas."

He released her, opened the door a few inches, and glanced out. "It's clear."

"Nicholas . . ."

Major Reynolds reached out to touch her cheek, freezing the words on her tongue. His mouth twisted wryly. "We must stop this," he said, as his gloved thumb moved across her skin, stroking, caressing.

Stop it?

His head dipped, his lips touched hers, and then he glanced out the door again and opened it more widely. "You first," he said. "I'll wait a few minutes."

Isabella hesitated. *You haven't answered my question.*

"Quickly," the major said.

The urgency in his low voice made her obey. She slipped through the opening.

The door closed behind her.

Isabella stood for a moment in the corridor. Absurdly, she wanted to cry. She turned away from the ballroom, heading for the ladies' dressing room.

Damn you, Major Reynolds. You didn't answer my question.

Nicholas collected his hat and walked down the steps to the street. He stood for a moment in the light of the flambeaux. He'd kissed Lady Isabella in the *library*. He winced, disgusted by the depth of his stupidity. *I should have known better than to take such a risk.* He *did* know better.

Except that when it came to Lady Isabella, it appeared that he didn't.

I look at her and my wits dribble out my ears, he thought sourly, hunching his shoulders against the cold night air and beginning to stride in the direction of Albemarle Street. The sound of his footsteps echoed flatly, thrown back at him by the tall stone façades of the houses.

He shook his head. No more. No more risks. No more kisses at balls. No more kisses at the opera.

At the opera.

He winced again in memory. He'd kissed Isabella at the *opera* of all places, in the back of a box, where anybody could have walked in and seen them. "I'm mad," he muttered. "Mad!"

A pedestrian, approaching, shied away, giving him a wide berth.

Nicholas scowled at him.

I'm a fool. A smitten, besotted fool, taking appalling risks for a few kisses, a few seconds holding her.

The scowl faded as he recalled the softness of Isabella's lips, the warmth of her mouth. Memory looped through his head: the leather-and-paper scent of the library, the dark shadows, the glimmer of diamonds in her hair, the way her lips had parted for him.

Nicholas turned into Albemarle Street. He halted outside his house and closed his eyes a moment, savoring the memory of Lady Isabella's kiss and the wash of heat that came with it. *Kiss me,* he'd said. And she had.

And then, afterwards, she had said, *I'm not the sort of woman you'd like to marry. Am I?*

Nicholas's eyes came open.

He stood for a moment, frowning, and then he climbed the steps slowly and let himself into the house. It was silent inside; he'd told the servants not to wait up for him. He stood for a moment in the dimness of the entrance hall. The silence and the shadows suited his mood.

I'm not the sort of woman you'd like to marry. Am I?

Nicholas grunted. Did she expect an answer?

He lit a candle from the lamp in the hall and climbed the stairs, shielding the flame with his hand. In his bedchamber he shrugged out of his coat and sat down to remove his shoes. Her question ran in his head, endlessly repeating itself as he untied his neckcloth and pulled his shirt over his head. *I'm not the sort of woman you'd like to marry. Am I?*

How the hell was he supposed to answer a question like that?

He fell asleep to the sound of her voice and woke several hours later with her question still turning in his head. *I'm not the sort of woman you'd like to marry. Am I?*

Nicholas stared up into the darkness. Clarissa Whedon was the bride he wanted. He could mold her into the perfect wife.

Lady Isabella was merely . . .

Epiphany came then, so bright that it seemed to light up the room. The flash of it seared across his retinas, making him blink. Isabella Knox was merely *perfect*.

The perfect friend, the perfect lover, the perfect wife.

I've been so blind.

Nicholas sat up abruptly and threw back the covers. He strode across to the window and jerked the curtains back. Moonlight streamed in.

The answer to her question was *Yes*.

He stared down at the empty street, frowning at the pool of light cast by the gas lamp. What made him think she'd say *Yes* if he asked her? Isabella Knox didn't want to marry; she had told him why, quite plainly, at the Worthingtons' masked ball. She had turned down many offers, from men far wealthier and more highly born than he was. Why would she choose to marry a scarred ex-soldier with a modest fortune?

Nicholas chewed thoughtfully on his lower lip. Her question turned in his mind. *I'm not the sort of woman you'd like to marry. Am I?*

Why had she asked it? Did it mean what he thought it

did? And what would Lady Isabella's answer be if he asked *her* that same question? *Am I the sort of man you'd want to marry?*

Nicholas woke to sunlight slanting in through the window—and with the sunlight, doubts. Was Isabella Knox really perfect? She was a Society lady, a darling of the *ton*. She enjoyed the whirl of the Season. Would she be happy on a country estate with no more excitement than being a wife and mother?

It seemed extremely unlikely.

Nicholas climbed out of bed and walked over to the window. He stared out at Albemarle Street, at the tall houses and the blank windows, the gray stone, the steep roofs, the coalsmoke smeared across the sky. Noises drifted up to him: the rattle of a hackney's wheels, the shrill shout of a crossing-sweeper.

We could live here, in London.

His reaction was deep and instinctive: a shudder, a *No* in his chest. He wanted expanses of blue sky, he wanted hills and valleys, meadows and woods. He wanted to inhale air that was rich with the scents of the countryside. He wanted his children to grow up climbing trees and fishing in creeks. He wanted them to know the smell of grass, of leaf mold, of hay drying in the sun.

Nicholas turned away from the window. *If I could have Isabella Knox, how much would I have to give up?*

Major Reynolds was frowning when Isabella stopped the phaeton for him that afternoon. The frown faded when he saw her, but his expression was unsmiling and almost stern as he stepped up into the carriage.

"Major," she said, in greeting. "How are you?"

"Very well." But the faint crease between his eyebrows and the set of his mouth belied the words.

Isabella set the horses in motion and wondered for what must be the hundredth time today how to get him to answer her question.

Should she be blunt? *Major, do you remember I asked you a question last night? I'd like to know the answer.*

Or should she try to turn it into a joke? *You never answered my question last night, Major.* And then a little laugh. *I'm curious as to your answer.*

She glanced sideways at him. He was patting Rufus.

Oh, for heaven's sake, just ask him!

Major Reynolds looked up and met her eyes. The frown still sat on his brow. "Lady Isabella," he said abruptly. "You enjoy town life."

Isabella blinked. "Yes. I do."

"Would you ever consider living in the countryside?"

Isabella blinked again. She transferred her attention to the horses. What an odd question. "The countryside? Of course!"

"But . . . you said that you like being in London, that you enjoy the Season."

"I do. But if you recall, Major, what I said was that I dislike being idle. One can be busy equally well in the country as in town." She glanced at him. His brow was no longer creased in a frown. If anything, he looked slightly taken aback. "I spend quite half the year in the country, you know."

He shook his head. "No, I didn't know." His fingers rubbed Rufus's head. "Ah . . . you enjoy it?"

"Yes." A barouche had halted by the side of the drive. Isabella guided her team neatly between it and the curricle coming in the opposite direction. "Very much. My eldest brother, Julian, lives in Derbyshire. I visit him often. In fact I've only just returned." And on her journey home, she had encountered Harriet Durham. Isabella bit her lip. She glanced at Major Reynolds. *Should I tell him now?*

No. Privacy would be best for that disclosure. To tell him now, under the gaze of the *ton,* would be the height of folly.

Isabella smiled brightly. "My other brother has a home in Kent, and of my sisters, one lives in Suffolk and the other in Somerset. You may believe that I spend a lot of time in the country."

"Somerset?" Major Reynolds said, a note of interest in his voice. "My estate is in Devonshire."

"Not far from my sister Amabel, then."

"No." His gaze was intent. He seemed on the verge of saying more.

Isabella glanced ahead. The landaulet approaching was a familiar one. "Lady Jersey."

An expression of frustration crossed Major Reynolds' face. He shifted slightly, so that they weren't sitting quite so closely together.

Lady Jersey had a lot—and very little—to say, as was her custom. It was quite ten minutes before they were able to part from her.

Isabella glanced at Major Reynolds. The polite smile he'd favored Lady Jersey with was gone. In its place was a small frown.

"Major—"

"Lady Isabella—"

Major Reynolds opened his hand. "After you."

"Will you tell me about your estate?"

The frown vanished from his brow. His eyes seemed to brighten with pleasure. "It's called Elmwood," he said, reaching down to pat Rufus. "I had it from my maternal grandparents. It's not large, but it has everything one could want."

Isabella drove slowly, nodding and bowing to acquaintances, enjoying the timbre of Major Reynolds' voice, the enthusiasm with which he described Elmwood. He loved his estate, that was very clear. She listened to his description of a lake and woods, the coastal cliffs, the salt tang of the breeze, hayricks in rolling fields, the red brick Jacobean house with its high ceilings and light-filled rooms. *I could be happy there.*

"It sounds very beautiful."

"It is. I hope . . . I hope my wife will love it as much as I do."

"How could she not?" Isabella said lightly. "Your wife will be very happy."

"I should try to be a good husband." His voice was diffident, and when she glanced at him she saw that he was looking at Rufus, not at her. "To, er . . . not treat my wife as if I own her." Major Reynolds' gaze lifted. His eyes met hers.

The intensity of his stare was unnerving. *Is there more to this conversation than I realize?*

Isabella moistened her lips and glanced ahead. Her groom stood beside the driveway. She drew the horses to a halt several yards distant from him. "Major Reynolds," she said, fingering the reins. "You are, by your own confession, an autocrat."

His eyebrows rose slightly. "I am?"

"Yes. At the Worthingtons' masked ball you said—"

"Ah . . ." Major Reynolds grinned. "So I did." As he looked at her, his grin slowly faded. His eyes were green and very intense. "I was joking. My wife will be free to be herself."

"But . . . you said that you would mold her—"

"I've changed my mind."

Is he saying what I think he is?

Isabella swallowed. "Major Reynolds . . . Nicholas . . . last night . . ."

She glanced down. Her groom was standing beside the phaeton.

"Yes," Major Reynolds said.

Her eyes flew to his. "Yes?"

"The answer to your question." Major Reynolds looked down at the groom, and then back at her. "I have a question for you, too, but now is neither the time nor the place."

Isabella clutched the reins more tightly. Her heart began to beat loudly in her chest.

"Tonight I dine with Colonel Durham." The major grimaced briefly. "Tomorrow . . . may I call on you?"

Isabella nodded, unable to speak.

"Two o'clock?"

She nodded again.

Major Reynolds made a slight movement, as if to lean over and kiss her, caught himself, nodded briefly to her, and descended.

Isabella watched him walk away. She felt dizzy, breathless, euphoric.

The groom climbed up into the phaeton and settled himself in the place Major Reynolds had just vacated.

"You drive, Cobb," Isabella said, handing him the reins. "I'm feeling . . ." *Quite light-headed.* "A little faint."

She sat back in the seat and clasped her hands tightly together. *Nicholas said yes.*

But mingled with the euphoria and the dizzy breathlessness was dread. Tomorrow . . . tomorrow she had to tell him about Harriet.

CHAPTER 18

It was one of the less enjoyable meals of Nicholas' experience. The food was good—almost as good as White's—and the wine excellent, but Colonel Durham wasn't the most pleasant of dining companions. His conversation consisted almost entirely of reminiscences about campaigns he had fought. In his minute and pedantic dissections of the errors of each battle, Colonel Durham never acknowledged any mistakes of his own—the blunders were always someone else's.

Everyone makes mistakes, Nicholas thought as he chewed on buttered lobster. *It's part of what makes us human.* He reached for his glass, swallowed a mouthful of wine, and looked sourly at the colonel. He'd had a commanding officer like Colonel Durham once. It had been an unpleasant experience. A good officer should acknowledge his errors, not push them off on someone else.

Interspersed with the reminiscences were heated animadversions about the slyness and dishonesty of his granddaughter. "I have nursed a viper in my bosom!" Colonel Durham declaimed, his face red with rage and alcohol, spittle forming at the corners of his mouth.

No blame, of course, attached to the colonel in his dealings with his granddaughter. He was guilty neither of bullying her into marriage, nor of refusing to listen to her pleas. The blame was all Harriet's. By the end of the evening Nicholas had conceived a deep and profound pity for her. He wished the girl well, wherever she was. He couldn't even whip up any animosity towards her benefactress; Harriet had needed rescuing, and whoever the woman was and whatever she had said regarding ogres, he no longer cared. Sometime in the past week his rancor had faded.

It was because of Lady Isabella, he thought, a smile playing on his mouth as he stepped from under the portico of the colonel's club. How could he be angry when he was so foolishly and fatuously in love?

A misting drizzle was falling, smearing the light of the gas lamps. Nicholas scarcely noticed. He strolled back to Albemarle Street, whistling softly under his breath. Mr. Shepherd had requested an interview tomorrow to report his findings. He would call the man off.

Let it rest, he thought as he turned the corner.

Mr. Shepherd arrived punctually at one o'clock. He entered the study, bowed, and bade Nicholas good day. "I've had some success in the matter of locating Miss Durham," he said.

"You have?" Nicholas said, not much interested. "Good." He opened one of the drawers in his desk and drew out a roll of guineas. "However, I've decided that the matter is less important than I'd thought. If you tell me what your expenses are, I can settle your account now." He gestured the man to a chair.

Mr. Shepherd drew a slim sheath of folded papers from his breast pocket and handed it to Nicholas. "A list of my expenses, sir. And a report detailing my findings."

"Thank you." Nicholas picked up the papers, unfolded

them, and glanced quickly through the sheets. The list of expenses was short, neatly written in copperplate, and came to a rather high total. He read through it. Ah, the man had taken the stage to Stony Stratford and stayed two nights.

The report was surprisingly long. Nicholas flicked to the last page. His eyebrows rose. An address in London.

He glanced at Mr. Shepherd, sitting quiet and nondescript on the chair in front of him. "She's here? At this address?"

Mr. Shepherd nodded.

Nicholas leaned back in his chair. Some success? Modesty was clearly one of Mr. Shepherd's virtues, along with efficiency and punctuality. "Tell me," he said, laying the report on the desk. "The brief version." As opposed to the pages of closely written notes.

Mr. Shepherd did so, succinctly. "I determined that Miss Durham took the stagecoach north and alighted at Stony Stratford, where she attempted to stay at the Rose and Crown, but having insufficient funds was turned away. However, a lady who was already residing at that establishment came to her aid, offering her a bed, and taking Miss Durham with her to London the next day."

Nicholas nodded. "Go on."

"I spoke to one of her Ladyship's servants yesterday. Miss Durham is still in residence with her in London."

Nicholas picked up the report again and turned to the last page. Clarges Street. That was where Lady Isabella lived.

His eyes narrowed suddenly. The street number . . .

Hastily he turned to the previous page. *Lady Isabella Knox,* he read. *Traveling with her servants and two outriders provided by her brother, the Duke of Middlebury*. "No," he said aloud. "You've made a mistake. This is wrong."

Mr. Shepherd was unruffled. "I assure you that my information is correct. Lady Isabella Knox is the person you seek."

Nicholas shook his head. "No."

"Lady Isabella was staying at the Rose and Crown on the night in question. She provided accommodation for Miss

Durham and took the girl to London with her." Mr. Shepherd's voice was light and dry and precise. "Miss Durham is presently residing with her in Clarges Street."

"No," Nicholas said again, putting down the report and leaning forward across the desk. "I've *been* to her house. I tell you, Harriet isn't there!"

"The cook assures me she is. Staying in the blue chamber on the third floor."

They matched stares, Nicholas's fierce, furious, and Mr. Shepherd's impassive.

He's wrong.

Wrong or not, Mr. Shepherd had spent twelve days—and not a little money—coming to his conclusions. Nicholas reached for the guineas, counted out what he owed the man, and handed them over. "Here," he said curtly. "Thank you for your work."

Mr. Shepherd accepted the money. He stood. "Read my report, Major Reynolds. It will all be quite clear."

Nicholas thinned his lips.

Mr. Shepherd bowed and exited the room.

Nicholas sat for a long moment after the door had closed, staring at the report. *Lies. It's all lies.*

But the problem was that it was entirely like Lady Isabella to rescue a penniless runaway. He could *imagine* her doing it.

No, he told himself firmly. It wasn't Isabella. She'd said she didn't know where Harriet was and he believed her. He *trusted* her.

Nicholas reached for the report, determined to read through it and find Mr. Shepherd wrong.

The first few pages detailed Mr. Shepherd's efforts to determine what mode of transport Harriet had taken in her flight from London, and where she had alighted: in Stony Stratford.

Mr. Shepherd's interview with the landlady of the Rose and Crown was brief and uninformative. In his opinion the woman had been bribed not to reveal any information concerning Harriet Durham—her manner had been adamant and defensive.

His subsequent interview with one of the porters, lubricated by several tankards of ale and a guinea, was much more interesting.

He showed Miss Durham into the taproom and fetched his mistress, Mr. Shepherd wrote. *Upon ascertaining that Miss Durham had insufficient funds for a room for the night, Mrs. Botham refused her accommodation, unswayed by the girl's tears and entreaties.*

At this point, another lady had entered the taproom. The porter had only heard the conversation through a partly closed door, but in his words the newcomer was "*awful polite*" and in less than a minute had "*routed the old besom.*" Mrs. Botham had been, in the porter's opinion, spitting mad, but far too afraid of offending the lady to cross her.

The porter's description of Harriet's benefactress was detailed. Mr. Shepherd produced it verbatim. Nicholas could almost hear the porter's voice in his head: *A prime 'un. A real beauty. Tall, with yeller hair, and so elegant you wouldn't believe.*

The porter knew her name, too: Lady Isabella Knox, a frequent guest on her way to and from Derbyshire. *A duke's daughter, but she looks like a princess,* the man had said.

No, Nicholas thought. *Not a princess; a goddess.*

The porter had also described the lady's dog: black and tan, with one blue eye and one brown, and a curling tail. *A mongrel if ever I saw one, but real well-behaved. Never bites anyone.*

Nicholas closed his eyes. He rubbed a hand over his face. Clearly Lady Isabella had been in Stony Stratford. And why shouldn't she? It was on her route south to London.

But she wasn't the lady who had rescued Harriet. He *knew* she wasn't. The porter had made a mistake.

Nicholas opened his eyes and turned the page, reading further.

Mr. Shepherd, not content with the porter's word, had interviewed an ostler. This man, similarly plied with ale and a guinea, had confirmed the identity of Harriet's benefactress, on account of her "*bang-up horses*" and liveried outriders. Both men had agreed that Lady Isabella Knox took up the girl into her carriage the next morning.

Nicholas put down the report. He pushed his chair back and strode across to the cluster of decanters on the sideboard. He poured himself a glass of brandy and stood for a moment, breathing deeply. *Calm,* he told himself. But anger was rising inside him and the brandy, burning down his throat when he gulped it, didn't help.

He strode back to the desk and read the rest of the report. Mr. Shepherd had spoken to a number of Lady Isabella's servants, both casually at the local tavern and more formally with the offer of money. All had refused to speak about any guests their mistress may or may not have had staying with her.

But yesterday Mr. Shepherd's luck had changed; he had managed a few words with the cook, a Mrs. Tracey, who had been quite happy to accept a few guineas in exchange for information concerning Lady Isabella's houseguest. Miss Durham, she confirmed, had inhabited the Blue Room for the past two weeks. Yes, she had arrived with Lady Isabella when she returned from Derbyshire. No, she hadn't left the house.

Nicholas closed his eyes. He pinched the bridge of his nose, hard. Isabella's image wavered behind his closed eyelids.

She had lied to him. For two whole weeks she had lied to him.

Nicholas opened his eyes. Mr. Shepherd concluded the report with a note concerning a Mr. Fernyhough, who, he said, had been in Stony Stratford several days before himself enquiring as to Harriet's whereabouts.

Who the devil is Mr. Fernyhough?

Nicholas put the report down. He rubbed his face. The ridges of the scar were hard beneath his fingers, smooth and rough.

Ogre.

He made a sound of disgust, lowered his hands, and turned

to the final page of the report. For a full minute he stared at the address, at each flourishing *s* and neatly looped *e*. Clarges Street.

*C*HAPTER 19

*I*sabella blew out a shaky breath. "How do I look?" she asked her maid, Partridge. She studied herself in the mirror. Did the yellow of the gown make her hair look dull? "Perhaps I should wear the blue after all."

"If you wish," Partridge said, her voice carefully neutral.

Five gowns lay on the bed. Isabella had tried them all on. The pink had been too girlish, the blue too plain, the white too formal, the green too severe, and the cinnamon brown too matronly.

The yellow had seemed hopeful, joyful.

Isabella glanced at the clock. She was trembling with a mix of apprehension and anticipation. It lacked ten minutes to two. This gown would do—it would have to do—there was no more time.

But I want to look perfect for him.

"Perhaps I should try the blue again."

"Miss Isabella," Partridge said, with something approaching frustration in her voice. "The yellow suits you perfectly."

Isabella swallowed and looked at the clock again. Nine minutes. And she still had to speak to her cousin and Harriet.

"Very well," she said. "Yellow it is."

She took a deep breath. She'd never imagined this moment

191

would come: waiting for a man, wanting to marry him. It was exhilarating. Terrifying.

She smoothed her gown with damp palms and turned towards the door.

"Are you all right, Miss Isabella?" Partridge asked, with the acuity of one who had known her from her girlhood.

Or perhaps it's not acuity. Perhaps I look as nervous as I feel.

"Perfectly," Isabella replied. She blew out another shaky breath. First Elinor and Harriet, and then Major Reynolds. She squared her shoulders, crossed the bedchamber, and opened the door. Rufus scrambled up from a sunny square of carpet and followed her, his tail wagging.

Isabella's steps were firm and purposeful as she walked along the corridor and down one flight of stairs. Her knock on the door of Mrs. Westin's parlor was firm and purposeful, too.

Mrs. Westin looked up from her knitting. "Yes, my dear?"

"Major Reynolds will be here shortly. I'm going to tell him about Harriet."

For a moment there was silence. Harriet stared at her, frozen, over the handkerchief she was embroidering.

Mrs. Westin nodded and laid down her knitting. "Very wise, my dear. Honesty is always the best course. As the good Lord said, *Thou shalt not lie.*"

"Tell him?" said Harriet, shrinking back in her chair. "But he'll find me!"

"He's not an ogre," Isabella said. "However much you imagine him to be."

Harriet shook her head. The blood had drained from her face.

Exasperation rose in Isabella's breast. How could the girl be so foolish? "You have nothing to fear from Major Reynolds."

Harriet shook her head again. Tears brimmed in her eyes, trembled on her lashes, spilled over.

Mrs. Westin tutted.

Isabella considered trying to convince Harriet of the major's good qualities. A few seconds' thought made her give up the notion as hopeless. The picture Harriet had painted of Major Reynolds was as inaccurate as it was ridiculous, but it would take more than a few words to persuade the girl she was wrong.

She gave her cousin a look of apology and left her to deal with the weeping Harriet. In the corridor she smoothed her gown again and took a steadying breath. A glance at her watch told her it lacked five minutes to the hour. Would Nicholas be on time?

Rufus took a step forward. His ears pricked.

Isabella walked to the head of the stairs. She heard the sound of men's voices in the foyer below: her butler, Hoban, saying something in welcome, Major Reynolds replying.

Isabella received Major Reynolds in the library. The morning room was sunnier and more pleasant, but the kittens were in residence. She left Rufus in the morning room, too. She wanted no distractions, no witnesses. *Just him and me.*

The apprehension, the anticipation, were a hard knot beneath her breastbone as she stood beside the fireplace. She concentrated on breathing, on not fidgeting, but even so, her heart began to beat much faster as the door opened and the butler ushered Major Reynolds into the library.

She was conscious of him—the green of his eyes, the weight of his presence in the room. And she was conscious of herself in a way she'd never been before, of her appearance, of her nervousness.

Isabella swallowed. "Nicholas."

"Isabella." His voice gave nothing away, nor did his face. No smile, no softening of his expression. Was he as nervous as she? As awkward?

"Please be seated."

He didn't sit. He walked past her to the window. He stood looking out for a moment, his figure silhouetted against the daylight, and then turned to face her. His features were in shadow.

Now.

Isabella took hold of her courage. She clasped her hands together and inhaled a deep breath. "Nicholas," she said. "There's something I must tell you. About Harriet Durham."

"I know," he said.

"You do?" Isabella began to walk towards him. Relief swelled inside her.

"Yes." Major Reynolds laughed. It was a harsh sound. He stepped away from the window.

Isabella halted. She saw his face, saw the hard glitter in his eyes, the tight line of his mouth, the anger. "Nicholas . . ."

His mouth tightened still further. "I *trusted* you."

The apprehension and anticipation were gone. In their place was something close to panic. "Nicholas—"

"Keep your friends close and your enemies closer." His voice made her flinch. "Congratulations, Lady Isabella. You succeeded admirably."

"No," she said. "It wasn't like that at all!"

His mouth twisted. "Wasn't it?" There was a derisive edge to his words, a bitter, mocking note.

"No!" Isabella cried. "Of course not! I was trying to make it *better,* to stop people laughing at you!"

The major's mouth tightened. His hand lifted to touch his left cheek. "I'd forgotten to thank you for my new name." He bowed, a sardonic movement. "Thank you for reminding me."

Shame flushed her cheeks. "It was a *mistake,* Nicholas. I never meant for any of that to happen!" She clutched her hands more tightly together. "I only said it once. Once! But Sarah Faraday heard me, and you know what her tongue is like. She—" Isabella bit her lip. *Stop. It sounds like excuses.*

Major Reynolds said nothing, he merely shook his head.

Anger was etched on his face. He turned away from her to look out the window again.

Isabella took a hesitant step towards him. She moistened her lips and spoke quietly. "I never intended to harm you, Nicholas. And once it had happened I did my very best to undo it."

He didn't look at her. "You lied to me." His voice was as quiet as hers had been.

"I'm sorry. I didn't mean to! But you were so angry. I was afraid to tell you—"

He turned to face her. His expression made her flinch. "You lied to me."

Isabella gripped her hands more tightly together, swallowed, and said, "Yes, I did. I'm very sorry, Nicholas."

He looked at her for a long moment, his eyes cold and hard and unforgiving, then bowed stiffly and stepped past her. "Good day, madam."

"Wait! Nicholas!"

"I have nothing more to say to you." He opened the door and closed it quietly behind him.

Isabella was left standing in the empty library. The silence seemed to echo with Major Reynolds' parting words: *I have nothing more to say to you.*

She smoothed her gown with trembling hands. The gown she had chosen so carefully, with such hope. Yellow.

The Sèvres figurines on the mantelpiece blurred. *I am not going to cry,* Isabella told herself fiercely.

It was too late. She already was.

Nicholas had never been so furious in his life. Furious with Lady Isabella for lying, furious with himself for being duped, for thinking her perfect when she clearly wasn't, for imagining himself in love with her. The afternoon passed in a blur: striding back to the hired house on Albemarle Street, ordering his horse brought around, riding as hard as he could out of London. Vaguely he noticed that paved streets had given way to winding dirt lanes, that tall buildings had been replaced by trees and hedgerows and paddocks where sheep grazed.

He chose an inn at random and shouldered his way into the busy taproom. A tankard of ale quenched his thirst; a second and third began to quench his anger. It came surging back, tiredly, when he remembered his defense of Lady Isabella to Mr. Shepherd. *Such a damned fool.* But he couldn't whip himself up into fury again. He stared at the empty tankard and rubbed his face wearily.

The shroud of rage that had cloaked him had kept the other patrons away from his corner of the taproom. They clustered at the counter, leaning against the scarred wood, their voices loud. Farmers in patched smocks, a blacksmith, a couple of coal-haulers with soot-stained clothes. *Where am I?*

It didn't matter. Nor did it matter, when he asked the publican if a bedroom was available, that the chamber he was escorted to was small and smelled of stale sweat. The mattress was lumpy, the pillow thin, and he had no idea whether the linen was clean or not, but it didn't matter. None of it mattered.

*C*HAPTER 20

*O*n Thursday morning, while they were still in the breakfast parlor, the postman in his scarlet coat and cockaded hat
delivered a letter for Harriet. It was postmarked from Penrith,
in the Lake District.

Finally, thought Isabella. But there was no relief, just
numbness. How long would the numbness last? Would she be
trapped forever in this empty, echoing place?

I hope so. Because under the numbness was pain. She was
aware of it, aware that it would hurt more than she could bear
if only she wasn't numb.

She watched without interest as Harriet broke open the
seal and almost ripped the letter in her haste to open it. Another letter fell out from the folded paper, falling to lie on the
tablecloth. Harriet's original letter. The one she'd sent to her
aunt more than two weeks ago. Unopened.

Isabella's numbness faltered slightly. *That doesn't look good.*

"It's from . . . it's from a Mrs. Jayne. She says—" Tears
suspended Harriet's voice entirely. She thrust the letter at
Mrs. Westin and ran from the room.

Mrs. Westin read the letter calmly. "Oh, dear," she said,
and then held it out to Isabella.

I don't think I want to read it.

She put down her cutlery and took the proffered letter.

Mrs. Jayne wrote briefly. Lavinia Mortlock had remarried two years ago and emigrated with her new husband to America. Mrs. Jayne had an address for her in Baltimore, which she enclosed. She apologized for the delay in replying; she had been laid up with the influenza.

Isabella refolded the letter and placed it neatly on the tablecloth. She closed her eyes. *What am I going to do with Harriet?*

She opened her eyes, picked up the knife and fork, and began to eat her eggs again.

"What shall we do?" Mrs. Westin asked.

"I don't know." *I don't care.*

But the numbness was beginning to fracture. Dear God, what *was* she going to do with the girl?

And beneath the worry, pushing determinedly through the cracks, was pain. Pain so intense that her throat closed.

Isabella reached for her tea. She took a sip. A second sip.

"You never said yesterday . . . how did Major Reynolds take the news?"

Her throat tightened. She drank another mouthful of tea. "Not as well as I had hoped."

"Ah," Mrs. Westin said. "A shame."

Isabella put down the teacup and looked at her plate. She had no appetite. She placed her knife and fork neatly alongside one another and folded her napkin.

"And how are you, my dear? Has your headache gone?"

"Gone?" Isabella said, staring at the congealing egg yolk on her plate. *What am I going to do about Nicholas? About Harriet?*

"You still look rather pale."

Isabella looked up at her cousin. She forced a smile. "A slight headache still. I believe I'll stay at home today." *And tomorrow. And the next day. I shall hide forever.*

She pushed back her chair and stood. The door was slightly open from Harriet's flight.

Harriet.

Dear God, what am I going to do about her?

Lieutenant Mayhew came to fetch the kittens just before noon. His sunny good humor was painful, as was his cheerful enquiry about Major Reynolds.

"I haven't seen him since yesterday afternoon," Isabella said. The smile felt stiff on her lips, but it fooled the lieutenant.

For a few minutes they were busy, capturing the two kittens, installing them in a wicker basket that Lieutenant Mayhew had brought with him.

"Wonderful!" the lieutenant said. "Thank you so much, ma'am. I'm indebted to you." He bowed over her hand, his eyes laughing at her.

"I hope they don't give you any trouble on your journey."

Lieutenant Mayhew had no such fears. He laughed and left, running lightly down the stairs, carrying the kittens. Their mews came indignantly from the basket.

Isabella stood at the top of the staircase, Rufus beside her, long after the lieutenant was gone. The conversation with her cousin looped in her head.

How did Major Reynolds take it?
Not as well as I had hoped.

Rufus sat down with a thump. He began to scratch himself vigorously.

"I should have told Nicholas earlier," she said to him. "He wouldn't have been so angry."

Rufus continued scratching, a strained grimace on his face.

Isabella sighed. "I should have never lied."

So many "should haves." But she had done what she had done—and the result was only what she deserved.

So what do I do about it?

Isabella came to an abrupt decision. She turned and headed upstairs. Rufus scrambled to his feet and bounded after her. "Partridge?" she said, opening the door to her bedroom. "I'm going out. I'd like you to accompany me."

They walked to Albemarle Street rather than take the carriage. Isabella told herself that it was because she needed the fresh air, but, truthfully, it was because she needed to muster her courage. Partridge walked silently beside her and Rufus trotted ahead, his ears pricked and his plumy tail wagging.

Isabella halted outside Major Reynolds' house. It seemed very tall, very stern. She took a deep breath and trod up the steps.

A butler with thinning gray hair and rather startlingly bushy eyebrows answered the door.

"My name is Lady Isabella Knox," she said. "I would like to see Major Reynolds."

"I regret that Major Reynolds isn't in town, ma'am."

"Not—?" Her momentum and her courage faltered. "Do you know when he'll return?"

The butler shook his head. "No, ma'am."

Had he left London permanently? Gone to Devonshire? No, the house would be closed then, the knocker off the door, the servants gone. *Unless the servants are packing up the house now.* Panic tightened her chest. "Do you expect him back?"

"Yes, ma'am."

Isabella expelled a shaky breath. "Where is he? Do you know?"

"No, ma'am. He didn't inform us of his destination."

Is he gone because of me?

"When did Major Reynolds leave?"

"Yesterday afternoon, ma'am," the butler said. "In something of a hurry."

Yes, he left because of me.

"Thank you," Isabella said. She turned away from the door and went back to Clarges Street, where she wandered from room to room—parlor, library, book room—unable to settle. She ended up in the morning room. Mrs. Early found her there half an hour later. "Lady Isabella?"

Isabella looked up from her listless observation of the last two kittens, sprawled on the floor with Rufus. "Yes, Mrs. Early?"

"I know who the thief is." The housekeeper's mouth was pinched, her expression grim.

Not now. "Who?"

"Mrs. Tracey."

Isabella straightened on the sofa. "The *cook*?"

"Yes, ma'am."

"But . . ." Mrs. Tracey had been in her employ for three years. "There must be some mistake."

Mrs. Early shook her head firmly. "No mistake, ma'am. I counted the wax candles this afternoon, and not five minutes later I saw Mrs. Tracey go down to the stillroom and come back with something in her apron pocket. I checked again and two candles were gone—the best beeswax!"

Isabella bit her lower lip. "You're certain? You didn't miscount?"

"I checked twice, ma'am."

Isabella sighed.

"Mrs. Tracey went to her bedchamber not long after that—to tidy her hair, she said—and when she returned, her pocket was quite clearly empty."

"But . . ." Isabella said again. *But why?* The woman earned a generous wage. She closed her mouth and struggled to think clearly. "Please ask her to attend me in my book room. I wish for you to be present, too, Mrs. Early."

The housekeeper nodded and withdrew.

Mrs. Tracey?

Isabella made her way purposefully downstairs. She sat behind the desk and folded her hands together on its smooth maplewood surface. She didn't have to wait long. A tap sounded on the door. "Come in."

Mrs. Tracey entered, followed by the housekeeper.

"Please be seated," Isabella said.

She watched as Mrs. Tracey sat. The woman was raw-boned, with a gaunt, ruddy face. Her hands were large, their backs knotted with veins. *Such clumsy-looking hands to create such dainty delicacies,* Isabella thought, not for the first time.

The cook looked at her. Her expression was politely enquiring, not defensive, not afraid.

"Mrs. Tracey," Isabella said. "We have a problem." She unfolded her hands and reached for the current ledger. "For several months now someone in this household has been stealing."

Mrs. Tracey's polite smile froze on her face.

"Beeswax candles," Isabella said, turning to the latest month's columns of figures. She glanced up at the woman. "And perhaps other things as well."

Mrs. Tracey said nothing. She sat stiffly in the wooden chair. A plain woman, hard-working. *And honest, I had thought*.

Isabella sat with her hands resting on the open page. "Is there anything you'd like to tell me, Mrs. Tracey?"

"Me, ma'am?" But there was a flat, false note to Mrs. Tracey's outrage. "Surely you don't think that *I* would steal anything!"

Isabella looked at her gravely. "You were observed taking two wax candles this afternoon."

"Wax candles? Me?" The cook's voice was affronted, but her expression was scared. Her cheeks, instead of flushing with indignation, had paled.

"I would like to check your room, please."

Mrs. Tracey swallowed convulsively. Her hands were tightly clenched in her lap.

Isabella stood. "Shall we do it now?"

"But my pastries! I need to get them out of the oven. I'm too busy for this now! Surely it can wait . . ." The woman's voice died out as Isabella shook her head.

Mrs. Tracey's room was downstairs, near the kitchen. The woman's manner became more flustered when they halted outside the door. "Lady Isabella," she said. "I can explain!"

Almost a confession. Isabella looked at her sadly. "Open the door, please, Mrs. Tracey."

The cook began to sob as she unlocked the door to her bedchamber. It was a large room, as befitted her status, with a half-canopy bedstead, a fireplace, and an armchair.

They stepped inside. Isabella glanced around the chamber, taking in the chest of drawers, the washstand, the sturdy pinewood trunk. "Can you open your trunk, please, Mrs. Tracey?"

The cook began to cry in earnest. She made no move to open the trunk.

Isabella turned to Mrs. Early. The housekeeper's plump face was somber. *She's enjoying this no more than I am.* "Mrs. Early? If you wouldn't mind?"

The housekeeper stepped forward and lifted the lid of the trunk. Blankets lay neatly folded inside. Mrs. Early rummaged with her hand, her mouth tight, as if she found the task distasteful. After a moment she stilled and looked up. "Ma'am?"

Isabella made herself step forward, made herself look. The beeswax candles were tucked down one side of the trunk. She turned to face the cook, but found herself unable to look at the woman. *I trusted you.*

She turned away. "Mrs. Tracey, you are dismissed. Please gather your belongings and depart this house within the hour."

"But ma'am, please . . ."

Isabella turned back to her. "You stole from me," she said quietly.

Mrs. Tracey's face was tear-stained. "But ma'am . . ."

Isabella stared at her. Was this how Major Reynolds had felt? This sense of disbelief, of betrayal, of disappointment so intense that it felt as if someone had kicked her in the stomach.

No, he had been angry, too. She wasn't angry. She was just sad. "Why, Mrs. Tracey?"

Mrs. Tracey gulped and sniffed back her tears. "My daughter's getting married soon. I wanted to give her a good start."

Isabella sighed. She turned away again. "One hour, Mrs. Tracey."

"You won't press charges?"

Isabella turned back to face her. She met the woman's eyes, saw the fear in them. No, not fear—terror.

She understood the terror: people had been sent to the penal colonies for stealing less. "No, Mrs. Tracey."

The cook subsided weakly on her bed. She began to sob again, noisily.

Isabella met the housekeeper's eyes. She made a slight beckoning gesture. The woman followed her outside into the corridor. "Stay with her, Mrs. Early, and see that she does as I've asked."

The housekeeper nodded.

"Would you like me to send for one of the footmen, just in case . . . ?"

"I don't think it will be necessary, ma'am."

No, Isabella didn't think the cook would create trouble, either. But then she hadn't thought the woman would steal. "After Mrs. Tracey has gone, can you please go to the registry office and see about engaging a new cook."

Mrs. Early nodded again. "Yes, ma'am."

"I'll speak with the kitchen maids, explain what has happened." Isabella rubbed her brow. "We'll dine plainly until there's a new cook. I think they'll cope for a few days. They're competent girls."

The housekeeper nodded her agreement.

"Thank you, Mrs. Early."

The housekeeper nodded again, then stepped back into the bedchamber and shut the door.

Isabella sighed. She needed to thank the housekeeper with more than words. A bonus, perhaps? A week's leave? She turned away. *I hate this.* To have one's faith in someone destroyed suddenly and utterly, to know that one's trust had been misplaced. It made her feel slightly ill.

She had done this to Major Reynolds.

Would he ever forgive her? *Could* he?

Isabella sighed and rubbed her face with both hands and headed for the kitchen.

*C*HAPTER 21

*I*sabella spent the rest of Thursday afternoon at the pianoforte, laboring over Beethoven's Sonata no. 14. There was no beauty in the music. The soft lamenting first movement, the stormy third, sounded equally flat and lifeless, the notes sliding from beneath her fingertips with one dull *clunk* after another, the hammers and strings making noise, not music.

Finally she gave up. She bowed her head, resting her forehead on the pianoforte, and closed her eyes. *What am I to do?*

A knock on the door jerked her upright. Rufus woke abruptly, scrambling to his feet, shedding the two kittens who'd been dozing on his flank.

"Yes?"

"The Duke of Middlebury," her butler said.

"Julian?" She stood as abruptly as Rufus. "Here?"

"I took the liberty of showing him to the library, ma'am."

"Thank you, Hoban," She hurried to the door. The butler stood back to let her pass. "Fetch up a bottle of the best claret, please."

Julian was standing by the window in the library, just as Nicholas had done. He turned at her entrance and came towards her, blond and tall, thickening slightly now that he'd reached forty, and engulfed her in a hug.

Isabella clung to him. *I am not going to cry.*

Julian released her. He looked down at her, smiling. "I'd thought you'd be in Hyde Park, showing off that phaeton of yours."

"Not today." Nor yesterday either, not after that shattering interview with Major Reynolds.

She pushed thought of Major Reynolds away. "Come," she said, taking her brother's hand and drawing him to the sofa. "Tell me how Marianne and the children are."

Julian sat down beside her, sinking back into the cushions, stretching his legs out with a sigh. "They're well." He looked towards the door as it opened. At the sight of the butler bearing a tray with a bottle and two glasses, he straightened slightly. "Claret?"

"Of course."

Julian examined the bottle and poured with careful reverence.

"I didn't know you were coming to town," Isabella said, as her brother took a first, savoring sip. His eyebrows rose in silent appreciation of the claret. "How long will you be here?"

"Just tonight," Julian said, lowering his glass. "I've put up at Grillon's."

"Grillon's? But you can stay here—" Abruptly she remembered that she had no cook. And that she had a secret guest upstairs.

"You'll be out anyway, if I know you. What is it tonight?" His voice held a teasing note. "A masked ball? The opera?"

"Nothing," Isabella said, looking down at the glass in her hand. "I'm rather tired. I shall be staying in tonight."

Julian said nothing. She glanced up to find his eyes on her face.

Isabella forced a smile. "Are you here on business?"

"No," he said. "I came to town because of you."

"Me," she said blankly. "Oh, the letter I sent you!" Hope rose sharply in her breast. Here was a solution for Harriet. "You have a vacant living?"

Her brother shook his head.

"Oh." Isabella tried not to show her disappointment. She bit her lip and looked at the wineglass again.

Julian laid his arm along the back of the sofa. His hand almost touched her shoulder. "I came because a number of people have mentioned your name in connection with a Major Reynolds."

Isabella's head jerked up. The wine slopped in her glass, almost spilling.

"In more than ten years I've not known you to show interest in any man, let alone make one your beau." Julian's expression was serious, but his eyes were smiling. "I would like to meet this Major Reynolds for myself."

"He has left town." *Because of me.*

"Ah." The smile faded from her brother's eyes. "A shame. I'd hoped to make his acquaintance."

Isabella bit her lip again. She looked down at the dark wine.

"Tell me about him."

Her gaze jerked to his. "About Nicholas?"

Julian's eyebrows rose. Too late, Isabella realized what that slip of the tongue told her brother. *Yes, I call him by his Christian name.* Faint heat flushed her face.

On the heels of that realization, came a second. *If I speak of Nicholas, I will cry.* She prevaricated: "What do you know of him?"

"Major Reynolds?" Julian swirled the claret in his glass. He looked at her a moment and then seemed to come to a decision. He put the wineglass down. "You're not in the habit of indulging in flirtations, so when I heard about this man I was curious. Very curious." He shrugged slightly. "So I asked a few people about him."

Isabella moistened her lips. "You did?"

Her brother nodded.

"What did they say?" she asked, clutching the stem of her glass more tightly.

"Everyone I spoke to thought highly of him. He was respected by the men he commanded, and by the men who commanded him. Respected and liked."

Isabella relaxed her grip on the glass. "Yes," she said. "He is a . . . a good man."

"I also heard that he would be a colonel, if he hadn't chosen to sell his commission."

"I didn't know that," she said, surprised.

Her brother's fingers tapped on the back of the sofa. He was frowning now. "He turned down a colonelcy—which isn't something most men would do." The frown deepened. "War can do things to a man, can unbalance—"

"Nicholas is not unbalanced," Isabella said firmly. "He left the military because he has had enough of death. He wants children. He wants a family."

Her brother's fingers stilled their tapping. He observed her face for a long moment and then asked quietly, "And are those things that you want?"

Isabella flushed. "I . . ." *Yes.* But she couldn't utter the word. Her throat had closed. Tears threatened. She swallowed and held tightly to her composure. *I am not Harriet. I am not going to cry.*

Julian waited for her to answer. When she didn't, he continued. "He has a reputation for fairness, your major, and a reputation for getting things done. A very competent man, by all accounts."

Isabella nodded. Very competent. She'd witnessed that. And then she frowned slightly. How *had* Major Reynolds discovered that she was sheltering Harriet?

"So, what I want to know is: is he worthy of you?"

Isabella swallowed again. "He is . . . the best of men." Her voice was only slightly unsteady.

Julian surveyed her thoughtfully. One of his fingers moved—*tap-tap*—on the back of the sofa. "May I ask what your intentions are with this major? Your name has been . . . rather closely linked with his." There was no censure in his voice or his expression. Instead she saw his concern, heard how much he cared for her. *He loves me. He's worried about me.*

"My intentions—" Her voice broke. Hastily she averted her face. She put down her wineglass with a shaking hand. *Don't let me cry in front of him.*

"Izzie," Julian said softly. His hand was on her shoulder, warm and comforting. "Is everything all right?"

She squeezed her eyes shut. *No. No, it's not.*

Julian shifted on the sofa. His arm came around her. "Izzie," he said again.

The composure she'd held onto so tightly fractured into tiny pieces. She began to cry, and as she'd feared, she couldn't stop.

"Hush," Julian said, holding her, one hand smoothing her hair as the sobs tore endlessly in her chest. "Hush."

The storm of grief passed finally, leaving her limp. Julian didn't release her. She leaned against him, her face pressed against his waistcoat. Tears seeped from beneath her eyelids. "I love him," she whispered. "And he . . . and he . . ." *He hates me.*

Julian's hand, stroking comforting circles on her back, stilled. She felt him stiffen. "Has he done anything to you? Has he—"

"It was me," she said, into his waistcoat. "I was the one who did something wrong. I lied to him."

"You? Lied to him?" But Julian didn't push her away; instead his arm tightened around her shoulders. His hand resumed its slow, stroking circles. "I've never known you to lie, Iz. You must have had good reason."

Isabella sighed. The sound was ragged, almost hiccupping. "I didn't mean to, but everything . . . it just . . ." She paused and inhaled a shaky breath. "It started in Stony Stratford, when I was on my way back from visiting you."

She told him the whole story: finding Harriet, her slip of the tongue in front of Sarah Faraday, the attempt she'd made to stop the ridicule, her growing friendship with Major

Reynolds. She left out only the kisses. Everything else—the lies, the little deceits—she recounted in a halting voice. Julian listened silently.

"I don't know what to do," she said, at the end of her recitation. "Nicholas has left town. I don't know if he'll come back. He was so *angry*." Tears threatened again. She bit her lip, holding them back.

"If he loves you, he'll come back."

Isabella gulped a breath. "You think so?"

"Yes." Julian stopped rubbing her back. He groped in his pocket and handed her a linen handkerchief.

Isabella blew her nose. "I'm sorry," she said, to his waist-coat. "I didn't mean to cry."

Julian tightened his arm around her. "I haven't seen you cry since you were a child. Not like that."

"No."

They were silent for a long moment, and then Julian said, "He means a lot to you, this Major Reynolds."

"Yes." *He means everything*. Isabella straightened and sat up. She wiped her face. "Would you like to meet Harriet?"

Julian reached for his wineglass again. "Yes." He didn't drink, though. "You did the right thing, helping her. If Felicity were ever in such straits . . ." His mouth tightened.

But his daughter never would be in such straits. She had parents who loved her. Whereas Harriet did not.

Isabella sighed. "Yes, it was the right thing. But I did everything wrong after that."

Julian didn't deny it. His mouth twisted in a wry grimace. He tilted the glass and swallowed a mouthful of claret.

Isabella reached for her own glass.

"Should I take her home with me? A companion for Felicity? They're the same age, you said."

Isabella paused, glass in hand. For a moment she felt lighter, as if a weight had lifted from her shoulders, then the weight settled again. She shook her head. "Thank you, but it's best that Harriet remains here. The fewer people who know, the easier it will be to keep this a secret."

If the *ton* found out . . .

Isabella sipped her wine slowly. The major's accusation echoed clearly in her head: *Keep your friends close and your enemies closer.*

The *ton* would think she'd done that, too. She could see it in her mind's eye: the sly amusement, the laughing whispers, the ridicule.

Her hand tightened on the glass. *I won't let that happen again. Not to Nicholas.*

Julian stayed to eat dinner with them, chicken fricassee and a raised giblet pie. With a seventeen-year-old daughter of his own, he managed—with no apparent effort—to put Harriet at ease. After they'd drunk tea together in the drawing room and discussed in detail the appetite and sleeping habits of his youngest son, three-month-old William, he took his leave, bowing to Harriet and Mrs. Westin. "I shan't see you again, Izzie," he said cheerfully. "I'm off early tomorrow morning."

Isabella accompanied her brother to the door. "I don't like this responsibility you've taken upon yourself," Julian said. The cheerfulness was gone. His face was serious.

"You don't like Harriet?"

"No, not that. What I meant was . . ." He frowned. "You've taken trouble upon your shoulders, and I can't see how it will turn out."

Neither can I.

"If you need help, you must tell me. Promise?"

"I promise."

Julian continued to frown. "If this major of yours is still angry when he gets back to town, if he's . . . difficult, I'll come at once."

If he wants revenge, you mean. If he tries to punish me. She remembered the moment in Hyde Park when Major Reynolds had asked after Harriet's benefactress, the expression on his face—implacable, hard, cold—and repressed a shiver. "Don't worry."

"Promise me," Julian said again.

Isabella bit her lip, looking at him. He was as tall as the major, as broad, but older, too. *Nicholas is more dangerous than Julian.* If it came to a duel—

"Promise me," Julian repeated, and his expression was as implacable as the major's had been.

Isabella sighed. "All right, I promise. But he won't be difficult. He's not that kind of man." *I think. I hope.*

Julian wished aloud that he had a vacant living to bestow on Mr. Fernyhough, kissed her cheek, and departed.

On Friday morning Harriet presented Isabella with a sheet of paper.

"What's this?" Isabella read the first item on the list—*Invalid's Companion*—and glanced at the girl.

"I need to earn my living." Harriet swallowed a sob. "I can't remain here forever."

Isabella read the next item on the list: "Seamstress?"

"I'm good at needlework," Harriet said, with a trembling smile.

That was undeniably true. Harriet was neat and quick with a needle. Isabella had lost count of the number of sheets and handkerchiefs the girl had hemmed in the past three weeks—tasks that would have bored her to tears but that Harriet apparently enjoyed.

The girl certainly had the skills to be a seamstress, but . . . Isabella shook her head. She read the next item—*Trimming*

Hats—and shook her head again. Yes, Harriet had the temperament to not mind being indoors all day, sitting and sewing, but . . .

Not an easy way to earn a living, bent over a needle and thread.

Lady's Maid was the next item on the list. And after that, *Kitchen Maid, Housemaid, Nursemaid,* and *Milkmaid.*

Isabella rejected those careers. She looked at the first item again. It was the most promising. *Invalid's Companion.* But such a position would be more arduous than the tasks the girl performed here: reading aloud to Mrs. Westin, hemming handkerchiefs and embroidering flowers at the corners. There'd be fetching and carrying, perhaps nursing her employer. *And she's only seventeen, far too young. A child still, not a woman.*

She put down the list and looked at Harriet. The girl looked back at her, anxiously. Tears brimmed in her soft brown eyes.

Isabella sighed inwardly. *What am I going to do with her?* Harriet had been raised to be a gentlewoman, not a servant—although that meant little in these days of economic crisis. Many an indigent gentlewoman eked out an existence as a governess or paid companion, or even a seamstress.

As if Harriet had read her thoughts, she said, "I didn't put down governess because . . ." She flushed. "Because my grandfather didn't think that girls need education."

Of course he didn't.

Isabella looked down at the list again and thought, not for the first time, how lucky she was. If she'd been born into a different family this would have been her fate: invalid's companion, seamstress. *Or wife,* she reminded herself. And that was the best solution for Harriet: marriage. The girl needed someone to look after her.

I need to find a vacant living for Mr. Fernyhough.

And until then . . . could the girl stay as Mrs. Westin's companion? But openly, without any of the secrecy of the past few weeks.

When Nicholas comes back, I'll ask him. He deserved a say in

Harriet's future. He had cared enough about the girl to want to marry her.

Harriet was still watching her, her expression anxious. Did she think she was in danger of being thrown out?

"I know you're dreadfully worried, but you mustn't be." Isabella folded the sheet of paper and gave the girl a reassuring smile. "We'll think of something. And until we do, you shall stay here."

"I don't wish to be a burden—"

"You're not," Isabella said firmly. "We like having your company."

Grateful tears trembled on the girl's eyelashes. "Thank you, ma'am." She bobbed a curtsy and left the morning room, quietly shutting the door behind her.

Isabella sighed. She looked down at the folded piece of paper in her hand. *Damn you, Nicholas. Where are you?*

CHAPTER 22

Nicholas had needed distance. Distance from London and Lady Isabella, but more than that, distance from *thinking*. The distance of simply existing in the moment, not remembering what had happened, not feeling any emotions. Yesterday he'd done just that: not thought, merely existed, sitting on the rough wooden bench in front of the inn, a tankard in his hand, the sign creaking above his head, watching the world go by.

Today it was time to make decisions. He chose the bench in front of the inn again and laid the facts out in his mind.

Firstly, Lady Isabella had sheltered Harriet.

For that, he could only thank her.

Secondly, she had named him for an ogre.

He grimaced at memory of Gussie's ball, the whispers and the sniggers, the sideways glances, his rage in discovering what he was being called. Ogre.

He waited for fury to resurface. It didn't.

So, Lady Isabella had named him for an ogre. But it hadn't been intentional. She'd said so, and he believed her. Isabella was someone who rescued kittens from rivers; she wouldn't deliberately harm anyone. A mistake, then. One that he could forgive.

Thirdly, she had lied to him.

That was the most painful memory. Lady Isabella had lied to his face. He could recall the moment, the time and the place: late afternoon in Hyde Park, with the sun low in the sky and a breeze lifting the leaves on the trees. He'd sat alongside her in the phaeton and spoken of his intention to find Harriet's benefactress. Isabella had been beautiful. And tense.

I was angry. And she was afraid.

And so she had lied to him.

In that context it was understandable. More than that, it was forgivable.

Nicholas sighed.

Isabella had planned to tell him, to reveal her lie. *Nicholas,* she had said. *There's something I must tell you. About Harriet Durham.*

But he'd been too angry to listen, too hurt by her deceit, too betrayed.

Nicholas grunted. *Idiot.* Isabella had made a mistake, several mistakes, but her intention had never been to harm him.

Everyone makes mistakes. It's part of what makes us human.

And he'd made a mistake, too, calling on her immediately after Mr. Shepherd's visit, allowing his hurt pride to rule him, accusing her of keeping her friends close and her enemies closer.

He could hear her voice, see the tears shining in her eyes: *It wasn't like that at all!*

And he *had* known that, even when he'd thrown the accusation at her. What had grown between them, the friendship, the laughter, the kisses—that had been genuine, it had been real, it hadn't been a game.

I love her. And I think she loves me.

No, he corrected himself. It was possible that Lady Isabella *had* loved him—and even more possible that she no longer did. Because the mistake he'd made on Wednesday was quite as bad as any she'd made.

Nicholas pushed to his feet and strode around to the stableyard, calling for the ostler. "My horse! As fast as you can!"

Isabella called at Major Reynolds' house in Albemarle Street on Friday afternoon. He was still out of town.

"Would you like to leave a message, ma'am?" the butler asked.

"No," Isabella said. No messages, no ink on paper.

She turned away and walked down the steps. Partridge said nothing. She was wearing her expressionless servant's face. What did she think of this second trek to Albemarle Street?

Rufus was easy to read. He didn't care. He lifted his leg against one of the steps—fortunately the butler had closed the door—and then pranced ahead of her, sniffing the fence railings in passing.

When they reached Clarges Street, Isabella's steps slowed. She halted outside her house.

Partridge halted, too, silent. Rufus sat on the doorstep and waited.

Isabella stared up at the house, at the blank windows. She didn't want to go inside, to sit with her regrets and her grief, her helplessness.

I need to face the world. She needed to *do*. Something. Anything.

Accordingly, at five o'clock, she drove to Hyde Park in her phaeton. Her appearance caused a slight stir. People stopped their carriages to greet her, to ask whether she'd been unwell.

Isabella smiled and kept her replies vague.

No one inquired whether her two-day disappearance from the parks and ballrooms had anything to do with Major Reynolds' abrupt departure from London, but she was certain some of them were thinking it.

Isabella found that she didn't care. The fresh air, the sunlight, the breeze on her face, lifted her spirits. *No more hiding,* she told herself as she climbed the stairs to her bedchamber. *From now on I face the world.*

She unbuttoned her gloves and pulled them off. "I shall be going out tonight, Partridge. The Griffiths' ball. I shall wear . . . the cream slip and the peony red robe." *Red for courage.*

"Very good, ma'am."

Isabella dined with her cousin and Harriet, and then went upstairs to change. She surveyed herself in the mirror once she was dressed—the cool folds of cream silk falling to her ankles, the red crêpe robe fastened over her bosom with rosettes of pearls, the long gloves, the satin dancing slippers, the pearl and ruby earrings dangling from her earlobes.

A maid tapped on her door. "The Washburnes' carriage is here, ma'am."

"Excellent," Isabella said. She took a deep breath—*Courage*—and picked up her reticule and fan.

The Griffiths' ball was one of the larger events of the Season, and the mood of the evening—gay, hectic—caught Isabella up almost as soon as she and the Washburnes entered the brightly lit ballroom. It was easier than she'd expected to lock her emotions away and fix a smile on her face. She enjoyed it all: the music, the conversation, the laughter, the dancing. Especially the dancing.

After a particularly energetic *contredanse*, Isabella retired to the side of the ballroom to drink a glass of champagne and fan herself. Gussie and Lucas joined her. Lucas was red-faced and panting. "I'm too old for this," he said. "If you have any compassion, Isabella, you'll lend me your fan."

Isabella laughed and handed it to him. "Where's yours?" she asked Gussie.

"Lucas stepped on it," Gussie said, pulling a face. "And it was made of ivory!"

"Not my night," Lucas Washburne said ruefully, fanning himself.

Gussie reached out and took his free hand.

The glance that they exchanged—loving, amused—made Isabella's throat close. She looked hastily away and swallowed a mouthful of champagne.

The dance floor was empty. Guests milled around the edges, talking and drinking and laughing. At the far end of the ballroom, a man paused beneath the arch of the doorway. His face was in shadow but he had a soldier's bearing, a soldier's way of standing quietly and observing.

He could almost have been Major Reynolds, except that the major wasn't in London.

Isabella averted her gaze. She took another hasty swallow of champagne. Her pleasure in the evening had evaporated. *I want to go home.*

"Nicholas is here," Gussie said.

Isabella looked around.

The man had stepped into the blaze of light from the chandeliers. He was walking towards them. His hair was brown, his face tanned. A scar was livid across his left cheek.

CHAPTER 23

Lady Isabella stood tensely, watching him approach. She was dressed in rich cream and deep, flowing red. Pearl and ruby earrings hung from her earlobes. A sybaritic outfit, if she hadn't been so pale, so tense.

"Evening, Gussie," Nicholas said. "Lucas. Lady Isabella."

The musicians struck the opening notes to a new dance as he bowed over Lady Isabella's gloved hand. A waltz.

"May I have this dance?" he asked her.

Lady Isabella seemed to grow even tenser, even paler. She swallowed. Her eyes meeting his were . . . what? *Scared,* he realized. *She thinks I'm still angry.*

He smiled to reassure her and repeated the question. "May I have this dance?"

Isabella hesitated. He watched her inhale a shallow breath, watched her swallow again. She nodded.

Nicholas held out his arm. After another hesitation she laid her hand on it.

They walked out onto the dance floor, something they'd done dozens of times before. Tonight it was different. Isabella was a queen in that outfit, the cream and the red, the rubies and the pearls, and yet she had shrunk into herself. She was tense, uncertain.

A bow, a curtsy, and her hand was in his, but their dancing was awkward tonight. Isabella's grace, the ease with which they'd matched steps, were gone. *This was a foolish idea.* He should have waited until tomorrow, waited to speak to her alone.

"Isabella," he said softly.

Her head was bowed. She didn't look up at him.

Words gathered on his tongue. *I forgive you for lying to me. I haven't come to upbraid you, I've come to ask you to marry me. I love you.*

Nicholas opened his mouth, looked up, and met the gaze of Lady Faraday. She was dressed in a frilled gown of jonquil yellow. The yellow made her look sallow, the frills old. Beneath a tall headdress of dyed ostrich feathers her eyes were bright and interested.

Nicholas shut his mouth. He steered himself and Isabella in the opposite direction.

"Nicholas." Her voice was low, so low he barely heard it.

He bent his head.

"Nicholas, I—" Isabella's voice choked. Her hand shook faintly in his. *She's trying not to cry,* he realized suddenly.

His throat tightened. Something clenched in his chest. He drew her more closely to him and guided her to the edge of the dance floor.

Isabella didn't look up when he halted, releasing her. "Nicholas," she said again. He heard tears trembling in her voice, as the ruby and pearl drops trembled from her earlobes.

"Not now," he said, placing a hand in the small of her back and guiding her with gentle pressure towards the nearest open door. It was the refreshment room, empty except for a liveried servant replenishing the lemonade.

"Forgive me," he said, lifting a hand to touch her cheek and then halting the gesture, aware of the servant. "I didn't mean to upset you."

"No." Her voice was low, rushed, barely audible above the strains of the waltz. "I'm sorry, Nicholas. For everything that happened."

Behind them the servant bustled, collecting used glasses on a tray.

"Nicholas . . ." She raised her head and looked at him.

Lady Isabella had looked at him like that once before, with tears shining in her eyes. Then, he had walked away; now, he had to clench his hands to stop from reaching for her.

"It was a mistake. I only ever said it once. Ask Gussie, she was there."

The servant departed with a tray of dirty glasses.

Nicholas unclenched his hands. He reached for Isabella, pulling her towards him. "I don't need to ask Gussie," he said, speaking the words against her temple. His lips brushed her skin. Her hair was soft against his cheek. "I believe you."

She inhaled a quick, shaky breath. He felt her tension, the faint shaking of her body. She was close to the humiliation of being seen crying in public. *My fault. I should have waited until tomorrow.*

"Did you come with Gussie?"

"Yes," she whispered.

"Go get your wrap. I'm taking you home." He released her, stepping back. "I'll tell Gussie."

Isabella nodded. Her head was bowed, gloved fingertips pressed to her mouth.

Nicholas clenched his hands again. He wanted to take her in his arms, to hold her as tightly as he could. "Go," he said. "I'll meet you in the vestibule."

Isabella lifted her head. She looked at him. "Nicholas . . ."

Tears, shining in those gray-blue eyes.

Nicholas cleared his throat. "Go," he said again, his voice hoarse, and he reached for her, cupping the nape of her neck with one hand, bending his head and kissing her brow, her skin smooth and warm beneath his lips, then he turned on his heel and strode from the refreshment room. A servant stepped back to let him pass, bearing a tray of fresh glasses. The waltz was still playing.

Lady Isabella was waiting for him in the vestibule. She stood pale and silent beside him as a linkboy hailed a hackney. Nicholas took her hand as soon as they were inside. The interior was musty and smelled faintly of onions.

"I apologize," he said. "I shouldn't have come tonight. It was ill-judged of me."

"I thought you were out of town." Her voice was a whisper. "Your butler said—"

His butler said that she had called twice, asking to speak with him.

"I was. I should have come back sooner. I'm sorry."

"Where were you?" A diffident whisper, as if she had no right to ask him.

"Getting some distance." Nicholas tightened his grip on her hand. "I apologize for leaving so abruptly on Wednesday." He'd been afraid he would say something unforgivable, had in fact come very close to it in his rage, in his hurt pride. "The things I said to you were—" *Unpardonable, inexcusable.* "I allowed my anger to rule me. Can you ever forgive me?"

Silence filled the carriage. He was acutely aware of its sway, of the rattle of wheels on stone, of the *clop* of the horse's hooves, and even more acutely aware of Isabella's silence. *She's going to say no.*

And then he realized that her head was bent, her free hand pressed to her face. "Isabella?" he said, reaching out to touch her cheek.

She was weeping.

Nicholas's heart clenched in his chest. He moved closer on the lumpy seat, putting an arm around her. "What is it? Please tell me."

She didn't lean into him, as he'd hoped. She stayed stiff and tense, miserable.

"Please," he said. "Isabella . . . tell me."

For a long moment she was silent, then she inhaled a shuddering breath. "You're asking me to forgive you, when it's all my *fault*—"

"Ah," Nicholas said, finally understanding.

"I called you an ogre," she sobbed.

"Yes," he said, stroking the nape of her neck lightly with his thumb. "You did."

"I wish I'd cut out my tongue before I said such a thing!" She was crying in earnest now.

Nicholas drew her closer. He put both his arms around her. "As I understand it, it was a mistake."

"And then I *lied* to you." Isabella was crying so hard that the words were hard to decipher.

Nicholas rested his cheek on her hair. "That was my fault," he said. "You were afraid of me."

She shook her head against his chest. Her sobs were deep and wrenching.

Nicholas held her, rocking her gently, his face pressed into her hair. *Have you been this miserable, my lady?* "Shh," he whispered. "It's all right."

Her head moved again, a shake, a negation.

"Yes," he said. "It's in the past. A mistake we made, you and I. And one day . . ." He drew in a deep breath—*Listen to me, Isabella. Hear what I'm saying.* "And one day, we will laugh about this. When we're married."

She heard. She became very still. Her sobbing shuddered to a halt.

"Isabella," he said softly. "Will you marry me?"

He held his breath, waiting for her answer, hoping.

For a moment Lady Isabella stayed stiff and tense in his arms, silent, and then the tension seemed to melt from her. She began to weep again.

"Is that a yes?" Nicholas asked.

She nodded against his shoulder.

Nicholas released his breath. He leaned back into the

corner of the hackney, drawing her with him. "Hush," he said, and laid a kiss on her soft hair.

"I *never* cry," Isabella sobbed, her face pressed against his waistcoat, her fingers clutching the lapel of his coat.

Nicholas uttered a shaky laugh. "You are now, my love."

She drew a deep, shuddering breath and stopped crying. He felt the effort it took her.

Nicholas tightened his grip on her. He glanced out of the window. They were turning into Clarges Street. "I think your servants had better not see you like this. We can go to my house. There's no one there. I gave everyone the night off." *Because I didn't know what you would do when I found you. You might have turned your back on me. You might have hated me.* And he'd wanted no witnesses to the man he would have been if she'd done that.

Isabella nodded. He released her reluctantly as she sat up.

"We've changed our minds," Nicholas said to the jarvey as the man opened the door. "Take us to Albemarle Street, please."

Isabella groped in her reticule and pulled out a handkerchief. She wiped her eyes, blew her nose, folded the handkerchief and placed it neatly back in the reticule.

Nicholas held out his hand to her. Isabella hesitated a moment, then took it, allowing him to draw her into his embrace again. She relaxed against him, her head leaning on his shoulder. "I apologize," she said. "I don't normally cry."

Nicholas stroked his fingers lightly down her upper arm. *Mine.* "No more apologies," he said. "Let us agree that we both made mistakes."

Isabella sighed. He heard a vestige of tears in that soft, shaky sound. "Yes."

They sat in dark, swaying silence for a long moment, then Isabella said, "Are you certain? I'm much older than you wanted."

"I don't care how old you are," Nicholas said firmly.

"But I'm almost thirty—"

"I don't care if you're almost forty." He shifted on the seat, pulling her closer, bending his head to kiss her.

Their lips clung for a moment. Isabella tasted of tears.

The hackney jolted to a halt. Nicholas raised his head. Albemarle Street.

The major didn't let go of her hand as he unlocked the front door. He drew her inside. Isabella glanced around. The house was silent, dark except for a lamp flickering on the marble-topped table in the entrance hall. A candle stood in a holder alongside the lamp. Major Reynolds lit it one-handed.

Ahead, a corridor vanished into darkness. To the right loomed the staircase. The major's bedchamber was up there, somewhere. Isabella was suddenly nervous. Did Nicholas think that they—?

"This way," Major Reynolds said, and the gentle pressure of his hand drew her down the corridor with him.

Isabella relaxed. Not his bedchamber.

The major ushered her into what was clearly a library. The walls were dark with books, the writing on their spines gleaming faintly in the candlelight. "There should be a fire laid," he said. "Ah, yes . . ." He released her hand with what seemed like reluctance, touching his knuckles to her cheek in a light caress. "Have a seat while I light the fire."

Isabella chose a sofa. It was upholstered in a soft fabric. Damask? She rubbed her fingers over it.

He asked me to marry him.

The rush of emotion was so strong that she had to close her eyes, squeezing back tears. *He came back. He forgave me.* Elation might come tomorrow; tonight there was just relief. Relief so intense that it took all her effort not to cry again.

Isabella let out a shaky breath. She opened her eyes and

watched Major Reynolds light the fire. He was silhouetted by the candlelight. She saw the breadth of his shoulders, saw the muscled length of his thighs as he crouched, saw his profile. *The best of men.*

"Brandy?" he asked, straightening and turning to her. "I know it's not a lady's drink, but—"

"Yes," she said. "Please."

The major poured them both generous portions. He handed her a glass and stood looking down at her. Firelight flickered on his unscarred cheek. "Drink," he said.

She did, no sip but a mouthful, and then a second one. The brandy burned down her throat and took up residence in her chest, warm. As the warmth spread, the urge to cry faded.

Isabella released a deep breath. She felt herself relax. "Thank you," she said. "I needed that."

Major Reynolds sat beside her, so close their thighs touched. He took her free hand and interlaced his fingers with hers. "When would you like to marry? I confess that my preference is for sooner, rather than later."

Isabella leaned her cheek against his shoulder. "There is the problem of Harriet."

The major sighed. "Ah, yes. Harriet. I'd forgotten about her. Is she still with you? Hasn't she gone to her aunt?"

"Harriet's aunt has emigrated to America."

"Ah . . ."

She didn't need to elucidate; he understood the problem. Harriet was penniless and homeless and needed someone to look after her.

Major Reynolds swirled the brandy in his glass. "What would you suggest?"

"Well . . . there is a Mr. Fernyhough—"

The major uttered a sound that was halfway between a grunt and a laugh. "Fernyhough."

"What?"

"His name came up a few days ago. I wondered who he was."

227

Isabella told him, while Major Reynolds traced light circles on the back of her hand with his thumb. She explained about the affection that existed between Harriet and Mr. Fernyhough, and about Colonel Durham's refusal to countenance such a marriage. "If Mr. Fernyhough weren't obligated to the colonel, he could take Harriet to Gretna Green and marry her," Isabella said. "But he's supporting a widowed mother and a number of brothers and sisters, so he daren't."

"I see," the major said. His voice was thoughtful.

"I asked my brother if he had a vacant living, but he doesn't." She nestled her cheek on Major Reynolds' shoulder. Such a nice solid shoulder. "We must find Mr. Fernyhough a new living. A good one. And then he can marry Harriet."

Major Reynolds was silent for a moment. When she looked at him she saw that his brow was furrowed in thought. "I have a feeling there's a vacant living on one of my brother's estates," he said slowly. "I wish I could remember . . ."

"We'll find one," Isabella said. "Whether your brother has one or not."

"We will?" The major glanced at her. She saw a glimmer of amusement in his eyes.

"Yes," she said firmly.

"And how can you be so certain?"

"Because . . ." She paused, struggling to find the words to describe how she felt, the certainty, the knowledge that everything was going to work out. "Because three weeks ago I would have said this was impossible."

"This?"

"Us." *Being together like this, loving each other.* "And two days ago I would have said it was even more impossible."

"Ah." The sound was almost a sigh. "Yes." His fingers flexed around hers.

"If *this* can happen, then anything is possible. We'll find Mr. Fernyhough a living."

The major uttered a soft laugh. "Yes," he said. "I believe we will." He put down his glass and turned to face her.

"Isabella . . ." One of his hands still held hers in a tight clasp, the other reached to touch her cheek lightly.

Isabella caught her breath. That half-smile on his mouth, the dark intensity in his eyes, were familiar. *He's going to kiss me.*

He did, dipping his head, touching his lips to the corner of her mouth.

Isabella reached out blindly, trying to find somewhere to put her glass. The major took it without lifting his head. She heard a faint *clunk* as he placed it on the table.

His mouth moved against hers, his tongue touched her lips lightly, a question.

Yes. Isabella kissed him back.

It started gently, but quickly became something else, something intense, almost urgent. He tasted of brandy, he tasted of Nicholas. Isabella clutched him to her, her fingers digging into his arms. *Don't leave me ever again.*

She was trembling, panting, when at last they broke apart. Major Reynolds' eyes glittered blackly. "Isabella . . ." His breathing was ragged.

Don't stop. She said it aloud: "Don't stop."

His laugh was unsteady. "Isabella—"

"Not yet," she begged. "Please don't stop."

Nicholas exhaled a shaky breath. *I should take her home.* But instead of drawing back, he bent his head and kissed Lady Isabella again.

Long minutes passed, minutes when he was oblivious to the world, blind and deaf to everything except pleasure: the pleasure of her mouth, the pleasure of his hands tangling in her golden hair, the softness of her lips, the smoothness of her skin, the tiny sigh she uttered when he kissed her throat, her fingers clutching his coat, the building intensity of his arousal . . .

Stop this. Now.

Nicholas drew back, releasing her. He stood abruptly and walked to the fireplace. He stirred the fire with the poker and tried to gather his control, tried to drag enough air into his lungs to breathe properly again.

When he had regained some semblance of control he turned back to Isabella. She was sitting on the sofa, watching him, her eyes dark in the firelight.

As he watched, she shivered.

"Cold?"

"A little."

Nicholas held out his hand to her and she came, rising to her feet, walking to him. He took her hand firmly. *Mine.* "Here," he said. "Take this armchair."

But Isabella preferred to sit on the rug before the fireplace, gypsy-like, with her legs crossed under her. Nicholas sat at an angle to her, his legs stretched out, leaning against the leather armchair, holding her hand, watching the firelight cast shadows over her face, over the column of her throat, the hollow of her collar bone.

The earrings swayed gently from her earlobes, ruby and pearl, barbaric in the firelight. He reached out with a finger and touched one.

She glanced at him and smiled. "You like them?"

"Yes." He liked the rosettes of pearls fastening the robe across her breasts even more. They gleamed against the dark red. *Unfasten me*, they begged.

He curled his fingers into his palm and tried to ignore the rosettes. *I should take her home now.* But there was deep contentment in sitting with Isabella like this, in quiet closeness, in firelight and shadows. He searched for a topic of conversation, something that would take his mind away from those glinting pearls. "Have you found a home for the last kitten?"

"I'm keeping her," Isabella said. "She purrs whenever I pick her up. I can't give her away."

"What will you name her?" What had she named the black one? Ah, that was it: Boots. "How about Puss?"

Isabella grinned at him. "I thought of that. But no."

The most beautiful thing about her face, Nicholas decided, was the crookedness of her lower teeth. Without that she would have been too perfect, untouchable; with it she was . . .

The shaft of desire was intense. The sense of possession was equally fierce. He tightened his grip on her hand. *Mine.* "What then?" he asked.

"Something beginning with M." Isabella touched her fingers to her forehead. "She has an M, right here."

Nicholas thought. "Martha."

"No," Isabella said, showing her teeth again in another grin.

"Matilda. Mary." If she grinned at him again he was going to have to kiss her. He focused his gaze on the fireplace. "Er . . . Minerva."

"Minerva!"

"I have an aunt called that," Nicholas said, risking a glance at Isabella. She was still grinning. He swallowed and looked away again. "How about . . . Methusela?"

Isabella laughed.

The sound drew his head around. He couldn't *not* look at her. And having looked at her, he couldn't not lean towards her and kiss her.

They kissed for long minutes until the pain of arousal made Nicholas draw back. "Isabella . . ." He was trembling. *I have to take her home.* He turned his face away from her and dragged air into his lungs.

"Don't stop," Isabella said. She touched the back of his hand with light fingers.

His laugh was unsteady. "I have to."

"No," she said. "Nicholas, please don't stop."

The tone of her voice registered: low, as breathless as he

was, and oddly serious. He turned his head and looked at her.

"Please, Nicholas," she said in that same serious tone. "Don't stop."

"Isabella . . ." He halted. She knew what she was asking. He saw the knowledge on her face.

Nicholas cleared his throat. "Why?" Was she giving herself to him as an act of penance? He tensed, ready to refuse.

Isabella removed her fingers from the back of his hand. "Because I want you," she said with her frank honesty. "I want all of you."

I want all of you, too.

Nicholas released the breath he'd been holding. *I should refuse. She deserves better than this.* He thought of wide beds, of clean white linen.

"Please, Nicholas."

And so he reached for her, knowing that this time he wouldn't stop. He kissed her mouth, her throat, the hollow of her collar bone, and then he undid the pearl rosettes and the red crêpe robe fell from her shoulders.

The minutes passed slowly, with low murmurs and soft whispers as they unfastened each other's clothing and laid it aside. His tailcoat first, and her cream silk slip. His neckcloth, her petticoat. His waistcoat, her half-stays and stockings. Nicholas removed his linen shirt, baring his torso to her, and then gently, slowly, peeled off her thin chemise. "Lie down," he whispered.

Isabella obeyed. She lay naked on the rug. Nicholas looked at her in wonder. She was Venus, pale and golden in the fire-light. His hands trembled as he touched her, skimming over that smooth skin. *Like warm silk.* And then he bent his head and kissed her, tasting her mouth again, tasting that firelit skin.

He touched her with his fingers, with his lips, with his tongue, learning her, worshiping her: the weight of her breasts as he held them cupped in his hands, the soft gasp she uttered when he took those rosy nipples in his mouth, the way her muscles fluttered beneath his hand as he stroked down her belly.

Arousal flushed her skin. She was quivering, trembling. "Nicholas, take off your breeches." Her hand was at his waist, trying to find the buttons.

"Not yet," he said, capturing her hand, kissing the palm, placing it above her head. He bent to kiss her breasts again, her belly. The faint fragrance of her arousal went straight to his groin. His cock was painfully hard, painfully hot. He squeezed his eyes shut, struggling for control—*not yet*—and then opened them, seeing pale skin gleaming in the firelight, the dip of her waist, the rich curve of her hip, the golden curls at the junction of her thighs. "Not yet," he said again, and slid his hand down her inner thigh.

Isabella caught her breath. She trembled.

"Not yet," he said a third time, whispering the words, sliding his hand back up the smooth, silken skin of her thigh.

He explored with his fingers, finding his way through those soft curls, stroking and teasing, delving inside her, watching arousal take hold of her, feeling the heat and urgency build, listening to her breathing become fast, become ragged. She arched against his hand. "Nicholas."

He lowered his head, inhaling her scent—and gave in to the temptation to taste her. At the touch of his mouth, she broke, pleasure shuddering through her. He almost broke, too, muscles clenching in his chest, in his groin. His cock strained in his drawers, hot and aching.

He rose on his elbow, reaching for her, holding her tightly. Isabella clung to him, her face buried in his shoulder. Her lips were parted. He felt her breath against his bare skin, felt her tremors ease. "Nicholas . . ." She swallowed. Her voice was steadier, firmer: "Nicholas, I think you should take off your breeches *right now*."

He laughed, a shaky sound, and released her and climbed to his feet. He stripped off his remaining clothing while she watched. His cock lunged free, desperately eager. He stood still for a moment and let Isabella look at him. Her eyes were wide as she examined his groin.

"Don't be afraid."

Isabella swallowed. "May I . . . ?" She reached hesitantly to touch him, her fingers brushing over the sensitized head of his cock.

Nicholas almost climaxed from that light touch. He captured her hand. "Later." When his control wasn't so precarious.

He stretched his body on the rug alongside her. Her hair lay tumbled, a golden spill in the firelight. The ruby and pearl earrings gleamed at her ears.

"I'll try not to make it hurt, but the first time—"

"I know," Isabella whispered, touching his scarred cheek with a fingertip. "Don't worry about it."

The words made him pause. "You know?"

"Parlor gossip." Her cheeks colored slightly.

Nicholas uttered a laugh. He bent his head to kiss her, brushing his lips lightly over her temple. "Parlor gossip? You discuss lovemaking with your friends?"

"Not now." Her breath hitched as he bit her earlobe gently. "My first Season. There was curiosity among some of the girls."

He laughed softly, and kissed his way along her jaw until he found her lips again. He deepened the kiss, losing himself in the taste of her mouth, stroking a hand down her body, pulling her close, fire-warmed skin to fire-warmed skin, and then he raised himself above her, in the darkness, in the firelight. *Take it slowly*.

His control held, barely, as he slid inside her. There was a moment when Isabella tensed, when he held himself motionless, panting, unable to speak, unable to ask if he was hurting her, and then she relaxed and her body opened to him.

Nicholas sank into her, into heat, into pleasure. A groan rose in his throat. He bowed his head and squeezed his eyes shut. *Control.* He tried to find the ability to speak. "Isabella . . . is it all right?"

"Yes." A single, breathless word.

Nicholas raised his head. He stared at her, at the dark eyes reflecting the firelight, at the flushed cheeks, the soft, parted lips.

Mine.

And then he released his control, stopped holding back, simply let go. His world narrowed to this woman, this firelit rug, to the movement of their bodies, to how perfect they were together, her hips lifting instinctively, matching his rhythm. He was no longer afraid he'd climax too soon. He could go on forever like this, glorying in the exquisite pleasure, the sheer perfection of making love to Isabella Knox.

Arousal built inside him, twisting tighter and tighter, so tight it almost hurt. Isabella climaxed, arching beneath him with a breathless cry, her sleek inner muscles milking his cock, tipping him over the edge. His climax rode a knife-edge between pleasure and pain. It left him dazed and breathless, trembling.

He held Isabella close as their breathing steadied. He was aware of his heartbeat slowing, sweat cooling on his skin, the scent of their lovemaking. He pressed his face into her hair and inhaled deeply. *Mine.*

"I hadn't realized it was that good," Isabella said against his shoulder.

Neither had I. If kissing Isabella had been incredible, making love to her had been a thousand times more incredible.

She pulled back from him slightly and looked at him. Her mouth was soft and smiling. She lifted her hand and touched his scarred cheek with light fingertips. "I love you, Nicholas."

"I love you, too."

"I never thought it would happen."

"Neither did I."

Her fingers traced the ridges of scar tissue across his cheek. "Lucky," she said quietly.

He smiled at her. "The luckiest man in England."

He saw the shine of tears in her eyes before her arms came

around him. She clung to him, her face pressed against his shoulder. Nicholas held her tightly. *Mine.*

"When can we do that again?" Isabella asked, her voice slightly muffled against his shoulder.

Nicholas laughed, and tightened his grip on her. "Every day, once we're married."

He allowed himself to imagine the future: taking Isabella home to Elmwood. They'd be friends, lovers, parents. The Jacobean house would echo with the sound of laughter and children's voices, with *life*.

His throat tightened in a sudden, intense rush of emotion. He closed his eyes and held Isabella close. He didn't want to let her go. Ever.

He listened to their breathing for several minutes, to their heartbeats, to the sound of the coals shifting in the fire, to the ticking of the bracket clock on the mantelpiece, before sighing and releasing her. "I have to get you home. Your servants will be wondering where you are." *And mine may return soon.*

He sat up.

Isabella sat up, too. He let his eyes feast on her for a moment. She was beautiful, dressed in nothing but shadows and firelight, the earrings glinting like barbaric pendants at her earlobes and her wheat-gold hair tumbling in long coils over her shoulders.

"Botticelli's Venus," he said aloud.

"What?"

"You look like Botticelli's Venus." *Rising naked from the sea.*

Isabella pulled a face. "I look like a Dresden china milkmaid."

The comment, the unexpected accuracy of it, surprised a laugh from him. The golden hair, the milk-white skin, the rosy cheeks . . . she was absolutely correct. "You don't like your coloring?"

"I would much rather be brunette," Isabella said frankly.

"But if you were brunette you couldn't be Botticelli's

Venus," Nicholas said, smiling at her. *You couldn't be* my *Venus.*

She made a sound of amusement. "True."

Nicholas pushed to his feet. He held out his hand. "Let me get you home."

*C*HAPTER 24

*O*n his way to Clarges Street the next afternoon, Nicholas passed the tall townhouse belonging to his brother. To his surprise, the knocker was on the door. Had Gerald returned to London?

On impulse he ran up the steps. His hand was still on the knocker when the door opened. Hampton, his brother's butler, and his father's butler before that, favored him with the slightest of smiles and gravely bade him enter.

"Is my brother in?"

"In the library, sir," the butler said, relieving him of his hat and gloves.

"No need to announce me." Nicholas strode down the corridor. His mood was buoyant. Isabella was right: the impossible was possible. If Gerald didn't have a vacant living at his disposal, someone else would. The problem of Harriet would be solved. It was only a matter of time.

He tapped once on the door to the library and pushed it open.

Gerald looked up from the newspaper he was reading. His heavily jowled face seemed to tighten. "Nicholas. I thought you were out of town."

And you wish I still was, Nicholas thought wryly. "I returned yesterday," he said, closing the door. "And you?"

"The same." Gerald folded the newspaper, a brisk, irritated rustle of sound. "What do you want?"

"I came to ask a favor of you."

Gerald uttered a bark of laughter, a humorless sound. "You?" he said, giving the word a bitter inflection. "Ask a favor of *me*?"

Nicholas stood silently for a moment, looking at Gerald, seeing the signs of anger: the pinched mouth, the flush of color rising in his brother's cheeks. "I'll come back later," he said, and turned to leave.

"No," his brother said, in a flat voice. "Ask me now. I want to hear this."

Nicholas turned back to face him. "Very well," he said mildly.

Gerald had been prepared for argument, his mouth already open. He sat for several seconds in surprise, bristling, and then closed his mouth.

Nicholas walked over to an armchair and sat. For a moment there was silence, broken only by the ticking of the clock on the mantelpiece. Was Gerald going to offer him something to drink?

Gerald folded his arms across his chest. "Well?" he asked. The word was short and pugnacious.

No drink, Nicholas thought wryly.

"What's this favor?"

Nicholas's thoughts strayed briefly to Lady Isabella. Some of his optimism returned. "I have a request," he said. "I don't know whether you'll be able to grant it or not."

His brother grunted.

Nicholas gave a brief account of Harriet Durham's predicament, carefully avoiding identifying Lady Isabella as the girl's benefactress. His pity for Harriet returned as he spoke. It was a dreadful fate she had found for herself: to be without family, with no means of supporting herself and with her reputation gone. He introduced Mr. Fernyhough's existence, and explained the man's dilemma. "If Mr. Fernyhough were to receive another preferment, then he'd be able to marry Harriet Durham."

"A jilt!" Gerald said. "What man would want to marry her?"

"Mr. Fernyhough, apparently. If he wasn't indebted to Colonel Durham."

Gerald sniffed.

Nicholas leaned back in the armchair. "So that's the favor. If you have a vacant living, would you consider conferring it on Mr. Fernyhough?"

Gerald's mouth was a thin line. One of his fingers flicked the arm of his chair, a sharp, angry sound: *tap-tap-tap*. "Why do you care about this girl? She made a fool of you!"

"I feel some responsibility for her," Nicholas said. "She was to be my wife."

Gerald sniffed again.

"I'd like to have her future assured as soon as possible." Nicholas eyed his brother—*Should I tell him now?*—and came to a decision. "I'm getting married."

"You are?" The tapping finger stilled.

"Yes," Nicholas said. "Isabella Knox has agreed to marry me." The emotions of last night—the joy, the exhilaration, the wonder—returned. He discovered he was grinning like a fool.

"Isabella Knox? You?"

"Yes," Nicholas said, his grin widening.

Gerald didn't congratulate him, instead he sat silently. His face seemed to swell, his cheeks to darken.

Nicholas's grin faded. "Gerald?"

"I have a vacant living," his brother said, his voice thick with rage. "But if you think I'll give it to your Mr. Fernyhough, you're vastly mistaken."

Nicholas stared at him blankly. "Gerald? Why—"

"Why?" Gerald heaved himself out of his chair. "Because it's what you deserve, you son of a bitch." His hands clenched into fists. "Don't ever ask a favor of me again!"

Nicholas stood slowly. "Gerald—"

"Get out of my house!"

Nicholas looked at his brother's face, congested with anger, and silently obeyed. He shut the door behind him and stood for a moment in the corridor. What had just happened?

He walked slowly back to the entrance hall. The butler met him with his hat and gloves.

"Lord Reynolds isn't in the best of moods today," Hampton remarked in a voice that was utterly expressionless.

"No," Nicholas said. He accepted his hat and stood holding it, staring back towards the library. What the hell had just happened?

"Master Harry has decided to join the army," Hampton said. "The Rifle Brigade."

"Ah," Nicholas said. Understanding dawned. He felt a brief flare of outrage. *He thinks I talked Harry into it. He thinks I broke my word.*

Nicholas took a step towards the library, halted, and turned back to the butler. "I'll come back later."

"Very good, sir." Hampton opened the door. A blustery wind gusted in.

Nicholas walked slowly down the steps. He stood for a moment on the street, turning the hat over in his hands, frowning. *Gerald thinks I broke my word.* He glanced up at the townhouse, at the flat, gray stone, the blank windows, and felt oddly disturbed.

Later. He gave himself a shake. He'd deal with Gerald later. Now, he was late to see Isabella.

His grimness stayed with him until he turned into Clarges Street, but with Lady Isabella's house in sight it was impossible not to feel the joy again. *She's mine. She'll be my wife.* And that word—wife—encompassed so many things: the person he would live the rest of his life with, would talk with and laugh with forever, would make love to and sleep beside. The person with whom he'd raise a family. The person he belonged to.

Wonder filled him. How had this come to be? That he belonged to Isabella Knox, and she to him?

Nicholas paused in front of Isabella's house. He recalled her words the evening they had met: *I'm an eccentric.* He shook his head in disagreement as he climbed the steps. Isabella was different from other ladies of the *ton,* but she wasn't eccentric; she was herself.

Now, if she took to dressing Rufus in clothing and letting him dine at the table . . .

He swallowed a laugh and plied the knocker to the door.

The butler bowed him in, took his hat, and told him he was expected. Nicholas trod up the stairs behind a footman with a light heart.

The footman opened the door to the morning room. Isabella stood at the window, bathed in sunlight. She turned to face him. The smile in her eyes—*For me alone*—made him breathless. She came towards him with her hands outstretched. He took them as the footman closed the door, drew her to him, embraced her. *Mine.*

When one of the kittens began to sharpen its claws on the major's boots, they broke apart laughing. Isabella picked up the kitten. It started to purr immediately, a warm rumble in the palm of her hand. "See?" She stroked a light finger over the kitten's brow, tracing the letter. "She needs a name that begins with M."

"Moppet," the major said, bending to pat Rufus.

Isabella sat on the yellow damask sofa, holding the purring gray-striped kitten. "She's not a Moppet."

Major Reynolds sat beside her, a smile in his eyes. *How did I ever think of him as hard-faced?* "Molly," he suggested.

Isabella shook her head. "One of the maids is called Molly."

The major leaned closer. "Marry Me," he said.

Isabella pursed her lips and pretended to think about this. "That doesn't really sound like a name for a kitten."

"How about, Kiss Me?" he asked softly, in her ear.

"That doesn't begin with M," Isabella said primly. She glanced at him, trying not to let a smile escape, and failed.

"Doesn't it?" One of his fingertips trailed along her collarbone. It traced a light, tickling path up the side of her neck, and then along her jaw, stopping beneath her mouth. "Are you certain?"

"Yes," she whispered, lifting her mouth, kissing him.

Long, lazy, sunlit minutes passed. The kitten fell asleep on Isabella's lap while Major Reynolds kissed her gently and thoroughly, and while she kissed him back, trying to tell him without words how much she loved him.

"I think Kiss Me is a good name," the major said, when at last he raised his head. He put an arm around her, settling her against the warmth of his body, and pressed a light kiss to her hair.

"Marry Me is even better," Isabella said, resting her cheek on his shoulder. She drank in the sensations—his warmth and solidity, the firmness of his shoulder and the strength of the arm that held her, his clean male scent. Contentment filled her, so pure it was almost painful.

She closed her eyes. *What did I do to deserve this man?*

"When would you like to marry?" the major asked, stroking her hair.

"As soon as you've met my brother, Julian. I think he'd be hurt if we married before he met you."

"Of course," the major said. "He lives in Derbyshire, doesn't he? Would you like to marry there?"

Isabella opened her eyes. "Yes. I'd like that very much."

"I'll get a special license," Major Reynolds said. "We can travel to Derbyshire next week and marry without waiting for the banns to be read." He paused, and then said, "About Harriet . . ."

A light, timid knock sounded on the door.

They pulled hastily apart.

"Come in," Isabella said, as the major stood and walked

to the window. The gray-striped kitten was mewing in her lap. She placed a hand on it, soothing, shushing, as the door opened.

Harriet stood in the doorway. Her face was pale and her eyes, as she looked from Isabella to Major Reynolds and back again, were dark and frightened.

"Harriet?" Isabella glanced at the major, standing at the window. His face was utterly expressionless.

"I . . . I wish to speak with you."

"With me?"

"With both of you, ma'am."

"Then please come in."

Harriet stepped inside and closed the door. Rufus trotted over to greet her. The girl shrank back.

"Rufus." Isabella clicked her fingers. *Poor Rufus,* she thought, rubbing the dog's warm, silky head when he came to her. *Nearly a month and she's still afraid of you.* "What is it, my dear?"

Harriet came no further into the room. She stood with her back pressed to the door. "I wish to . . ." She swallowed. Her gaze flicked to Major Reynolds and away. An emotion crossed her face too swiftly for Isabella to identify it. Fear? Revulsion? "I wish to apologize for jilting you, Major Reynolds." She spoke the words to his shoulder, not his face.

"Thank you, Miss Durham." The major bowed slightly. His voice was light and pleasant, polite.

"And . . ." Harriet clasped her hands tightly together and visibly gathered her courage. "And I wish to marry you."

Isabella saw the astonishment on Major Reynolds' face, saw his blink of surprise.

"It was wrong of me to disobey my grandfather, and wrong of me to jilt you, and I'm very sorry, and . . . and I wish to make it right and marry you." Harriet finished in a rush, still not looking the major in the eye.

Isabella exchanged a glance with Major Reynolds. She was too shocked to speak. Fortunately, the major wasn't. "I'm sorry,

Harriet," he said gently. "I'm betrothed to someone else now. I can't renew my offer to you."

The words brought Harriet's gaze to his face. She stared at Major Reynolds. Isabella saw her dismay, saw tears well in her eyes.

"Lady Isabella and I are getting married," Major Reynolds said, even more gently.

Harriet's gaze jerked to Isabella.

Isabella attempted a smile.

"Oh," Harriet said, the sound almost a sob. "I wish you happy." She gave a tragic, watery smile, then turned and ran from the room.

There was a long moment of silence, and then Major Reynolds turned to Isabella, his expression baffled. "Why the devil does she want to marry me now?"

"I imagine she's afraid for her future." Isabella scooped the kitten from her lap and stood. "I'd best go after her."

The major caught her hand. "Give her some time." He drew her into an embrace.

Isabella didn't try to pull free. She felt quite shaken. "Nicholas, are you certain that—"

"If you dare to ask whether I'd rather marry Harriet than you—if you dare even to *think* it—then I swear to God that I'll beat you soundly."

Isabella managed a weak chuckle. Some of her tension eased.

The major's grip on her tightened. He whispered in her ear, "I will never beat you."

"I know," she whispered back. And then she sighed. "Why do I feel guilty? As if I've stolen you from her?"

"You haven't," he said. "So don't think it."

"No." She sighed again.

Major Reynolds rested his cheek on her hair. "Harriet Durham may have been my first choice and Clarissa Whedon my second, but you, Isabella Knox, are my *best* choice. Don't ever doubt it."

*C*HAPTER 25

*I*sabella thought she understood why Harriet had changed her mind about marrying Major Reynolds. Her grandfather had disowned her, her aunt had emigrated, and her last communication with Mr. Fernyhough had been a letter of farewell.

Harriet was afraid of the major, but she was even more afraid of earning her living.

Isabella remembered the list the girl had given her yesterday: *Invalid's Companion, Seamstress, Trimming Hats, Lady's Maid.* A daunting future for a gently reared girl.

Viewed dispassionately, marriage to Major Reynolds was a sensible choice. He might be an ogre, but he was an ogre who would take care of her. Isabella couldn't despise the girl for her change of heart. Many women in England had made similar decisions.

Harriet was in her bedchamber. One glance at the girl's face told Isabella that she'd been crying.

"Harriet? May I come in?"

Isabella had been afraid that Harriet might have cast her in the rôle of villain, but the girl appeared to have taken that mantle for herself. "What must you think of me?" she whispered, wringing her hands.

"I think that you're very afraid of your future," Isabella said. "But you have no reason to be, my dear. You have a home here until I see you safely established somewhere."

"You can't want me in your house!" the girl cried, mortification suffusing her face. "Not now!"

"Why ever not?" Isabella said, smiling at her. "Because I'm marrying Nicholas?"

Harriet gripped her hands even more tightly together, the knuckles whitening. "You must hate me."

Isabella laughed. "Quite the contrary. If not for you I would never have met Nicholas—or fallen in love with him."

"You *love* him?" Harriet said, her expression somewhere between disbelief and awe.

"I do." Far more than she had ever loved Roland. "So I'm very grateful to you, and I hope to return the favor and see you united with Mr. Fernyhough."

Harriet's eyes filled with tears. She looked away. "Malcolm and I can never marry," she whispered. "My grandfather—"

"I have every reason to believe that Mr. Fernyhough will come into possession of another living before long," Isabella told her.

"He has no connections," Harriet said, hunting for her handkerchief.

"He has me," Isabella said. "And through me, my brother—and he's a duke, you know. Between us we'll find Mr. Fernyhough a new living."

But this statement didn't have the effect she'd hoped for. More tears gathered in the girl's eyes. "I'm sorry to be such a burden, ma'am."

"You're not a burden," Isabella said. "Any more than the kittens are! Do you think I'd cast them out onto the street when they needed me? Of course not. And I shan't cast you out, either." She stroked a strand of hair back from the girl's flushed, tear-stained cheek. "Come now, my dear. Don't lose hope. Everything will sort itself out."

Harriet dabbed her eyes with the handkerchief and gave a wan, valiant smile.

Next, Isabella broke the news of her betrothal to Mrs. Westin. "I can't deny that I've longed for this moment," her cousin said, laying down her knitting. "It's troubled me to see you live your life alone."

"I've been perfectly happy," Isabella said, taken aback.

"You'll be much happier with a husband to guide and protect you."

Isabella opened her mouth to tell her cousin that she wasn't marrying Major Reynolds for either of those reasons— and decided it would be a futile argument. She changed the subject instead. "You may stay in this house once I'm married. It's yours for as long as you like."

"Thank you," Mrs. Westin said, picking up her knitting again. "But if you no longer require a chaperone I shall move to Bath. I prefer it to London."

"Oh," Isabella said, even more taken aback. "You never said so."

"Of course not," Mrs. Westin said, smiling gently. "Why would I?"

Isabella had no answer to this question. She listened to the brisk *click-click-click* of the knitting needles and plucked at a fold of her gown, pleating the muslin between her fingers, then said, "About Harriet . . ."

The knitting needles stilled.

"I know you've disliked the secrecy, Elinor."

Mrs. Westin gave a nod.

Isabella twisted the muslin between her fingers. "Once I'm married there's no reason for us to keep Harriet's presence hidden, only . . . I'm afraid it would invite gossip if she were to live with Nicholas and me, given her history with him."

"Gossip? Yes." Mrs. Westin pursed her lips in distaste.

"So, I was wondering . . . may Harriet stay with you as your companion? It wouldn't be for long," she said hastily. "Only until we find Mr. Fernyhough a new living."

The knitting needles began clicking again. "Of course she may stay with me."

"Thank you," Isabella said, relieved.

Sunday passed as Sundays generally did: quietly. Isabella attended church in a happy glow. Gussie cornered her after the service. "Well?" she asked.

"Well, what?"

"Are you all right? You left the Griffiths' so suddenly, and you weren't at the Fothergills' last night."

"I'm perfectly well," Isabella assured her. She bit the tip of her tongue, wishing she could tell Gussie her news. "Gussie, would you and Lucas like to come into Derbyshire next week?"

Gussie's eyebrows lifted in astonishment. "Derbyshire?"

"I know it's the middle of the Season, but . . . I thought you might like to."

Gussie subjected her to a quizzical stare. "We might? Why?"

"There might be a . . . a small celebration you'd like to attend," Isabella said, and felt herself blush betrayingly.

Gussie's eyes grew wide. Her mouth opened.

"You mustn't say anything!" Isabella said hurriedly. "I have to tell Julian first."

Gussie visibly swallowed whatever words she'd been about to utter. After a moment she said, "We'll come to Derbyshire. I promise." And then she grinned, looking as if she'd like to burst with excitement. "Hurry up and write to your brother!"

Isabella obeyed this dictate. Once home, she sat down and

penned a letter to Julian. *Nicholas and I are coming to Der-byshire to marry. Look for us next week. There's still the problem of Harriet's future to be dealt with, but she can live as Elinor's companion until a living is found for Mr. Fernyhough.* Next, she wrote to her sisters and to her brother, addressing Simon's letter to Naples and wondering when he would receive it.

As an afterthought, she sent a note around to Gussie, asking whether Lucas had a vacant living in his gift, and received the reply half an hour later: No.

She didn't tell Harriet. The girl had been extremely sub-dued all day.

Isabella went in search of her, and found her weeping over the newspapers. "Come now," she said gently. "There's no need for tears. Everything will work out."

Harriet made a heroic attempt to halt her sobs. "I'm sorry to be such a nuisance, ma'am. You must wish me gone. Espe-cially after yesterday."

"Don't worry about yesterday," Isabella said. "The major wasn't upset by it, and neither was I. Now, come help me with the kittens. The little rascals need feeding again. Did I tell you I've decided on a name for the gray? She's to be Mimi."

On Monday morning, Nicholas sat down at his desk and studied the list of things that needed to be done. Applying for a marriage license at the Archbishop of Canterbury's office at Doctors' Commons was the most important item on the list, but there was also the journey into Derbyshire to be arranged, and a multitude of other things, too. His marriage to Lady Isabella might be somewhat hasty, but it would be done *well.*

He lifted his head at the sound of voices in the corridor. "Don't bother to announce me," someone said cheerfully.

A tap sounded on the door, and his nephew strode into the study, grinning. "Sir! I have something to tell you!"

"You've joined the Rifle Brigade," Nicholas said, putting the list to one side. "Yes, I know."

Harry's grin widened. He pulled up a chair in front of Nicholas's desk and sat, leaning forward, words tumbling from his mouth as he explained with eager detail his decision to become a soldier. Nicholas watched his face, youthful, alight with enthusiasm, and felt a faint stirring of apprehension. *This could make a man of him, or kill him.*

"Did Mayhew put you up to this?" he asked, in the first pause that was offered.

Harry looked affronted. "No one put me up to it! I decided myself."

Nicholas stroked his ruined cheek with a finger. "It's not a game. You know that?"

"Of course I do," Harry said, looking even more affronted. "I'm not a child, sir."

A month ago you were a sullen boy. But the Harry seated in front of him bore little resemblance to the Harry of last month.

"No, you're not, are you?" Nicholas stood and offered Harry his hand. "I wish you all the best."

Harry grinned. The excitement lit his eyes again. "Thank you, sir." His grip was firm.

Nicholas resumed his seat. "How did you purchase your commission? I understood your pockets were to let."

Harry flushed and laughed. "It was a horse, sir, at the races." His flush deepened and his expression became half-embarrassed, half-defiant. "Its name was Ogre's Luck."

Nicholas grunted a laugh.

Harry looked relieved. "You don't mind, sir?"

"Ogre?" Nicholas shook his head. It was a connection he had with Lady Isabella, one that no one knew about. *She named me.* He touched two fingers to his scar. "Half of London calls me that now." But with no malice, no hint of ridicule. It was a nickname, nothing more. He shrugged. "It doesn't bother me."

Another ten minutes passed before Harry stood to leave. "You must be busy, sir."

Nicholas looked down at the list on his desk. He read the first item. *Obtain marriage license.* "I'm getting married."

"Lady Isabella Knox? Lord, as if we hadn't all guessed that! The pair of you smelling of April and May."

Nicholas felt himself blush faintly. "That obvious, was it?"

"Blindingly," Harry said. "Congratulations, sir." He shook Nicholas's hand enthusiastically and then took his leave. His footsteps, as he crossed the study, were brisk and eager.

A thought occurred to Nicholas as his nephew opened the door. "Harry?"

Harry halted. "Sir?"

"Do me a favor. Tell your father that your decision to join the Rifles wasn't at my persuasion."

Harry pulled a face. "He's in a foul mood."

"He's afraid for you."

Harry made a scoffing sound and looked away.

"He's your father and he loves you, and he's afraid of you dying on a battlefield."

Harry's gaze came back to him. He was silent for a long moment, and then he nodded. "I'll talk with him, sir." He raised his hand in a gesture that was vaguely like a salute, and closed the door behind him.

Nicholas listened to the sound of his footsteps fade, and then looked down at the list again. *Obtain marriage license.* He'd get started on that this morning, make his application at the archbishop's office.

Isabella saw Major Reynolds three times on Monday, once to give him her full name and her father's full name for the marriage license, once to drive in Hyde Park, and lastly when he escorted her and Mrs. Westin to the opera. He didn't steal a kiss in the shadows at the back of the box this time, but he did discreetly hold her hand during the performance, and it was magical: sitting alongside the major, listening to the music, holding his hand.

On Tuesday morning Harriet didn't join them for breakfast. Isabella eyed the empty seat. Was the girl upstairs crying? *I must find a way to cheer her up.* But how?

Isabella set that problem aside to ponder later, poured herself a cup of tea, and allowed herself to think of Major Reynolds. She ate her eggs without noticing, drank her tea without noticing. She jerked back to reality when Mrs. Early entered the breakfast parlor. The housekeeper's plump face was flushed, her manner flustered. "Ma'am," she said to Isabella. "Miss Durham isn't in her bedchamber."

"Not? Have you checked the morning room? The kittens—"

"She left these," Mrs. Early said, laying two letters on the breakfast table. "One for you, ma'am, and one for Mrs. Westin."

Isabella met her cousin's eyes. She snatched up the letter addressed to her, tore it open, and read swiftly and with a growing sense of shock. *You are too kind to say it, but I know I am a burden and an affliction,* Harriet wrote in a looping, childish hand. Tear stains blotched the ink. *I cannot repay your generosity and your many kindnesses by remaining in your house.*

"Harriet says that she's borrowed some money from my reticule," Mrs. Westin said in an astonished voice. "She promises to repay me." She looked up at Isabella. "Wherever can she have gone? And why?"

"She's gone because she thinks she's a burden." Isabella pushed up from her chair. "Mrs. Early, who's been waiting on Miss Durham? I wish to speak with her."

The new housemaid, Molly, had been attending to Harriet's needs. Miss Durham, she said with wide and anxious eyes, had asked her to run two errands for her.

"I posted a letter for her, ma'am," the housemaid said,

pleating her apron nervously between her fingers. "I didn't know it was wrong."

"It wasn't wrong," Isabella said, with a reassuring smile. "Do you remember the address?"

The housemaid shook her head, still looking frightened. "I don't read that well, ma'am."

"And the other errand?"

"I bought a ticket for her, on the stage. Had her name put on the waybill. Miss H. Durham. She wrote it down for me."

"Do you remember where she was going?"

"Chippenham," the housemaid said. "I'd never heard of it before." And then she added helpfully, "The stage left this morning, quite early."

"I see," Isabella said, trying to keep her tone even. "Is there any reason why you didn't inform Mrs. Early or myself that Miss Durham was leaving today?"

"I thought you knew, ma'am." Molly's eyes became even wider and more anxious. She twisted her hands in her apron. "Don't turn me off, please."

"I'm not going to turn you off." Isabella managed to smile at the girl. "Thank you. You may go."

When the maid and housekeeper had gone, Isabella looked at her cousin. "Chippenham? Why there?"

"I think I know," Mrs. Westin said, in a quiet, worried voice. She rose and left the room, returning in a few minutes with a newspaper. "There was a position in Chippenham for a lady's companion. Applications in person, it said." But the page with the advertisement was gone.

"I have to go after her," Isabella said, pushing to her feet. "She's far too young to go to Chippenham by herself." And too pretty, too innocent, too poor. The girl would be prey to all sorts of fiends.

She pulled the bell rope. "Have my carriage brought around," she told the footman. "Immediately." She halted in the doorway, looking back at her cousin. "Do you wish to come with me, Elinor?"

254

Mrs. Westin shook her head. "You'll be faster without me."

Isabella acknowledged this truth with a nod; Mrs. Westin was a poor traveler. She shut the door, picked up her skirts, and hurried upstairs. "Partridge! My carriage dress, quickly!"

*C*HAPTER 26

*N*icholas ran lightly up the steps to his front door, the marriage license in his pocket and a whistle on his lips.

"These were delivered while you were out, sir," his butler told him, presenting two letters. "By hand."

Nicholas took them. He recognized the handwriting on one of them: Gerald.

He opened Gerald's letter as he headed for his study, tearing the paper slightly, unfolding it one-handed as he reached for the brandy decanter.

He poured himself a glass and read the note, grunting when he reached the end. The living at Halvergate was his to dispose of if he wished. *An apology, Gerald?* If so, it was perfectly timed.

Nicholas put Gerald's letter aside and opened the second one, taking slightly more care, managing not to rip it. He raised the brandy glass to his mouth and read the first lines.

Nicholas,

Harriet has run off to Chippenham to apply for a position as a lady's companion.

Nicholas put the brandy glass down. He read swiftly. "Frye!" he shouted, striding from the study. "When was this letter delivered?" He thrust it at the man.

"About an hour ago, sir."

An hour. Nicholas reread the final line. *I'm departing London immediately and have hopes of catching her by Marlborough,* Isabella had written.

"Have my curricle brought around," Nicholas said, refolding the letter. "At once!"

By the time Isabella reached Hungerford, she was a mere half hour behind the Bristol stagecoach. One of the serving maids at the inn confirmed that Harriet had been aboard. "Little thing with brown hair?" she said, wiping her hands on her apron. "Looked as if she'd been crying." Harriet had purchased a glass of lemonade, but declined the ham sandwiches offered by the establishment.

Isabella glanced up at the sky. Clouds were gathering on the horizon. She wrapped her traveling cloak more tightly around her and climbed back into the carriage.

By Froxfield, they had gained further on the stage. The clouds had gained, too, massing darkly, their bellies almost resting on the ground.

"It left fifteen minutes ago?" Isabella asked.

"Yes, ma'am," the ostler said.

A long blast on a horn sounded, signaling a traveler wanting a change of horses. "'Scuse me, ma'am," the ostler said, and hurried off.

A curricle clattered into the yard, its horses streaked with sweat. Isabella's heart leapt. "Nicholas!"

Major Reynolds thrust the reins at his groom and jumped down, his driving coat flaring, the many capes fluttering like little wings. "I thought I'd have caught up to you before this," he said, reaching for her hands. "You must have been springing your horses."

257

"I have been," Isabella said, returning the pressure of his fingers. "We're only fifteen minutes behind them."

"Do you wish to ride with me?"

Isabella glanced at the sky, at the rain misting the horizon. "Yes."

She gave orders to her coachman while fresh horses were harnessed to the curricle, and climbed up into the seat vacated by Major Reynolds' groom.

The ostler stood away from the horses' heads and deftly caught the coin Major Reynolds tossed him.

"So Harriet wants to be a lady's companion?" the major said as he negotiated the turn onto the main street.

"No, not at all."

"Then why . . . ?"

"It's a Noble Sacrifice. She thinks she's a burden to me." Isabella pursed her lips thoughtfully. "But I think a great deal of it has to do with us. You and me."

The major overtook a wagon. "Us?"

"Our attachment. Harriet felt the awkwardness of Saturday quite acutely."

"Saturday?" He huffed a laugh. "Yes, it was more than a little awkward."

The major kept a sedate pace until they were out of Froxfield, then he let the horses have their heads. Hedgerows and ditches flashed past. Air scented with the smells of the countryside—grass, manure, woodsmoke—tugged at her bonnet. Isabella put a firm hand on it. The major snatched a glance at her, and grinned. "Feels a bit like a French farce, doesn't it?"

Isabella choked back a laugh at this unexpected humor. "A French farce?"

"Can't you imagine it at the theater? Everyone chasing each other across the stage?" He sent her another swift, grinning glance. "We have almost a full cast of characters. The damsel in distress, the cruel guardian, the loathsome suitor, the dashing hero waiting in the wings for his cue."

"Earnest hero," Isabella said. "Not dashing. Mr. Fernyhough is an earnest hero."

"Earnest hero, then," Major Reynolds said, feathering the reins as the curricle swept around a bend.

"What's my rôle?" Isabella asked him, amused.

"It's a puzzle. I'm not quite sure what Botticelli's Venus is doing in a French farce." He cast her another grin. "Perhaps you're meant to tame the loathsome suitor's ogreish heart?"

Isabella's own heart skipped a beat. *I love this man.*

A long stretch of road opened before them. Half a mile ahead was another coach. "Ah," the major said. "This looks promising."

Isabella held onto her bonnet as Major Reynolds urged the horses in a ground-eating gallop. The distant vehicle resolved itself into a large, top-heavy coach, moving with sluggish speed, and then, as they drew closer, into the Bristol stagecoach, piled with luggage and with three miserable passengers hunched on the outside seats.

Major Reynolds drew alongside and shouted at the coachman to stop. The man stared steadfastly ahead, ignoring him.

The major muttered under his breath. The curricle surged past the swaying coach and swung in front of it. Major Reynolds slowed his horses to a trot, keeping the curricle firmly in the middle of the road, with no room to pass.

Isabella clutched her bonnet even more tightly as the stagecoach loomed behind them. Noise enveloped her—the thunder of hooves and wheels, the shouted voices of men— and then the stagecoach slowed, too.

Major Reynolds brought his horses to a walk, and then a halt. "Here," he said, thrusting the reins at her. "Hold them."

Isabella did, twisting in the seat to watch as the major strode back to the coach. He overrode the coachman's indignant voice. "Looking for a runaway," he said curtly, and wrenched open the heavy door.

The reins tugged in her hand as one of the horses pulled at its bit. Isabella glanced at it, and then back at the stagecoach.

Major Reynolds was closing the door. His expression was frowning. He spoke with the driver. Isabella couldn't hear the words, but from his gestures he was describing Harriet.

The coachman shook his head. His answer was brief.

"Where is she?" Isabella asked as Major Reynolds climbed up into the curricle and reclaimed the reins.

"She got off at Froxfield," he said, guiding the curricle to the side of the road. The stagecoach rolled past, the outside passengers craning their necks to look at them.

"Froxfield? But she was booked to Chippenham. Why on earth would she get off early?"

"She was in conversation with a man. Not a passenger; a man who was at the inn. And she got off the stagecoach and asked for her luggage."

"A man?" Alarm leapt in Isabella's chest.

"Yes," the major said grimly, turning the horses. "We'd better get back to Froxfield. Fast."

Isabella glanced at his face, and past him to the undulating hills. They weren't far from where Harriet had grown up. "Perhaps Colonel Durham? Did the coachman say how old—"

"A young man."

"Did . . . did he say whether Harriet knew him?"

"He said that she was upset. Crying."

"Oh."

They drove in tense silence, pausing only to redirect her carriage when they met it. "Back to Froxfield," Major Reynolds instructed her coachman, not waiting to give an explanation.

Froxfield came into view. Isabella kept her eyes anxiously on the church spires, watching them grow nearer. At the inn, she scrambled down from the curricle before it came to a complete halt. She ran across the courtyard and pushed open the door, almost knocking over the innkeeper. "A girl," she said breathlessly. "A girl got off the stage. About half an hour ago. She met with a man." She was conscious of Major Reynolds behind her, blocking the doorway, huge in his driving coat. "Do you know where they are?"

"They're in the parlor, ma'am." The innkeeper gestured down the corridor. "But—"

Nicholas pushed past them both. His footsteps rang on the flagstones. He wrenched open the door to the parlor and stepped inside.

"Excuse me," Isabella said, and hurried after him. "Harriet—"

She halted in the doorway, taking in the scene: the small parlor with a sofa and two armchairs and a little oak side table, the man standing silhouetted against the window, his face freckled and earnest, his mouth half-open in shock, Harriet shrinking back on the sofa, a handkerchief clutched in her hand, and Major Reynolds standing in the center of the parlor. He was a tall man, and in this low-ceilinged room seemed even taller. A giant, in that many-caped driving coat. An ogre. He stood silently, not moving, and yet he filled the room with his rage. The sense of threat was so palpable that she understood Harriet's cringing terror.

"Mr. Fernyhough," Isabella said, stepping into the room. She closed the door on the innkeeper. "How very glad I am to see you."

The major's head swung around. His expression relaxed slightly. "Mr. Fernyhough?"

"Yes." Isabella smiled at the young man. She held out her hand. "How do you do?"

Mr. Fernyhough glanced at Major Reynolds, swallowed, straightened his spine, and pushed away from the window. He skirted the major warily.

I don't blame you, Isabella thought, as Mr. Fernyhough bowed over her hand. *I would be frightened of him, too.* How did Nicholas do it? There had been no shouting, no bluster, and yet he was clearly and quite unmistakably dangerous. "What are you doing here?"

Mr. Fernyhough glanced nervously at Major Reynolds again. "Harriet . . . that is to say, Miss Durham wrote to tell me that she was leaving London to seek employment in

Chippenham." His chin rose. The look he sent Major Reynolds was slightly defiant. "So I came to stop her."

"How very good of you," Isabella said warmly. She looked at Harriet, huddled on the sofa. The girl looked pale enough to faint. "Shall we partake of refreshments while we talk? Nicholas, if you wouldn't mind asking the innkeeper?"

Major Reynolds gave a short nod. With him gone, the level of tension in the room dropped markedly.

Isabella untied the ribbons securing her bonnet and removed it. She placed it on the little oak table and laid her gloves alongside. "Harriet, my dear," she said, going to sit beside the girl. "There was no need in the least for you to leave."

"I couldn't stay, ma'am," she whispered. "I just *couldn't*."

Major Reynolds reentered the parlor. His expression was mild, but both Harriet and Mr. Fernyhough flinched slightly. Isabella lost her smile. *Can't they see past the scar?*

Harriet's gaze darted to the major's ruined cheek and fell. She stared down at her handkerchief.

"Mr. Fernyhough," the major said, with a gesture at the door. "A word in private, if you don't mind."

Mr. Fernyhough swallowed audibly. "Of course, sir."

Harriet began to sob as the door shut behind the men. "He'll kill him—"

"Of course he won't!" Isabella said. She took a deep breath and made herself smile at the girl. "My dear, while I appreciate that you left my house with the best of intentions, I must tell you that it was completely unnecessary."

"I've been such a nuisance for you," Harriet said, weeping despairingly into her handkerchief.

"Nonsense," Isabella said. "My cousin has greatly enjoyed your company, and as I told you earlier, I'm indebted to you; I wouldn't have met Nicholas otherwise."

But these words didn't stem the flow of Harriet's tears.

How do I stop her crying? Isabella thought helplessly. To her relief the door opened again. Mr. Fernyhough stood on the threshold. His expression made her look at him more closely. Joy? She glanced enquiringly at Major Reynolds, standing behind him in the doorway.

"Harriet," Mr. Fernyhough said, stepping into the parlor. "There's no need to cry."

Harriet gulped and stopped sobbing.

"I think we can safely leave Miss Durham in Mr. Fernyhough's company," the major said, with a faint smile. He held out his hand to Isabella.

Isabella rose gratefully. She let Major Reynolds take her hand and draw her out into the corridor. "What . . . ?" she asked, glancing back at the parlor as the major closed the door.

"Mr. Fernyhough has something of a private nature to say to Miss Durham." The major led her down the corridor to the coffee room. It was empty.

"But what—?"

"I believe he's asking her to marry him." Major Reynolds escorted her to a cushioned bench beneath the window. Rain streaked the tiny panes.

"Marry?" Isabella said, sitting. "But he's beholden to Colonel Durham."

"Not any longer." The major felt in a pocket, and pulled out a letter. "The earnest hero has received his cue and will be sweeping the heroine off to Gretna Green later this month."

Isabella unfolded the letter and read swiftly. "A living in Norfolk?" She glanced up at him. "Oh, Nicholas!"

"What did I tell you?" he said. "A French farce. The hero and heroine have their happy ending and the curtain can now fall." He reached into his pocket again and handed her another letter. "This is *our* happy ending," he said softly.

Isabella unfolded the second letter—and discovered that it wasn't a letter at all, but a marriage license with the Archbishop of Canterbury's seal affixed to it. For a moment she couldn't breathe. Her gaze flew to him. "Nicholas . . ."

Major Reynolds sat beside her on the bench and drew her

into his arms. "Sometimes the villain gets to live happily ever after, too."

"You're not a villain!"

He grinned at her. "It's generally my rôle in plays."

"You might be Harriet's villain," Isabella told him, clutching the marriage license tightly, "but you're *my* hero."

The major laughed, and dipped his head and kissed her. "I love you."

"I love you, too." She breathed in his scent—dusty roads and horses—and then said fondly, "Ogre."

"The luckiest ogre in England," he said, and kissed her again.

Lieutenant Mayhew's

CATASTROPHES

A NOVELLA

CHAPTER 1

The stagecoach door banged shut and the guard gave a final blast of his horn. Willemina Culpepper only just managed not to wriggle with excitement. It was finally happening. Her journey had begun and in a few short seconds the miles would start to roll away beneath the carriage wheels.

Willie let out a tiny sigh of happiness. She wanted to bounce in her seat and say to her fellow passengers, *Oh, isn't it so marvelous to be traveling again!*

But she was twenty-five years old, and twenty-five-year-old ladies didn't wriggle or bounce or blurt out remarks to utter strangers. And, sadly, none of these strangers appeared to share her enthusiasm for travel. The stout matron alongside her sighed and muttered as she rummaged through her reticule. Dawn wasn't quite yet upon them. The carriage was full of shadows, only the faintest of illumination coming from the lamps outside, but there was enough light to see the matron dab the contents of a small vial onto her handkerchief.

A scent wafted its way to Willie's nose. Lavender. It mingled with the other smells in the narrow confines of the carriage: perspiration old and new, tobacco, ale, and for some reason that Willie couldn't fathom, marmalade.

The stout matron pressed the handkerchief to her nose and closed her eyes. A poor traveler, Willie deduced.

With a loud clatter of iron-shod hooves on cobblestones the stagecoach lurched into motion.

"Late," the other female in the stagecoach muttered. "Two whole minutes late already!" She was as thin as the matron was stout, her mouth pinched shut in a way that gave it wrinkles all the way around.

The stout matron sighed. So did the thin woman. Two different sighs. One long-suffering, one annoyed.

Willie bit back a smile. Not at the stout matron's discomfort or the thin lady's irritation, but a smile of gladness that she was in this carriage with them, that she was *moving* again.

She turned her attention to the final passenger. It was from him that the smells of tobacco and ale came. He wasn't sighing like the matron and the thin woman; he was already asleep, his chin pillowed in the folds of a rather dirty muffler.

The stagecoach navigated the tight corner onto the street, swaying ponderously as it did so. The matron moaned and pressed the scented handkerchief more closely to her nose.

Willie didn't mind the swaying in the slightest. She would have preferred to be up on the roof, where the swaying was at its worst, but respectable young ladies didn't travel on the roofs of stagecoaches, where their faces might become dusty and sunburned and their hair windswept, and where every Tom, Dick, and Harry might gawp up at them.

But even if she couldn't be on the roof, her heart beat as fast as the horses' hooves, a quick tempo of anticipation and happiness. Today, she was in London. Tomorrow, it would be Owslebury. And next month, she was off to the continent again!

Willie couldn't quite prevent a squirm of excitement. Fortunately, no one noticed.

The coach halted at the Bell and Crown, its final stop in London, and three more passengers came aboard: a woman and her young son, and a soldier.

The soldier was wearing the familiar green uniform of the Rifle Brigade, with the epaulettes of a lieutenant.

Willie's breath caught in a moment of pure homesickness. Although, could it be called homesickness when it wasn't a single place she missed, but many? She missed Egypt and South Africa and even the disaster that had been South America, and most of all she missed the people who'd been in those places. Men like her father. Men like the officer now settling himself opposite her. Men who'd worn uniforms. Men who'd trained and fought and endured hardship, who'd laughed and joked and lived with enthusiasm because they knew that death might be just around the corner.

Willie released a silent sigh. How she *missed* the army. Missed the people and the purpose, the busyness, the travel and the places, and yes, even the discomfort of being on campaign, the heat and the cold, the mud and the rain.

But not the deaths. She didn't miss those. What she *did* miss was the sense that every minute of every day was to be treasured, even if it contained sleet or choking dust or saddle sores, because today one was alive and tomorrow one might not be.

"*Three* minutes late, now," the thin woman said, as the guard secured the door.

That was another thing she missed: the stoicism of army life—and the jokes that went with that stoicism. Here in England, people complained if it rained, or if their shoes got muddy, or if a stagecoach was three minutes behind schedule. Soldiers didn't complain about the little annoyances of life; they joked about them. A lot.

Willie *did* miss the jokes.

"All aboard the coach to Southampton!" the guard cried, and gave a blast of his horn. Willie's heart lifted, while the stout matron sighed into her handkerchief and the thin woman looked at her timepiece and tutted sourly and the man with the dirty muffler snored faintly in his corner.

The mother was fussing over her young son, settling him

carefully on her lap, and the lieutenant was taking almost as much care with the covered basket he was carrying. He held on to it firmly, as if something breakable were inside.

The lieutenant glanced up, caught her gaze, and smiled cheerfully. "Good morning."

"Good morning," Willie said. She wanted to say more, wanted to say, *Tell me how things are with the Rifle Brigade. How's Colonel Barraclough? How's Charles Pugsley? What's it like in France right now?*

She would have asked those questions under other circumstances, but there was enough dawn light now leaking into the carriage to see the obvious appreciation in the lieutenant's gaze, and Willie had learned years ago that when men looked at her like that it was best not to encourage them. It had been true when her father was alive and was doubly true now that he was dead.

She was a female, she was alone, and she was on a public stagecoach, and as much as she wished to talk about the Rifle Brigade with this lieutenant, it was wisest not to.

Willie smiled politely at him as the stagecoach rolled out of the Bell and Crown's yard, springs creaking, wheels rattling, harness jingling jauntily. She turned her attention to the window and the glimpses of London it afforded—brick and stone façades, windows and doors. Dawn was pink above the roof tops. Her heart beat a happy rhythm. *It's started. I'm on my way.*

A tiny, shrill squeaking drew her attention. Not the squeaking of springs or wheels or harnesses, but a squeaking that sounded alive, and not only alive but *inside* the carriage.

A mouse?

Mice didn't scare Willie, but she didn't particularly wish to be in a stagecoach with one. Not once her fellow passengers realized there was a rodent aboard. The thin lady would undoubtedly have the vapors. Probably the stout matron, too.

She cocked her head, trying to determine the location of the sound . . . and realized that it came from directly opposite her. More precisely, from the basket that sat on the lieutenant's lap. The covered basket that he held so firmly and so carefully.

There wasn't something breakable inside, she realized. There was something *alive.*

The sound came again, high-pitched, more mew than squeak.

Willie glanced at the lieutenant. Their eyes met again in the half-light, and he gave her a wide, cheerful smile. He reminded her so much of the young officers who'd been under her father's command that her heart gave another great pang of homesickness.

"Your basket is making noises," the little boy seated on his mother's lap observed.

"So it is," the lieutenant agreed.

"What's in it?"

There was just enough light for Willie to see the lieutenant wink at the boy. "Baby monsters."

There was also enough light to see the little boy's eyes grow wide. "Monsters?"

"Monsters with teeth as sharp as needles," the lieutenant said, with utmost gravity. "And claws that would tear your clothes to shreds."

"Oh," the little boy said.

The lieutenant lowered his voice and said in thrilling accents, "I daren't let them out of the basket for fear of the havoc they would wreak."

The boy's eyes were now as round as saucers.

"Do you want to know what type of monster they are?" the lieutenant asked.

The boy nodded cautiously.

The lieutenant winked at him again and laughed, a merry sound. "They're kittens, my young friend."

The little boy laughed, too, a trill of delight. "Kittens?"

"A kitten apiece for my niece and nephew."

"Can I see them?" the boy asked eagerly.

"When we stop," the lieutenant said. "Kittens and carriages

don't mix." He smiled at the boy's mother. "And only if your mother allows."

There was enough light, too, to see the boy's mother blush upon receipt of that smile, as well she might; the lieutenant was a good-looking man, with his fair hair and his easy smile and his green rifleman's uniform. Quite dashing, in fact. But Willie had grown up following the drum. She had met a great many officers, handsome and otherwise, and she knew better than to judge men by their smiles. The lieutenant certainly *looked* attractive, but she knew nothing of his character.

Except that he was cheerful. And he liked to joke. And he gave kittens as presents to his nephew and niece.

They changed horses at Twickenham and again at Chertsey, and stopped for a meal at Bagshot. The lieutenant was first out. He set his basket on the cobblestones, then helped the stout matron, the thin lady, and the mother and her son to descend. When he held up his hand to Willie, she took it, even though she was perfectly capable of climbing down from a stagecoach by herself.

It would have been discourteous not to.

The lieutenant was even more handsome in full daylight than he'd been in the gloom of the coach. His eyes were a warm, laughing brown with flecks of gold.

Those laughing eyes and that charming smile and the smart green uniform made her heart flutter a bit. But only a *very* tiny bit.

"Can I see the kittens now?" the little boy asked. "Please?"

"Certainly," the lieutenant said. "Anyone who wishes may make their acquaintance." His smile included Willie.

Willie decided that she would quite like to see the creatures. Purely because she liked kittens. It had absolutely nothing to do with the lieutenant's eyes or his smile.

CHAPTER 2

*F*or a sixpence, one of the ostlers was willing to let Mayhew decant the furry monsters in an empty horse stall. He ushered his audience inside: child, mother, and one very pretty governess. At least, he assumed she was a governess. She was clearly well-bred, yet she was traveling on a stagecoach, and in Mayhew's experience respectable young ladies who traveled by stagecoach were usually governesses.

"They're a brother and sister," he told his audience, kneeling on the straw and unfastening the strap that held the basket closed. "Someone I know found them in a creek. Tied up in a sack."

"In a sack?" the little boy echoed, his eyes wide with dismay.

"He saved them all," Mayhew reassured him. "And a lady took them home and looked after them, and now they're big enough to have homes of their own. See?" He lifted the lid.

Two furry monsters blinked up at him and opened their pink mouths and mewed.

"Oh," his audience breathed in unison, drawing closer.

"Come on out, little rascals," Mayhew told the kittens. "Time to stretch your legs." And hopefully they'd pee into the straw while they were at it.

The fluffy black-and-gray female scrambled up the side of

the basket with the speed and determination of a foot soldier storming a defensive line, which Mayhew had expected. Her less fluffy gray-striped brother stayed where he was, in the warm nest of the basket, which Mayhew had also expected.

"Come along, my lazy friend," he said, lifting the little tabby out. "You can't sleep *all* day."

"What are their names?" the boy asked eagerly.

"I call this one Mr. Bellyrub," Mayhew said, and then he demonstrated why, cupping the kitten belly-up in his hand and rubbing his fluffy stomach.

Mr. Bellyrub immediately began to purr.

"Oh," his audience breathed again.

"Would you like to hold him?" Mayhew asked the little boy.

"Yes! Yes!"

The boy's hands were too small for Mr. Bellyrub to lie in, but his arms made a perfect cradle. Mayhew carefully transferred the kitten. Mr. Bellyrub didn't mind at all. He kept purring.

They made an adorable pair, child and kitten. The governess must have thought so, too, because she smiled—which made dimples spring to life in her cheeks, making *her* adorable, as well.

Mayhew admired her for a few seconds—the nutbrown ringlets peeping from beneath her bonnet, the straight little nose, the rosy lips. *Very* pretty. It was a shame she wasn't the type to make eyes at soldiers. A little flirtation would have whiled away the journey to Southampton most enjoyably, but he knew women well enough to know when they wanted to flirt and when they didn't, and this governess definitely didn't.

He turned his attention to the basket. The nest of rags was still clean and dry. Excellent. He looked around for Mr. Bellyrub's sister. Predictably, she'd vanished. "Uh-oh."

The governess cocked her head at him.

"The exploring officer is on the loose. Careful where you put your feet."

The governess's dimples made a reappearance. "Exploring officer?"

"She was born to be a reconnaissance scout." Mayhew climbed to his feet. "That's my name for her: Scout. Now, where did she get to . . . ?"

The fluffy kitten was at the back of the horse stall, relieving herself. "Well done," Mayhew told her. "Your timing is perfect."

Scout ignored him, and set out to investigate the rest of the horse stall. Mayhew wondered if she was hungry. "I'll fetch some milk," he told the governess. "Would you mind keeping an eye on her?"

"I shan't let her escape," the governess promised.

One of the inn's kitchen maids gave him two saucers of milk, a bounty that both kittens consumed eagerly, and then it was time to restore the furry monsters to their basket. Scout protested shrilly about her incarceration, but Mr. Bellyrub didn't appear to mind at all. In fact, Mayhew thought he was asleep before the basket lid had even closed.

There wasn't much time left for them to eat. Mayhew managed to secure a half-pint of ale and a slice of ham on bread, then the guard blew his horn and it was time to climb aboard. "We should have left ten minutes ago," the Friday-faced old lady scolded the guard. "Ten minutes!"

Mayhew swallowed the last of his ale, then went to help the young mother and her son to ascend.

The guard blew his horn again, a loud *blat* of sound.

"I shall complain to the company!" Mrs. Friday-Face told the guard.

The guard ignored her. "All aboard!" he cried.

Mayhew handed the governess up into the coach. The last of the roof passengers were scrambling into their places and horses were stamping and snorting, impatient to be off. He held out his hand to Mrs. Friday-Face. She ignored it in favor of berating the guard.

Mayhew shrugged, picked up his basket, and climbed

aboard. He settled himself on the narrow seat, bumping knees and elbows with his fellow passengers. One of the kittens mewed.

"Last call for the stage to Southampton!" the guard bellowed.

Mrs. Friday-Face finally climbed aboard, bristling with indignation. "Scandalous," she muttered, as she settled herself. "No attempt to keep to the time-bill at all."

Mayhew bit back a smile, and glanced at the governess. She was trying not to smile, too. He saw a dimple quiver in her cheek and—aha!—a tiny roll of her eyes, and then she realized he was looking at her and the dimple vanished. She averted her gaze.

The stagecoach lurched into motion, sweeping out of the inn yard. Mrs. Friday-Face examined her watch. "Twelve minutes late. *Twelve!*"

CHAPTER 3

*I*t appeared that the thin lady was going all the way to Southampton. She didn't get off in Frimley Green with the mother and her son, or in Basingstoke, when the man with the dirty muffler left the carriage. The smell in the stagecoach changed with each new passenger. Coffee when the attorney's clerk settled into his seat. Cabbage and sweat when the farmer came aboard.

At every stop the stagecoach fell a little further behind schedule—a fact that the thin lady didn't fail to remark on. Each time she did, Willie had to bite her lip a little bit harder to stop from laughing out loud.

The stout matron left the carriage at North Waltham, taking with her the scent of lavender. Her replacement was a sailor, and he was drunk. Willie knew that fact even before he climbed aboard. His too-loud voice told her, and the way he slurred his consonants.

The only vacant seat was next to Willie.

She drew her shawl more tightly around her shoulders and reminded herself that discomforts were part of travel.

"Move over," the lieutenant said in a low voice, as the sailor fumbled to heave himself into the carriage.

Willie glanced at him, and there was something so

authoritative in his face that she obeyed, shifting sideways into the warm spot the matron had left. The lieutenant moved, too, taking the place she'd vacated, and by the time the sailor had negotiated the steps, the empty seat was neither next to Willie nor opposite her.

She breathed a silent sigh of relief and loosened her tight grip on the shawl, while the sailor settled himself clumsily and then belched.

The guard closed the door and blew his horn, the driver cracked his whip, and the stagecoach lumbered into motion again. Beside Willie, the thin lady sniffed. "Seventeen minutes," she muttered.

The carriage had been small and cramped before. With the sailor in it, it was even smaller and more cramped. Or perhaps that was because the lieutenant was alongside her now. He seemed to take up more space on the seat than the stout matron had, although that couldn't actually be possible; the matron had been *very* stout, and the lieutenant was quite lean. But Willie was aware of him in a way she hadn't been aware of the matron, aware of his body pressed against hers—his arm, his thigh—and she was aware, too, of his strength and his heat and his maleness.

Willie felt suddenly self-conscious and awkward. Her cheeks grew a little warm.

To distract herself from the lieutenant, she discreetly observed the sailor. He was unshaven and bleary-eyed. The smell of gin wafted strongly from him. He belched again. His gaze drifted past Willie—and then swung back. He looked her up and down, a blatant leer. "You're a spruce one, you are."

"I suggest you keep your tongue between your teeth while you're aboard," the lieutenant said coldly.

The sailor took note of the rifleman's uniform and sneered. "Oh, you do, do you, swoddy?" Then his gaze rose to the lieutenant's face. The sneer faded so quickly that it was almost comical.

Willie bit her lip to prevent herself laughing.

"I do," the lieutenant said. His voice was hard and flat and dangerous, and Willie wasn't at all surprised that the sailor looked away.

Five minutes later, he was snoring.

"Thank you," Willie told the lieutenant, in a low whisper.

"You're welcome," the lieutenant whispered back. His voice sounded like it had before the sailor had climbed aboard, friendly and cheerful.

He'd be a good officer, Willie thought. The sort of officer that men respected. He knew when to laugh and joke, but he also knew when not to. And he knew how to make people obey him.

The lieutenant was still disconcertingly large and warm alongside her, but Willie no longer felt self-conscious. She felt safe. On the heels of that realization came a decision: at the next halt, she'd ask him about the Rifle Brigade. Yes, the lieutenant liked her looks, but she was no longer worried that he'd leer at her like the sailor had, or try to flirt with her, because he wasn't merely an officer; he was a gentleman.

They halted for another meal at Abbots Worthy. The lieutenant leapt down lightly, then turned to help the thin lady to descend. Willie gathered up her reticule and descended, too. This time she took the lieutenant's hand without a second thought, and noted again that yes, he did have *very* nice eyes.

She inhaled a deep breath that smelled of horses and horse dung and woodsmoke and roasting meat, while behind her the thin lady told the guard off. "Twenty-three minutes behind schedule! I shall complain to the company, don't you doubt it!"

Willie wasn't particularly hungry, nor did she wish to spend the allotted half hour sitting in a stuffy coffee room. "I'll help you with the kittens," she told the lieutenant.

His face lit up in a smile, and Willie told herself that her heart had *not* fluttered, although she was rather afraid that it had.

The lieutenant spoke to an ostler, a coin changed hands, and half a minute later she, the lieutenant, and the basket were in an empty horse stall. Alone.

For a moment Willie doubted her decision, and then she remembered his behavior in the carriage. The lieutenant was a gentleman and as long as *she* didn't flirt with him, *he* wouldn't flirt with her.

He crouched and opened the basket. Kittens blinked up at them. Willie smiled involuntarily, and crouched, too.

"Come on out, little monsters," the lieutenant said, and the kittens did, one after the other, mewing loudly. "I wager they're hungry. I'll fetch some milk."

"I shan't let Scout escape," Willie promised.

The lieutenant gave her a grateful smile and left the stall, careful to close the door behind him.

"Hello, sweethearts," Willie said softly, once he was gone.

The kittens mewed back at her. Monsters or not, they were darlings, with their round little bellies and bright blue eyes, their tiny pink tongues and sharp white teeth. Scout was quite fluffy, with patches of black and gray, while her sleeker brother had smart gray stripes. Willie laid her reticule to one side, picked Mr. Bellyrub up, turned him over, and rubbed his belly. To her delight, he immediately began to purr.

Willie stroked him, and felt the reverberation of his purr, and watched while his bolder sister staggered across the straw, apparently determined to explore all four corners of the stall.

Mr. Bellyrub closed his eyes and Willie felt him relax in her hand, a soft, warm bundle of contentment. By the time the lieutenant returned with two saucers of milk, the kitten was practically asleep, but he roused and mewed loudly to be let down.

Willie set him on the straw and he attacked the milk with so much enthusiasm that he stepped into the saucer.

Willie laughed, and so did the lieutenant. He had a very nice laugh. Her awareness of him spiked again, and with it, the awkwardness.

Idiot, she scolded herself. The lieutenant *was* very attractive, but she was in this horse stall because of the kittens and because she wanted to talk about the Rifle Brigade, not for any other reason. Accordingly, she said, "When did you join the Rifle Brigade, Lieutenant?"

He glanced at her, and she saw his surprise.

"My father was in the army," Willie told him. "He was invalided out in 1806."

The lieutenant sat back on his heels and looked at her, still with surprise on his face. "That was the year I joined the Rifles."

"You were on the Peninsula, then?"

He nodded.

She named several battles: "Salamanca? Vittoria? Tarbes?"

He nodded again.

Willie bit her lip, and then asked, "Badajoz?"

The lieutenant grimaced faintly. "Yes." He looked down at Mr. Bellyrub, then glanced back at her, hesitated, and said, "You know what happened there, I take it?"

"I do. My father corresponded regularly with Colonel Barraclough. He said—Barraclough, I mean—that the events at Badajoz brought discredit to the entire army."

"They did."

"Barraclough also said that he was proud of his officers, that they did everything they could to halt it."

It. An entirely inadequate word for the violence and rapine that had occurred after Badajoz fell.

"We did," the lieutenant said. "For what it was worth." He grimaced faintly again, then cocked his head and said, "Who is your father? What regiment did he serve in?"

"The Sixty-Ninth," Willie said. "He died last year. His name was Culpepper."

The lieutenant's jaw dropped. "Culpepper? Not . . . Colonel Culpepper?"

It was Willie's turn to be surprised. "Yes."

The lieutenant stared at her for a moment, open-mouthed, and then said, in a disbelieving voice, "You're Colonel Henry Culpepper's daughter?"

Willie nodded again.

The lieutenant finally remembered to close his mouth. He looked down at Mr. Bellyrub lapping his milk, and then back at her. This time his gaze wasn't friendly or appreciative; it was something much more penetrating. He looked at her—truly *looked* at her—a head-to-toe glance that was nothing like the drunken sailor's leer. Then, he shook his head and laughed. "So *you're* Sweet Willie."

Embarrassed heat rose in Willie's cheeks. "Wherever did you hear that name?"

The lieutenant shook his head again, laughed again. "The fellows who were in South America used to talk about you. A *lot.*"

"They did not," Willie said, as her cheeks grew hotter.

"They most certainly *did,*" the lieutenant said. "It was 'Sweet Willie this' and 'Sweet Willie that' the whole first year I was in the Rifles. Some of 'em are *still* talking about you. Barraclough, for one. Pug Pugsley, for another. And Sergeant Jones, remember him?" Then his expression became serious, solemn. "They're still talking about your father, too. By all accounts, he was a remarkable soldier. My condolences on his death."

Willie's cheeks cooled. "Thank you," she said quietly.

The lieutenant eyed her, a faint frown on his handsome face. "What are you doing on a stagecoach, Miss Culpepper? You're not a governess, are you?"

The disapprobation in his voice made Willie smile. "Not quite. I'll be more of a companion. My charges are sixteen and seventeen."

"But surely . . ." He halted, and looked a little abashed.

Willie answered the question that he clearly felt he couldn't ask. "I don't need a position, Lieutenant; I *want* one."

His frown became tinged with confusion.

Willie tried to explain: "England bores me. I want to travel again, and Sir Walter Pike, who's employing me, is a diplomat. The family is off to Vienna next month."

"Your father became a diplomat, I understand? After his injury."

Willie nodded. Colonels of infantry regiments needed two hands, but members of the Foreign Office didn't. "Yes. We were in Constantinople, then Russia, and lastly Brussels. If Father hadn't died when he did, we'd have been in Brussels during the Battle of Waterloo."

The lieutenant grimaced again, not the faint grimace he'd accorded Badajoz, but something much grimmer that thinned his lips and twisted his mouth. "Be glad you weren't there. Waterloo was . . ." He shook his head and reached for the basket.

"I heard it was bad," Willie said cautiously, as she examined the nest of rags.

"Very bad." The lieutenant looked down at the basket a moment longer, then glanced at her. "Have you ever seen an illustrated version of Dante's *Inferno*, Miss Culpepper?"

Willie nodded.

"Waterloo was like that. Only worse."

He was telling the truth—she could see it clearly on his face: the pinching at the corners of his eyes, the pinching at the corners of his mouth.

Willie acknowledged what he'd said with a nod, for it seemed to her that nothing she could say would be meaningful. The Battle of Waterloo had happened. It had been a terrible slaughter. Those were irrefutable facts, and platitudes and words of condolence wouldn't be in the least bit helpful now, nearly twelve months after that battle.

The pinching at the lieutenant's mouth and eyes faded. He looked down at the basket again and put it aside.

Willie changed the subject. "You're on furlough, I take it? Where are you stationed?"

"France." The lieutenant shook off his grimness and smiled at her. "Two of our battalions are there right now; the third's in Ireland."

They talked about army life while the kittens lapped their milk. The lieutenant told her some of the stories he'd heard about her and Willie had to confess that they were all true, and then he told her some of *his* misadventures. It was the most enjoyable conversation Willie had had in years. She couldn't remember when she'd last laughed so much. She heard the first warning blast of the guard's horn with something close to disbelief. Had she and the lieutenant been talking for half an hour?

She scrambled to her feet. "Where's Scout?"

The lieutenant stood, too. "She was in that corner, last I saw her. Probably made herself a nest." He scooped up Mr. Bellyrub and placed him in the basket.

Willie began searching in the straw for Scout. "I still don't know your name," she told the lieutenant.

"Mayhew," he said. "William Mayhew."

"William?" Willie said.

He grinned at her. "We share a name. Almost. I'm a Will, not a Willie." He rifled through the straw and called softly, "Here puss, puss, puss."

But Scout didn't poke her head up and mew at them.

The guard's horn sounded again.

Lieutenant Mayhew began to grope through the straw more urgently. "Go, Miss Culpepper."

"Nonsense," Willie said, widening her search. She checked one corner, and another. "Here she is!"

"Thank God." The lieutenant grabbed the basket and held it out to her—and said, "Uh-oh. Where's Bellyrub?"

The guard's horn blasted a third time.

Lieutenant Mayhew took Scout from her. "Go!"

Willie ignored him.

"Miss Culpepper—"

"I see him," Willie cried. She seized hold of the kitten, thrust him into the basket, then snatched up her reticule and ran to the front of the horse stall, drawing back the bolt and flinging the door open.

They burst from the stables, out into the yard, just as the stagecoach disappeared from view.

The clatter of hooves and jingle of harnesses faded from hearing. There was a long moment of silence, and then, "They left without us," the lieutenant said, a note of indignant disbelief in his voice.

CHAPTER 4

Miss Culpepper took it exceedingly well, Mayhew thought. But then, the daughter of Colonel Culpepper would. She didn't have hysterics or fly into a temper, she merely said, "Well, *that's* a slight setback," and turned to one of the ostlers and inquired about hiring a gig to take them to the stagecoach's next scheduled stop, which was Winchester.

By the time that Mayhew had fastened the basket lid properly, Miss Culpepper had ascertained that the inn did have a gig, that it was available for hire, and was in negotiations as to the price.

The ostler, no doubt thinking that they were pigeons to be plucked, named an extortionate sum. Mayhew opened his mouth to object, and then listened in admiration as Miss Culpepper proved that she was no pigeon. In fact, he suspected that the price she beat the ostler down to was less than anything he'd have managed.

But when she opened her reticule to pay, he said, "Absolutely not, Miss Culpepper. *I* shall pay for the gig."

Miss Culpepper, proving her intelligence further, didn't argue with him.

Mayhew handed over the coins. "The fastest horse you

have," he told the ostler. "And there's a half crown in it for you if we're gone in five minutes."

The ostler headed for the stables at a run.

The gig was ready in four minutes. Mayhew handed Miss Culpepper up onto the seat, passed her the basket, climbed up himself, and tossed the ostler the half crown he'd promised him.

They left Abbots Worthy at a brisk trot. Mayhew estimated that they were six minutes behind the stagecoach, possibly seven.

"I apologize," he said. "This is my fault."

"It's no one's fault," Miss Culpepper said cheerfully, clutching the basket with one hand and her reticule and shawl with the other. The tassels that fringed her shawl fluttered in the warm summer's breeze, and the ribbons on her bonnet did, too. "We'll catch up before the next stop."

Mayhew knew that they would. One horse pulling a light gig was faster than four horses pulling a heavy stagecoach. The chestnut was young, fresh, and perfectly willing to stretch its legs in a gallop. At every bend in the road, Mayhew expected to see the stagecoach ahead of them—until the horse went lame half a mile past Headbourne Worthy.

They went from tooth-rattling gallop to hobbling walk in the space of a few seconds.

Uh-oh, he thought.

Mayhew drew the gig to one side of the road, handed the reins to Miss Culpepper, and jumped down to examine the chestnut, hoping it was just a pebble lodged in a shoe.

But no, they weren't so lucky.

"Damnation," he said under his breath, and then, more loudly, "It's cast a shoe."

"At least it hasn't thrown a splint," Miss Culpepper said, which was a much better reaction than he'd expected.

"We'd best turn back to Headbourne Worthy," he said. "I'm sorry, Miss Culpepper."

"Don't look so worried, Lieutenant," she said, with surprising equanimity. "It's not the end of the world."

"But your employer—"

"Sir Walter is meeting me in Twyford tomorrow. As long as I'm at the coaching inn by nightfall, all will be well. And Twyford can't be more than a dozen miles from here. Even if I have to walk, I'll get there before dark."

The prospect of walking a dozen miles didn't seem to perturb her in the slightest, and Mayhew was reminded once again that she *was* a soldier's daughter.

"You won't have to walk that far," he promised her.

They did have to walk the half a mile back to Headbourne Worthy, though, leading the horse and gig. But although they were headed *away* from Winchester, and although it was now impossible that they'd catch up with the stagecoach, Mayhew couldn't regret it. He'd never enjoyed a walk more. He liked Miss Culpepper. He liked looking at her and he liked talking with her, and if they hadn't missed the stagecoach, and if the horse hadn't cast a shoe, then he'd have been wholly delighted to spend his time in her company. As it was, he was partly delighted and partly worried. Miss Culpepper shouldn't be wandering the countryside with him; this was how young ladies lost their reputations.

But no one would ever know, and he *would* get her to Twyford by nightfall.

Headbourne Worthy was very small. It didn't have a posting inn, but it did have a blacksmith. They left the horse and gig at the smithy, with instructions that both were to be returned to the inn at Abbots Worthy. Mayhew forked over some coins, retrieved the basket with the kittens, and asked the blacksmith how best to get to Twyford.

The man ruminated on this question, his jaws moving as if he were chewing cud, and then said, "Farm cart."

The blacksmith was a man of few words, but with a great deal of chewing and a great many pauses, he informed them that his aunt's brother-in-law's son would shortly be driving his cart from Headbourne Worthy to Winnall, that Winnall was only a mile from Winchester, and that in Winchester they could easily hire a carriage to take them to Twyford.

"When will the cart be leaving?" Mayhew asked.

"Once it's loaded."

"And you think we'd be able to reach Twyford by nightfall?"

The blacksmith chewed and thought and then gave his considered opinion: "Yes."

"Excellent," Mayhew said. "Where can we find this cart?"

They found the cart in the blacksmith's aunt's farmyard. The young farmer's load wasn't vegetables, as Mayhew had supposed, but pigs. *Uh-oh*, he thought for the second time that afternoon. He glanced at Miss Culpepper.

She interpreted his glance correctly. Dimples sprang to life in her cheeks. "Don't look so worried, Lieutenant. I have no objection to traveling with pigs."

"You don't?"

"No. Now, come along; it's time to haggle for our ride." She flashed him a smile and stepped into the farmyard.

Mayhew watched her pick her way through the mud and the puddles, and had a moment of astonished insight. Miss Culpepper was actually *enjoying* this.

CHAPTER 5

If their luck had been out earlier, it was now in. The cart was loaded and the farmer ready to depart. Five minutes later and they'd have missed him. As it was, they left Headbourne Worthy perched on the box seat of a cart carrying pigs. Nine pigs, altogether. Willie had counted. And handsome pigs they were, too. Black, with a white stripe over their shoulders.

The farmer was as garrulous as the blacksmith had been taciturn. He talked about his pigs and his other livestock and his crops and the spring just past and the summer they were having. Willie sat on the wooden seat and simply enjoyed it all: the fresh country air, the trees and the hedgerows, the grassy verges studded with wildflowers, the birdsong, the noises the pigs made, the slow *clop-clop* of the horse, the farmer's conversation, his broad Hampshire accent.

Headbourne Worthy to Winnall wasn't a post road; consequently it was not in good repair. The horse picked its way slowly, walking, not trotting. The cart jolted and lurched over ruts and through potholes and puddles, but Willie didn't mind the slowness, or the jolting, or the pigs. She drank it all in—the sights and sounds and smells. Traveling by farm cart was a thousand times better than sitting in a stagecoach, she decided, and perhaps she ought not to be relishing this unexpected little adventure as much as she was, but it was impossible *not* to relish it, partly because it reminded her of being in the army, and partly because there would be no opportunities to ride in farm carts with lieutenants who were carrying baskets of kittens once she was in Sir Walter's employ.

She liked this lieutenant. More, perhaps, than she ought to. She'd only just met him and yet for some reason Lieutenant Mayhew didn't feel like a stranger; he felt like a friend.

They came to a section of road where the ruts on one side had merged into a deep trough. "Hold tight," the farmer said, and jumped down to guide his horse. Willie braced herself. The cart tilted sideways as the wheels on the left descended into the trough and the wheels on the right didn't. The wooden seat was worn so smooth that Willie almost slid off it.

"Careful, Miss Culpepper!" the lieutenant said, and put his arm around her.

Willie's heart beat a fast *pitter-patter* that had nothing to do with the angle of the cart and everything to do with Lieutenant Mayhew's arm around her waist, strong and warm, and then the cart lurched its way up out of the trough and he released her.

"That's the worst of it," the farmer said, clambering back up into the cart. He'd plucked a stem of grass, which he now set between his teeth.

"How much further to Winnall?" Mayhew asked.

The farmer sucked thoughtfully on his grass stem, and then said, "Mebbe half an hour?"

Willie savored every minute of that half hour. In fact, she wished that the afternoon would never end, that the sun would remain halfway across the sky, and that the rutted, muddy lane would go on and on and on, and she'd sit next to Lieutenant Mayhew on this hard wooden seat forever.

Which was a little alarming. Forever? With a man she barely knew?

Don't lose your head over a uniform and a handsome face, Willie scolded herself, as she climbed down from the cart in the farmer's yard. But she didn't think she'd done that. It wasn't Mayhew's uniform or his face that she liked so much—although his eyes were very nice—it was his character, his cheerfulness, the way he'd protected her from the sailor, changing seats, putting the man in his place with a few words and a look.

The farmer wouldn't take payment for the ride. "I were a-comin' home anyways," he said. They drank cool water from his well and the kittens lapped at a little milk, and then the farmer gave them directions to Winchester. "Quickest way's across ol' John Plum's paddock," he said, and then proceeded to tell them exactly how to find John Plum's paddock.

Two minutes later, they were walking along a country lane. The spires of Winchester were visible across the fields, and Willie knew that Twyford was only a few miles beyond those spires.

She also knew that once they reached Twyford, she and Lieutenant Mayhew would part.

It wasn't in Willie's nature to feel melancholy, but she did feel a little melancholy about reaching Twyford. She almost wanted to sigh. She suppressed the urge and strode briskly along the rough little lane and told herself that she was *excited* about reaching Twyford. Excited about starting her position. Excited about returning to the continent.

"This looks like it," Mayhew said, as a paddock planted with turnips came into view.

Willie agreed: It did look very much like Old John Plum's paddock.

They started across. Willie picked her way carefully, holding her hem up. *Squelch. Squelch.* Within a dozen steps, her half boots were heavy with mud. It was almost like ice skating—slip and slide, slip and slide.

Her half boots became heavier, her slips and slides more erratic.

"Perhaps this wasn't the wisest idea," the lieutenant said.

"Perhaps not," Willie admitted.

The lieutenant stopped. "Your choice, Miss Culpepper: keep going, or turn back."

Willie looked at what lay ahead, and then glanced behind them. It was a mistake; one of her feet slid sideways.

Lieutenant Mayhew caught her upper arm in a strong grip. "Steady, there."

Willie's other foot slid in the opposite direction. She clutched the lieutenant's green jacket and tried not to fall.

He set down the basket, but didn't release his grip on her arm. "I think we'd best turn back."

"Yes." Willie planted her right foot firmly in the mud, and then her left.

"Got your balance?"

"Yes." She cautiously let go of his jacket.

Mayhew waited a moment, then released her and reached for the basket—and skidded wildly, windmilling his arms.

Willie grabbed one of his elbows and he grabbed one of hers. He gave a great, sliding, sideways lurch, and she lurched with him, and it was as if they were dancing a clownish jig. The lieutenant's feet slid and her feet slid and they swayed left and then right and then left again.

Finally, they both caught their balance, clutching each other in the middle of the muddy field. Willie bit her lip and tried not to giggle, and failed.

The lieutenant grinned at her. "May I have this dance, Miss Culpepper?"

"It would be my pleasure, Lieutenant," Willie said, and she would have dipped him a curtsy if she'd been more certain of her footing, but she didn't quite dare let him go yet, let alone dip funning curtsies.

The lieutenant's grin faded, and his expression changed slightly. Not the casually appreciative look he'd given her when he'd climbed aboard the stagecoach in London, but something warmer and faintly regretful.

Willie felt that regret, too. If she and Lieutenant Mayhew

had met under other circumstances, if she wasn't going to Vienna, if he wasn't going back to his regiment . . .

But these were the circumstances under which they'd met, and the likelihood of them ever seeing each other again after today was infinitesimally small—and there was nothing at all that could be done about that.

Willie released his arm.

"Back to the lane?" the lieutenant said.

"Back to the lane."

Lieutenant Mayhew let go of her. He shifted his weight. His left foot shot out from under him. His left hand shot out, too, grabbing her again. Together, they toppled over backwards into the mud.

Willie blinked up at the sky.

"Well, that was unfortunate," the lieutenant said, after a moment of silence. "Please accept my apologies, Miss Culpepper."

Willie began to giggle, and then to more than giggle. She laughed—laughed from her belly, laughed until her ribs ached and tears streamed down her face—and the lieutenant lay alongside her in the muddy turnip field and laughed, too.

Finally, Willie stopped laughing. She caught her breath and wiped her eyes and sat up.

The lieutenant sat up, too, alongside her. "Thank heavens you have a sense of humor, Miss Culpepper."

"It's just mud," Willie said, smiling at him. "It will wash off."

"So it will." He smiled back at her, and there was such warmth in his brown eyes, such approbation, that her breath caught in her throat and she realized that she didn't just like him, she liked him *a lot*.

And he liked her a lot, too.

Which didn't change the fact that she was headed to Vienna and he was headed back to his regiment.

The last of Willie's amusement snuffed out. She felt rather sad. She looked around for the basket. It was sitting where the lieutenant had left it, lid firmly fastened. "It's fortunate you weren't carrying the kittens when you fell."

"Yes." The lieutenant carefully climbed to his feet, extended a hand, and helped her to stand. Then he picked up the basket. Together they slipped and slid their way back the way they'd come. Ironically, now that they were both caked in mud, neither of them fell over.

"The farmer must have hobnails on his boots," the lieutenant said, when they reached the lane.

"Undoubtedly." Willie looked around for a stick, found one, and set to work removing the mud from her half boots. That task accomplished, she took off her bonnet and examined it. It was liberally besmirched, as was her shawl and, yes, even her reticule. She only needed to look at the lieutenant's filthy rifleman's jacket to know what the back of her gown looked like.

But it was only mud, and mud could be brushed off and washed off. Nothing was ruined. The next time she wore these clothes, the mud would be just a memory.

As would the lieutenant and his kittens.

Willie tried not to sigh. She put the bonnet back on and retied the ribbons.

"Right," the lieutenant said, after he'd scraped the worst of the mud off his boots. "Let's get to Winchester as quickly as we can."

They set off at a brisk pace. Willie didn't bother trying to keep her hem clean anymore. The lane curved right, then left, then dipped down to a ford where water flowed swiftly.

They halted. "This would be why the farmer recommended the paddock," Lieutenant Mayhew said.

Willie eyed the water and tried to estimate how deep it was. Six inches? Twelve?

"I'll piggyback you across," Mayhew said.

"Piggyback?" Willie said. Her voice sounded a smidgeon higher than it usually was.

"Would you prefer wet feet?"

Willie bit her lip. No, she wouldn't prefer wet feet, but being piggybacked by a man she barely knew while on a public lane where anyone might see—being piggybacked *at all*—was not something that a respectable lady would do.

But neither was traveling in farm carts carrying pigs.

Or falling over in muddy turnip fields.

The lieutenant was still looking at her, eyebrows slightly raised, waiting for her decision.

"I would prefer to keep my feet dry," Willie admitted.

Mayhew grinned at her, and set down the basket. "Let me just check how deep it is, Miss Culpepper." He waded into the ford and cast about to find the shallowest spot. Willie was relieved to see that the water didn't come over the top of his boots.

The lieutenant returned and hunkered down with his back to her. "Climb aboard," he said cheerfully.

Willie glanced over her shoulder, made certain that the lane was empty of spectators, hiked her gown up past her knees, and scrambled onto Lieutenant Mayhew's back.

"Hold tight," he said, and stood.

Willie held on tightly, her arms around his shoulders, and the lieutenant held tightly to her, too, his hands gripping her legs just above the knees, where her garters were tied, and Willie realized that if he hadn't been wearing gloves, his hands would have touched her *bare skin.*

She shivered at this thought. Not a shiver of revulsion or unease, but a tingling, warm shiver that made her pulse accelerate. She held her breath as Lieutenant Mayhew navigated the ford, not merely because she was afraid he might lose his footing, but also because he was *touching her legs* and it felt deliciously exciting.

Once he'd gained the other side, the lieutenant crouched again. Willie scrambled down and smoothed her gown hastily past her knees again. She knew she was blushing; her face felt quite hot.

The lieutenant didn't notice. He was already heading back

for the kittens. Willie watched him. He was very well put together, with those long limbs and those broad shoulders, and—as he turned around—that cheerful grin, a flash of white teeth in his tanned face.

Mayhew picked his way back across the ford, holding the basket. One of the kittens was mewing indignantly. "Poor Scout," he said. "She wants out, and I can't say I blame—"

He sat down suddenly in the water.

Willie stood frozen for a brief second, her mouth open in a soundless *Oh* of shock, and then she cast aside her reticule and splashed into the ford, dry feet be damned.

"Your shoes—"

"Kittens are more important than dry shoes," Willie told him, taking the basket, which he fortunately hadn't dropped. She heard two tiny voices, wailing their disapproval at the sudden change in elevation.

She waded back to dry ground and set the basket down. "It's all right, little ones," she said soothingly, and then she splashed back to the lieutenant. Her wet hem wrapped itself around her ankles.

She held out her hand. Mayhew took it and climbed to his feet. "Are you all right?" she asked.

"I believe my uniform's a little cleaner, now," he said.

Willie laughed, and he laughed, too, and as she laughed her foot slipped and she abruptly sat down.

The lieutenant was still holding her hand, so he sat down again, too.

There was a loud splash, and then silence. Willie bit her lip, and glanced at the lieutenant, sitting alongside her in the ford. His lips twitched. Her lips twitched, too, and then they were both laughing again, because really, what else *could* one do when one had just sat down in a ford?

"Well," the lieutenant said, when he'd caught his breath.

"Well," Willie agreed.

They helped each other to their feet. Willie's gown was

quite sodden. Water streamed off it. "Are you all right?" the lieutenant asked.

"I believe my gown's a little cleaner, now," Willie said.

He grinned, recognizing his own words, and she grinned back at him, and then his grin faded, and hers did, too, and they just stood there in the ford, with water flowing around their ankles, looking at each other.

He's going to kiss me, Willie thought, and then she thought, *And I'm going to kiss him back.*

But at that moment a farm cart came around the corner, heading towards them.

Willie and the lieutenant stepped away from each other and sloshed to dry ground. The cart slowed, splashed through the ford, and halted alongside them. A stout, grizzled farmer man gazed down at them, a pipe clamped between his teeth. He removed the pipe. Its stem was well-chewed. "Dearie me," he said. "Dearie, dearie me."

CHAPTER 6

The farmer took them home with him, where his wife fussed over them and bore Miss Culpepper off to the inner reaches of the farmhouse. When they returned, Miss Culpepper was wearing one of the farmer's wife's dresses. It wasn't just two sizes too large for her, it was *ten* sizes too large. Miss Culpepper looked as if she was wearing a tent.

But at least it was a dry tent.

The farmer loaned Mayhew a shirt and breeches, and they were tent-like on him, too, and they sat in the kitchen and drank cowslip wine while their clothes dried by the fire.

They stayed for three hours. Mrs. Penny, the farmer's wife, fed them bread and butter and the last of a knuckle of ham, and apologized that she had nothing better to give them. Mayhew told her of the time the commissariat's wagons had taken the wrong route and he'd had to eat acorns for his dinner, which made Mrs. Penny cluck with dismay. She stopped apologizing for the plainness of her fare, but she pressed bread and butter and ham on them until Mayhew feared that he would burst.

He could have stayed in that warm, cozy kitchen forever, seated at the table alongside Miss Culpepper, eating bread and butter and sipping cowslip wine, while Mr. Penny chewed on his pipe and Mrs. Penny bustled to and fro.

He watched Scout explore the kitchen, watched Bellyrub curl up and fall asleep on Mr. Penny's lap, watched Mrs. Penny knead dough and chop vegetables, but mostly he watched Miss Culpepper. He watched her eat, he watched her smile, he watched her enjoy being in this rustic kitchen, he watched her simply be *happy.*

She was good at being happy, Mayhew thought. Good at taking things in her stride. Today she'd missed a stagecoach, become separated from her luggage, traveled with pigs, fallen over in a muddy turnip field and again in a ford, and now she was wearing a coarse, country dress that didn't fit her—and she was happy.

Most young ladies would have had the vapors given any one of those events, let alone all of them, but Miss Culpepper hadn't. She hadn't even complained. Not once. Instead, she'd *laughed.*

Right now she was chuckling as Mrs. Penny described the time her children—three daughters—had decided to wash the hens. "A bigger mess you never did see. Feathers everywhere. Wet as fish, they all was. Wet as fish."

Mayhew watched the dimples come and go in Miss Culpepper's cheeks. He watched her sip cowslip wine and nibble bread-and-butter. She was enchanting. Utterly enchanting. The most enchanting female he'd ever met, and even though she was a colonel's daughter and he was merely a lieutenant, a tiny seed of hope flowered in his breast.

The Pennys had a nephew in the 2nd Regiment of Foot, and they asked about the Peninsula campaign. Mayhew told them stories of Spain and Portugal and France, and then he said, "But Miss Culpepper's been further afield than I have. Tell us about South America, Miss Culpepper."

She did. And then she told them about Constantinople and Russia, about chandeliers dripping with diamonds and plates made from gold, and she told them about dining with the tsar and dancing with princes.

The Pennys listened, openmouthed. Mr. Penny forgot to

chew on the stem of his pipe. Mrs. Penny forgot to knead her dough.

Mayhew listened, too, and quietly let go of the hope that had flowered in his breast. To think that a colonel's daughter would marry a lowly lieutenant was foolish. To think that a diplomat's daughter who'd danced with princes and supped with the tsar might marry a lowly lieutenant wasn't merely foolish; it was laughable.

"Lordee," Mrs. Penny said, when Miss Culpepper had finished. "I'm quite betwattled! To think that you're sittin' at me own table, and you've dined with *royalty*."

"Your cowslip wine is better than anything I had in Russia," Miss Culpepper assured her.

Mrs. Penny went pink with pleasure.

"Do you miss diplomatic life?" Mayhew asked, even though he already knew the answer. Of course she missed it. She missed it so much that she was taking steps to return to it. As companion to Sir Walter's daughters, she would move in diplomatic circles again. She'd rub shoulders with attachés and ambassadors, and before very long a diplomat destined for a lifetime of dining off golden plates would snap her up.

"No." Miss Culpepper shook her head, a decisive movement that set her ringlets dancing. "It's army life that I miss."

"It is?" Mayhew said doubtfully.

She nodded.

"Why?"

Miss Culpepper frowned and gave the matter some thought, and even frowning she was enchanting. "Life is plainer in the army. Simpler. More real."

"More uncomfortable," Mayhew pointed out.

Laughter flashed across her face. "A great deal more uncomfortable!" The amusement faded, and Miss Culpepper's expression became serious. She looked down at the scrubbed wooden tabletop and circled a knot with one fingertip. "I know this will sound silly, but . . . I think I *like* to be a little bit uncomfortable. If one is forever wrapped up in luxury,

301

one forgets to appreciate things like being warm and dry and fed. You never forget to do that when you're following the drum. When you have food, you're happy for it. When you have a dry bed, you're happy for it. When you don't have lice or fleas or saddle sores, you're happy for it." She rubbed her fingertip back and forth, tracing the grain of the wood. "Army life is frequently dirty and disagreeable, and sometimes it's terrifying and sometimes it's heartbreaking, and I know it's not sensible of me to miss it, but I do. It made me feel alive, and not only that, it made me feel *glad* to be alive."

There was a long moment of silence while they all digested her words. Mayhew heard the fire mumbling in the kitchen hearth. He heard Mr. Bellyrub purring. He heard a rooster crowing outside in the yard. And while he heard those things, hope began to cautiously flower in his breast again.

Miss Culpepper *liked* army life.

Mr. Penny removed his pipe from his mouth. "Ye've a soldier's heart, lass."

"I do," Miss Culpepper said, with a rueful laugh. "But alas, I can't be a soldier."

You could be a soldier's wife, Mayhew thought.

He glanced at his pocket watch, which had fortunately survived his impromptu dip, and saw, with a sense of shock, that it would be dark in two hours.

He tilted the watch toward Miss Culpepper, letting her see the time.

Her lips tucked in at the corners, a tiny, regretful movement, and he realized that she wanted to remain in this cozy kitchen as much as he did.

"We must be going," Mayhew told the Pennys. "Miss Culpepper needs to be in Twyford by nightfall."

All became hustle and bustle. Miss Culpepper gathered up her clothing and retired to dress. Mayhew gathered up *his* clothing and retired to dress. His shirt was dry, his rifleman's pantaloons merely damp. His jacket was rather more damp, as were his boots, but Mayhew was used to wet jackets and wet boots.

When he returned to the kitchen, the kittens were already in their basket. "I took them outside," Miss Culpepper told him cheerfully. "They both did their business, and Mrs. Penny has put butter on their paws, so they're perfectly content."

"Thank you," Mayhew said. He went out into the yard and discovered that the sky was dark with clouds. He also discovered that Mr. Penny had harnessed his cob to the gig again. "I'll take ye to the Morestead bridge," the farmer said. "It's but a mile to Twyford from there."

"That's very kind of you," Mayhew said, with another glance at those threatening clouds. He reached into his pocket and fished out a shilling.

"Put that bob away, young feller," Mr. Penny said. "No need to pay me. I'd take ye all the way to Twyford if I could, but ol' Dobbin here won't cross the Morestead bridge." He clapped the cob on the shoulder. "Took a fright there ten year ago and ain't crossed it since."

Mayhew laughed, and put the shilling back in his pocket. He heard footsteps behind him and turned. It was Miss Culpepper. "Mr. Penny has offered to drive us to Morestead," he told her. "From there, it's only a mile to Twyford."

CHAPTER 7

It was nearing twilight when they reached Morestead. The gloaming hour. That was a word Willie had always loved: gloaming. It sounded a little magical, a time of lingering daylight and long shadows and dusk slowly deepening in the hollows.

Morestead was too small to be called a village. It possessed a small church, a crossroads, a bridge, and that was all. The gig slowed as they approached the bridge, going from brisk trot to slow walk to complete standstill. The horse planted its hooves firmly, put its ears back, and refused to take another step.

Lieutenant Mayhew laughed. "I see what you mean."

"Aye," Mr. Penny said, around his pipe stem. "Stubborn as an ox, our Dobbin. Ain't no doin' nothin' about it."

Mayhew jumped down from the gig and held up a hand to Willie. She took it and jumped down, too.

"See that spire?" the farmer said, with a nod to the west. "That's Twyford, that is. Ye'd best walk fast, though. I don't like the look of them clouds."

"Thank you," the lieutenant said, lifting down the kittens' basket.

"There's another ford, jes' round the corner, but there's a footbridge alongside. Don't fall in, now."

The lieutenant laughed, and so did Willie. "We shan't," she assured Mr. Penny.

"Thank you," Lieutenant Mayhew said again. "We're very much obliged to you. You've been prodigiously kind, you and your wife."

The farmer chewed on his pipe and looked both pleased and bashful. "Godspeed."

By the time they'd crossed the humpbacked little bridge, the gig had turned around and was headed back towards Winnall. Willie watched it out of sight. "There are some very nice people in the world."

"There are." The lieutenant smiled down at her. "Come now, let's get to Twyford before it rains."

They turned right at the crossroad, walking briskly. No sound came from the basket. The kittens were snugly asleep.

Willie saw a line of oak trees ahead, and behind those, a church spire. Twyford.

She took a deep breath and set herself to enjoying this last mile of her journey—the gloaming, the mud and the puddles, the hedgerows on either side of the lane, the fields beyond that, the clouds heavy with approaching rain, the warm summer's breeze. And most of all, Lieutenant Mayhew's company.

"Here's the ford," he said.

"Yes." Willie eyed it as they approached. The ford was shallower than the one they'd fallen in, but wider and a great deal muddier.

"Footbridge," Mayhew said, with a tilt of his head.

Footbridge was perhaps too fine a word for that single, warped wooden plank, but at least their footwear wouldn't get wetter than it already was.

The lieutenant went across first, carrying the basket. He paused at the end of the plank, then took a long, leaping stride. He set the basket on the ground and turned to back her. "Have care, Miss Culpepper. It's wobbly, and there's a great puddle at the end."

Willie picked up her skirts and stepped onto the plank.

It *was* a little wobbly, but not enough to upset her balance. She crossed quickly—and discovered that the puddle at the far end was not only larger than she'd thought, but also most unfortunately situated, precisely where she needed to step.

"Take my hand," Lieutenant Mayhew said.

Willie took hold of his outstretched fingers. "If I fall short, it's no matter. My shoes are still wet."

She jumped, but she didn't jump quite far enough. Her left foot landed in the puddle, and it wasn't merely a puddle, it was a *hole*.

Willie went in it up to her knee, lost her balance, and sat down. Fortunately, she let go of the lieutenant's hand, so she didn't pull him in, too. Muddy water enveloped her to the waist.

"Miss Culpepper!" Mayhew exclaimed, and he looked so aghast that Willie had to laugh.

"Are you all right?" he asked anxiously, crouching.

"Perfectly," Willie said, and then she shook her head and laughed again, because honestly, what else *could* one do when one had just sat in a muddy puddle in front of a man one was attracted to? She gave him her reticule and took his hand.

Mayhew helped her to stand. Water streamed off her. "Are you *certain* you're all right?"

"My pride has received a mortal blow," Willie told him. "But other than that, I'm perfectly well." And then she put her weight on her left foot and discovered that she wasn't perfectly well. She couldn't hide her wince.

The lieutenant saw it. "You're hurt?"

Willie bit her lip, and then confessed, "My ankle."

Mayhew picked her up as if she were a bride being carried over a threshold, crossed the lane to where there were no puddles, and set her down on the grass verge. "Let me see."

Willie sat silently while he knelt and unlaced her half boot and removed it. "Where does it hurt?" he asked.

Willie pointed.

Mayhew examined her ankle through her muddy stocking,

probing with his fingers, testing the joint. There was no levity on his face now; his eyebrows were drawn together, his eyes slightly narrowed, his mouth a flat line. This was his serious face, Willie realized. His soldier's face.

"Does it hurt when I do this?" he asked, and flexed her ankle, watching her face as he did so.

"No," Willie said, and thought how *very* nice his eyes were. Quite the nicest eyes she'd ever seen. And then she scolded herself for mooning over Lieutenant Mayhew's eyes while he was examining her ankle. If one thing was certain, it was that at this moment *he* was not mooning over *her*. Not while he was kneeling in the mud and holding her foot in its wet, filthy stocking. If anything, he was probably annoyed at her for being so clumsy.

Willie shook her head at herself.

"What?"

"Just telling myself off for being so clumsy." She wrinkled her nose and attempted a joke: "This will teach me not to try to impress people with my athletic prowess."

He grinned at her. "You were trying to impress me, Miss Culpepper?"

Willie felt herself blush. "No, of course not."

The lieutenant's grin widened, and she had a horrible feeling that he didn't believe her, but he said nothing. He returned his attention to her ankle, rotating the joint carefully. It hurt, but not too much.

Willie told him that, and then she said, "I think it's just a sprain."

"So do I." He released her foot and sat back on his heels. "Thank God. I was afraid you'd broken it." He smiled ruefully at her. "Today has been a chapter of accidents, hasn't it? One catastrophe after another."

"They've been trifling catastrophes," Willie said. "Not full-grown ones."

Mayhew cocked his head. His smile changed, becoming faintly playful. "*Kitten*-astrophes?"

Willie's heart actually skipped a beat. How was it possible for a man to be so attractive? Especially when kneeling in the mud uttering appalling puns? But attractive he was. Incredibly attractive. Not because of the symmetry of his features, but because of the boyish tilt of his head, the twinkle in his eyes, that impish smile.

Willie tried to pretend that she wasn't flustered. She shook her head at him, uttering a chuckle that absolutely did *not* sound breathless, and said, "Allow me to inform you, Lieutenant, that puns are not your forte."

He shrugged, unabashed. "It made you laugh."

"Because it was so *bad*."

Mayhew grinned at her, and then his expression sobered and he climbed to his feet. "I'll run ahead to Twyford and fetch a carriage. You can't walk half a mile on that ankle, let alone a mile."

"I might be able to," Willie said.

The lieutenant looked doubtful, but he helped her to stand—and Willie took a few steps and discovered that her ankle actually did hurt rather a lot. She tried not to wince, but she knew that she *had* winced—and she also knew the lieutenant had seen it. "You're not walking to Twyford," he said, in a voice that brooked no argument.

"No," Willie said, with a sigh.

A puff of warm wind gusted along the lane. In its wake, a fat raindrop hit the ground. *Plop.* A moment later, came another one. *Plop.*

Plop. Plop.

Mayhew frowned, and looked around. Willie looked around, too. She saw trees and hedgerows and that distant church spire, and on the other side of the nearest hedgerow, a small barn.

The lieutenant saw the barn, too. He picked Willie up and set off for it at a brisk pace.

"The kittens," Willie protested.

"I won't let them get wet," Mayhew said. "I promise."

A few raindrops pattered down while he carried her—*plop, plop-plop*—erratic and desultory, vanguard of the approaching storm. Willie eyed those dark clouds as Mayhew rounded the end of the hedgerow and headed across a rutted stretch of muddy ground, but it was difficult to pay attention to clouds or raindrops or even sprained ankles while Lieutenant Mayhew was carrying her. He was so *strong.* So steady on his feet. He smelled of wet wool. Perhaps it could be argued that one damp woolen garment smelled like another, but her nose told her that his green jacket smelled of *soldier,* and the familiarity of that scent brought a rush of homesickness.

"Roof looks sound," Mayhew said, when they reached the barn.

The barn was small and dark and smelled of hay and turnips, even though there were no turnips that Willie could see. There was a lot of hay, though. Several piles of it.

Mayhew crossed to one pile, crouched and settled her carefully atop it, then said, "Won't be a moment," and headed back to the ford at a jog. Two minutes later he returned, panting, with the basket, Willie's half boot, and her reticule. He set all three items down. Outside, wind gusted, rattling the shutters.

"I'll run in to Twyford," Mayhew said. "Are you cold? The storm's almost upon us."

Willie shook her head. "It's a warm wind."

"Even so, take my jacket. It's not dry, but it's dryer than what you're wearing."

Willie wasn't at all cold, but her gown was soaked from the waist down, and part of her shawl was, too, so she made no protest when he peeled off his jacket. Mayhew crouched and settled it over her shoulders, not with brisk indifference but gently and almost tenderly, as if her comfort was important to him. As if he *cared* about her.

Willie slipped her arms into the sleeves and felt emotion tighten her throat.

The jacket was far too large, damp and heavy and warm

from his body. The *soldier* smell of it was strong—and that made her throat tighten even further.

Mayhew looked at her, an anxious crease on his brow. "How do you feel? Warm enough?"

Willie didn't quite trust her voice. She pulled the jacket closed at her chest and nodded.

"Good." He stood. "I'll be back as soon as I can. Should be less than twenty minutes." But he didn't depart. He stood looking down at her, frowning. "I don't like leaving you on your own, Miss Culpepper."

"I'll be perfectly fine," Willie said firmly.

His frown deepened. She saw conflict on his face, saw that he truly *didn't* want to leave her, saw how much it worried him—and saw, too, that he knew he had to if he was to help her.

"Go," she said.

Mayhew hesitated a moment longer, then gave a curt nod, and as he nodded the wind gusted so strongly that it made the shutters bang against the walls and sent scraps of hay dancing madly across the dirt floor. On the heels of that mighty gust of wind came a burst of rain. Heavy rain. *Very* heavy rain. A downpour, in fact.

Willie raised her voice to be heard over the drumming on the roof. "You can't go out in that!"

Lieutenant Mayhew grinned, and shrugged. "It's a warm rain," he said, echoing her earlier words. "I'll be as fast as I can. Half an hour at the most." Then he plunged out into the deluge and was gone.

Willie opened the basket. The kittens blinked up at her. Did that loud roar of rain frighten them? She thought it probably did. "Hello, sweethearts," she said. "Come and sit with me while we wait."

Her gown was wet, but her shawl was still mostly dry, so she wadded it up and made a bed for the kittens on her lap and settled them there. Scout mewed up at her, but Mr. Bellyrub was silent. Willie petted them and murmured reassurances,

"You're safe, I promise," and then she drew the damp green rifleman's jacket snugly around them all. She couldn't hear the kittens purring over the rain, but she felt it in the palm of her hand.

Gloaming was past, full night swiftly approaching. It was difficult to make out the interior of the barn—the piles of hay, the rusty implements, the abandoned buckets—but Willie wasn't afraid. She'd only been acquainted with Lieutenant Mayhew for a few scant hours, but she knew that if he said he'd be back within half an hour, he would be. Until then, she'd sit and enjoy the kittens on her lap and the smell of Mayhew's jacket and the noisy, turbulent drama of the storm. It reminded her of the humid, sultry storms she'd experienced in South America—

A figure loomed out of the semi-darkness. Willie started violently and let out a squeak of alarm—and then she recognized that grinning face. It was Lieutenant Mayhew. Water streamed off him.

"Your ride is here, m'lady," he said, with a flourishing bow.

"But you were gone barely two minutes!"

"Met a wagon in the lane." Mayhew crouched and helped her swiftly return the kittens to the basket. Poor Mr. Bellyrub squeaked his displeasure at this change in circumstance—or at least, Willie *thought* he did. She saw a flash of white teeth as his mouth opened, but couldn't hear anything over the rain. "Driver didn't want to stop for us," Mayhew said. "But I persuaded him to." He stood and held out a hand to her.

Willie climbed to her feet. Her left ankle gave a sharp twinge of protest.

Mayhew swept her up in his arms and carried her out into the storm. Warm wind gusted and warm rain poured down. When they reached the lane, a shape materialized in the gloom: a horse and wagon. Willie saw to her relief that the wagon was covered.

Mayhew lifted her over the tailboard, deposited her carefully in the wagon, and disappeared into the gloom. He was back in less than a minute with the kittens and her reticule and half boot.

Willie heard him shout something to the driver. The wagon lurched into motion, and they were off. Mayhew scrambled up into the wagon, wet and panting. "We'll be at Twyford in a few minutes, Miss Culpepper." She thought he was grinning, but it was too dark to be certain.

Willie felt a pang of regret. Which was absurd. How could she possibly regret arriving in Twyford, where a bath and a soft bed awaited her, and a trunk filled with dry clothes?

Willie frowned to herself, and examined her emotions.

She *was* relieved to be reaching Twyford—but not nearly as much as she ought to be, considering how wet and filthy she was.

It appeared that she didn't want this misadventure to end. If her father were still alive, he'd shake his head and laugh at her.

Willie did it for him: a shake of her head, a silent inner laugh. *Idiot*, she told herself. *Be thankful for the clean clothes and dry bed you'll soon have.*

And she was grateful for those things, she *was,* it was just . . .

She would miss Lieutenant Mayhew, miss his smile and his warm, brown eyes and his sense of humor and his chivalry.

Willie sighed at her foolishness, and as she sighed, she heard a crash that was louder than the storm.

The wagon halted abruptly.

"What was that?" she said, alarmed.

"I'll find out," Mayhew said, jumping down from the wagon.

He disappeared into the storm. Rain drummed down on the canvas overhead. Willie heard shouted voices, and then Mayhew returned. "A tree's come down across the road."

"Thank heavens it didn't fall on us!"

"Indeed." His voice was slightly grim. "It's an old oak, too big to move and we can't go around it. I'm going to help turn the wagon. Hold tight."

Willie nodded, but he was already gone. After a moment, the wagon began to move slowly backwards.

It took five minutes to turn the wagon, then Mayhew scrambled up alongside her again. "Where are we going?" Willie shouted over the roar of the storm.

"Morestead," Mayhew shouted back. "We'll see if we can find someone to take us in for the night."

Willie nodded, although it was too dark for him to see it.

Three minutes later the wagon was back to the ford—where it halted again. Mayhew jumped down. Willie stayed where she was, clutching her reticule and the basket, listening to the rain beat on the canvas. She heard Mayhew shout something, heard the driver reply, and then Mayhew returned. "Too deep to cross. We'll have to stay the night in the barn."

"The barn?" Willie stared at his dark shape in dismay. Now that a dry bed and clean clothes were impossibilities, she discovered that she *did* rather want them.

"I'm very sorry, Miss Culpepper."

Willie reminded herself that she was a soldier's daughter. "It's not your fault, Lieutenant," she told him, as cheerfully as she was capable of. "We're fortunate that there *is* a barn for us to stay in."

CHAPTER 8

*T*he wagon driver was as big as a bear—and as surly as one. When Mayhew asked him to unhitch his horse and ride to Twyford for help, he refused. The horse was a massive beast, with powerful hindquarters and a great deal of feathering on its lower legs. A draft horse. Mayhew eyed that broad back. "Then let me and Miss Culpepper ride to Twyford," he said. "We'll stable your horse there overnight and I'll bring him back in the morning."

"Me 'orse ain't goin' nowhere," the wagon driver growled. "No while there's trees a-blowin' down."

Frustration flared in Mayhew's chest, but he held his tongue. In his experience, losing one's temper never helped a situation. He turned his attention to Miss Culpepper: lifting her down from the wagon, carrying her into the barn, carefully setting her on a pile of hay.

"At least the roof doesn't leak," she said, in the buoyant tone of someone determined to make the best of things. "And we have all this hay to sleep on. We're really very lucky!"

Water trickled down Mayhew's cheek and dripped off his nose and chin. He wiped his face and reminded himself that they *were* lucky: they could be lying squashed under an oak tree right now.

He mustered a smile, because even if it was too dark for Miss Culpepper to see it, she'd hear it in his voice. "We are indeed lucky," he agreed. "I've slept in worse places in my time." And it was true; he'd slept in *far* worse places while on campaign.

Come to think of it, Miss Culpepper probably had, too.

He fetched the kittens, then helped the driver maneuver his wagon out of the rain as much as was possible, and then, praise be, the man produced a lantern and lit it.

The barn became almost cozy in that flickering golden light.

The wagon driver unhitched his horse and set to work rubbing the beast down with handfuls of hay. After a moment, Mayhew joined him. They worked in silence, while the rain hurled itself at the barn and the lantern cast dancing shadows. *Thank God it's summer,* Mayhew thought as he rubbed his way down the horse's hind leg. *Thank God it's warm.* The night was going to be uncomfortable, but if it had been winter and they were stranded here, soaked to the bone, it wouldn't have been merely uncomfortable, it would have been dangerous.

There was no risk of anyone freezing to death tonight. If anything, he was almost too warm.

He glanced across at Miss Culpepper. She'd removed her bonnet and gloves, but she still wore his jacket, so perhaps she was a little cold?

She didn't look cold. Or miserable. Or in pain. She was smiling, dimples dancing in her cheeks, her attention on something in her lap. A kitten, he guessed.

Thank God her ankle isn't broken, Mayhew thought, and then: *Thank God she's who she is. Thank God she's taking this all in her stride.*

In fact, there were a great many things to be thankful for tonight—the most important being that the oak tree hadn't fallen on them.

He crouched down to rub the long, wet hair that feathered

the horse's lower leg, then stood and wiped his sweaty brow. "Done?" he asked the wagon driver.

The driver grunted and turned away, heading for his wagon.

Had the man *no* manners at all? Mayhew huffed out a soundless laugh and tossed away his handful of hay. He crossed to Miss Culpepper and crouched. "How's your ankle?"

She looked up at him and smiled, and despite the damp, bedraggled ringlets he thought she was the most beautiful woman he'd ever seen. "It doesn't hurt as long as I don't move it."

"I'm relieved to hear it."

Mr. Bellyrub was curled up in Miss Culpepper's lap, his eyes half closed, an expression of blissful contentment on his tiny face. Of his sister, there was no sign.

"Where's Scout?"

"Doing what she does best," Miss Culpepper said. She pointed, and he spied Scout investigating one corner of the barn, where a rusted hoe and several battered buckets lay discarded. "You were right; she ought to be a reconnaissance officer. She's absolutely fearless."

The driver had been rummaging in the back of his wagon; now, he returned with a rough woolen blanket, which he laid over his horse's broad back.

"Do you have another one of those?" Mayhew asked.

The man scowled at him, and produced a second blanket, which he handed over so grudgingly that Mayhew was hard put not to laugh. "Thank you," he said, and shook it out.

The blanket smelled strongly of horse, but it was thick and warm and dry. Mayhew placed it carefully around Miss Culpepper's shoulders.

"Thank you," she said, and then she pointed and said, "Look."

The wagon driver turned to look. So did Mayhew. He watched, incredulous, as Scout approached the draft horse. Her tail was high and her ears were pricked. She looked alert and inquisitive and wary. The horse saw her and pricked its ears, too, and dipped its great head for a closer look. Scout froze, every hair on her body bristling with cautious curiosity.

Their noses touched. Kitten and horse sniffed one another. Scout stopped bristling.

The great horse nudged Scout gently, knocking her over.

Scout scrambled upright. She didn't retreat; instead, she frisked around the horse's front hooves, discovered the long feathering hairs, and reached out a daring paw and patted, as if those hairs were playthings.

Mayhew hastily retrieved her. The horse's hooves were far larger than Scout was. One misstep and the kitten would be dead.

Miss Culpepper was smiling. So was the wagon driver, although he scowled and turned away as soon as Mayhew caught his eye.

Mayhew deposited Scout on Miss Culpepper's lap. "Best keep her close. I'd hate for her to be squashed."

Scout wanted to continuing exploring, but Miss Culpepper distracted her with a long strand of hay. Soon the kitten was leaping and pouncing. Mr. Bellyrub joined in and they had a grand game. Miss Culpepper was laughing, and Mayhew was laughing, and he was pretty certain that the kittens were laughing, too, as they dashed around in the hay.

He didn't think the wagon driver was laughing, although he couldn't be certain because the man had his back to them. Mayhew kept an eye on him, watching as he gave his horse two armfuls of hay, then picked up one of the discarded buckets and went outside to fill it with water.

He lowered his voice: "Miss Culpepper, I promise I won't leave you alone with him for so much as one second."

"I don't think he's dangerous," she whispered back. "Just ill-tempered."

That was Mayhew's assessment, too, but he wasn't going to take the risk.

The driver returned and set the bucket in front of his horse. Then, he clambered up into his wagon. A minute later he emerged and crossed to where Mayhew and Miss Culpepper sat. "Here," he said brusquely, holding something out. "For the tibbies."

Mayhew held out his hand—and received a small piece of cheese. He blinked at it, too astonished to speak.

"Thank you," Miss Culpepper said.

The driver grunted and turned away.

Miss Culpepper's lips twitched, as if she found the man's complete lack of manners amusing.

Mayhew broke the cheese into crumbs and laid it down for the kittens. Mr. Bellyrub found it first, his little nose twitching. Soon both kittens were eating ravenously.

He glanced at Miss Culpepper. She was biting her lip. Her dimples were deep. She looked as if she was trying not to laugh.

"What?" Mayhew asked her.

She leaned close and said in an undertone, "He fed the animals, but not *us*," and then she went into a peal of laughter.

Her laughter was contagious. Mayhew had to laugh, too, because it really *was* damned funny, but when he'd stopped laughing he climbed to his feet and went across to where the wagon driver was gathering a pile of hay, presumably for his bed.

"Do you have any more food?" he asked. "We'll pay you for it."

The man scowled, and grudgingly produced more cheese and some coarse bread.

"Thank you," Mayhew said. "What's your name? Mine's Mayhew, and my companion is Miss Culpepper."

"Williams," the man said gruffly.

With anyone else, Mayhew would have commented that his given name was William, and Miss Culpepper's was Willemina, and what were the odds of all three of them having variations on the same name? With this man, he didn't bother. He simply returned to where Miss Culpepper sat and offered his spoils.

"Excellent!" she said.

They ate their meal while the wagon driver finished assembling his bed. Mayhew didn't fail to notice that the man had chosen to sleep as far from them as was possible. Had he done that out of misanthropy? Or courtesy to Miss Culpepper?

He decided it didn't matter what the man's reason was. Even if the wagon driver *had* located his bed with Miss Culpepper's sensibilities in mind, there was no way in Hades that he was going to leave her alone with the man for twenty seconds, let alone the twenty minutes it would take to run in to Twyford and bring a horse back—always supposing he could find his way there and back in the dark *and* that he could get a horse past that fallen tree.

They were only half a mile from Twyford, but they might as well be on the moon for all the likelihood they had of reaching the coaching inn tonight. His most pressing concern at this moment—his *only* concern—was to keep Miss Culpepper safe.

Mr. Bellyrub climbed into Miss Culpepper's lap again. Mayhew watched her stroke the kitten. Lord, but she looked beautiful, the lantern light playing softly over her face. She looked happy, too. As happy as Mr. Bellyrub was right at this moment—which was exceedingly happy. Despite the storm, despite her wet clothing, despite her sprained ankle, despite the series of catastrophes that had befallen them today, she *glowed* with contentment. If she were a cat, she'd be purring right now.

She's remarkable, Mayhew thought. *Quite remarkable.* And then he shook that thought out of his head. He wasn't in this barn to make sheep's eyes at Miss Culpepper; he was here to keep her safe. And if he could make her laugh while doing so, so much the better.

To that end, he said, in a mock-lugubrious tone, "Has it occurred to you, Miss Culpepper, that we're doomed never to reach Twyford?"

She glanced sideways at him, still stroking Mr. Bellyrub. A dimple appeared in her cheek. "Doomed?"

"Doooomed," Mayhew repeated, drawing out the word.

Her lips twitched into a smile. "We are *not* doomed," she told him. "This is merely another kitten-astrophe."

Mayhew leaned back on one elbow in the hay and smirked. "I knew you liked that pun."

"It's a *dreadful* pun."

"Dreadful?"

"*Monstrously* dreadful. *Prodigiously* dreadful."

He laughed. "Please, don't spare my feelings."

Miss Culpepper rolled her eyes at him. He could tell from her dimples that she was struggling not to smile.

Mayhew laughed again. And then he stopped laughing. This felt dangerously like flirting, and he couldn't flirt with Miss Culpepper. Not under circumstances like this. Not when she was injured and dependent on his protection. Only a cad would do that, and he was not a cad.

Scout climbed up on his damp knee, her claws digging into his green pantaloons. Mayhew winced and carefully detached her. He sat up again, laid some hay on his lap, and let her settle there. She turned around three times, curled up in a tight ball, and closed her eyes.

Mayhew cupped a hand over her and felt the warm vibration of her purr. He glanced at Miss Culpepper. *No flirting,* he reminded himself. "How's your ankle?"

"Not bad at all."

"Are you warm enough?"

"Yes. Are you?"

He was. Wet, but warm. He cast about for a subject. "Where else have you been, Miss Culpepper, other than South America and Constantinople and Russia?"

Her face lit up. "We were in Egypt for four years. I was only a girl, but I still remember it."

They talked about Egypt, and briefly about South Africa, where Miss Culpepper's mother had died of a fever, and then she told him about Kingston upon Thames, the village outside London where her aunt lived, and where she'd spent the past year.

"You don't like it there," Mayhew said, when she'd finished.

Miss Culpepper pulled a wry face. "Is it that obvious?"

He nodded, and stroked Scout.

Miss Culpepper hesitated, and then said, "Kingston upon Thames is very picturesque and very quiet—and I know that most people would love to live somewhere picturesque and quiet—but my parents didn't, and I don't either." She sighed, and looked down at Mr. Bellyrub, asleep in her lap. "It would be much easier if I did. I could be married and settled there right now."

Mayhew's hand hesitated in its stroking of Scout. "Married? You had a suitor in Kingston Upon Thames?"

Miss Culpepper nodded. "They did me a great honor, but . . ." Her lips pressed together regretfully.

They?

Mayhew waited for her to continue, but she didn't. "They?" he prompted carefully.

Miss Culpepper colored. "Yes."

"How many is 'they'?" he asked, even more carefully.

She looked away. "It sounds braggish."

"I promise I won't think you're puffing yourself off."

Miss Culpepper looked back at him and hesitated, and then said, "Six."

Mayhew felt his eyebrows rise. "Six?" His voice might have risen a little bit, too.

Miss Culpepper had had *six* suitors in Kingston Upon Thames?

"Yes." Her lips pursed regretfully again. "First was the vicar. Then the squire's son. Then Mr. Hanslow, who's secretary to Baron Allen. Then the baron's youngest son. Then Sir Peter Frost, and the very last was Mr. Mannering."

Mayhew digested that list for a few moments. *Six.* "May

I ask why you didn't wish to marry them? If it's not too impertinent?"

Miss Culpepper frowned down at Mr. Bellyrub and stroked him several times and then said, "They were all perfectly nice men, respectable and amiable and upstanding and . . . and well-born and . . . and . . ."

"Boring?"

"Yes." She sighed. "They all want to live in Kingston upon Thames. Forever! And you may tell me that I'm a fool for not wanting that—my aunt certainly told me often enough—but unfortunately, I'm my parents' daughter. I felt as if I was *suffocating* in that village."

"There's nothing unfortunate about it," Mayhew said firmly. He ran through the list of suitors in his head: vicar, secretary, squire's son, baron's son. "Your suitors sound very much like my brothers."

She cocked her head at him. "They do?"

"My father's a baron," Mayhew told her. "My oldest brother will make a worthy successor when it's his turn. My next oldest brother is a rector, and the one after that is a vicar, and the one after that, too. And the youngest one, John, is secretary to an earl."

"You have *five* brothers?"

"Five brothers and one sister. Do you have any?"

She shook her head.

"Well, my brothers all live in the same county—in fact most of them live within ten miles of each other." He smiled at her. "They're exactly like your suitors: amiable and upstanding, and they don't want to leave Wiltshire, let alone leave England."

"But you're not like that."

Mayhew shook his head. "I want to see the world, and I want to be *challenged*." He hesitated, and then said, "What you said to the Pennys . . . that's how I feel, too. I love army life. Even when it's awful and heartbreaking." He rubbed between Scout's ears, gently and meditatively. "Waterloo was worse than awful. It was . . ." He grimaced at memory of that carnage. "A lot of fellows sold out afterwards, and I considered it myself, but . . . I couldn't. A soldier is what I'm meant to be. It's who I *am.*"

Miss Culpepper nodded, as if she understood exactly what he was attempting to say. "It's who my father was, too."

He rubbed Scout's little head again. "I wish I'd met him."

"He would have liked you," Miss Culpepper said.

"I hope so." He stroked Scout once, twice. "From what I've heard, your father was everything a good commander should be. He led from the front, he was scrupulously fair, and he kept a cool head. Colonel Barraclough says that your father always said it was better to fix things than lose one's temper over them."

Miss Culpepper's smile was soft, a little sad. "Yes, he did say that."

"And Barraclough says he didn't play favorites." Which was, in Mayhew's opinion, almost as important as courage and cool-headedness in a commanding officer.

"Father? Heavens, no! Which isn't to say that people didn't try to pour the butter boat over him, because they most certainly *did.*" Miss Culpepper chuckled, as if at some memory, and then her smile slowly faded, becoming soft and sad again. She looked down at the folds of rough blanket spilling around her and plucked a horse hair from the coarse weave. "That was the hardest thing for him when he moved in diplomatic circles—all the flummery and the puffery. Father much preferred bluntness."

Lamplight caressed her face. She plucked another horse hair from the blanket, and another, and she looked rumpled and lovely and pensive, and it struck Mayhew suddenly that she was an orphan, and not just an orphan but an only child, too, and that she was alone in a way that he, with five brothers and one sister, could never be. Her aloneness seemed suddenly so dreadful, so terrible, that his throat clenched and his heart clenched and the urge to put an arm around her was almost overwhelming. He wanted to tell her that she wasn't alone, tell her that he thought he'd fallen in love with her, that he wanted to marry her, and that if she married him she'd never be alone again, that she'd have him and the whole of the Rifle Brigade as her family.

But only a cad would put his arm around a young lady under circumstances like this, when she was vulnerable and under his protection, and only a fool would blurt out a proposal after an acquaintance of only a few hours.

Mayhew swallowed past the lump in his throat and looked away. "What sort of man is this baronet who's hired you?"

"Sir Walter Pike? He's . . ."

He glanced back at her. Miss Culpepper's expression was no longer pensive, but thoughtful, as if she was searching for a word. "He's very genteel," she said, finally.

Genteel? Mayhew gave a soundless snort. If Sir Walter Pike was so damned genteel, why was Miss Culpepper traveling by stagecoach? Surely a *genteel* employer would hire a post-chaise for his daughters' companion?

Dare he ask her that question?

He gave a mental shrug, and decided that he would. "Why are you traveling to Twyford by stagecoach?"

"Sir Walter was going to book me on the Mail," Miss Culpepper said. "But the waybill was full."

"If the Mail was full, why didn't he hire a post-chaise for you? Or send one of his own carriages?"

She shrugged. "More expensive."

Mayhew gave another soundless snort. Sir Walter might be genteel, but he was also a damned penny-pincher. "What time is he meeting you tomorrow?"

"Ten o'clock."

"You'll be in Twyford before that, Miss Culpepper. I give you my word." He'd make certain of it. Even if he had to carry her, she'd be there on time. *Before* time, because she needed to wash and change her clothes before she met Sir Walter.

He hoped to God that her trunk had been set down at

Twyford. That would be a disaster he couldn't mend by ten o'clock.

Mayhew sent up a brief prayer for Miss Culpepper's trunk to be where it was meant to be, then glanced over at the wagon driver. Mr. Williams appeared to be asleep on his pile of hay. The great horse had one hip cocked as if it was sleeping, too.

He looked back at Miss Culpepper. "Why don't you get some rest? I promise that you'll be safe."

"What about you?"

Mayhew shook his head. "I'll keep watch."

Miss Culpepper leaned closer, lowering her voice so that he barely heard it over the hammering rain. "You should sleep, too, Lieutenant. Our friend may possess a churlish disposition, but I don't believe he'd harm us."

Mayhew didn't think the wagon driver would harm them either, but he wasn't prepared to risk Miss Culpepper's safety. "I'll keep watch," he repeated, firmly.

Miss Culpepper must have heard the implacable note in his voice, because she didn't try to persuade him to change his mind. She simply nodded, and said, "Here," and shucked his jacket and gave it to him.

"I'm not cold—"

"I have the blanket, so you must take this."

Mayhew heard the implacable note in *her* voice, and decided not to argue. He accepted the jacket.

Miss Culpepper removed the single half boot she was wearing, placed it alongside its mate, and settled herself and Mr. Bellyrub on their bed of hay, beneath the heavy horse blanket. She smiled at Mayhew, a cheerful smile, as if she wasn't wet and muddy, as if she didn't have a sprained ankle, as if this day hadn't been one disaster after another, as if she was *happy* to be in this barn with him and England's surliest wagon driver while a storm raged outside.

Mayhew smiled helplessly back at her.

Miss Culpepper snuggled deeper into the blanket and closed her eyes.

For some reason the fact that she'd closed her eyes made a lump grow in Mayhew's throat again.

Miss Culpepper trusted him not to touch her. She trusted him to keep her safe.

She *trusted* him.

Mayhew looked away and found that he needed to clear his throat and blink a little moisture from his eyes, which was rather embarrassing. He was a soldier, for heaven's sake. He didn't get mawkish over something as simple as someone closing their eyes.

Unless that someone was Miss Culpepper.

He glanced back at her. Emotions surged through him. Protectiveness was foremost, but there were a multitude of others: admiration, tenderness, longing, hope, respect. Love.

Mayhew lifted his jacket to his nose and inhaled, hoping to catch Miss Culpepper's scent. All he smelled was wet wool.

Idiot, he told himself, with a self-conscious glance around the barn. But no one had seen him. Not the wagon driver. Not Miss Culpepper. Not even the horse.

CHAPTER 9

*W*illie woke to the sound of low voices. She blinked her eyes open and saw hay and daylight. Memory came sweeping back. She sat up hastily, dislodging Mr. Bellyrub. He uttered a squeaking meow, clambered to his feet, and shook himself from head to toe.

"Sorry," Willie said, stroking his tiny head, and it appeared that Mr. Bellyrub wasn't one to hold grudges, for he butted against her fingers and purred. Then he yawned widely and shook himself again.

Willie yawned, too, and rubbed her face and put her hand to her hair, which felt as tangled as a briar patch. Lieutenant Mayhew and the wagon driver were at the barn door. The lieutenant said something, his voice too low for her to catch the words, but it sounded like a question. The driver replied gruffly.

Willie plucked out her hairpins. She ran her fingers through her ringlets and found them as snarled and messy as she'd feared. She needed a mirror and a comb if she was to repair that, but neither of those things was available right now, so she replaced the hairpins as best she could and made inventory of her situation.

One: chaotic hair.

Two: her gown was still damp, the muslin stained with mud and puckered into a thousand wrinkles—but she could do nothing about that, so there was no point worrying about it.

What *was* worth worrying about was her ankle.

Cautiously, Willie flexed it. The resultant twinge barely qualified as pain.

So, that was all right. In fact, it was *better* than all right.

A bath, a comb, and fresh clothes, and she would almost be as good as new.

Lieutenant Mayhew turned his head, saw that she was awake, and crossed swiftly to her. "Miss Culpepper. Good morning."

"What time is it?" Willie asked.

"Nearly seven o'clock." He crouched alongside her, smiling. He looked rumpled and disreputable—hair disheveled, golden stubble roughening his cheeks—but not nearly as rumpled and disreputable as she knew that *she* looked.

Willie told herself there was no point in vanity in situations like this, but she did wish she could wash her face and tidy her hair.

"The rain stopped about an hour ago," Mayhew said. "Mr. Williams has been out to check the road. The ford's still flooded, so we can't go that way, and the oak that came down is too large for his horse to move, but he thinks that you and I can climb over it, and from there it's less than half a mile to Twyford."

Willie nodded.

"We'll be in Twyford by eight thirty," he promised. "I'll carry you."

"I don't think that will be necessary. My ankle feels much better today."

His eyes lit with hope. "May I examine it? Do you mind?"

"Of course not." Willie extended her leg and pulled up her hem a few inches, revealing her filthy stockinged foot and ankle.

The lieutenant examined it as he had yesterday, probing gently with his fingers. It felt ridiculously intimate. Willie's pulse hammered in her throat and her face felt hot. No, it wasn't just her face that felt hot; her whole *body* felt hot.

Lieutenant Mayhew carefully rotated her ankle joint through its range of movement, a thoughtful frown on his face.

"It really doesn't hurt much at all," Willie told him, and to her relief her voice was steady, not breathless.

"Let's see how it feels when you put weight on it," Mayhew said, releasing her ankle. "Let me put your half boots on." He did just that, carefully sliding them onto her feet and lacing them up. Willie should have felt like a child, to have him do that, but she didn't. She felt . . . a little self-conscious and desperately aware of him—his proximity, his deft fingers, the way his eyebrows drew together as he concentrated—but mostly, she felt cared for, a sensation that she hadn't felt since her father had died. A sensation that made her throat constrict and her eyes sting.

Willie blinked several times and looked away, then back. The glinting golden stubble on Mayhew's cheeks made him look more flesh-and-blood man and less dashing lieutenant. It made him look older, too. She caught herself wondering how old he was. Twenty-seven? Twenty-eight?

Mayhew tied the laces into neat bows, stood, and extended his hand to her. "Here, I'll steady you."

Willie let him pull her to her feet—and realized that neither of them was wearing gloves any longer. Her fingers tingled at his touch.

Willie held on to his hand and tried to ignore the tingle and the way it elevated her heart rate. She took a cautious step. Her ankle gave a throb of discomfort, but that throb was nothing like the raw, stabbing pain of yesterday. "It feels a thousand times better. I don't think you'll need to carry me, Lieutenant." And *that* was a blessing for which she was deeply thankful. If her fingers tingled when he touched them for a few seconds, imagine how she'd feel if he carried her half a mile?

Mayhew released her hand and Willie should have felt relieved, because the tingle snuffed out, but perversely she felt sorry for that loss of contact.

"I'd feel better if you had a crutch or walking stick." Mayhew cast a frowning glance around the barn, then his face brightened. "How about that hoe, Miss Culpepper?"

He brought it to her, flipping it so that the blade pointed to the ceiling. "Blade's rusted, but the handle looks strong."

Willie accepted the hoe and leaned on it and took a careful step.

"Well?" the lieutenant asked, a hopeful note in his voice.

"It will do perfectly," Willie said.

Mayhew grinned at her—a grin that took her breath away—and rubbed his hands together briskly and said, "Right, let's be off!" And then he lost his grin and went faintly pink and said hesitantly, "Or, do you need to, *er* . . ."

Yes, Willie did need to, *er*.

She hobbled outside and around to the back of the barn, thanking God for the hoe with every step that she took. Imagine if Mayhew had had to carry her out here to do this?

She spent her penny, as the saying went, and hobbled back, and discovered that Lieutenant Mayhew had fetched a bucket of water for her to wash her hands and face in. The thoughtfulness of that shouldn't have made her eyes sting, but it did.

She also discovered that the wagon driver had put down some cheese for the kittens, which was no surprise—the man clearly liked animals more than he liked people. What *was* a surprise was that he offered her and the lieutenant food without being asked.

They ate quickly, then Mayhew fetched fresh water and they drank, and it was time to go. Mayhew folded up the horse blanket she'd slept under and gave it to the wagon driver while Willie caught Scout and put her in the basket. She closed the lid and looked around for Mr. Bellyrub.

"All set?" Mayhew said, turning to her with a smile.

"Once we find Mr. Bellyrub, yes."

"Ah." He lost his smile.

Mr. Bellyrub wasn't where the cheese had been. He wasn't in the nest of hay where Willie had slept. He wasn't in the nest of hay where the wagon driver had slept, either. He wasn't making the acquaintance of the draft horse. He wasn't under the wagon. He wasn't in any of the four corners of the barn.

The sense of déjà vu was strong. This was how it had all started: searching for a kitten while precious minutes ticked away.

Willie began to feel slightly frazzled. She thought the lieutenant was feeling frazzled, too; she heard him mutter something that was probably a curse as he pawed through the hay.

"Perhaps he went outside?" Willie said, after it seemed that every strand of hay in the barn had been turned over at least three times.

Mayhew strode out and made a hurried circuit. He shook his head when he reentered the barn. "We'll leave the kittens here."

"But—"

"I'll come back for them, Miss Culpepper. I promise. But I need to get you to Twyford. That's the most important thing right now."

"He's here somewhere," Willie insisted, rifling urgently through the hay.

"Miss Culpepper," the lieutenant said, in the sort of stern voice her father had used when telling her to do something he knew she wouldn't like.

"Five minutes!" she begged.

It took four and a half minutes, and it was the wagon driver who found Mr. Bellyrub. He was fast asleep inside a bucket that lay abandoned on its side. A bucket that Willie *knew* both she and Mayhew had checked earlier. "You little rascal," she told him sternly.

Mr. Bellyrub twitched his ears, but didn't bother to open his eyes.

"Into the basket, little man," Mayhew said, scooping the kitten up.

Mr. Bellyrub didn't object to his change in circumstance; he purred as he was placed in the basket. His sister tried to scramble out. Mayhew closed the lid ruthlessly. Willie heard Scout's indignant squeak.

Mayhew fastened the strap, sat back on his heels, and blew out a breath. Then he stood and checked his pocket watch. "Quarter to eight. We'll be in Twyford by half past, Miss Culpepper, I *promise* you." He turned to the wagon driver. "Thank you, Mr. Williams. We're extremely grateful for your help."

Mr. Williams grunted and turned away.

Willie almost burst into helpless giggles. She met Mayhew's eyes and saw laughter leap across his face. His lips twitched and a muscle jumped in his jaw. He said, with barely a quiver in his voice, "Shall we depart, Miss Culpepper?"

"Yes," Willie said, and her voice was almost as steady as his. "Let's." She picked up her reticule and looped it over her wrist—and then her amusement snuffed out, because this was the end of their adventure together.

The lieutenant carried her across the rutted, muddy stretch of ground between the barn and the lane, set her carefully on her feet, and ran back for the kittens and the hoe. He returned, grinning, and handed her the hoe with a flourish. Willie tried to grin back, but it felt unnatural on her face, an imitation of cheerfulness.

They set off together, Willie using the hoe as a walking stick, the lieutenant slowing his pace to match hers. Water sparkled on grass blades and tree leaves and hung in spiders' webs in bright, trembling drops. The world seemed fresh and new and clean. Birds sang and grasshoppers chirped and with every step that Willie took her spirits should have risen; instead, they sank.

All too quickly, they reached the fallen oak. It was bigger

than Willie had thought, a colossus of a tree, its trunk thicker than she was tall.

She looked at that great trunk and the shattered branches and the squashed hedgerows on either side of the lane. "We're very lucky," she said soberly.

"Yes," Mayhew said, equally soberly.

The oak lay squarely across the road. There was easy no way around, not unless they backtracked and ventured into the muddy paddocks on either side of the hedgerows. "We'll climb over it," Mayhew said, setting down the basket.

And that was what they did: they climbed over the great, slain oak, finding a path through the tangle of branches, clambering and crawling, and always Mayhew was there with a hand outstretched, ready to steady Willie, to brace her, to help her.

He jumped lightly down on the other side and held up both hands to her. "Slide. I'll catch you."

Willie perched for a moment on the gnarled trunk, and then did as he bid, sliding, her gown snagging on the rough bark. Mayhew caught her, his hands around her waist, and set her carefully on the muddy ground. "All right?" he said, smiling down at her.

"Yes," Willie said breathlessly, terribly aware of his hands at her waist.

Mayhew released her, and scrambled back up into the oak. "Won't be a minute," he said, and he was true to his word: less than a minute later he reappeared, with the hoe and the kittens and her reticule.

He lowered all three items to her, then jumped lightly down. "How's your ankle?"

"I barely notice it," Willie said.

"Good," he said, and glanced past her. "We're almost there."

Willie followed his gaze: the curve in the lane, the church spire peeking from behind the trees. "Yes," she said, and felt a pang of something that might have been sorrow.

The bell in the church spire struck the quarter hour—eight

fifteen—and as the echo died away, a horse and cart came around the bend in the lane.

"Cross your fingers, Miss Culpepper," Mayhew said. "We may not have to walk."

The cart was small and crude and filled with firewood, but there was room for them to both perch on the tailboard.

Mayhew lifted her up, handed her the basket, then helped the driver to turn the vehicle. "Our luck has finally turned," he said, climbing up alongside her.

"Yes," Willie said. But she didn't feel lucky as the cart rattled towards Twyford; she felt an absurd sense of loss, and a sadness that was close to grief.

Mayhew sniffed, scenting the air, then sniffed again, and she saw that he'd caught the lingering aroma of cow dung.

He glanced at her, clearly hoping she hadn't recognized that smell.

"And they rode into town in a dung cart," Willie said jauntily.

Lieutenant Mayhew huffed a surprised laugh and Willie laughed, too, at the expression on his face—but deep inside, she felt like crying.

CHAPTER 10

Five minutes, Mayhew told himself. They'd be in Twyford in five minutes. And that was good. It was better than good; it was excellent. Miss Culpepper's trunk would be waiting for her, and she'd have time to bathe and change into clean clothes. Right now, she looked as if she'd been dragged backwards through a hedge, but by ten o'clock she would once again be the respectable, faintly aloof young lady he'd met yesterday morning: her hair tidy, her gown unwrinkled, everything about her pristine and immaculate.

He preferred her as she was now, perched alongside him on this dung-cart-turned-firewood-cart, with her messy ringlets and her grubby clothes. This young lady was the Sweet Willie he'd heard so much about, the girl everyone in the second battalion had loved for her spirit and her resilience and her *joie de vivre.*

Not that the respectable Miss Culpepper of yesterday morning hadn't been attractive. She had been. Just not as attractive as this muddy, messy, vividly alive young woman beside him.

The horse's hooves clopped and the wheels turned and the cart jolted and splashed its way through ruts and puddles, and now it was only four minutes to Twyford, probably less.

Resolve had been gathering in Mayhew's belly for hours, slowly accreting into something solid and weighty, but now that Twyford was mere minutes away, it put out claws and took hold of his innards and grabbed hard, no longer resolve, but *urgency.*

Urgency, because once they reached the coaching inn, they would say their farewells.

Urgency, because Miss Culpepper was off to Vienna next month.

Urgency, because he might never see her again.

Another fifty yards rattled away beneath the cart wheels, while his urgency grew until he simply *had* to speak, even if it was foolish and even if he had no chance.

Mayhew took a deep breath. "Miss Culpepper? I know it's irregular, but . . . while you're in Vienna, may I write to you?"

It was more than irregular. It was, in fact, verging on improper. Single young ladies and single young men did not correspond with one another. Not without the permission of the young lady's parents. Not unless there was an acknowledged connection between them.

But Miss Culpepper had no parents and she was perfectly capable of making her own decisions.

She didn't reply immediately, but she did look at him. Her gaze was serious and he saw that she understood that he wasn't merely asking to correspond with her; he was asking to court her. A year of letters, perhaps two years, and then, when she'd fulfilled her commitment to the Pikes and he'd obtained his captaincy, he would ask for her hand in marriage.

Mayhew held his breath. His heart thumped loudly with hope. Miss Culpepper had turned down six offers in the past year and she could very well turn him down, too. She hadn't wanted to marry a baronet, or a baron's son, or a vicar, but maybe, just maybe, she *did* want to marry a soldier.

He tried to look as if her answer wasn't desperately important to him. If she said *No,* he'd smile and say something light and friendly, and then in three minutes' time, when they reached the inn, he'd help her down from the cart and bow politely over her hand and let her go. A chance lost forever.

"Yes," Miss Culpepper said. "I would like that."

Mayhew's heart gave a great leap. "You would?"

"Yes."

A smile grew on his face. Miss Culpepper liked him. She liked him so much that she'd agreed to correspond with him. She *wanted* to correspond with him.

Mayhew felt jubilant, felt like laughing aloud, and then he *did* laugh out loud, because it really was too absurd to have made the equivalent of a proposal while perched, damp and filthy, on the tailboard of a dung cart.

Miss Culpepper laughed, too, dimples dancing in her cheeks, and then their laughter faded and their grins faded and they just sat there, looking at each other, smiling ever so faintly.

Mayhew had never felt anything quite like this—the warmth in his chest, the joy, the hope, the sheer wonder that he'd met this particular woman out of all the women in the world and that possibly, hopefully, in a year—or perhaps two—they would marry.

If Miss Culpepper didn't meet someone else in Vienna. *If* she didn't lose interest in him. *If* nothing untoward or—heaven forbid—disastrous happened to one or the other of them.

He suddenly wanted, quite desperately, to ask her to marry him *now*, right this very instant. Mayhew bit the words back. He couldn't ask her to marry him today, or even this week or this month. Not when Miss Culpepper was bound for Vienna. Not when he was still merely a lieutenant.

But if he couldn't ask her to marry him now, he could take her hand, and so he did.

Miss Culpepper didn't object. On the contrary, she gripped his hand back, a firm grip, a grip that said *I am yours and you are mine,* a grip that made him feel even more hopeful about the future. The world glowed with sunshine and happiness.

They could do this, he and Miss Culpepper. It would be hard, a year apart, perhaps even two years, but they could do it. He *knew* they could do it.

The first houses of Twyford came into view. Mayhew released her hand, because it wasn't acceptable for unmarried young ladies to be seen to be holding hands with unmarried young men. "When do you leave for Vienna?" he asked.

"In two weeks."

"I'll write to you before then," he promised. "I'll write to you tomorrow. Where should I address it?"

She barely had time to tell him before the cart slowed to a halt. Mayhew looked up at the sign swinging overhead in the breeze. This was it, the place they'd been trying to reach for what seemed like forever: the coaching inn in Twyford, where Miss Culpepper would meet Sir Walter Pike in . . . He pulled out his pocket watch and saw, with relief, that she still had an hour and a half before that appointment.

He shoved the watch back in his pocket and jumped down from the cart, lifted Miss Culpepper down and set her carefully on her feet, then retrieved the basket and the hoe. One of the kittens mewed plaintively. Most likely Scout.

Mayhew checked that Miss Culpepper had her reticule, then raised his hand in thanks to the farmer.

The man nodded back, flicked his reins, and the cart clattered off, with its load of firewood and its aroma of cow dung and the tailboard upon which Mayhew had sat while he'd asked what was perhaps the most important question of his life.

"Do you need the hoe?" he asked Miss Culpepper. "Or will my arm suffice?"

She smiled up at him. "Your arm will suffice. It's only a few steps."

Mayhew leaned the hoe against the brick-and-plaster wall, made a mental note to have one of the ostlers return it to the barn, and gave Miss Culpepper his elbow. Together they entered the inn. It was low-ceilinged, warm and dimly lit and fragrant with the smells of coffee and baking bread.

The plump, smiling innkeeper welcomed them and confirmed that yes, Miss Culpepper's trunk had come yesterday on the stagecoach and was upstairs, and that yes, her room was ready for her, and that yes, water would be heated immediately for a bath, and that yes, he did have a walking stick that she might use while she was here.

Mayhew inhaled the smell of baking bread and knew that finally, after nearly twenty-four hours of mishap and misfortune, things were going their way.

He placed the basket on the floor and took Miss Culpepper's hands, while the innkeeper bustled off to fetch the walking stick. This moment felt like an end, but he knew it wasn't. It was a beginning. *Their* beginning. His and Miss Culpepper's. He could wait a year for this woman. Two years, if he had to. Because she was worth it.

"Well," he said. "I guess this is good-bye."

"It's au revoir," Miss Culpepper told him. "*Not* adieu."

They smiled at each other a little foolishly, and Mayhew wished that he could bend his head and kiss her, but he couldn't. Not with the innkeeper standing there, plump and smiling, holding out a walking stick.

Reluctantly, he released Miss Culpepper's hands. Reluctantly, he picked up the basket again. Reluctantly, he took a step back.

"I'll write to you every week," he said, and what he actually meant was, *I'm madly in love with you.*

"It'll write to you, too," Miss Culpepper said, taking the walking stick from the innkeeper.

She looked utterly disreputable, with her uncombed hair and her grubby shawl, her wrinkled gown and those filthy half boots—and at the same time, she looked extraordinarily lovely. Sweet Willie. *His* Sweet Willie. The Sweet Willie who'd be his wife in a year. Or perhaps, two.

If everything went well.

Mayhew didn't want to say goodbye. He wanted to blurt a proposal, wanted to beg her to marry him today. But marriage today wouldn't have been possible even if she *hadn't* been going to Vienna with Sir Walter Pike's daughters. Not without a special license, not without his commanding officer's permission.

Mayhew took another reluctant step back. One of the kittens squeaked faintly in the basket. "Goodbye, Miss Culpepper."

"Goodbye, Lieutenant."

He managed a smile. "Enjoy Vienna."

A door opened behind her, giving Mayhew a glimpse of a private parlor. A stout, well-groomed man emerged—and halted abruptly. "Miss Culpepper!" he exclaimed.

CHAPTER 11

*M*iss Culpepper jerked around. Her face paled. She looked as appalled as the man did.

Mayhew didn't need an introduction to know who this newcomer was. It was blindingly obvious. The man was Sir Walter Pike.

What was also blindingly obvious was that their disasters weren't over yet. In fact, the expression on Pike's face told Mayhew that the greatest disaster of all might be upon them.

Miss Culpepper clearly realized that, too. She put a hand to her damp, misshapen bonnet, as if she wished she could somehow hide her appearance, but it was no use. Everything about her was unkempt. And bedraggled. And grimy.

Mayhew put the basket down on a wooden bench and took a hasty step forward. "Sir Walter Pike? I can explain everything."

The man looked him up and down, visibly dismissed him, and turned his attention back to Miss Culpepper. "*You,*" he said, a whiplash of anger in his voice. "You are *dismissed,* Miss Culpepper."

"It's not what it looks like," Mayhew said, and in contrast to Sir Walter, his voice was calm and reasonable.

Sir Walter ignored him. "You were meant to arrive last night!" he snapped at Miss Culpepper.

"We missed the stagecoach at Abbots Worthy," Mayhew said. "It was my fault."

Sir Walter paid him no attention. "You are *late*," he said, his voice sharp with accusation. "Late and untrustworthy and *slatternly* and—"

Rage ignited in Mayhew's chest. "And *you* are out of order, Sir Walter. You know absolutely nothing about what befell Miss Culpepper yesterday!"

"I know enough that I don't want her anywhere near my daughters," Sir Walter Pike said, and his tone wasn't merely disrespectful, it was *exceedingly* disrespectful: a verbal sneer of contempt.

Mayhew took a step closer. "You would be *lucky* to have Miss Culpepper as companion to your daughters," he told the man. "She's the most outstanding female I've ever met. She has more fortitude and more character than you will *ever* have! She's too *good* for you and your daughters, you small-minded, pompous *prat.*"

Sir Walter stopped glaring at Miss Culpepper and glared at Mayhew instead. He drew himself up. "You are out of order, Lieutenant!"

"No, *you* are!" Mayhew thundered back. "You've jumped to conclusions—*offensive* conclusions—without even *asking* what happened, and *then* you've had the insolence to insult a lady *to her face.* Heaven help the Empire if you're an example of His Majesty's diplomats, because you're an ill-bred, ill-mannered *buffoon.*"

Sir Walter flushed an ugly shade of red. "Who the devil are you?" he demanded, trying to look down his nose at Mayhew, which, given that he was a good four inches shorter than Mayhew, didn't work.

"Lieutenant William Mayhew," Mayhew informed him. "*Lord* Mayhew's son." And he enjoyed saying that 'Lord,' because this stout, pompous man was merely a baronet. "*I* am the person responsible for Miss Culpepper missing the stagecoach, and *I* am responsible for her appearance. She is entirely blameless! Which you would *know,* if you'd bothered to *ask* her what happened, instead of assuming the worst!"

Sir Walter flushed even redder, and glared at Mayhew.

Mayhew glared back at him and realized, suddenly, that they had accumulated a sizable audience. At least a dozen people were watching agog from the doorways to taproom, coffee room, and kitchen.

Sir Walter came to the same realization a split second later. The color in his face mounted until it was almost puce. He took a step sideways, towards the street.

Mayhew stepped sideways, too, planting himself firmly in the man's path. "Apologize to Miss Culpepper," he said, in a hard voice.

Sir Walter firmed his jaw. "Out of my way, Lieutenant."

Mayhew didn't move. "*Apologize to her.*"

Sir Walter glowered at him, and then turned to Miss Culpepper and said, stiffly and insincerely, "I apologize if my words were offensive, Miss Culpepper."

She nodded coolly. "Your apology is accepted, Sir Walter."

Sir Walter turned back to Mayhew, his face still puce with rage and humiliation. "Your commanding officer will hear about this, Lieutenant," he said in a low, threatening voice.

"I hope so," Mayhew said. He bared his teeth at the man in a smile. "Colonel Barraclough, of the Rifle Brigade. He's a stickler for *gentlemanly* behavior."

Sir Water flushed even redder, which Mayhew hadn't thought possible. He lifted his chin, sidled around Mayhew, and headed for the door to the street. His gait was more scurry than strut.

Mayhew watched until the door swung shut behind the man, then turned back to Miss Culpepper. His audience was still staring at him, agog. Miss Culpepper was staring at him, too. He couldn't quite discern her expression. She didn't look angry, although she had ample reason to be. Not only was he the author of every misfortune she'd experienced in the past day and night, he had just subjected her to an extremely unpleasant and very public scene.

"I beg your pardon," he told both Miss Culpepper and the innkeeper.

"Not at all," the innkeeper said, and Mayhew had the feeling that the man held no very high opinion of Sir Walter.

Miss Culpepper said nothing.

The innkeeper clapped his hands briskly. "Back to work."

Half their audience disappeared. The other half didn't.

Mayhew looked at Miss Culpepper, and at those lingering spectators, and at the open doorway to the private parlor that Sir Walter had occupied.

"May we?" he asked the innkeeper, tipping his head at the parlor and the privacy it offered.

"Of course," the innkeeper said. "I'll set the water heating for you, Miss Culpepper. Your bath will be ready shortly."

"Thank you." Miss Culpepper glanced at Mayhew, her expression still indecipherable, then turned and entered the parlor, leaning lightly on the walking stick.

CHAPTER 12

$\mathcal{M}$ayhew made to follow Miss Culpepper, remembered the kittens, and caught up the basket. He stepped hastily into the parlor, closed the door behind him, set the basket down again, and turned to face her.

Miss Culpepper had crossed to the small diamond-paned window casement and was looking out. Her back was to him and he could see every mud stain, every wrinkle, every snagged thread.

No wonder Sir Walter had assumed the worst.

"I'm very sorry," Mayhew said contritely. "I shouldn't have said half of what I said and I *definitely* shouldn't have said it so loudly and so publicly."

Miss Culpepper turned to face him. To his astonishment, he saw that she was smiling. It was a small smile, not enough to set the dimples dancing in her cheeks, but enough to tell him that she wasn't furious with him.

Which she really *ought* to be.

She'd been harangued in public because of him. She'd lost her chance to go to Vienna because of him.

"I'm very sorry," Mayhew said again. He felt a rising tide of shame, and on the heels of shame, dismay. He'd accused Sir

Walter of ill-breeding, but *he'd* been ill-bred, too, losing his temper like that.

It's better to fix things than lose one's temper—Colonel Culpepper's maxim, that, and Mayhew had indisputably lost his temper. Even worse, he couldn't fix this mess. Miss Culpepper's position with the Pikes was irrevocably lost.

But he *would* fix the things that *could* be fixed.

"May I escort you back to Kingston upon Thames, Miss Culpepper? That is . . . if my behavior hasn't given you a repugnance of me."

Miss Culpepper cocked her head at him. "Repugnance?"

"Your father disapproved of displays of temper. I must presume that you do, too."

Miss Culpepper's dimples finally made an appearance. "Do you think my father never lost his temper, Lieutenant? You'd be wrong, then, for he most certainly did!"

"You're not angry with me?" Mayhew asked cautiously.

"Angry?" Miss Culpepper's dimples deepened. "Lieutenant, you were shockingly uncomplimentary to Sir Walter, but you were *exceedingly* complimentary to me."

Some of the tension in Mayhew's chest eased.

"If my father had been here, he'd have given Sir Walter exactly such a raking down as you did," Miss Culpepper said.

"He would have?"

"Yes." She pursed her lips thoughtfully. "Although he probably would have been louder."

"But . . . your position in Vienna—"

"It would have been interesting to live in Vienna for a spell," Miss Culpepper said. "But I doubt I would have enjoyed being part of Sir Walter's household. As you so eloquently put it, he's a pompous prat."

Yes, he had called Sir Walter that. Loudly.

Mayhew didn't know whether to grimace or laugh, so he did both. Then his laughter faded and his grimace faded and he just stood in the middle of the private parlor, looking at

Miss Culpepper. "I meant it," he said quietly. "You are the most outstanding female I've ever met."

Miss Culpepper's cheeks became an adorable shade of pink. She looked down at the muddy toes of her half boots.

"The last eighteen hours have been both irksome and uncomfortable. Most people would have complained, but you haven't. Not once! Not when you missed the stagecoach. Not when you got muddy and wet. Not even when you *hurt* yourself and had to sleep in a barn! You've borne everything with fortitude and good humor."

Miss Culpepper's cheeks became even pinker. "You make me sound like a paragon, but the sad truth of it is that I've enjoyed it, Lieutenant." She glanced up at him through her eyelashes, not flirtatiously, but a little uncertainly, as if she was doubtful of his reaction. "Even the mud. Even the storm."

"I'm shocked," Mayhew said, a smile growing on his face. "Deeply shocked." He took a step closer. "And extremely relieved. And . . . enchanted."

Miss Culpepper blushed ferociously at that last word. She fixed her attention on her half boots again.

Mayhew laughed softly and reached out and tipped up her chin.

Her eyes met his shyly, and Mayhew felt an almost overwhelming urge to bend his head and kiss those rosy lips.

The urge was so strong that he almost succumbed to it—but he'd just comprehensively upended Miss Culpepper's life and he needed to mend that before he did anything else.

"What would you like to do now?" he asked her. "Tell me, and I'll make it happen. Would you like to return to your aunt? Or would you like to come to Southampton with me? You can stay with my sister and her husband—there would be no impropriety, I assure you!—they're *very* respectable. He's a magistrate, you know."

"Southampton?" Miss Culpepper said.

"Yes." Mayhew's lungs squeezed tight. "And . . . if you

wish . . . I can apply for permission to marry you." He felt himself blush, and continued resolutely on: "But I'll only do that if it's what you truly want, because we don't know each other very well and perhaps we ought to correspond for a while, and I *am* only a lieutenant."

"My father was only a lieutenant when he married my mother," Miss Culpepper said.

Mayhew's heart gave a hopeful leap. Did that mean what he thought it meant? "Tell me what you'd like to do, Miss Culpepper. What you would *most* like to do."

She smiled at him. "What I most want to do is marry you."

"Now?" he said cautiously. "Or in a year—"

"Now."

Mayhew's heart didn't just leap in his chest, it soared. "Are you certain?" He searched her face for doubts, for hesitancy.

"I'm certain," Miss Culpepper said. "Maybe I don't know everything about you, but I *do* know that we're cut from the same cloth, you and I."

"Indeed, we are." He lifted one hand and touched her cheek, ghosting his thumb over the spot where her dimple was hidden.

"I think I could search all of England and not find someone who suits me as well as you do," Miss Culpepper told him.

"Nor I you." Mayhew stroked her cheek again, lightly, reverently, marveling at the softness of her skin.

She smiled, and a dimple sprang to life beneath his thumb. "And it's not just because you're a soldier. I think I should wish to marry you even if you weren't."

"You do, do you?" he teased her. "Are you certain about that?"

The dimple deepened. "Yes."

"I'm very pleased to hear it," Mayhew said. "Because I've decided to sell my commission and become a farmer. A pig farmer. In Wiltshire."

Miss Culpepper laughed. "No, you haven't."

"No, I haven't," Mayhew agreed. He gave in to temptation and tipped up her chin and kissed her lightly. Her lips were exactly as he'd imagined, soft and warm, but also shy and trembling, which he hadn't expected, and a sudden realization flashed through him: Willemina Culpepper had never been kissed before.

Mayhew drew back slightly and looked down at her.

Miss Culpepper gazed back, shyness written on her face, and it made his heart squeeze in his chest to think that he was the first man to kiss this remarkable woman.

Shyness wasn't the only thing written on her face. Trust was there, too, but trepidation and fear weren't—which didn't surprise him, because his Willie didn't have a timid bone in her body. His Willie was brave and confident and indomitable—and gazing at him not just with shyness and trust, but also with *expectancy*.

Mayhew could see that she wanted him to kiss her again, so he did, bending his head, touching his lips to hers. It was a kiss that was gentle and tender and friendly, affectionate. A kiss that said *hello* and *I love you* and *this is our beginning*. Then he drew back and took both her hands in his. "I know I'm only a lieutenant, but I *have* been tapped for a captaincy. I'll be a major within five years, and a colonel before I'm forty. I promise you."

"I don't mind if you're a lieutenant forever," Miss Culpepper told him. "But I have no doubt that you'll be an excellent colonel."

"I hope to be."

"I *know* you'll be," she said. "I have confidence in you. And I have confidence in *us*. You and I were destined to be together."

Mayhew laughed at that and kissed her again, lightly, and whispered, "I have confidence in us, too," against her mouth, and then he kissed her again, not quite so lightly, and her lips parted for him and the tip of her tongue touched the tip of his and a shiver went through him from head to toe.

Mayhew drew her closer. He kissed her in wonder and joy and delight, and she kissed him back eagerly. His arms were around her, drawing her close, and her hands were fisted in his jacket, pulling him even closer, and the dance of their mouths became deeper and more intimate, more urgent . . .

Mayhew reluctantly broke the kiss. He lifted his head and tried to catch his breath, tried to catch his wits, but it was practically impossible to do either when Miss Culpepper was clutching his jacket and gazing up at him, looking flushed and breathless and utterly adorable.

Much as he wanted to keep kissing her—much as he wanted to do a *lot* more than merely kiss her—now was not the time and here was not the place.

It took effort to let her go, effort to uncurl her fingers from his jacket, pick up the walking stick from where it had fallen on the floor and hand it to her, effort to take a half step back.

Miss Culpepper looked as disappointed as he was, but she didn't protest. She knew as well as he did that a servant could enter the parlor at any moment.

Mayhew took her free hand in his. "A postponement," he said, sealing the promise by laying a light kiss on her knuckles. "Hopefully not a long one, but I *do* need permission to marry. I can't imagine Barraclough will refuse. He knows you, after all! He is in France, though, and it'll take time." He grimaced at thought of exactly how *much* time. Weeks, damn it. "But I'll try at the Horse Guards first. It's possible someone there will give me permission. General Seaton is a family friend. He sponsored me into the Rifles. He might—"

"General Sir George Seaton?"

Mayhew nodded.

"Seaton was a good friend of my father's."

"Was he?" Mayhew began to feel more hopeful. "I'll apply to him first, then. If he feels he can't sanction it, we'll have to wait for Barraclough's permission, but I *know* we'll get that."

Miss Culpepper nodded. She'd grown up in the army; she

understood how these things worked. Officers couldn't marry without permission.

Mayhew released her hand and made himself take another step back, when what he really wanted to do was step closer and gather Miss Culpepper in his arms and kiss her until they were breathless and dizzy. "What's going to happen now is that you're going to go upstairs and have a bath and change into dry clothes," he told her. "And then we'll go to Southampton, and tomorrow I'll return to London and speak with General Seaton." He waited a beat, and then said, "If that meets with your approval?"

She nodded. "It does."

"Good." Mayhew crossed to the door and took hold of the handle.

Miss Culpepper came to join him, leaning on the walking stick. Her nearness, the smile on her lips, the smile in her eyes as she gazed up at him, made his heart feel as if it had grown several sizes in his chest.

"May I call you Willie?" he asked.

She nodded.

"May I call you *Sweet* Willie?"

She blushed, and nodded again. "If you wish."

He did wish. Very much. "I hope you'll call me Will," he said.

"Will and Willie." She laughed at that and shook her head, and then she tucked her free hand into his, a gesture of trust and familiarity that made Mayhew's heart leap absurdly. "We really *were* made for each other, weren't we?"

"We were."

"I'm glad we missed the stagecoach in Abbots Worthy," Miss Culpepper told him. "And that the horse cast a shoe. And that we fell in the ford and got caught in that storm and had to spend the night in a barn. I'm glad for *all* of it."

"So am I," Mayhew said, and he was. More glad than he'd ever been of anything in his life.

He gazed down at her, knowing that this was a moment to be treasured: the coaching inn, this parlor, Willemina Culpepper holding his hand. And then he realized that while this moment was wonderful, what was even more wonderful was that they'd be able to hold each other's hands for the *rest of their lives.*

Mayhew's throat tightened and it became ridiculously hard to swallow. He managed it, though, and then he released her hand and opened the door and said, "Go and take your bath. I'll wait here. Would you like me to order breakfast sent up to you?"

"Yes, please." Miss Culpepper smiled at him, grubby and bedraggled and vivid and beautiful.

Mayhew smiled back, feeling so damned *happy* and so damned *lucky.* How had this happened? This combination of mischance and pure good fortune? How had he ended up betrothed to Sweet Willie Culpepper?

A maid appeared and bobbed a curtsy. "Are you wantin' to go to your room, ma'am?"

"Yes, please."

Mayhew watched them cross the vestibule and climb the stairs—the tidy maid in her apron and mob cap, and the unbelievably messy colonel's daughter in her mud-stained dress and bedraggled bonnet, limping ever so slightly, leaning on the walking stick. Miss Culpepper sent him a smile before disappearing from sight and Mayhew smiled helplessly back. Then he uttered a laugh of disbelief and wonder and sheer joy, and went in search of the innkeeper to arrange for a hot breakfast for Miss Culpepper, and a hot breakfast for himself, and milk for the kittens, and a carriage to take them the ten miles to Southampton, where *his* dry clothes were waiting.

*C*HAPTER 13

Six days later . . .

*W*hen Mayhew had said that his brother-in-law was a magistrate, Willie had pictured someone serious and stern, with gray sideburns. Sir John Belton *did* have gray sideburns, but thereafter reality had diverged from what she'd imagined. Sir John was jolly rather than stern and his eyes twinkled with good humor. His wife had twinkling eyes, too, and their six-year-old twins were giggling, harum-scarum delights.

The Beltons had welcomed her into their home without question, and it should have been awkward, staying with people who were practically strangers, except that after the first half hour the Beltons hadn't been strangers at all. They'd been friends. They'd been *family*.

The time while Mayhew was in London had passed swiftly. Willie had rested her ankle for the first day, then spent the next two days in a blur of kittens and hide-and-seek and building forts out of furniture. They'd been good days, wonderful days even, but nothing had equaled the moment when Mayhew had returned, and she'd run down the sweeping curve of the marble staircase and seen him standing in the entrance hall, handsome in his green Rifleman's uniform.

Willie had laughed and cried when she'd greeted him, and she'd laughed and cried some more when Mayhew had told her that he had a special license in his pocket and General Seaton's permission to marry. And then she'd hugged him again, and again, and *again.*

She'd kissed him, later that afternoon, when they'd had a moment alone together in the drawing room, and that was how she'd measured the rest of their time in Southampton: by kisses. Two the day he'd arrived. Three more the next day. And then yesterday, six. *Six.* Because yesterday had been special. The day before their wedding, the day the Beltons had hosted a dinner party in their honor.

There'd been dancing after the dinner, with a small orchestra, and Willie had stood up with Sir John Belton twice, but she'd danced all the other dances with Mayhew, because it was a private ball and it was the night before her wedding and she could dance every single dance with her fiancé if she wished to—and she *had* wished to.

Mayhew had kissed her after the ball, and he'd kissed her this morning before the wedding ceremony, and again afterwards, and he'd kissed her quite a few times in the six hours since they'd departed from Southampton. So many times, in fact, that Willie had quite lost count of today's kisses.

Last week, when she'd left London on the stagecoach, she'd been so excited that she'd been hard pressed not to wriggle in her seat. Today, as she sat in a post-chaise while afternoon ripened into early evening, she wasn't excited in a wriggle-in-her-seat way; she was excited in a huge, uplifting way. She almost felt as if she was floating.

As of ten o'clock this morning, she was *married.*

She was no longer Willemina Culpepper. She was Willemina Mayhew, and she was sitting in a post-chaise with her husband, en route to Oxfordshire to meet Mayhew's parents and brothers, and then they were going to Kingston upon Thames so that he might meet her aunt, and *then* they were going to France. Home to the army. Home to the Rifle Brigade.

Willie turned her head and found Mayhew watching her. "Hungry?" he asked. "Tired?"

Willie shook her head. "Neither. Happy."

He grinned at her and leaned in for another kiss. "So am I," he whispered against her lips.

The post-chaise slowed to a trot while they kissed, and then slowed further. The wheels rattled over cobblestones. They drew apart. Mayhew looked out the window. "We're coming into Nettlebed."

Nettlebed, where they'd break their journey for the night. Nettlebed, where they would consummate their marriage.

Willie gave a tiny shiver that was equal parts anticipation and excitement, with a dash of nervousness thrown in.

She gave another of those delicious little shivers when they climbed down from the carriage, and yet another when the innkeeper showed them to their bedchamber. It was a handsome room, with a washstand and a dressing table and a four-poster bed hung with green curtains.

"Does it meet with your approval?" Mayhew asked, smiling down at her.

"It does," Willie said, and another tingling shiver ran through her, from her scalp to the tips of her toes.

"The private parlor is taken, but you'll be quite comfortable dining in the coffee room," the innkeeper said, and showed them where the coffee room was, and while he was doing that more travelers arrived, an elderly man and his wife.

The man could have been anything in his younger days—a clerk, a farmer, an apothecary—but Willie looked at his weather-beaten face and his bearing, upright despite the way age had curved his spine, and thought *soldier.*

"We're full, sir," the innkeeper said. "Try one of the other inns."

"We have. We've tried them all." The old soldier's voice held a Yorkshire brogue and an indefinable hint of something that Willie's ears identified as *sergeant.*

"Then I'm afraid you'll have to drive on to Nuffield, sir."

"We'll take anything," the old sergeant said. "Even truckle beds in the stables." He looked exhausted, and his wife even more so.

The innkeeper hesitated. "I have a room up in the attic, but it's only fit for servants."

Willie exchanged a glance with Mayhew. He lifted his eyebrows fractionally, a silent question to which she returned a nod.

"We'll take it," the old soldier said.

"No, *we'll* take it," Mayhew said. "You and your wife may have our room."

Three pairs of startled eyes swung around to look at him.

"Thank you, Lieutenant," the old man said, assessing Mayhew's rank with the merest glance at his shoulder. "But it's not necessary."

"We insist," Mayhew said. "Which regiment were you?"

The man hesitated, and then said, "The Fifty-First."

"You were a sergeant?" Mayhew asked.

"Yes."

"Well, Sergeant, we'd be pleased if you would take our room."

"You'd prefer not to climb all those stairs, I think," Willie said, with a smile at the elderly couple.

The old soldier wavered for a few more seconds, then gave a stiff, courteous bow. "Thank you, we would be most grateful."

Their original bedchamber had been well-appointed. Their new one was not. The ceiling sloped so steeply that Mayhew had to duck his head, the floorboards were bare, the bowl in the washstand was chipped and the four-poster bed was missing one of its posts, but the room had the quaintest of tiny-paned windows through which the setting sun cast a golden glow.

There were dust balls on the floor and the bed linen wasn't clean, a fact that discomfited the innkeeper greatly. He went as red as a lobster, promised to have the floor swept and the sheets changed immediately, and hurried back down the steep, narrow stairs, shouting for his servants.

Mayhew glanced at her. "What do you think?"

Willie looked at that delightful little window and the bed with its three posts. "I love it," she declared.

He laughed, and said, "Of course you do," and she could tell from his expression that he was thinking about kissing her again.

Willie stepped closer and tucked her hand into his. "Thank you for changing rooms. You don't mind, do you?"

"Mind? Of course not." Mayhew drew her even closer and bent his head—and then stepped back as someone clattered up the uncarpeted stairs. A maid hurried into the room with a broom. On her heels was another servant bearing an armful of bed linen.

Willie and Mayhew retreated downstairs. The coffee room was comfortably snug, with a low-beamed ceiling and a small fire burning in the grate. Two of the little tea tables were occupied by other travelers, and the hearth was occupied, too—by a basket containing half a dozen kittens.

"Look!" Willie said, and headed for the kittens.

Dusk fell, that magical gloaming hour. Willie sat near the fire with her husband alongside her and a tortoiseshell kitten on her lap, drinking home-brewed cider. The cider was crisp on her tongue, tart and sweet at the same time. She sipped it and felt happy enough to burst.

They ate a raised pie for their dinner, and the pastry was buttery and the meat tender and fragrant, and while they ate, Willie said, "I think the Fates were watching over us the day we met."

Mayhew smiled at her over the rim of his tankard. "The Fates?"

"Yes," Willie said, and although she was joking, she also

357

wasn't *quite* joking. "I think they made certain that we had enough time to become properly acquainted."

"They did, did they?"

"Yes," she said again. "Because if those things hadn't happened—the horseshoe and the storm and the tree falling over—then we'd have sat in the same carriage for a whole day and never known we're meant to be together." Her throat tightened at that thought.

Perhaps Mayhew's throat tightened, too, because he didn't laugh at her; instead, he raised his tankard. "To the Fates," he said. "And to *us*."

They touched brims and drank, and despite that fact that it was mostly a joke, the moment felt weighty and ceremonious.

Servants cleared their plates, lit the candles, and closed the shutters. Other guests came and went, eating, drinking, reading the *Gazette* beside the fire. A kitten found its way onto Willie's lap again, the same kitten that had been there before: a tortoiseshell with one ginger paw. She stroked it and listened to the tiny vibrato of its purr and thought that no one had ever had such a good wedding day as she was having.

A faint melody crept into the coffee room, teasing her ears. "Where's that music coming from?" Mayhew asked, when a servant came to place more coals on the fire.

"Taproom," the woman said. "The Barrett brothers brought their fiddles in again."

Mayhew glanced at Willie. "Would you like to listen for a while?"

If Willie had been by herself she would never have dared venture into a taproom; in the company of her husband, she did. A rollicking jig spilled out when Mayhew opened the door. Willie looked around with interest, but the taproom was no dangerous den of iniquity; it looked very much like the coffee room, although the furniture was a little rougher, trestle tables and wooden benches instead of tea tables and chairs. The clientele was a little rougher, too, and quite a lot rowdier.

Not rowdy in a bellicose way, but rowdy in a loud, cheerful way, people stamping and clapping in time to the music.

They found space at a bench and a servingman brought them more home-brewed cider. Willie settled in to enjoy herself. The tunes weren't tunes she knew, but they were lively and infectious, and she sipped her cider and tapped her feet to the music and felt happiness bubble in her veins.

Mayhew got up to speak with one of the fiddlers, and when he returned to their bench he didn't sit, but held out his hands to her.

Willie let him pull her to her feet.

The fiddler struck up a new tune, and called out, "A dance for the newlyweds! Married today, they was."

A whoop went up, and the second fiddle joined the first, and thus it was that Willie danced her first dance as Mrs. Mayhew.

She had danced in a private ballroom last night, wearing pearls in her hair and silk slippers on her feet. Those dances had been formal—the waltz, the quadrille, the cotillion. To-night's dance wasn't formal at all. It was fast and foot-stomp-ing. Mayhew whirled her around and around, while the fiddlers fiddled and their audience clapped and stamped and whooped, and when it was over, Willie clung to her husband, breathless and laughing, and she just *knew* that no one had ever had such a marvelous wedding day as she was having.

They returned to their wooden bench. Mayhew put an arm around her shoulders and Willie leaned into the heat of his body and enjoyed this gift of an evening: the strangers, the music, the good cheer.

She sipped the last of her cider and smothered a yawn.

"Time for bed?" Mayhew asked.

"Time for bed."

They went up the steep, narrow stairs and discovered that their luggage had been brought up, the candles lit, and the bedclothes turned back. Mayhew eyed the three-poster bed somewhat dubiously. "We can wait, you know. It doesn't have to be tonight."

"It's good luck to consummate one's marriage in a three-poster bed," Willie told him.

His eyes creased at the corners with amusement. "Is it, now?"

"*Very* good luck. Quite auspicious, in fact."

Mayhew laughed. "Auspicious?"

"Exceptionally auspicious."

He took both of her hands in his and smiled fondly down at her. "Well, then. Let's not wait."

*C*HAPTER 14

*M*ayhew had undressed a woman before, but it had never been like this, unhurried, a sweet and slow disrobing, minutes slipping by in quiet murmurs and gentle touches, in the whisper of fabric sliding over skin, in the feather-light brush of his fingertips across the nape of Willie's neck, in reverent kisses placed on her bare shoulders.

When they were both standing naked Mayhew couldn't help but gaze at Willie, because she was so damned beautiful, all creamy skin and slender curves, sweet rosy lips and sweet rosy nipples.

Willie gazed back, taking him in from head to toe, a blatant perusal that made his balls tighten and heat flush beneath his skin. Then she tilted her head and said, "You look very fine, Lieutenant Mayhew."

Mayhew laughed—somewhat breathlessly, and said—somewhat hoarsely, "You look a great deal more than fine, Mrs. Mayhew."

She laughed, too, and Mayhew realized in that moment that his hands were trembling slightly. He wasn't sure whether the tremble came from his eagerness to make love to Willie or his fear of hurting her. He swallowed past the sudden lump in his throat. "It might hurt a little bit."

"I know," Willie said. "Your sister told me about it."

Mayhew blinked at her. "My sister did?"

Willie nodded. "She said it would probably hurt the first time, maybe even the first few times, but after that it would become a lot more enjoyable."

Mayhew stared at her, bemused. His *sister* had talked to Willie about *sex*?

His expression appeared to amuse Willie, because she laughed, and then she climbed up on the three-poster bed, giving him a tantalizing glimpse of her derrière as she did so. "Come to bed, Lieutenant Mayhew."

Mayhew did.

He'd never felt shy when making love to a woman before, but he found himself a little shy tonight. Willie was shy, too, of course—shy and blushing, but she was also eager and trusting. She laughed at him while he worshiped every one of her fingertips with kisses, and she giggled when he nipped and teased his way down her throat, and she gasped and squirmed as he kissed his way up her inner thighs.

He did his best not to hurt her, entering her more slowly than he'd ever entered a woman before, more carefully. He watched her face intently while he sank in those final inches and he thought that he'd mostly succeeded. Willie looked flushed and wide-eyed and a little disconcerted, but not pained.

"How does it feel?" he asked.

Her lips pursed thoughtfully. "Odd."

It didn't feel odd to Mayhew; it felt unbelievably good.

Willie shifted her hips slightly, making the breath catch in his throat. She heard it, and grinned up at him. "How does it feel to you?"

"Good," Mayhew said, and the word was almost a groan. He was trembling—the muscles in his belly, in his thighs, in his arms as he braced himself above her. Trembling with the need to move and the equally strong need to stay still until he was certain he wasn't hurting her.

He bent his head and kissed Willie. Their lips clung together for a long moment, and then he began to move—slow slide, slow glide—coaxing a rhythm between them.

Willie enjoyed it. He could tell from the way she gasped and the tiny, guttural moans she uttered, and also from the way that she moved, clutching his arms, arching into him—and he could tell from the way she laughed at the moment of her climax. Mayhew laughed when she laughed and climaxed when she climaxed, because it was impossible not to do either, and then he held her tightly while they both floated down from that soaring high.

He would have liked to have stayed inside her all night, but he couldn't, so he carefully withdrew and cleaned her with a handkerchief, and then he blew out the candles and crawled into bed and tucked Willie into the curve of his body, her back pressing snugly to his chest, his arm securely around her waist.

They lay curled together in the cozy warmth of the three-poster bed. Willie stroked the back of his hand. "I know your sister said it would get better, but I honestly can't imagine it."

Mayhew couldn't imagine it either.

When he woke, it was dawn and his wife was still in his arms. He pressed his face into her hair and inhaled her scent—orange blossom—and wondered how he'd been so damned lucky as to meet Sweet Willie Culpepper, let alone marry her.

Mayhew tightened his arm around her, but only a little bit; he didn't want to wake her. But it appeared that she was already awake, for her fingers intertwined with his. "Careful," she whispered. "Don't disturb the kitten."

"Kitten?" He lifted his head and peered over her, and there

on the pillow was a tortoiseshell kitten, curled up asleep. He found that he wasn't surprised. It felt almost like fate. "How long has it been there?"

"I don't know. It was there when I woke."

Mayhew was fairly certain it was the same kitten that had sat on Willie's lap in the coffee room. "It must like you."

Their voices woke the kitten. It blinked its eyes opened and yawned, pink-tongued and sharp-toothed. It looked adorable. Almost as adorable as Willie.

Willie slipped her hand free from his clasp and reached out and stroked the kitten. "It was born a marmalade tabby, I think, but someone took it by the paw and dipped it in a cauldron of magic and stardust, and now it looks like the night sky."

Mayhew huffed a laugh. "Very poetic." And accurate, too; the kitten's coat did look like a night sky speckled with stars. Except for that one golden paw.

Willie carefully rubbed between the kitten's ears. Mayhew heard the tiny rumble of its purr. "My brigade major had a kitten that looked a bit like that," he told her. "He found it at Badajoz, carried it around with him for months."

"He did?" Willie said, and he heard her surprise.

"He did. His name's Reynolds. Major Reynolds." Mayhew smothered a yawn. "Actually, it was Reynolds who rescued Scout and Mr. Bellyrub." Or Princess Plum Blossom and Prince Purr-a-lot, as they'd been renamed by the twins.

"Is he on furlough, too?"

"Sold out after Waterloo. Henry Wright's our brigade major now. He's first rate. You'll like him."

"I'm sure I will," Willie said, and then, "Colonel Barra-clough didn't mind one of his officers keeping a kitten while on campaign?"

"Not at all. He was rather fond of it. Was forever bringing scraps for it to eat."

"Was he now?" Willie said, her tone thoughtful.

Mayhew yawned again. "I think Barraclough likes cats."

Willie was silent for a moment, and then she said, "Good," and tickled the kitten under its chin with a fingertip.

Mayhew watched her fingertip and heard that tiny purr and made a belated realization. "We're taking the kitten with us, aren't we?"

"Yes," Willie said. "It's our wedding gift from the Fates."

Mayhew didn't laugh at that statement because he had a feeling she might be right. "What shall we name it?"

"Stardust," Willie said, and tickled the kitten under its chin again.

Mayhew pressed his face into his wife's hair and inhaled her orange blossom scent, and then he laughed softly, his breath stirring her messy ringlets. "I love you," he told her.

Willie stopped stroking the kitten. Her fingers intertwined with his again. "I love you, too."

Mayhew inhaled another orange-blossom-scented breath and thought that he couldn't possibly be any happier than he was at that moment, lying in a three-poster bed, holding his wife, while a kitten purred on the pillow alongside them.

Then he remembered that this was the first of many such mornings together, and he discovered that it *was* possible to be even happier. He gathered Willie closer, tucking her warmth and her soft, slender curves in tightly to his body. "This is going to be so good," he whispered in her ear. "Us, together, forever."

"It most certainly is!" Willie said.

And it was.

$\mathcal{T}$HANK $\mathcal{Y}$OU

Thanks for reading *Love and Other Surprises*. I hope you enjoyed it!

If you'd like to be notified whenever I release a new book, please join my Readers' Group, which you can find at www.emilylarkin.com/newsletter.

I welcome all honest reviews. Reviews and word of mouth help other readers to find books, so please consider taking a few moments to leave a review on Goodreads or elsewhere.

I invite you to read the first chapter of *My Lady Thief,* a novel about an heiress with a dangerous pastime and a bachelor who thinks very highly of himself.

My Lady THIEF

*C*HAPTER *O*NE

*T*he thief stood in front of Lady Bicknell's dressing table and looked with disapproval at the objects strewn across it: glass vials of perfume, discarded handkerchiefs, a clutter of pots and jars of cosmetics—rouge, maquillage; many gaping open, their contents drying—two silver-backed hair brushes with strands of hair caught among the bristles, a messy pile of earrings, the faceted jewels glinting dully in the candlelight.

The thief stirred the earrings with a fingertip. Gaudy. Tasteless. In need of cleaning.

The dressing table, the mess, offended the thief's tidy soul. She pursed her lips and examined the earrings again, more slowly. The diamonds were paste, the sapphires nothing more than colored glass, the rubies . . . She picked up a ruby earring and looked at it closely. Real, but such a garish, vulgar setting. The thief grimaced and put the earring back, more neatly than its owner had done. There was nothing on the dressing table that interested her.

She turned to the mahogany dresser. It stood in the corner, crouching on bowed legs like a large toad. Three wide drawers and at the top, three small ones, side by side, beneath a frowning mirror. The thief quietly opened the drawers and let her fingers sift through the contents, stirring the woman's scent from the garments: perspiration, perfume.

The topmost drawer on the left, filled with a tangle of silk stockings and garters, wasn't as deep as the others.

For a moment the thief stood motionless, listening for footsteps in the corridor, listening to the breeze stir the curtains at the open window, then she pulled the drawer out and laid it on the floor.

Behind the drawer of stockings was another drawer, small and discreet, and inside that . . .

The thief grinned as she lifted out the bracelet. Pearls gleamed in the candlelight, exquisite, expensive.

The drawer contained—besides the bracelet—a matching pair of pearl earrings and four letters. The thief took the earrings and replaced the letters. She was easing the drawer back into its slot when a name caught her eye. *St. Just.*

St. Just. The name brought with it memory of a handsome face and gray eyes, memory of humiliation—and a surge of hatred.

She hesitated for a second, and then reached for the letters.

The first one was brief and to the point. *Here, as requested, is my pearl bracelet. In exchange, I must ask for the return of my letter.* It was signed Grace St. Just.

The thief frowned and unfolded the second letter. It was written in the same girlish hand as the first. The date made her pause—November 6th, 1817. The day Princess Charlotte had died, although the letter writer wouldn't have known that at the time.

Dearest Reginald, the letter started. The thief skimmed over a passionate declaration of love and slowed to read the final paragraph. *I miss you unbearably. Every minute seems like an hour, every day a year. The thought of being parted from you is unendurable. If it must be elopement, then so be it.* A tearstain marked the ink. *Your loving Grace.*

The thief picked up the third letter. It was a draft, some words crossed out, others scribbled in the margins.

~~My dear~~ Miss St. Just, ~~I have~~ a letter ~~of yours~~ you wrote to a Mr. Reginald Plunkett of Birmingham has come into my possession. ~~If you want it back. In exchange for its return~~. I should like to return this letter to you. In exchange I ~~want~~ ask nothing more than your pearl bracelet. You may leave ~~it~~ the bracelet ~~for me~~ in the Dutch garden in the Kensington Palace Gardens. ~~Place it~~ Hide it in the urn at the northeastern corner of the pond.

The thief thinned her lips. She stopped reading and picked up the final letter. Another draft.

Dear Miss St. Just, thank you for the bracelet. I find, however, that I ~~want~~ require ~~the necklace~~ the earrings as well. You may leave them in the same place. Do not worry about ~~the~~ your letter; ~~I have it~~ it is safe in my keeping.

The thief slowly refolded the paper. Blackmail. There was a sour taste in her mouth. She looked down at the bracelet and earrings, at the love letter, and bit her lower lip. What to do?

St. Just.

Memory flooded through her: the smothered laughter of the *ton,* the sniggers and the sideways glances, the gleeful whispers.

The thief tightened her lips. Resentment burned in her breast and heated her cheeks. Adam St. Just could rot in hell for all she cared, but Grace St. Just . . . Grace St. Just didn't deserve this.

Her decision made, the thief gathered the contents of the hidden drawer—letters and jewels—and tucked them into the pouch she wore around her waist, hidden beneath shirt and trousers. Swiftly she replaced both drawers. Crossing the room, she plucked the ruby earrings from the objects littering Lady Bicknell's dressing table. The rubies went into the pouch, nestling alongside the pearls. The thief propped an elegant square of card among the remaining earrings. The message inscribed on it was brief: *Should payment be made for a spiteful tongue? Tom thinks so.* There was no signature; a drawing of a lean alley cat adorned the bottom of the note.

The thief gave a satisfied nod. Justice done. She glanced

at the mirror. In the candlelight her eyes were black. Her face was soot-smudged and unrecognizable. For a moment she stared at herself, unsettled, then she lifted a finger to touch the faint cleft in her chin. That, at least, was recognizable, whether she wore silk dresses or boys' clothing in rough, dark fabric.

The thief turned away from her image in the mirror. She trod quietly towards the open window.

Adam St. Just found his half-sister in the morning room, reading a letter. Her hair gleamed like spun gold in the sunlight. "Grace?"

His sister gave a convulsive start and clutched the letter to her breast. A bundle of items on her lap slid to the floor. Something landed with a light thud. Adam saw the glimmer of pearls.

"Is that your bracelet? I thought you'd lost—" He focused on her face. "What's wrong?"

"Nothing." Grace hastily wiped her cheeks. "Just something in my eye." She bent and hurriedly gathered several pieces of paper and the bracelet.

A pearl earring lay stranded on the carpet. Adam nudged it with the toe of his boot. "And this?" He picked up the earring and held it out.

Grace flushed. She took the earring

Adam frowned at her. "Grace, what is it?"

"Nothing." Her smile was bright, but her eyes slid away from his.

Adam sat down on the sofa alongside her. "Grace . . ." he said, and then stopped, at a loss to know how to proceed. The physical distance between them—a few inches of rose-pink damask—may as well have been a chasm. The twelve years that separated them, the difference in their genders, seemed insurmountable barriers. He felt a familiar sense of helplessness, a familiar knowledge that he was failing in his guardianship of her.

He looked at his sister's downcast eyes, the curve of her cheek, the slender fingers clutching the pearl earring. *I love you, Grace.* He cleared his throat and tried to say the words aloud. "Grace, I hope you know that I . . . care about you and that I want you to be happy."

It was apparently the wrong thing to say. Grace began to cry.

Adam hesitated for a moment, dismayed, and then put his arm around her. To his relief, Grace didn't pull away. She turned towards him, burying her face in his shoulder.

It hurt to hear her cry. Adam swallowed and tightened his grip on her. She'd grown thinner since their arrival in London, paler, quieter. *I should take her home. To hell with the Season.*

The storm of tears lessened. Adam stroked his sister's hair. "What is it, Grace?"

"I didn't want to disappoint you again," she sobbed.

"You've never disappointed me."

Grace shook her head against his shoulder. "Last year . . ." She didn't need to say more; they both knew what she was referring to.

"I was angry—but not with you." He'd been more than angry: he'd been furious. Furious at Reginald Plunkett, furious at the school for hiring the man, but mostly furious at himself for not visiting Grace more often, for not realizing how lonely she was, how vulnerable to the smiles and compliments of her music teacher.

The anger stirred again, tightening in his chest as if a fist was clenched there. *I should have horsewhipped him. I should have broken every bone in his body.*

Adam dug in his pocket for a handkerchief. Grace had come perilously close to ruin. Even now, six months later, he woke in a cold sweat from dreams—nightmares—where he'd delayed his journey by one day, where he'd arrived in Bath to find her gone. "Here," he said, handing her the handkerchief.

Grace dried her cheeks.

Adam smiled at her. "Now, tell me what's wrong."

Grace looked down at her lap, at the papers and the pearls. She extracted a sheet of paper and handed it to him.

~~My dear~~ Miss St. Just, ~~I have~~ a letter ~~of yours~~ you wrote to a Mr. Reginald Plunkett of Birmingham has come into my possession. ~~If you want it back. In exchange for its return.~~ I should like to return this letter to you. In exchange I ~~want~~ ask nothing more than your pearl bracelet.

"What!" He stared at his sister. "Someone's blackmailing you?"

Grace bit her lip.

Adam's fingers tightened on the sheet of paper. "Why didn't you tell me?"

Her gaze fell.

Because you were afraid I'd be angry at you, disappointed in you. Adam swallowed. He looked back at the blackmail letter without seeing it. He rubbed his face with one hand. "Grace . . ."

"Here." She handed him another piece of paper. The writing was the same as the first, the intent as ugly.

"You did what this person asked? You gave them your pearls?" His rage made the sunlight seem as sharp-edged as a sword. The room swung around him for a moment, vivid with anger. He focused on a chair. The rose-pink damask had become the deep crimson of blood, the gilded wood was as bright as flames. *How dared anyone do this to her?* The sheet of paper crumpled in his fist. *I'll kill them—*

"Yes." Grace gathered the bracelet and the earrings within the curve of her palm.

Adam blinked. His anger fell away, replaced by confusion. "Then why—?"

"Tom returned them to me."

"Tom?"

He blinked again at the elegant piece of paper she handed

him, at the brief message, the signature, the cat drawn in black ink at the bottom of the page. His interest sharpened. *That* Tom.

I believe these belong to you, Tom had written. *I found them in Lady Bicknell's possession.*

"And the letter to Reginald Plunkett?"

Grace touched a folded piece of paper in her lap.

Adam read the note again. *Tom.* "The devil," he said, under his breath. He fastened his gaze on his sister. "Was there anything else? Anything that might identify him?"

Grace shook her head.

Adam touched the ink-drawn cat with a fingertip. It stared back at him, sitting with its tail curled across its paws, unblinking, calm.

He lifted his eyes to the signature, and above that to the message. "Lady Bicknell," he said aloud, and the rage came back.

"Apparently," Grace said.

The blackmail letters were clearly drafts. "You have the ones she sent you?"

Grace shook her head. "I burned them."

Adam reread Lady Bicknell's letters, letting his eyes rest on each and every word, scored out or not. "She'll pay for this," he said grimly. "By God, if she thinks she can—!" He recollected himself, glanced at his sister's face, and forced himself to sit back on the sofa, to form his mouth into a smile. "Forget this, Grace. It's over."

"Yes," said Grace, but her expression was familiar: pale, miserable. She'd worn it four years ago when her mother died, and she'd worn it last November when she'd learned the truth about Reginald Plunkett.

Adam reached for her hand. "How odd, that we must be grateful to a thief." He laughed, tried to make a joke of it.

Grace smiled dutifully.

Adam looked at her, noting the paleness of her cheeks, the faint shadows beneath the blue eyes. "Grace, would you like to go home?" Away from the press of buildings and people and the sly whispers of gossip.

Her face lit up, as if the sun had come from behind a cloud. "Oh, yes!"

"Then I'll arrange it."

"Thank you!" She pulled her hand free from his grasp and embraced him, swift and wholly unexpected.

Adam experienced a throat-tightening rush of emotion. He folded his sister briefly in his arms and then released her. *How did we become so distant?* He cleared his throat. "Have you any engagements today? Would you like to ride out to Richmond?"

"Oh, yes! I should like that of all things!" She rose, and the pearls tumbled from her lap onto the damask-covered sofa. A much-creased letter fluttered down alongside them. It was addressed to Reginald Plunkett in Grace's handwriting.

The delight faded from his sister's face, leaving it miserable once more.

Adam gestured to the letter. "Do you want to keep it?"

Grace shook her head.

"Shall I burn it for you? Or would you prefer—"

"I don't want to touch it!" Her voice was low and fierce.

Adam nodded. He scooped up the pearls and placed them in Grace's palm, curling her fingers around them, holding her hand, holding her gaze. "Forget about this, Grace. It's over."

Grace nodded, but the happiness that had briefly lit her face was gone.

Adam stood. He kissed her cheek. "Go and change," he said, releasing her hand.

When she'd gone, he picked up the pieces of paper: Grace's love letter, Tom's note, Lady Bicknell's blackmail drafts. He allowed his rage to flare again. Lady Bicknell would pay for the distress she'd caused Grace. She'd pay deeply.

But some of the blame was his. The distance between himself and Grace was his fault: he'd been his sister's guardian, not her friend. She'd been too afraid of his disappointment, his anger, to ask for help.

Adam strode from the morning room. His shame was a physical thing; he felt it in his chest as if a knife blade was buried there.

He had failed Grace. Somehow, without realizing it, he'd become to her what their father had been to him: disapproving and unapproachable.

But no more, he vowed silently as he entered his study. *No more.*

Adam grimly placed the letters in the top drawer of his desk. He put Tom's note in last and let his gaze dwell on the signature. "I would like to know who you are," he said under his breath. And then he locked the drawer and put the key in his pocket.

Arabella Knightley, granddaughter of the fifth Earl of Westwick, paused alongside a potted palm and surveyed the ballroom. Lord and Lady Halliwell were launching their eldest daughter in style: hundreds of candles blazed in the chandeliers, a profusion of flowers scented the air, and yards of shimmering pink silk swathed the walls. An orchestra played on a dais and dancing couples filled the floor, performing the intricate steps of the quadrille. The débutantes were distinguishable by their self-consciousness as much as by their pale gowns.

Grace St. Just wasn't on the dance floor. Arabella looked at the ladies seated around the perimeter of the ballroom, scanning their faces as she sipped her lemonade. Her lip lifted slightly in contempt as she recognized Lady Bicknell.

The woman's appearance—the tasteless, gaudy trinkets, the heavy application of cosmetics—was reminiscent of her dressing table. Her earrings . . . Arabella narrowed her eyes. Yes, Lady Bicknell was wearing the diamond earrings she herself had discarded as worthless.

If the woman's appearance was in keeping with her dressing table, her figure brought to mind the mahogany dresser: broad and squat. *Like a frog,* Arabella thought, watching as Lady Bicknell's wide, flat mouth opened and shut. She was declaiming forcefully, her heavy face flushed with outrage. One of the ladies seated alongside her hid a smile behind her fan; the other, a dowager wearing a purple turban, listened with round-eyed interest.

Telling the tale of Tom's thieving, Arabella thought, with another curl of her lip. The woman certainly wouldn't mention the other items that had gone missing last night: the pearl bracelet and earrings, the blackmail letters.

Arabella dismissed Lady Bicknell from her thoughts. She continued her search of the ballroom, looking for Grace St. Just.

She found her finally, seated alongside a St. Just aunt. The girl wore a white satin gown sewn with seed pearls. More pearls gleamed at her earlobes and around her pale throat. She was astonishingly lovely, and yet she was sitting in a corner as if she didn't want anyone to notice her.

Arabella was reminded, vividly, of her own first Season. It was no easy thing to make one's début surrounded by whispers and conjecture and sidelong glances.

And I had advantages that Grace does not. She'd had the armor her childhood had given her; armor a girl as gently reared as Grace St. Just couldn't possibly have. And she'd had advice—advice it appeared no one had given Grace.

Arabella chewed on her lower lip. She glanced at the dance floor, trying to decide what to do. Her eyes fastened on one of the dancers, a tall man with a patrician cast to his features. Adam St. Just, cousin to the Duke of Frew.

She eyed him with resentment. St. Just's manner was as aloof, as proud, as if it was he who held the dukedom, not his cousin. *How could I have been such a fool as to believe he liked me?* She should be grateful to St. Just; he'd taught her never to trust a member of the *ton*—a valuable lesson. But it was impossible to be grateful while she still had memory of the *beaumonde*'s gleeful delight in her humiliation.

Arabella watched him dance, hoping he'd misstep or trample on his partner's toes. It was a futile hope; St. Just had the natural grace of a sportsman. His partner, a young débutante, lacked that grace. The girl danced stiffly, her manner awkward and admiring.

Arabella's lips tightened. No doubt St. Just accepted the admiration as his due; for years he'd been one of the biggest prizes on the marriage market, courted for his wealth, his bloodline, his handsome face.

She looked again at Grace St. Just. The girl bore little resemblance to her half-brother. Adam St. Just's arrogance was stamped on him—the way he carried himself, the tilt of his chin, the set of his mouth. Everything about him said *I am better than you.* Grace had none of that. She sat looking down at her hands, her shoulders slightly hunched as if she wished to hide.

I really should help her.

Arabella looked at St. Just again. As she watched, he cast a swift, frowning glance in the direction of his sister.

He's worried about her.

It was disconcerting to find herself in agreement with him.

Arabella swallowed the last of her lemonade, not tasting it, and handed her empty glass to a passing servant. No one snubbed her as she made her way through the crush of guests, her smiles were politely returned, and yet everyone in the ballroom—herself included—knew that she didn't belong. The satin gown, the fan of pierced ivory, the jeweled combs in her hair, couldn't disguise what she was: an outsider.

Music swirled around her, and beneath that was the rustle of silk and satin and gauze, the hum of voices. Her ears caught snippets of conversation. Much of tonight's gossip seemed to be about Lady Bicknell. Opinion was divided: some sympathized with Lady Bicknell; others thought it served her right.

There was no doubt why Tom had paid her a visit last night.

"That tongue of hers," stated a florid gentleman in a waistcoat that was too tight for him.

"Most likely," his wife said, glancing up and meeting Arabella's eyes. For a brief second the woman's smile stiffened, then she inclined her head in a polite nod.

Seven years ago that momentary hesitation would have hurt; now she no longer cared. Arabella smiled cheerfully back at the woman. *Only four more weeks of this.* Four more weeks of ball gowns and false smiles, of pretending to belong, and then she could turn her back on Society. *But first, I must help Grace St. Just.*

The girl looked up as Arabella approached. She was fairer than her half-brother, her hair golden instead of brown, her eyes a clear shade of blue. She was breathtakingly lovely—and quite clearly miserable.

"Miss St. Just." Arabella smiled and extended her hand. "I don't believe we've met. My name is Arabella Knightley."

Grace St. Just flushed faintly. She hesitated a moment, then held out her hand. *Her brother has warned her about me.*

Arabella sat, ignoring the St. Just aunt who frowned at her, lips pursed in disapproval, from her position alongside Grace. "How are you finding your first Season?"

"Oh," said Grace. She sent a darting glance in the direction of the dance floor. "It's very . . . that is to say—"

"I hated mine," Arabella said frankly. "Everyone staring and whispering behind their hands. It's not pleasant to be gossiped about, is it?"

Grace St. Just stopped searching the dance floor for her brother. She stared at Arabella. "No. It isn't."

"Someone gave me some advice," Arabella said. "When I was in a similar position to you. If you don't think it impertinent of me, I should like to pass it on."

She had the girl's full attention now. Those sky-blue eyes were focused on her face with an almost painful intensity. "Please," Grace St. Just said. Even the aunt leaned slightly forward in her chair.

"It was given to me by Mr. Brummell," Arabella said. "If he were still in England, I'm certain he'd impart it to you himself."

"The Beau?" Grace breathed. "Truly?"

Arabella nodded. "He said . . ." She paused for a moment, remembering. The Beau's voice had been cool and suave, and oddly kind. "He said I must ignore it, and more than that, I must ignore it *well*."

It was the only time Beau Brummell had spoken to her. But he had always nodded to her most politely after that, his manner one of faint approval.

"And so I did as he suggested," Arabella said. "I gave the appearance of enjoying myself. I smiled at every opportunity, and when I couldn't smile, I laughed." She smoothed a wrinkle in one of her long gloves, remembering. A slight smile tugged at her lips. "I believe some people found it very annoying."

She looked up and held Grace St. Just's eyes. "So that's my advice. However difficult it may seem, you must ignore what people are saying, the way they look at you. And you must ignore it *well*."

"Ignore it?" Tears filled the girl's eyes. "How *can* I?"

"It isn't easy," Arabella said firmly. "But it can be done."

Grace shook her head. She hunted in her reticule for a handkerchief. "I would much rather go home." Her voice wobbled on the last word.

"Certainly you may do that, but if I may be so bold, Miss St. Just . . . the rumors are just rumors. Speculation and conjecture. If you shrug your shoulders, London will find a new target. But if you leave now, the rumors will be confirmed."

Grace looked stricken. She sat with the handkerchief clutched in her hand and tears trembling on her eyelashes.

"It   doesn't   matter   whether   you   committed whatever indiscretion London thinks you did," Arabella said matter-of-factly. "What matters is whether London *believes* it or not."

Grace St. Just bit her lip. She looked down at the handkerchief and twisted it between her fingers.

"Be bold," Arabella said softly.

"Bold?" The girl's laugh was shaky. "I'm not a bold person, Miss Knightley."

"I think you can be anything you want."

Arabella's voice was quiet, but it made the girl look up. For a moment they matched gazes, and then Grace St. Just gave a little nod. She blew her nose and put the handkerchief away. "Tell me . . . how you did it, Miss Knightley. If you please?"

Arabella was conscious of a sense of relief. She sat back in her chair and glanced at the dance floor. Adam St. Just was watching them. She could see his outrage, even though half a ballroom separated them.

It was tempting to smile at him and give a mocking little wave. Arabella did neither. She turned her attention back to Grace St. Just.

Adam relinquished Miss Hornby to the care of her mother. He turned and grimly surveyed the far corner of the ballroom. His sister sat alongside Arabella Knightley, as she had for the past fifteen minutes.

They made a pleasing tableau, dark and fair, their heads bent together as they talked, Miss Knightley's gown of deep rose-pink perfectly complementing his sister's white satin.

Adam gritted his teeth. He strode around the ballroom, watching as Grace said something and Miss Knightley replied—and his aunt, Seraphina Mexted, sat placidly alongside, nodding and smiling and making no attempt to shoo Miss Knightley away.

Grace lifted her head and laughed.

Adam's stride faltered. Arabella Knightley had made Grace *laugh*. In fact, now that he observed more closely, his sister's face was bright with amusement.

She looks happy.

Arabella Knightley had accomplished, in fifteen minutes, what he had been trying—and failing—to do for months. How in Hades had she done it? And far more importantly, *why?*

Miss Knightley looked up as he approached. Her coloring showed her French blood—hair and eyes so dark they were almost black—but the soft dent in her chin, as if someone had laid a fingertip there at her birth, proclaimed her as coming from a long line of Knightleys.

His eyes catalogued her features—the elegant cheekbones, the dark eyes, the soft mouth—and his pulse gave a kick. It was one of the things that annoyed him most about Arabella Knightley: that he was so strongly attracted to her. The second most annoying thing was the stab of guilt—as familiar as the attraction—that always accompanied sight of her.

Adam bowed. "Miss Knightley, what a pleasure to see you here this evening."

Her eyebrows rose. "Truly?" Her voice was light and amused, disbelieving.

Adam clenched his jaw. This was the third thing that annoyed him most about Miss Knightley: her manner.

Arabella Knightley turned to Grace and smiled. "I must go. My grandmother will be wanting supper soon."

Adam stepped back as she took leave of his sister and aunt. The rose-pink gown made her skin appear creamier and the dark ringlets more glossily black. A striking young woman, Miss Knightley, with her high cheekbones and dark eyes. And an extremely wealthy one, too. But no man of birth and breeding would choose to marry her—unless his need for a fortune outweighed everything else.

She turned to him. "Good evening, Mr. St. Just." Cool amusement still glimmered in her eyes.

Adam gritted his teeth and bowed again. His gaze followed her. Miss Knightley's figure was slender and her height scarcely more than five foot—and yet she had presence. It was in her carriage, in the way she held her head. She was perfectly at home in the crowded ballroom, utterly confident, unconcerned by the glances she drew.

Adam turned to his aunt. "Aunt Seraphina, how could you allow—"

"I like her," Aunt Seraphina said placidly. "Seems a very intelligent girl."

Adam blinked, slightly taken aback.

"I like her, too," Grace said. "Adam, may I invite her—"

"No. Being seen in her company will harm your reputation. Miss Knightley is not good *ton*."

"I know," said Grace. "She spent part of her childhood in the slums. Her mother was a . . . a . . ." She groped for a euphemism, and then gave up. "But I *like* her. I want to be friends with her."

Over my dead body.

"Shall we leave?" Adam said, changing the subject. "It's almost midnight and we've a long journey tomorrow." To Sussex, where there'd be no Arabella Knightley.

He began to feel more cheerful.

"I've decided to stay in London," Grace said.

Adam raised his eyebrows. "You have?"

"Yes," Grace said. "This is my first Season, and I'm going to *enjoy* it."

Like to read the rest?
My Lady Thief is available now!

$\mathcal{A}$CKNOWLEDGMENTS

A number of people helped to make this book what it is. Foremost among them is my developmental editor, Laura Cifelli Stibich, but I also owe many thanks to my copyeditor, Maria Fairchild, and proofreader, Martin O'Hearn.

The cover and the formatting are the work of the talented Jane D. Smith. Thank you, Jane!

Emily Larkin grew up in a house full of books. Her mother was a librarian and her father a novelist, so perhaps it's not surprising that she became a writer.

Emily has studied a number of subjects, including geology and geophysics, canine behavior, and ancient Greek. Her varied career includes stints as a field assistant in Antarctica and a waitress on the Isle of Skye, as well as five vintages in New Zealand's wine industry.

She loves to travel and has lived in Sweden, backpacked in Europe and North America, and traveled overland in the Middle East, China, and North Africa.

She enjoys climbing hills, reading, and watching reruns of *Buffy the Vampire Slayer* and *Firefly*.

Emily writes historical romances as Emily Larkin and fantasy novels as Emily Gee. Her websites are www.emilylarkin.com and www.emilygee.com.

Never miss a new Emily Larkin book. Join her Readers' Group at www.emilylarkin.com/newsletter and receive free digital copies of *The Fey Quartet* and *Unmasking Miss Appleby*.

$\mathcal{O}$THER $\mathcal{W}$ORKS

THE BALEFUL GODMOTHER SERIES

Prequel
The Fey Quartet novella collection:
Maythorn's Wish
Hazel's Promise
Ivy's Choice
Larkspur's Quest

Original Series
Unmasking Miss Appleby
Resisting Miss Merryweather
Trusting Miss Trentham
Claiming Mister Kemp
Ruining Miss Wrotham
Discovering Miss Dalrymple

Garland Cousins
Primrose and the Dreadful Duke
Violet and the Bow Street Runner

Pryor Cousins
Octavius and the Perfect Governess

OTHER HISTORICAL ROMANCES

The Earl's Dilemma
My Lady Thief
Lady Isabella's Ogre
Lieutenant Mayhew's Catastrophes

The Midnight Quill Trio
The Countess's Groom
The Spinster's Secret
The Baronet's Bride

FANTASY NOVELS
(Written as Emily Gee)

Thief With No Shadow
The Laurentine Spy

The Cursed Kingdoms Trilogy
The Sentinel Mage
The Fire Prince
The Blood Curse

Printed in Great Britain
by Amazon